LUCKY FIVE

Lucky Five
Copyright © 2022 Lynn Harrod

For information contact :
www.deerwoodpress.com

Book and Cover design by Lynn Harrod
Edited by William McCoy

ISBN: 978-1-7367234-5-6 (ePub edition)
ISBN: 978-1-7367234-6-3 (Paperback edition)

First Edition: February 2022

LUCKY FIVE

a crime novel

LYNN HARROD

For Nathan and his wealth of skill and talent

1

The Games People Play

The Horseshoe Lounge looked like any other dim, smokey watering hole, with its worn, padded booths, wobbly barstools, and neon beer signs hung on walls of cheap wood panelling. A few patrons sat scattered about the room, slumped over beers they'd been nursing for hours. Classic Rock from the 80s played on an old boom box sitting atop an even older jukebox that had its swan song nine years prior.

At this lonely hour, rocker Billy Idol crooned wildly to no one, his distinct, raspy voice occasionally drowned out by the teasing chimes and beeps of the upright slot machines along the front wall and the inviting bells and chirps of the gaming terminals built flush into the bar top.

Besides the ample slots, ribbons of lottery tickets hung from clothespins clipped to shelves beside the cash register, and sports betting forms sat stacked beside the seven beer taps. These options weren't the only means of gambling in that old Las Vegas lounge for even in The Silver State of Nevada - a state where gambling was not only legal but widespread and highly encouraged - people still sought illegal bets. For some, it's not enough of a thrill to risk their wallet, they must also skirt the law, the allure of forbidden fruit.

In the middle of the lounge, six anxious men had gathered chairs around a cocktail table built for two, faced off three-versus-three in a contest of wills with a disregard to wits.

Sitting to one side of the table was a young man named Billy White. He wore Ray Ban Wayfarers atop his mop of auburn hair and a gold chain necklace out and over his oversized UCLA sweatshirt. With a determined scowl, he pinned his right elbow to the table as if about to arm wrestle his opponent.

Across from Billy sat Benjamin Parr, a pudgy middle-aged man in a navy Polo shirt, brown slacks, and bright yellow trail running shoes whose soles had only felt the cold cement of his driveway, the plush carpeting of his office, and the heated hardwood laminate flooring of his suburban Sacramento home. He met Billy's scowl with peering eyes that poorly masked an uncomfortable grimace.

"Not feelin' well, Mr. Parr?" Billy asked in his rough, chain-smoker voice, raising a shot glass to his lips. "Lemme know if you wanna call it quits. I know your guts must be rockin' and rollin' after all those Cajun shrimp cocktails." Billy took his third shot, squinted his eyes tight as it slid down his gullet, and slammed his shot glass onto the table. "Goddamn, that burns goin' down, don't it, Mr. Parr?"

Benjamin shook his head as he also took his third shot, swallowing it in restrained agony. He slammed down his shot glass as his opponent had before him.

"Your buddies are right, Mr. Parr," Billy said. "You really do have an iron stomach. I might've finally met my match."

Billy's friends stood behind him, two loud, rambunctious men introduced as his classmates and brothers from the hallowed halls of Delta Sigma Phi. They circled the table like hyenas jockeying for better reach of fallen prey.

Roscoe Wilson counted fifty dollars to match Billy's stake, tossing it onto the table. He wore baggy jeans and a USC hoodie, his youthful outfit contrasting with his weathered, wrinkled face. Rodney Finch towered over the table in green camouflage pants topped with a long Cal Poly T-shirt, his thinning hair contradicting his college persona.

If only Benjamin Parr or his friends had spotted the fraternity brothers' discrepancies.

Billy slid the two empty shot glasses together. "How about a joke to help wash down the next one?" He read the faces of the three older men across from him, knowing his facade held as he poured the fourth pair of shots of a thick, bright red drink.

"Let's hear it," Benjamin said, clearing his hoarse throat, his first words during their ten minutes together.

"So this farmer has a daughter, 'cause it's always about a farmer having a daughter. She's a mute. Ain't spoke a word in years."

To Benjamin's left stood his coworker Carl Pendergrass, Office Manager at Morgan Business Machines, who'd missed the company's last three Christmas parties in Vegas in order to attend gatherings with in-laws out of state. He defied his wife's obligations that year not only to finally join the annual staff retreat but to celebrate his fiftieth birthday in grand style. Dressed in a tan fedora, plaid button-up shirt, and slim-fitting jeans - an outfit he'd purchased specifically for their wild night out - Carl objected to the little contest the college boys had proposed ten minutes earlier. He'd been waiting all year for this weekend and the last thing he wanted was his night of freedom and debauchery sidelined by a friend taken out of commission early in the evening by three college kids.

To Benjamin's right stood Gene Renfrow, Lead Accountant at Morgan Business Machines, whose notion of dressing to impress comprised a leather bomber jacket and aviator sunglasses adorning his head, concealing his dyed-black comb-over. Gene had known Benjamin seven years longer than Carl and felt confident in his friend's invincible "iron stomach," a legend at the office. When the frat brothers approached them with cash and a big red bottle, Gene patted Benjamin's rotund stomach and boasted of his eating and drinking prowess, citing his First Place trophy in Sacramento's famous "The Whole Kit and Caboodle" burger-eating contest at the Pitch and Fiddle. Seeing his friend now wavering, facing his fourth shot, he whispered advice and encouragement.

"The farmer will pay anyone who can make his daughter speak," Billy said, continuing his joke. "So three guys show up, 'cause it's always about three guys showin' up. White guy, Black guy, Mexican." Billy took his fourth shot, barely getting it down. He slammed his glass to the table as Benjamin raised his.

Lynn Harrod

Benjamin gathered his courage and took his shot, nearly vomiting from the burning sensation. After a moment of taunts in front of him and praise behind him, he swallowed both the thick drink and his mouthful of puke, gently placing his shot glass beside his opponent's with a shaky hand. Frat boys Roscoe and Rodney howled in excitement while office managers Carl and Gene sighed in relief.

As if part of the torture, Billy took his time pouring two more shots of the dreaded red "drink" - Insane Dwayne's Diablo Death Sauce - a cruel condiment whose primary ingredient was the Carolina Reaper chili pepper, scoring a ludicrous 2.2 million heat units on the Scoville Scale. It made Benjamin's six o'clock Cajun-style shrimp cocktails taste like ketchup in comparison.

"Four down," Billy said. "Get ready for Lucky Number Five."

Neither the wild frat brothers nor the timid office managers at the table noticed the lone patron watching from the bar, like an apex predator sizing up a herd. The silent giant had slicked black hair and wore a black tailored suit and matching wool coat, a small Armani shopping bag sitting within reach. He sipped a glass of Scotch, smoked a cigar, and checked the time on his gold watch, careful not to miss any details as he observed the juvenile contest from afar.

The large man in black didn't care who won or lost, or who would first become violently ill from ingesting half a pint of Carolina Reaper. What piqued his curiosity was the fact that the college boys had been picking the pockets of the mature men while feigning interest in the drinking challenge.

"White guy goes into the daughter's bedroom," Billy said. "Comes out ten minutes later. Not a peep. Black guy goes in for ten minutes, comes back. Nothing." Billy slammed another brutal shot of Insane Dwayne, taking a full painful minute to swallow. Roscoe and Rodney screamed in triumph. "Mexican guy goes in. Five minutes later the girl yells 'water!' The farmer can't fuckin' believe it!"

Benjamin raised his glass and took a moment to focus, but the smell of the pungent pepper stopped him cold. He set his glass down on the table between the bottle of Insane Dwayne, a carton of milk, and the stack of cash.

Carl exhaled in relief.

Gene frowned in disappointment.

"Game, set, match," Billy said with a devilish grin as he scooped up the cash and gulped down the milk - a soothing bonus for the winner. His friends nodded, wide smiles on their impudent faces. "Farmer asks, 'How the hell did you do it?' Mexican guy smiles and tells the farmer..." Billy did his best Speedy Gonzales voice. "It's an old Tijuana trick. I put hot sauce on my cock."

Billy alone laughed at his vile joke. Without a word, Benjamin Parr stood and exited the Horseshoe Bar, his revolted coworkers following him out the door. It wouldn't be until nearly half an hour later, when they finished their long walk back to the Luxor Hotel and Casino and sat together at a roulette table, that they'd finally realize they'd been fleeced.

Roscoe and Rodney joined their leader at the small table, counting the money they just won - and stole - from the three clueless tourists.

"Dude, it looked like you were about to barf for a moment there!" Rodney said.

"For sure, Billy, you had me convinced." Roscoe smelled the extreme hot sauce and grimaced. "I thought you might've accidentally drank some. I felt like backing away just in case!"

"David Blaine ain't got shit on me," Billy said, revealing a glass tube that held plain tomato juice, one of ten that he used to substitute for Insane Dwayne in a seamless display of sleight of hand. Holding the tube behind the bottle gave the convincing illusion that the contest was fair. "All that scrunching up of my face was just to fuck with him."

Roscoe motioned to put the cash away when he noticed the large man in black at the bar, his stare piercing through a shroud of cigar smoke like the eyes of the Devil. The three con men sat frozen, unsure, eyeing the exit only twenty feet away.

"Who the fuck is that?" Rodney asked in a lowered voice.

"Cop?" Roscoe asked, ready to bolt.

Billy stared back in defiance, assessing the well-dressed, intimidating giant. "Ain't no cop. He woulda popped us already, and he wouldn't have let the fish leave."

"We in somebody else's territory?"

"Nah, the Horseshoe is our bar."

"Think he made us, Billy?"

"Only one way to find out." Billy White, career confidence man, thrill seeker, and leader of a small crew of grifters, shoved caution aside and waved to the mysterious man at the bar, gesturing for him to join them at their table. The man downed his last swallow of Scotch, picked up his Armani shopping bag, and puffed his cigar while walking across the bar as if he owned the joint.

Stepping into the well lit center of the room, Rolo Marino stood six-foot-four, his hands like baseball gloves, his stout frame draped with a full-length coat blocking the light from the neon signs and overhead lamps. The intimidating Italian loomed over the three thieves for a moment, allowing them a good long look, waiting to see if they recognized him. Judging from their curious, grinning faces, they apparently didn't know who the hell Rolo "Moonlight" Marino was or that *his* crew had taken over Vegas during the past year.

That night in the Horseshoe Bar, away from the main drags of town and the grand casinos of the luxury resorts that had become his playground, away from the Castle District that served as his underworld empire, Moonlight Marino stood alone, face-to-face with three clueless con men. Their petty operation was beneath him, but he saw an opportunity to test something long on his mind.

"Good evening, gentlemen," Rolo said, his deep voice startling, seizing command of the room. "Got any other games going on?"

"That depends," Billy said. "You a cop or a Soprano?"

"You know, I get that a lot. I'm just a tourist. Like you."

Billy laughed, amused by this arrogant man who clearly had more wealth and bravado than sense, having no idea what he was walking into. Roscoe and Rodney watched the awkward exchange unfold, ready to sprint for the door in a heartbeat. Billy sensed his friends' trepidation and waved it away without taking his eyes off who he believed could be their juiciest mark of the week, a man who could be taken advantage of by preying on his hubris.

Billy extended his hand. "Billy."

"There we go," Rolo said. "Civility. You call me Rolo." He gestured to take Billy's hand but puffed his cigar instead.

"Rolo. My favorite candy." As before, Billy laughed alone. "Sorry, I bet you get that a lot."

"Actually, no. Where I'm from, 'Billy' would get kicked around." Rolo again checked the time on his gold watch. "I noticed your friendly little wager. Three bright young college boys out on the town playing games in a dive bar off the Strip. What is it, Pledge Week or Hell Week or something like that?"

"Something like that." Billy smiled, taking back his unrequited handshake.

"I bet you have a whole playbook of this shit. I have some time to kill and I'm looking to try something... a little crazy."

"You ever hear of a Marshmallow Run?"

"Is that where a bunch of queers run around with candy up their asses?"

Billy pointed to the bottle of Insane Dwayne. "How about Hot Shots?"

"Not crazy enough."

Intrigued, Billy turned to consult with his partners. "Ideas? What haven't we played in a while?"

"Toad in the Hole?" Roscoe said.

"He's too tall."

"Teddy Bear Scare?"

"Do you see any women here?"

"Caesar's Skinny Dip?"

"Nothing with water," Rolo said. "I don't feel like getting wet."

"What about 'The Gotcha Game'?" Rodney asked.

Billy thought about the idea for a moment. "That's it. The Gotcha Game. It's crazy and it's a classic. Fifty to buy in. The more green you put up, the more interesting it..."

Rolo silenced Billy by reaching into his coat and pulling out his wallet, bursting at the seams with cash. He tossed down three Hundreds.

"Dude, can we cover that?" Rodney asked.

"I think we can manage," Billy said. "I'll cover your share if that's what you're in a tizzy about."

Rolo checked the time on his gold watch. "I'd sit but I have a feeling this game ain't happening here."

Billy slid the money from the table, shoved it in his pocket, and grinned.

* * *

The giant neon signs and bizarre skyline of the Las Vegas Strip shone in the distance, like an immense board game beckoning tourists across the dark desert. Billy White and his cronies walked with Moonlight Marino down an industrial street past storage yards surrounded by barbed wire to the Lady O' Luck Motel, a decrepit Irish-themed two-story relic from the 1960s, its large, rusted shamrock sign missing most of its neon tubing. The glory years of accommodating visiting families long past, the Lady O' Luck was now reduced to being one of those foreboding motels that rented rooms by the hour.

"Nice joint," Rolo said, tossing his cigar to the ground.

"Hey, it's the cheapest place in town," Billy said. "We may be college students, but we ain't trust fund babies."

"I figured that much."

It didn't occur to Billy that any other mark would have hesitated walking into such a seedy place on the dark side of Sin City, that any other man would have thought twice about following a group of strangers on his own. All he could imagine was Rolo's overstuffed wallet in his hands, his gold watch on his wrist, and the little Armani shopping bag that surely held something of value.

As they entered the nearly vacant parking lot, Billy made a call on the cell phone he lifted from Benjamin.

"We'll be there in a moment," Billy said on the phone. "We're playing the Gotcha Game... well get ready... I don't give a shit, wake his ass up... we got a game going on... tell him I said no... hell, we're almost there!"

Billy hung up, frustrated with his other "frat brothers." He guided Rolo to Room 23, the only room with lights on, but stopped short of turning the knob. "I don't mean to insult you, big guy, but I think we'd all feel better if..."

Rolo laughed and raised his arms, allowing Rodney to frisk him head to toe. Satisfied, Rodney nodded, and Billy unlocked the door, gesturing for Rolo to walk in first.

They entered the small motel room, where three other men dressed in mismatching college gear drank cans of beer from a case sitting on the bed.

Ricky Bronco, a musclebound behemoth in a UC Irvine tank top, sat at the foot of the bed. Beside him sat Ruben Fykes, tall and lean in a UC Santa Cruz T-shirt, covered in crude prison tattoos. They watched softcore porn on a small TV bolted to the wall.

"Meet our new player," Billy said, annoyed by his partners' distraction. "He already bought in, three bills, so now we're playin' Gotcha... so shut that fuckin' thing off!"

Ruben clicked off the TV and rose to his feet, his height nearly matching Rolo's. Ricky slammed the rest of his beer, crushed the can, and tossed it into the bathroom.

"This is Ruben and Ricky," Billy said.

"Nice to have friends," Rolo said. "The consistency with the 'R' names is cute."

"Well, Sleeping Beauty over here is 'Skinner'... hey, didn't I say to wake his ass up?"

Scott "Skinner" Boggs slept on the bed, shaved bald, his black tank top, ripped jeans, and combat boots clashing with the clean-cut college theme of the grift. His emaciated frame and face full of pock marks made him a startling sight.

Skinner sat up groggy and pissed off. He shot Billy a look of daggers as he stood to approach their new mark, locking eyes with the giant.

"He's clean," Rodney said. "I patted him down."

"Big boy, ain't ya?" Skinner said to Rolo with a distorted, high-pitched voice like knives on a chalkboard. "Bet that's a custom suit. Bet you gotta get all your shit custom made. Ain't nothing that fuckin' big at JC Penney."

"I could pick my teeth with you," Rolo said.

The frat brothers laughed at Rolo's joke and defiance, something Skinner clearly wasn't accustomed to.

"Let's get this over with," Skinner said, brushing past Rolo to dead-bolt the door.

Rolo checked the time again on his gold watch.

Billy grabbed a beer from the case on the bed and walked into the bathroom, returning with a duffel bag. He unzipped the bag and fished around inside. "Gentlemen, get ready to play..." He pulled a revolver from the bag and pointed it at Rolo's face. "Gotcha!"

The six grifters laughed in a sustained uproar as Rolo stood helpless in the center of the room. He knew these men were con artists but wasn't yet sure if the gun posed a threat or just a juvenile joke. Ricky Bronco searched his coat and yanked out his thick wallet, assuring him that the affront was real. Rolo offered no resistance as Ruben grabbed his Armani shopping bag and tossed it across the room to Skinner.

"Something told me you guys weren't college kids," Rolo said.

"Congratulations, dumb shit!" Billy said, nearly doubled over in laughter. "You're the single biggest fish we caught yet! Sure beats weekend warrior dads and convention fools."

Ricky smiled wide as he thumbed through the thousands of dollars in Rolo's wallet before tossing it to Billy. Skinner pulled four matching jewelry boxes from the Armani bag. Rolo again checked his gold watch, barely catching the time as Ruben snatched it from him only for Skinner to immediately take it for himself. He placed it on his slender wrist, laughing at how oversized it looked on him, sliding up past his elbow to the amusement of his comrades.

"You boys familiar with the Castle District?" Rolo asked. A few heads suddenly turned, concerned, but Billy dismissed it with a smirk. "That's where I'm from, and punk-ass pranks don't sit well where I'm from. Walk away while you can."

Skinner opened the jewelry boxes, revealing four more gold watches identical to Rolo's. He tossed them back in the shopping bag and reached into the duffle for a roll of duct tape. The thin man stood and approached Rolo, pulling out a few feet of tape.

"This ain't no prank, big boy," Skinner said. "And we ain't where you're from, and we ain't walkin' away 'cause we're jus' gettin' started."

His gun still raised, Billy held his beer up in a mock toast. "To Tony Soprano!"

The crew of grifters laughed as Skinner walked up to Rolo, ready to duct tape his mouth. Rolo stood motionless, eyeing his gold watch on Skinner's upper arm as a tinny sound came from it.

BEEP BEEP.

1:21 A.M.

In a flash, Rolo grabbed Skinner like a rag doll, wrapped the duct tape twice around his eyes, and slammed his face to the wall.

With the frat boys taken off guard, Rolo stalked the small motel room in a rage, suddenly unconcerned with the gun pointed at him. Billy panicked and fired a shot, missing Rolo, nailing Roscoe in the neck.

Rolo slugged the behemoth Ricky Bronco, kicking down on his lower leg, snapping it like a broomstick. Ricky screamed in pain as he crumpled to the floor. Billy fired and missed

Lynn Harrod

again even though Rolo stood just fifteen feet away. He could only watch in horror as Rolo grabbed Ruben's arms and cruelly broke them backward at the elbows. Billy fired a third time and missed again as Rolo clutched Rodney's skull, broke his neck, and shoved his head through the TV screen.

Billy clutched his gun with trembling hands as he backed into the bathroom doorway, confused, terrified, his men bleeding, broken, screaming. "Don't move! Don't you fuckin' move!" Rolo paused in the middle of the room and stared down Billy, striking him with the fear of the Devil. "I'm warning you, motherfucker! Stay back!"

Rolo stood unblinking as Billy raised his gun with two hands and took dead aim. He fired another shot directly at Rolo's head, but Skinner - blind from the duct tape - stumbled by at that precise moment and took the bullet to his temple. Rolo knelt down and took back his gold watch from the dead man's thin arm. He looked up in time to see Billy scramble out the bathroom window.

Behind the motel, Billy White tumbled out through the window, landing hard to the ground, still clutching his worthless revolver. He ran for his life down a dark alley, scampering through a gap in a chain link fence and into a storage yard. He sprinted to the rear of a warehouse, his lungs about to burst, but his escape was cut short by a bizarre, frightening obstacle.

Out of the darkness in front of Billy sat a giant clown head, twenty feet tall, an old, burnt out casino sign. Written across its long teeth were the words "Feeling Lucky?" Billy tried to squeeze past it, tried to climb over it, but quickly realized he was trapped. He turned to see the silhouette of the demonic Rolo blocking his only exit.

"Gotcha!" Rolo said.

Billy pointed his weapon, his only option. "Get back! Get back, godammit! I'm the one with the fuckin' gun!" He shook uncontrollably, held his breath as he took careful aim. He fired again, impossibly missing his target in such close quarters. Rolo rushed forward and grabbed Billy by the throat with one hand, lifting him up the giant clown face. Billy shoved the gun under Rolo's chin.

"One bullet left, Billy. Time's almost up."

Billy pulled the trigger.

CLICK CLICK.

Rolo grabbed the gun and backed away, his eyes aflame. Billy fumbled in his pocket and pulled out Rolo's wallet, tossing it to him along with his own, hoping to appease this monster.

"Now here's a classic game for you," Rolo said, opening the chamber of the revolver. He showed the chamber to Billy. As he said moments before, one bullet indeed remained. He spun the chamber and slammed it in - Russian Roulette.

"Don't do it!" Billy said. "Don't fuckin' do it! Please!"

Rolo checked his gold watch one last time as he raised the gun to Billy's face. "You tell 'em how you got your boys killed by one of the horsemen of the apocalypse. Tell 'em of all the guys in Vegas, you singled out the king of the Castle District, chief of the Mojo Boys, leader of the Lucky Five. You tell 'em nobody can touch Moonlight Marino no more."

"Tell who?" Billy asked, shutting his eyes tight.

BEEP BEEP.

1:26 A.M.

"Whoever's waiting for you on the other side."

BLAM!

2

One-Upping Bonnie and Clyde

Thursday, December 20, 2001, 8:14 a.m.

The opulence of Brewer Manor started with its towering brass gates, continuing down a driveway lined with Greek statuary and topiary animals that led to the majestic house. The property's French Renaissance design might seem fitting in Neuilly sur Seine or Versailles, but stood out like a garish vanity project in the working class town of Easton, California, even nestled in the well-to-do neighborhood of North End. Doctors, bankers, and lawyers lived on those streets, not royalty, though some would say the master of the manor lorded over the city until last night.

On that cold December morning - nearly a year after Moonlight Marino dispatched a crew of grifters on the outskirts of Las Vegas - the driveway glistened from an all-night downpour. The house staff and security detail, confused and aghast, gathered under a large canopy set up for questioning. Yellow crime scene tape blocked entry instead of the wide open gates.

Manuel Sanchez sat in the passenger seat of a white panel van beside his new supervisor, George Armand. George shifted the van into Park as they waited for an Easton police officer to undo the yellow tape, allowing them access to the grounds.

"We got the call this morning," George said, his wheezy voice still half-asleep. "Maid almost had a goddamn heart attack when she walked in. Don't bother shooting her, Manny. Staff photos are already on file."

Manuel introduced himself as "Manny" when he first met George, a nickname he hadn't used since his childhood in Modesto, California. Though Easton sat only a few hours south of his hometown, it felt like another world. He hoped that a new city and new name would help reboot his life.

Manny prepared his two cameras, a Minolta and a Pentax, professional-grade 35mm workhorses past their prime and facing obsolescence in the burgeoning era of digital photography. They were handed down to him by his father as a graduation present, cameras that served Manuel Sr. well, covering high school and college sports in the Bay Area. Manny promised himself he'd use his father's old shooters for a greater purpose, imagining accolades from National Geographic and Time Magazine. Covering crime back in Modesto and now Easton fell below his ambitions, but paid the bills.

Manny struggled to load his Minolta as the van lurched forward on the cobblestone driveway. As much as he wanted to upgrade and repair his gear - the Pentax succumbed to moisture years prior and was only there for show - he'd only started working with Easton P.D. that week and had yet to save the money he needed.

"Do us a favor, Manny," George said, squinting at the rising sun peeking over the mansion's roof. "Get yourself a decent rig."

"Would the department flip the bill? Maybe deduct it from my pay in installments?"

"Sure, if you were shooting bullets instead of pictures. A rookie photog's gotta wait six months before pitching equipment requests. Forensics got the short end of the fucking budget cuts." George reached between the buttons of his shirt and scratched his belly as he parked the van near the open front door of the house. He shut off the motor and turned to his new assistant. "Ever been out to North End before?"

"First time," Manny said, finally securing his Minolta's load door. "I haven't seen much of Easton yet, to be honest. Other than the lab, all I've seen is a few streets around the Castle." In Manny's first week on the job, he snapped pictures of a hit-and-run on Clay Avenue and an argument at a birthday party that ended in manslaughter on Butler Road, gang-ridden streets south of the infamous Castle District.

"Lately, North End feels like Beverly Hills for crooks," George said, scratching his belly. "The only reason we ever come up here is for a mob hit. No domestic disturbance calls, no drunks, no wife-beaters. You never see North End on *COPS*."

Lynn Harrod

Stepping out of the van, Manny took pictures of a champagne-colored SUV and matte black luxury sedan parked nearby. He knew their owners were lieutenants of a local mob, but he didn't yet know of their infamy.

"Come on," George said. "We can get the grounds later. We gotta capture the poor devils inside before they clean up and take 'em to the fridge."

* * *

Entering through the decorative double doors, George nearly fell against a wall as two uniformed officers bumped into him while wrestling with a frantic African-American woman desperate to be heard.

Marissa Washington yelled at the officers as she tried to yank herself from their grip. Her frayed brown afro and runny makeup atop her tall, slender frame draped with a disheveled dress gave her the appearance of a feral junkie. The maid found her upstairs, ransacking the master bedroom. "Godammit! Fuckin' listen to me! He said he wanted me to have it! It's here somewhere! I gotta find it!"

George grabbed his assistant and took him to the next area of the house, a place listed on their itinerary as the "Game Room." The ornate recreation room had a long granite bar, pool table, poker table, big-screen TV, and abstract paintings adorning the mahogany walls.

Overwhelmed, Manny raised his camera and took pictures of the many peculiar items in the room. Cards and cash sat on the poker table, denoting the abrupt end of a game. A silver spade earring sat between them atop the unclaimed pot of clay gaming chips. Two pistols lay on the floor. Behind the bar, a broken antique grandfather clock forever approached eleven o'clock. The actual time - a quarter to nine - displayed on a large wall clock that resembled a giant pocket watch.

Perhaps out of fear or an attempt to control his unease, Manny captured the odd objects in the room before addressing the two bodies on the hardwood floor.

Teddy "Prime Time" Brewer, a young Caucasian male in a silk shirt and slacks, lay dead from a gunshot to the gut.

Rolo "Moonlight" Marino, the large Italian man from the rampage at the Lady O' Luck, lay beside him, dead from a gunshot to the chest, his white button-up shirt contrasting with the blood spattered across it.

Manny had worked many grisly crime scenes and knew what to expect but still didn't feel comfortable with them. Though these victims had clean deaths compared to the multiple stab wounds and laceration of gangbangers he'd captured before, something about these two bodies filled him with dread, their lifeless stares and blood-soaked clothing at odds with the elegance of the house.

Turning to ask George about the scene, he realized he stood alone in the Game Room. He heard his supervisor speaking with someone farther into the house. He followed the two men's voices into a massive room lined floor-to-ceiling with bookshelves.

"What kind of book?" George asked.

"She doesn't know," Detective Bruce said in frustration. Manny took notice of Bruce's gray suit with no tie and

Lynn Harrod

unbuttoned collar, an outfit that seemed more informal than Manny's regulation blue Polo shirt and beige slacks.

"She connected?" George asked.

"We think she was hired by Brewer for the evening, but she's claiming to be the love of his life."

"Gimme a fucking break."

"Hey, more power to her. A godfather and a casino king are lying on their faces in there. If I was a working girl who just happened to be here, you bet I'd want a piece of the action."

Manny shook his head in disbelief, realizing where he was and who he'd just taken photos of.

"If we don't find this mystery book of hers, she'll just write her own," George said.

"Instant best-seller. *Prime Time Brewer Was My Lover.*"

"Hell, I'd buy a copy."

"This is his house?" Manny asked, interrupting the casual exchange. "Brewer's?"

"Bruce, this is Manuel Sanchez. He's on my detail now."

Detective Bruce shook Manny's hand. "Good to have you."

"Call me Manny."

"Been working forensics long?" Detective Bruce asked.

Manny disliked small talk, asking how long he'd been shooting crime scenes or whether he'd been to North End before, questions that suggested he was young and green and in need of guidance. "That was him in there?" he asked again, ignoring the chit chat. "Teddy Brewer?"

"Prime Time Brewer, that's right," Detective Bruce said, amused by Manny's star-struck expression. "And that big guy cuddling next to him is..."

"Moonlight Marino," Manny said in awe.

"Biggest stinks since Capone," George said, getting caught up in his assistant's fascination. "You're shooting history, Manny. Imagine the cameraman at the Bonnie-and-Clyde showdown. Now imagine one-upping that guy."

George and Detective Bruce left the room, George gesturing for Manny to shoot the library before joining them. Manny raised his Minolta and took a picture of the cathedral window, but his old camera jammed. He felt a mild panic run through him. He finally had his chance to shoot something important, something more than the aftermaths of petty crimes or his father's local football games, but his equipment threatened to thwart his moment. Manny wanted to impress George and prove himself worthy of covering such a high-profile case, and he cursed the fact that his backup Pentax camera was a worthless brick.

Desperate, he gently banged his Minolta with the butt of his palm, but it failed to dislodge the shutter. He placed the camera on the windowsill before him and banged the top of the camera body twice more, jostling loose a small wooden board underneath the sill.

"Fuck!" Manny felt his plight deepening. Not only did his equipment fail, he just damaged property at an active crime scene. Looking around to ensure there were no witnesses, he knelt to the floor and tried to shove the board back under the sill.

Sunlight beamed through the stained glass cathedral window, reflecting off his camera lens onto a flash of gold that caught his eye. He realized he hadn't broken the windowsill but opened a secret storage compartment.

Lynn Harrod

Peering inside with a pen flashlight, he spotted a book. He turned his head to call out for George, but couldn't get the words out. Instead, he reached into the narrow space and pulled out the book, a massive journal bound in red leather, a large gold "Q" embossed on its cover.

He knew he should have immediately brought the book to his supervisor's attention and that he was tampering with evidence, but something took hold of him, keeping the book firmly in his grasp. He looked around the lavish room, at the ornate book, and his busted camera sitting on the sill.

"Manny, you almost done in there?" George said from the next room. "Let's get the cars and the grounds now."

Manny placed the wooden board back in place, concealing the hidden storage.

The book remained in his hands.

"On my way."

3

Four Walls

Standing in the doorway of his studio apartment, his camera bag still slung over his shoulder, Manny could see everything he owned in one glance. Canned soup and boxes of sugary cereal sat on a shelf in the "kitchenette," a cute term that meant a small refrigerator sat beside a two-coil electric stove and a single-basin sink, all tucked in the southeast corner to the left of the door. A square Formica dining table with two matching chairs separated the kitchenette from the cracked faux leather sofa sitting under the lone window in the northeast corner, which faced the thirteen-inch TV sitting on a crate in the northwest corner. Built into the wall opposite the door stood the Murphy bed that came with the apartment, folded up and out of sight for the day. Each morning, Manny made the queen-sized bed and raised it up and into the wall for if he hadn't there would be no space to move about. His only view of the world were two small windows on either side of the bed. The three-quarter bathroom comprised the southwest corner, to the right of the door, a green vinyl floral curtain providing minimal privacy.

Manny had called that cramped apartment home for three months, living off meager savings from Modesto that dwindled away with instant ramen noodles and frozen burritos and cans of chicken noodle soup, all while waiting for a follow-up call from Human Resources at Easton P.D. The afternoon they offered him a position with the department should have been cause to celebrate, but his desperate relief eclipsed any joy he might have felt from being employed again.

He tossed his camera bag onto the sofa and grabbed a bottle of beer from the fridge. The full six-pack gave him a sense of stability and normalcy, allowing him to forget for a moment that he lived day-to-day, check-to-check. His sister alone knew the details of his struggle, worried that he accepted a life of surviving versus living.

Sipping his beer on the sofa, Manny reached into his bag and pulled out his stuck Minolta, his dead Pentax, and the thick, priceless book he stole from Brewer Manor. He stared at the red leather cover, its large, gold embossed "Q" staring back. He hadn't taken the book for its black market value, fetching a hefty price with collectors of mafioso memorabilia, nor had he taken it for detailed photos of each page for the sake of preserving a piece of history before it could be buried in the department's evidence cage. Confused, Manny wasn't sure at all why he quickly tucked the book in his camera bag at the mansion, as if compelled to keep it safe and secret.

Setting down his beer, careful not to risk spilling a drop on the pristine journal, he opened it to find the mad, nearly illegible scribblings of someone named "Buckner." Wanting to get straight to Prime Time Brewer's entries, he bypassed those first two-hundred pages to one bookmarked by a photograph. It fell out onto his lap, showing Marissa Washington - the frantic woman from the mansion - arm in arm with Brewer. The couple looked happy and healthy in breezy summer clothes, standing in front of the famous "Welcome to Las Vegas" sign that greeted tourists arriving from the south.

"Well, shit, maybe you were special to him," Manny muttered, scrutinizing the photo. It showed Marissa as pretty and pleasant, before her fall to drugs, and the infamous Prime Time Brewer as an ordinary guy in blue jeans, before his rise to the heights of the FBI's Most Wanted.

His curiosity piqued, Manny turned the next page and read the first of Teddy Brewer's entries, eerily noting that its date of December 20, 2000 was exactly one year before Brewer's death the night before.

"You won't believe a lot of what I have to say, but it doesn't matter. I'm not continuing Quickie's journal for the New York Times Best Seller List. I'm writing to get everything out of my head before it drives me over the cliff, and I think I've been failing. Again, it doesn't matter. Nothing matters because I'll be dead. The only way this book will rest in anyone else's hands is if I'm done and checked out for good. I'm not going to prison to rot

until I die of old age or a heart attack or a shiv in the shower. I'm not flying overseas to waste away in a third-world beach hut like an exiled king. None of that will do anymore. I'm likely staying here in Easton's precious North End, surrounded by a cul-de-sac of upper-class pricks, and I'll probably die in this gaudy, forsaken house."

Manny uprighted the journal, turned the page, and felt something else slide down into his lap from farther into the book. A torn, soiled Ace of Spades covered the photo of the loving couple, as if to block out their salad days. From what he knew of Brewer's life, that simple playing card surely served as far more than a simple bookmark. He continued to read.

"You ask yourself, what would you do if you were king for a day? Money? Fame? Easy enough, I'm sad to report. But what if you were a god for five minutes a day? I can tell you. I dream of Marissa. It's always the same. We're downtown, dancing late night at the Brickhouse Bar. Then I take her up to Crow Canyon for midnight steak-and-eggs and nickel slots. I wish I could live in those dreams. They're a relief from all the waking nightmares since Long Green Hour. I wanna pluck it all out of my mind, but part of me never left that fucking bank."

4

I'm The One With The Gun

Like many American cities, Easton enjoyed a downtown full of architectural wonders, from its early days in the 1850s to its metropolitan prime in the 1920s. As the population grew to over half a million, urban sprawl pushed real estate development north, leaving behind a once-central downtown suffering from inner-city crime, neglect, and decay. Over the years, most of the businesses relocated or shuttered completely. The Victorian hotels, Art Deco restaurants, Beaux-Arts storefronts, and Neoclassical city hall were covered in plaster, enclosed in metal facades, or razed to the ground, concealing a rich history, Easton's sesquicentennial heritage.

Easton Monument Bank stood as one of the last stalwart symbols of the city's former glory, its domed painted ceilings depicting an impressionist paradise of white clouds and flocks of geese soaring across a blue sky above a picturesque woodland sanctuary. Along the marble tile floor, fifteen teller stations made of brass and oak serviced the bank's members, none of whom noticed any of the building's beauty as their personal time ticked away and the late-afternoon rush hour loomed ahead. The line seemed exceptionally long as the staff balanced customer service with the needs of the bank's special biennial date known internally as "Long Green Hour."

The line of four dozen impatient members stretched down the length of the immense bank, from the "Next in Line" sign near Teller One to the front double doors that led to Royal Street, the main thoroughfare of Old Downtown. So preoccupied with their upcoming transactions and the long commutes home to follow that not one patron noticed the large man at the back of the line wearing black pantyhose over his head, watching the second hand of his gold watch. By the time the last in line turned to see the startling sight of the masked criminal standing behind him, firearm ready in hand, it was too late to scream for help.

BEEP BEEP

4:02 P.M.

"Hello Easton Monument!" Rolo "Moonlight" Marino yelled like a showman to the stunned line of patrons, his deep voice echoing across the bank as if his watch's alarm had transformed him. Though his face looked distorted behind the tight pantyhose, his wide smile was clearly seen.

An old, lone security guard stood frozen, unsure, as four more thieves wearing similar pantyhose masks and gold watches, carrying identical handguns, burst into the bank behind Rolo.

Teddy "Prime Time" Brewer, the apparent leader of the gang, pointed his gun at the line of tellers. "Your alarm's out for the count! Bash those hidden buttons all you want, but I'm not bluffing. You'll soon learn that I never bluff."

Behind Teddy stood the rest of his partners, comprising a tall African-American man, a bald Caucasian man, and a young Mexican woman, their statures, genders, and skin tone the only traits that could be discerned through their masks.

Angelica "Tea Time" Cruz looked around for her position but couldn't decide where to stand. She yelled at Teddy. "Prime, where you want me?"

"You know the drill, anywhere up high where you can see everything."

While Teddy corralled the frightened staff behind the teller stations, Angelica jumped atop a desk in the middle of the room, sure to scan everyone and everything during what would be the gang's final heist. Of all the people in that crowded bank, it wasn't the customers or the staff that Angelica watched, rather her partners. She didn't dare break sight of them for a moment.

One glance away could bring disaster.

Bart Reed, the nervous security guard, stood motionless with his hands raised to his shoulders, bewildered by the gang spreading out across the bank as if his guard uniform and gun were inconsequential. The bank staff knew Bart as a friendly old fellow who resembled country music star Kenny Rogers and worked part-time as a guard in his retirement years. They never once wondered if he'd ever pointed his weapon at someone before, much less fired it, or if he'd have the courage to do anything other than comply during a robbery. They assumed he served as their fully qualified guardian with experience and training from twenty-eight years with the police. None of them knew Bart served his first seven years in Parking Enforcement and subsequent fourteen in Dispatch, nor that he had never felt like a genuine police officer. A year prior to his retirement party, he planned his winter years, applying for comfortable jobs guarding warehouses, hotels, and banks. He imagined sitting and standing for five hours a day, pacing the floor in his clean, pressed uniform, sipping coffee, opening doors for customers, and greeting the employees with a polite "Good morning" or "Nice clear day, today, isn't it?"

Not once did Bart Reed imagine actually having to guard anything, so his verbal command tumbled out with confusion and fear as he gripped his pistol with both hands, pointing it at Rolo Marino. "Don't move!" The threat proved to be futile and dangerous, not only because the thieves outnumbered him, but because for the next few minutes - unbeknownst to Bart - no force on Earth could stand in their way.

Rolo glanced at the armed retiree only to turn away to speak to his comrade, the bald, pale Enzo "High Noon" O'Day.

"Look at this place, Noon," Rolo said. "Amazing."

"It's like Caesar's Palace up in here," Enzo said, his wide smile seen through his mask. He forgot to cover his thick Boston accent. "It's kinda pretentious, in a way. Not sure how I feel about it."

"Hell, I love it. Most banks are pathetic and plain, but this is a palace, worthy of my money." Rolo walked up to Bart as if to include him in the conversation. "This is a nice place you got. It's an elegant fortress. It's what a bank should be. You know, I never got the flip-flop with churches and banks. A church should be simple. It's a house of worship, a place to be humble. But a bank should be majestic. It should slap you in the face *money*."

Bart stared at the large, disturbed thief in front of him, his gun still raised, desperate to remember his training.

"I think you're supposed to let us do our thing," Rolo said, as if he could read the guard's mind. "I mean, you don't want bodies hittin' the floor, do you? But who am I kidding? That Beretta in your mitts might as well be a squirt gun."

Bart took Rolo's blunt advice as a personal insult and felt twenty-eight years of self doubt swell inside him. With Rolo standing ten feet away, and nearly thirty years of fear and regret bubbling to a head, the old guard pulled the trigger.

CLICK CLICK.

His gun misfired, as if its hammer was worn to a nub. Now committed, Bart whipped out his radio to call for help.

BLAM!

The radio flew out of his hand, its shattered case and components scattering across the floor onto the kneeling customers who screamed in terror.

BLAM!

A second shot took the old guard's hat high into the air, landing it onto a nearby desk. Bart instantly collapsed flat to the floor, joining the customers, his arms over his head.

From her high, central position, Angelica lowered her gun, her precision shots unnecessary during her Five. Rolo shook his head and muttered "show off" not realizing that her shots were meant to scare the old guard into submission, to save him from earning Moonlight's famous wrath. She'd seen the aftermath of his short fuse and wanted to avoid bloodshed.

"Leave him be, Moon!" Angelica said. "He ain't no threat to nobody!"

Her distinct urban Spanish accent sounded familiar to Nora Castillo, a senior citizen sitting cross-legged on the floor in the middle of the subdued crowd, clutching a tote bag that held "Pee Wee," her anxious Chihuahua puppy. Nora focused on Tea Time standing above her, searching for a name to place with the voice.

Behind the tellers' counter, Teddy scanned the two dozen employees dressed in beach wear - jeans, Hawaiian T-shirts, straw hats, canvas shorts - to help celebrate the bank's new location in the Central Coast city of Monterey, California.

Larson "Rooster" Williams, the tall African American thief, also scanned the staff until he found who they were looking for. He nodded to his partner. "Prime, I think I found her."

Teddy approached Alice DeVoss, the employee Rooster singled out, a middle-aged woman standing behind her beach-going coworkers, her makeup running from tears and sweat. Unlike the rest of the staff, Alice wore a blue pant suit and heels.

Teddy grabbed Alice by the back of her neck. "You must be Miss Manager. When you don't get in the spirit of Casual Friday, you give yourself away." Alice stared at the pantyhose-masked menace clutching her.

On the main floor, Rolo - confident beyond logic - unfurled a long burlap sack and held it out to the customers sprawled on the floor. "Today's your lucky day because you get to tell all your friends that you were at a real life robbery! The biggest in the history of Easton! You get to tell 'em you had the honor of being robbed by the Lucky Five. Hell, you might even make the evening news."

During Rolo's boisterous control of the room, Robbie Sullivan, a man in a New York Yankees baseball cap and matching Yankees shirt, lay flat on the floor, slowly moving the fingers of his right hand under his stomach, across his belt, to his loaded firearm. He watched as Rolo relieved the customers of their wallets, making his way down the line toward him.

Enzo noticed the Yankee's refusal to ready his wallet. "Moonlight, we got resistance over here. Careful, he might be a tough guy."

"Wonderful," Rolo said, smiling wide. "Tough guys are my kind of people." He gestured for Enzo to gather the rest of the wallets while he made a beeline for Sullivan. As he held the sack out to him, the man kept his hand on his hidden gun, staring up at the giant before him. Rolo read the Yankee's angry, determined face, and spoke to him like a friend. "Fella, I understand where you're comin' from. There are times you feel the need to stand your ground and other times where you bend your knee and live to see another day. I know, 'cause I been there many times, and I strongly recommend you choose the knee 'cause you gotta understand where I'm comin' from."

"And where's that?" Sullivan asked defiantly.

"Your piss-ant wallet ain't even one percent of one percent of the take. But it's a matter of principle. It wouldn't be fair to the others if I let you slide just because you're giving me a fuckin' Dirty Harry look." Sullivan kept his right hand on the grip of his concealed gun, pressed between his belly and the floor.

Rolo paused his booming showman voice, knelt down, and leaned into the man. "Just so there's no confusion," Rolo said, "I'm the one with the gun."

After a tense moment, the Yankee complied, removing his hand from his hidden gun to pull his wallet from his back pocket.

Behind the counter with the tellers, Teddy manhandled the frightened Alice, guiding her to the vault, sealed tight for the moment.

"I can't... I mean..." Alice said, her words stumbling over each other. "I can't... with that gun.. I don't..."

"Godammit!" Teddy said. "Don't they give you guys crisis training?"

Unlike his partner, Larson seemed more at ease, almost monotone, as he checked the time on his gold watch. "Prime, time's burning. We need that cow."

"Someone get the fuckin' cow!" Teddy said. "Tellers! You're gonna dump your trays!" The staff stood frozen, hesitant to move out of fear of a misstep that could trigger the unstable leader of the gang. Rather than bark more orders at them, Teddy looked Alice in the eye. "What's your name, Miss Manager?"

"Al... Al... Alice," she said, trembling.

"Well, Al-Al-Alice, I hope you're a great boss. I hope your employees respect and adore you, because if they don't dump their fuckin' trays, and I don't see a rolling cow in front of me, I'm gonna put a bullet through that river of mascara."

The indirect threat moved the tellers to quickly obey his orders. One of them ran into another room and brought out the "cow," a small wheeled cart built like a miniature armored tank, used to transport unusually high amounts of money from the teller stations to the vault on that date every two years. To Teddy's dismay, the cow sat empty in front of the locked vault. "Tea Time! Make sure you can see everything!"

From her vantage point out on the main floor, Angelica yelled "Yep!" Exactly as ordered, she merely stood and watched everyone, particularly Nora Castillo, the old woman who kept staring at her. "Shit," Angelica said, muttering to herself, suddenly scared.

"Now the vault!" Teddy said to the tellers. "Who's gonna assist me? Alice? You can still save that pretty face."

Mascara dripping down her cheeks, Alice shook her head in defeat and dread. "None... none of us can open... the vault is timed..."

"Let me read your pretty face, Alice." Teddy took a moment to judge whether this frightened woman spoke the truth, concluding that she hadn't tried to play him. "Tea Time! I'm gonna need you back here after all!"

Rolo tied the burlap sack full of wallets and watched as Angelica jumped off her central desk and hurried to the vault. She kept eye contact with him until she ran behind the tellers' counter, out of his sight.

Suddenly concerned, Rolo checked his gold watch and quickly pointed his gun at security guard Bart Reed. "You just stay cool, friend. No need for two tough guys today." Bart felt confused as the fearless criminal now considered him a threat.

Angelica joined Teddy at the vault. "What the hell?" she asked. "I'm supposed to be out there!"

"I need you to open it."

"But I've never..."

"You can do it," Teddy said, assuring her. "This is your Five, not mine."

Angelica took a breath, placed her fingers on the vault's combination dial, and fumbled with it, slowing her shaking hand to a careful movement.

"Prime!" Rolo yelled from the main floor, his unsure tone betraying his bravado. "What the fuck is going on? Tea Time? Somebody talk to me!"

"Hold on!" Angelica yelled back.

"Clock's ticking!"

"Hold on!"

Rolo "Moonlight" Marino, who held the bank firmly in control moments before, felt sweat beading on his forehead. He turned to Bart, now sitting on the floor. "Noon, grab his piece."

Enzo approached the old man with his hand out. "Sorry, buddy, gotta take that old-school gat of yours. They're hazardous for your health, trust me." Bart relinquished his gun, sliding it to Enzo's feet.

While Rolo watched, distracted, Robbie Sullivan finally pulled his gun out from under his belt. He carefully sat upright and aimed at Rolo.

Angelica eased the vault's dial until she felt something give. After another half-inch turn, the lock made a soft click. She swung open the massive vault door, amazed that she pulled it off. "Got it!"

"Then get your ass back out here!" Rolo yelled. "We got under a minute before..."

BLAM! BLAM! BLAM!

Rolo shut his eyes. He slowly opened them, surprised to still be alive and standing. Robbie Sullivan sat puzzled. The shots from his smoking gun somehow missed the large criminal standing fifty feet away.

Rolo turned, relieved to see Angelica once again making eye contact with him through a teller window.

Teddy and Larson wheeled the cow into the vault and shoved shelves of cash into it, stacks of Hundreds falling into the wheeled tank, an unknown fortune for the taking. Their moment of euphoria ended when Larson checked his watch and pointed out the time to Teddy. The two men immediately abandoned the rest of the money. They wheeled the cow out onto the main floor, rejoining their partners.

Robbie Sullivan clutched his exposed gun tight, not sure what the hell was happening. "Don't move! Stay right there!" To his bewilderment, the reunited ring of thieves ignored his command.

"All of it?" Rolo asked.

"Not all," Larson said.

"Then get the fuck back in there!"

"No time," Teddy said, wheeling the cow to the bank's side exit.

"Godammit!" Rolo's eyes fixed on the Yankee, his gun still raised.

"I said hold it right there!" Sullivan yelled again. He pulled the trigger on the gathered gang.

CLICK CLICK.

Rolo ran up to Sullivan and grabbed his gun. Both men clutched the weapon as Rolo muscled it toward the Yankee's head.

"Just so there's no confusion..." Rolo said, seething.

BLAM!

5

Back Rent

Thursday, December 20, 2001, 3:39 p.m.

BAM! BAM! BAM!

Manny slammed the journal shut and stared at the door as if trying to see through the peeling wood to whoever pounded it with clinched fists. He imagined a disappointed George and an angry Detective Bruce standing in the hall with several other officers, having just seen surveillance footage of the Brewer journal being stolen from an active crime scene.

Manny looked at his reflection in the dormant TV. What a fool, to steal something that had not only become a vital piece of a double-murder investigation but a priceless artifact of history. George had compared him to the first photographer on the scene at the infamous Bonnie-and-Clyde

Lynn Harrod

ambush, but that man didn't dare swipe Bonnie Parker's purse or ever consider pocketing Clyde Barrow's wallet.

"Sanchez!" An old man yelled from the hall. "I know you are home inside! I see you come carry bags!" The thick, angry Armenian accent and wheezing cough put Manny at ease. He slid the journal under the sofa cushions, walked the length of his studio apartment in eleven steps, and answered the door.

"Gregor," Manny said, pushing forward the best smile he could manage. "I know what day it is. I'm sorry..."

"You call me 'Gregor' when you move in," the old man said, standing alone in the hall in his pajamas, oxygen tubes snaked around his shoulders into his nostrils. "You call me 'Gregor' when you pay deposit and rent. Today is two months late. You call me 'Mr. Azizian.'"

"I'm sorry but this coming Friday..."

"You say 'I have rent now, Mr. Azizian, sir.' You don't say Friday, you say now."

The monthly rent for Manny's rat-hole studio on Broadway Avenue, on the southern outskirts of the Castle District, seemed like a steal at $650. When his amiable landlord allowed Manny some breathing room two months ago, he'd hoped to save enough money to either repair and upgrade his equipment or purchase all new gear, but that forgiving old man lost patience and felt pressure to bring the eighty-year-old four-unit building to code in time for the upcoming annual County inspection.

"Inspector come Monday," Gregor said. "Pay rent now or maybe we all live on street."

"If you really need it, I can pay for October."

"I really need it October and November."

"I can cut you a check for six-fifty right now."

Gregor interrupted a mounting rant, inhaled deep through his oxygen tubes, and looked his young tenant in the eye. "Bro, I understand." The old man often called people "bro" when he tried charm over demands. "I know you are new to town and new job, but I need full payment. The owner, he will be pissed. If he know I let you pay late, he will be pissed."

"I'll pay you the late fees and an advance on next month if I could just..."

"I don't care about late fee, bro. I just need full payment. You and me don't want to evict."

Defeated, Manny looked at his broken equipment spilling out of his camera bag onto the sofa. He needed a solid rig to work, to earn the money he promised, but he also needed a keep that rat-hole. Finding an apartment within his meager budget had been a challenge. Gregor had been generous with him, forgoing the usual requirement of first and last month, plus deposit. Manny knew the old man's dilemma with the County. He couldn't ask for more slack.

Reaching into a coffee can under the kitchen sink, Manny retrieved the full cash payment of $1,300 and handed it to the old man.

Gregor nodded, knowing that his tenant just handed over every dollar he had. After writing out a receipt for the double payment, the old man walked down the hall, returning to his apartment. As he opened his door, he turned to Manny with a look of apology. "You will figure out, Sanchez. I know you will. Good luck."

The two men shut their doors. Manny felt as empty as the coffee can in his hands, nearly all of his savings gone. He hoped George would help him with equipment, but that had been a touchy subject for weeks, and his supervisor often reminded him he was still on probation, that four other candidates stood in line behind him for the position.

Teddy Brewer's journal waited for him in its hiding spot within the sofa cushions. Until the next morning, when Manny could beg his new boss for aide, all he could do was continue reading a mobster's life story. He pulled out the journal and instantly found the page and line where he left off.

"I'm starting this journal with a glass of cognac and a cigar, sitting in a house too big and too classy for a guy like me, having stolen a life in Easton's North End that passes for success. But I need to rewind, back to the poor souls of the Lucky Five that started with a cup of burnt coffee and a borrowed cigarette at a broke down school."

6

If You Believe in Luck

Friday, August 27, 1999, 8:10 p.m.

Clarke Adult School began life in 1956 as Hamilton High School. Its students all grown up and moved on, the school fell to decades of disrepair and had been scheduled for demolition twice before the city reopened it, first as a community center, followed by a short stint as an ambitious, privately owned events center. In 1997, the school returned to the city's care, reborn and renamed after one of Easton's founding fathers as a place for high school dropouts to gather at night to earn their General Education Development certificates in hopes of course-correcting their wandering lives.

As a full moon rose above the hills, a group of twenty students bundled in coats and scarves stood on the front steps of the school under a light drizzle of rain, waiting for

Lynn Harrod

their teacher to arrive. Mr. Roman was known to arrive late, and that night cemented his reputation.

Teddy Brewer stood apart from the pack, draped in a green trench coat from a thrift-store window and black cotton gloves from a bargain bin. He lit his third White Knights cigarette and sat on the first step of a small set of bleachers, his feet on the perimeter of the basketball court, as he watched a young woman play handball against the north wall of the administration building.

"You ain't cold, Ang?" Teddy asked, his breath condensing, drifting away, like the ribbons of smoke from his cigarette.

Angelica hurled her three-inch rubber ball with venom for the two-hundredth time, working herself up into such a sweat that she'd removed her puffy nylon jacket and dropped it on the bleachers beside Teddy sixty throws prior. "The jacket slowed me down."

"I used to play, before I moved out here."

"For reals?" Angelica asked. "Like pro ball?" Her distinct urban Spanish accent landed somewhere between East Coast and East L.A.

"No, but if there was professional stoopball, I'd be holding the cup."

"What the hell is 'stoopball'? Is this more New York stuff, Ted?"

Angelica Cruz - the woman who would be later known by both her friends and the FBI as "Tea Time" - had the pitiable honor of being Teddy Brewer's only friend in the world and former friend of his old flame Marissa Washington. Teddy met them both at the Brickhouse Bar, his first stop upon moving to Easton six years prior. When Marissa left Teddy, she also fell out with Angelica who didn't approve of her new friends in the Castle District, her new job as an exotic dancer, and her downward spiral into drugs.

During the trio's first meeting - an evening of light beer, Long Island Iced Tea, and brisket nachos over three rounds of pool - Teddy saw Angelica as confident and tough without being full of herself, each trait an exact opposite of Marissa's, he'd later realize.

Angelica grew tired and allowed the ball to get away from her. Teddy instantly snatched it from the air and threw it squarely against the center of the wall, back into play. His friend had never seen him move so fast.

"Shit, Ted, maybe you weren't bluffin' me about being good at 'stoopball' or whatever you call it."

"One thing you'll come to learn about me, Ange, is that I never bluff."

While Teddy and Angelica waited for Mr. Roman a short distance away from the rest of the students, Rolo Marino waited by the fence, watching the occasional car drive by, their tires kicking up spattering rain. Far from the wool overcoat and custom suit he would later be known for, Rolo wore a cracked leather jacket, jeans, and brown boots. He held a cigarillo, pausing his casual smoke to eavesdrop on the two figures on the basketball court, as if gathering intel on them. Something Angelica said piqued his interest.

"You're from New York?" Rolo asked Teddy. "I was born there. Best years of my life."

"I was born here, lived there for a while, then I had to move back here."

"Had to?" Rolo asked, seizing on that curious wording. Before Teddy could recall his cover story regarding his move back to California, their math teacher arrived.

Mr. Roman's blue step-side truck bypassed the faculty parking lot and stopped directly in front of the school, a mere fifty feet from the cluster of adults waiting for him in the light rain. He ran to the school's entrance and unlocked the door. After dark, the school's many doors and hallways were bolted, a nuisance only the night students had to contend with, along with a dormant climate control system and a shuttered cafeteria. Attending night school at Clarke meant enduring in a cold classroom with no food service during breaks.

"Can anyone tell me the average rainfall in Easton on this date?" Mr. Roman asked while fumbling through an immense ring of keys, as if starting a discussion on statistics as they entered the school would lessen his tardiness. "Anyone watch the news?"

"Seventeen?" Angelica said. "I mean, it's been raining for a few hours now."

Mr. Roman sighed at his one vocal student who hadn't learned a damn thing in the month she'd been coming to class, twice weekly.

* * *

Mr. Roman sat at the front of the classroom, laying out the evening's lesson on a spartan desk he shared with five other rotating teachers. He'd written "Statistics 1A" on the whiteboard behind him, claiming a meager fourth of the board for the next hour. Surrounding it were auto repair diagrams, algebra formulas, cake recipes, and Shakespearean characters - lessons from other classes - each with "save" written above them. Roman dared not erase any of it for fear of backlash from his underpaid peers.

Roman's cell phone buzzed, prompting him to drop his paperwork and answer the call. He spoke to someone in a hushed tone while his students settled in their seats.

Near the door, Teddy poured coffee into a Styrofoam cup, twelve ounces of burnt, black sludge that would have to do if he was to keep his eyes open for the sixty agonizing minutes. He briefly considered the coffee offered by a vending machine in front of the dark cafeteria, but it sat across campus and was likely depleted for the day. Even if the machine still had provisions, the coffee that spewed out of it tasted like mud mixed with corn syrup. More likely, the old machine might simply eat his seventy-five cents and mock him by opening its little door and dropping an empty cup.

Teddy took his steaming cup from the teacher's decrepit drip machine and walked to his desk at the back of the room. He passed the tired faces of his classmates, faces that just finished a double shift at a downtown diner, a long day of picking grapes in the fields of Ashton, and a droning drive from nearby Brawley. Besides day jobs, many of them had spouses and children waiting for them at home. Many more of them had only their night classes and food stamps and the hopes of something better than their unfulfilling lives of regret. Most were in their late twenties. After years of drifting from job to job, living check to check, nothing is more motivating than one's biological clock about to strike thirty.

Teddy sat at his desk and looked at all those worn faces. He saw average joes who learned the hard way that ambition, natural skill, and born talent meant nothing in this world without a G.E.D. What was unfortunate, he surmised, was that most of those ignorant fools didn't even have natural skills or born talent and would end up dropping out of school all over again, their inability to endure class dooming them to repeat history. School proved hard enough to a teenager whose daily life revolved around learning. It proved ever more difficult to an adult who had to worry about paying bills, buying diapers, and putting food on the table.

Like most of the students, Teddy had a day job, part-time work at the Trevorrow General Motors car dealership, washing and detailing Cadillacs and Buicks. He considered it monkey work typical of an uneducated slob who'd wasted his early potential. With no upward growth, no respect, no real pay, he enrolled at Clarke Adult School to become what he called a "second lifer," just like his father - a blue collar trying hard to be white.

Teddy shook away his self-pity and turned to Angelica sitting beside him. "Did you study for the test?"

"There's a test?" Angelica asked, still not comprehending the fact that they were tested biweekly.

Mr. Roman ended his phone call and stood to address his students, pulling a quarter from his pocket.

"I have a family crisis," Roman said. "One of my Great Danes has lost his mind and is trying to eat his own leg. So, thanks to Cartier, we're getting out early. Here's a quickie. Let's talk odds. Heads or tails?"

Mr. Roman flipped the quarter high in the air, slapping it onto the back of his hand. For the first time in weeks, Teddy perked up as gambling odds always intrigued him. The other students shouted "heads" or "tails," waiting for Roman to uncover the coin.

"If I flip this coin twenty times, what are the odds of all Heads? Or thirty times? Or a hundred times?"

"It's gotta be Tails sometime," Angelica said, as always his one vocal, oblivious student.

"Fifty-fifty. That's the answer. Even if you get a hundred Heads in a row, that next flip is fifty-fifty. The odds reset each time."

"Unless you're lucky," Teddy said, his first words offered in class. The rest of the students laughed, nodding in agreement.

"If you believe in luck, you're gonna need it," Mr. Roman said. "Here's a story. A woman sits at a slot machine for seven hours, one of those machines networked with five-hundred others. She pulls that handle and drains away her nest egg. Same machine. Seven hours. Nature eventually calls, so she goes to the ladies' room. That moment, a man walks up, puts in a buck, pulls the handle, wins a cool fifty-three million." He paused for a dramatic effect, giving his stunned students a moment to let it sink in. "True story. Reno. Nine years ago."

"Fifty-three mill," Teddy said, "must have been a Megabucks machine."

"Ask yourself, would the Seven-Hour Woman now be rich if she'd held her pee for just one more turn? Think about it.

Lynn Harrod

This is what makes Vegas Vegas. Thousands of people on thousands of machines, all thinking, hell, it's gotta come up cherries sometime. People play their kids' birth dates in the lotto for years thinking that their numbers gotta win one day." He uncovered the quarter in his hand, not yet revealing it. "Nope. The odds reset each time."

"Did it come up Heads?" Angelica asked, craning her neck to spy the coin, completely missing the point of the lesson. She seemed disappointed to see the coin had landed on Tails.

"Time to go," Mr. Roman said, glancing at the clock on the wall. "Homework is Chapter Five. Read it. Take notes. Split into groups. Make charts for your hobbies, something personal, so you get into it. They'll be a big chunk of your grade. They should complement each other, so get to know your group. See you next week."

Mr. Roman shoved his papers into his satchel and was out the door within a minute. The students looked to each other, splitting into the same groups formed earlier in the rain.

Rolo rose from his rear corner desk and approached Teddy and Angelica. He simply stared at them, at Angelica's puzzled expression and Teddy's Styrofoam cup of burnt coffee.

"Two's company," he said. "Three's a gang."

7

Three's A Gang

Friday, August 27, 1999, 9:19 p.m.

Teddy had been to the Brickhouse Bar every weekend since he moved to Easton, and each time he opened its door he was sure to approach carefully, looking through the windows to be sure no one was on their way out as he reached for the ornamental handles. This instinct arose from his first time at the bar, reminding him of the first smiling face to greet him.

* * *

Six years prior, Teddy arrived in Easton on a Friday night behind the wheel of "Maxine," his old, red Jeep Wrangler. The small utility vehicle had no trunk yet still held his every possession. He pulled off Interstate 5 and into a rural gas station for a fill-up and a tall can of Mexican lager, the closest thing to a flavorful craft beer the desolate all-night mini mart offered. While filling Maxine's tank, an attendant emptied the trash cans at the pumps. Teddy asked him where "real beer" could be had in Easton. The young attendant pointed him to Lighthouse Row, a hip, bustling neighborhood of bars, restaurants, and clubs a few miles down I-5, named after the majestic Lighthouse Theater that anchored the nightlife.

Upon reaching the lively street, a banner advertising an upcoming poker tournament brought him to the Brickhouse. Teddy walked down the crowded sidewalk to the old bar and reached for the door only to get slammed in the forehead by it as a young African American woman rushed out with her friend.

Marissa Washington laughed, distracted by her high school friend Angelica Cruz who recalled a funny story about an old man who kept flirting with her at the gun range, offering to take her to his house in the hills for a tour of his safari trophy kills and rare imported firearms. With Marissa turned toward her friend and the door having no transom arm to slow its swing, she'd beaned Teddy on the head, nearly knocking him to the sidewalk.

Angelica grabbed Teddy's arms and kept him on his feet. Marissa apologized and offered to buy him anything he wanted to drink. As Teddy's daze subsided, his vision focused on Marissa's warm smile, bright eyes, and flawless skin, her expression tipsy from five green apple martinis over the past two hours.

"Tell him to surprise me," Teddy said to her, nodding to the concerned bartender behind them who'd just witnessed the collision. Marissa and Angelica took Teddy to the barstools they just left, luckily still vacant in the packed pub.

The Brickhouse was a Hofbrau-style bar with the college kitsch of beer mascot inflatables dangling from the ceiling and small neon signs adorning the back wall near the pool tables. Hardly the type of drinking hole that Teddy normally sought - his tastes leaned toward classic lounges that Dean Martin would consider home - he soon warmed to the atmosphere, if only for the company he enjoyed.

In addition to the bartender's surprise drink - a mix of dark rum and fruit juices fittingly called a "Painkiller" - Angelica ordered three Long Island Iced Teas, telling the barkeep that the drinks should be free considering she'd warned them about that goddamn wild door several times. No dice. Teddy's Painkiller alone was on the house.

Teddy spent the rest of that Friday evening with Marissa, Angelica, and the bartender, Enzo O'Day, a short, bald Caucasian with a permanent smile and a joke a minute, fresh from working the bars of South Boston, the man who would later be known as the notorious criminal "High Noon."

After drifting across the country, living out of his Jeep in small towns and roadside motels on the outskirts of capital cities throughout the Midwest, Teddy felt he may have finally found a place to call home, a welcoming feeling he never thought he'd experience again after leaving his old New York neighborhood of Coney Island. Not once during that year of roaming did he enjoy company and conversation with people he actually wanted to get to know. He settled in Easton and returned to the bar every weekend in search of that friendly, fleeting feeling again.

Lynn Harrod

* * *

Arriving at the Brickhouse on that rainy August night, after a ten-minute drive from Clarke Adult School, Teddy entered the familiar pub with Angelica and Rolo. He'd never confess it, but opening the door for the 300th time still brought Marissa to mind, the woman who took him by the hand, sat him in a barstool beside hers, and spent the next four years in his arms and his two-bedroom apartment, planning marriage and a move to Reno to start anew. For a while, he thought he could make it work.

"Impossible," Rolo said. "Can't be done."

Angelica had given a homeless man in the parking lot five bucks moments before, sparking a conversation about whether vagrants could still fit in with a society that shunned them.

"It's not impossible, you snob," Angelica said.

"Sure it is, and it ain't about being a snob."

"Hey, I was friends with a homeless guy. Ted, remember Minnesota Mark?" Teddy didn't hear her, still thinking of his ex-girlfriend.

"Saying 'hi' and 'bye' outside 7-Eleven doesn't count," Rolo said. "The only way you can be friends with a bum is if you were a bum, too."

"Why you gotta call them 'bums'?"

"'Cause that's what they are."

"See what I mean? You're a snob, Rolo."

"He's talking Tribalism," Teddy said, finally joining the conversation as they took seats at the bar. There were a few patrons scattered about, sitting in booths, listening to a Miles Davis marathon coming from a bookshelf stereo by the beer taps.

"Damn straight," Rolo said. "If you live in the Hamptons, guess what? Your friends live in the Hamptons. If you live in the ghetto... different worlds."

"It's all the same world, man," Angelica said.

"Same planet, country, state, town, but different worlds. You said you're from out in Whitesbridge, right? I grew up in The Castle. Just a bus transfer between us, but sweetheart, it's night and day."

"Castle District is pretty rough territory," Teddy said. "What was that like?"

"Picture the Castle District," Rolo said, "with me, I'm Italian, my brother's Italian. Everyone else was in one of the gangs - Black, Mexican, Russian. Different worlds."

"So you and your brother were the Italian gang," Angelica said with a grin. Rolo laughed, not elaborating further.

Teddy thought about Rolo's point and wandered into memory. "I was that one welfare kid in the big rich school. Upstate New York. After I graduated, I bumped into a guy from there, a grade below me. David Something. Trust fund baby, Porsche in the garage, summer home in the hills. A full ride. The guy had the soft touch his whole life. We reminisced about our high school. Damn, if you heard his stories and you heard mine... like Rolo said, different worlds."

"Let's raise a glass to Trust Fund David Something," Rolo said. He and Teddy knocked their drinks together - a glass of Scotch for Rolo, a mug of black coffee for Teddy.

"Forget him and his daddy's Porsche," Angelica said, trying to lighten the mood, knowing the nostalgia wounded her friend more than he let on. "We're getting our educations in order, right? We keep our noses in our books, Teddy whips up our charts, and we make with the happy graduation speeches."

"There's no speeches for a G.E.D., Ange," Teddy said. "No cap and gown, no ceremony, just a piece of paper sent to you in a big manilla envelope, mixed in with the junk mail."

"Shit, don't be so down on it."

"You know what 'G.E.D.' stands for? 'Good Enough Diploma.' That's what we'll be after all the studying and all the anxiety about being on time to class and taking notes and barely passing their fucking tests. We'll be just good enough."

"You're making a new life, Ted."

"You could do it the Castle way," Rolo said. "You hustle, make some scratch, get some juice, get a name."

"You do talk like a gangster," Angelica said with a smile.

Enzo the bartender poured Teddy another coffee. "Here you go, Ted, fresh brew just for you," Enzo said in his thick Bostonian accent. "At this time of night, I mean that literally. The carafe is all yours, free of charge. I'm just gonna toss it, anyway."

Rolo turned away, failing to hide his grimace. "Come on, man, let me buy you a man's drink." He offered the blue bottle of Scotch Enzo left for him. "It goes down smooth."

Teddy shook his head "nah."

"You can buy me one," Angelica said, "but forget him. Big Ted's been dry, what, a year now?"

"Sorry, I didn't know it was a 'wagon' thing," Rolo said.

"Well, now it's the coffee wagon," Teddy said. "And you, Ange, you might want to join me in a cup. You're knocking back a lot for someone who weighs a buck-and-change."

"Hey, some of us can handle a 'man's' drinks, thanks."

Angelica stumbled out of the ladies' restroom in the back hall of the bar, bumping into a decommissioned British telephone booth used for storing cases of beer and spirits. She slapped her palms to the red vintage phone booth, trying not to collapse to the floor for all to see. She'd metered her drinking with intermittent sips of water, as she always did, but her trusted pacing method normally involved pilsners and lagers, lightweights compared to the blended blue-label Scotch Rolo kept pouring.

The big man remained relatively centered and quiet across the evening, and it encouraged Angelica to match him glass-for-glass. She failed to consider that Scotch was ten times as strong as her usual lagers, and that her new friend stood three times her size, accustomed to enjoying such potent fare. By her fifth glass, she knew following his example was folly, destined for disaster, but still had a lovely time along the way.

During the four evening hours she spent with Teddy and Rolo, they occasionally talked about Mr. Roman's Statistics assignment but mostly spoke of old neighborhoods, former lovers, career goals, and the difference in balance between a muzzle-heavy and stock-heavy handgun - drunken random topics and the tangents thereof.

With the after-dinner crowd gone, the bar held only the most diehard patrons, regulars who remained late into the night through Last Call and the dimming of the house lights. Rolo sat at the end of the bar, nursing his sixth and final drink, mumbling to Enzo about the pointless pursuit of higher education and the thankless efforts of reinventing oneself. Teddy meanwhile sat alone at a side table, observing a nearby poker game.

Dealing and holding court over the five other players entrenched in Texas Hold 'Em sat Larson Williams, the bespectacled African-American man with the monotone voice - a perfect, permanent poker face - the man who would later be known on the FBI's Most Wanted list as "Rooster."

"Theodore, you sure you don't want in?" Larson asked Teddy, shuffling the deck. "The cards have been running cold for us all evening. Maybe you're the lucky one tonight, son."

"If you believe in luck, you're gonna need it," Teddy said, parroting Mr. Roman's earlier lesson on gambling odds.

"I know you don't actually believe that."

"Maybe I'm just not in the mood."

"And you know I don't actually believe *that*," Larson said as he dealt a new hand.

"Not even you know everything, Larson. Sometimes, even the hungriest of dogs can be full."

"We're not dogs, Theodore. People call serious card players 'sharks' for a reason. We never get full. We keep swimming, looking for more unsuspecting little fish to devour." Larson paused and glanced at the other players. "No offense to present company."

"Is that how you see me? A shark like you?"

"You don't really know a man until you play him Heads Up, and we've faced off across this table enough times that I can confidently say I know exactly what you are, son."

Teddy couldn't deny Larson's assessment of him. Indeed, they'd played cards together countless times over the years, often ending with 'Heads Up' - two cowboys left at the table in an Old West standoff after all the others folded. From such showdowns, Teddy became a local legend. He knew the correct play against every possible hand in every form of poker, whether it be with a few rookies or a loaded table of seasoned gamblers who just came from cleaning house at Crow Canyon Casino up in the hills. Never letting his emotions get away from him, never chasing his money down a dead end streak, he always stuck to the odds. In a purely statistical sense, Teddy's play was flawless. What he lacked was Larson's analytical prowess. The tall, stone-faced man who many considered a human lie detector could see through anyone, reading their faces and body language with perfection, as if their cards were double-sized and transparent. It came as no surprise when Teddy learned long ago that his friend earned the bulk of his income "working" at the many tables - both public and private, legal and otherwise, - across Easton, Ashton, and Brawley.

"You're right, as usual," Teddy said. "But let's just say I need to take a vacation from the tables for a while."

"I get it," Larson said, winning the new hand with a Full House of Queens over Tens. "Let's just say that."

On wobbly legs, Angelica reached Teddy's table and pulled out a chair, but sat a second too soon, landing her hard on the polished concrete floor. Teddy rushed to help her into the chair, sliding a glass of water in front of her.

"This ain't no Rolling Rock!" she said. "Gimme a beer, Ted!"

"Sorry, Ange, they're fresh out of beer."

"Don't sass me, Mr. Clean and Sober. You think you're better than me?"

"Yep," Teddy said with a grin.

"Listen," Angelica said, searching for his face, leaning in close. "I know why you're really going to night school, and it ain't for no Good Enough Diploma."

"You're not being real ladylike."

"I guess I'm not a real lady." Angelica stood, knocking over her chair. Teddy bolted to his feet, ready to catch her, unsure if he could.

"Let's fight for a beer, Ted. Makes it taste better 'cause I earned it."

"How about I call you a taxi?"

"How about I call you a bastard? A taxi? Am I made of money? Are we the Jeffersons?" She swiped a spoon from the table and held it like a microphone. "We're movin' on uuuuuup!"

Hitting the high note of the classic TV theme song, Angelica's body stiffened like a board as she fell onto the poker table, sending cards, gaming chips, and drinks flying everywhere. The players sat stunned. Larson laid down his now-useless hand of three Jacks.

"Sorry fellas, she had a few too many," Teddy said.

"She's always had a few too many," Larson said in a dry, disapproving tone. "Take her home, Theodore."

"Yeah, take me home, Theodore," Angelica said, her words slurring into each other. "I promise, I won't tell Marissa."

* * *

Teddy drove west of Easton into rural Whitesbridge, his top-down Jeep Wrangler rambling down a crumbling two-laner devoid of street lights or traffic signals. Creedence Clearwater Revival crooned about being in a traveling band, their classic rock anthem blasting down from 6x9 speakers mounted to the roll bar above. The dark country road stretched into the farmlands, cutting through miles of flat vineyards whose grapes were perfectly fine on a plate but barely passable in a glass, not that it discouraged the half-dozen family wineries in the area. Irrigation canals lined the old road, providing water for the crops and serving as a moat for the many cemeteries between farms.

"There's only two things in Whitesbridge," Teddy said, looking out at what he deemed a wasteland. "Cheap hobo wine and the dead."

Angelica sat in the passenger seat of the convertible, groggy but coherent, looking up at the stars and the tops of cypress trees that stood at the entrances of the cemeteries like rows of green sentinels. She batted at Teddy's fuzzy red dice hanging from the rear view mirror.

"The air feels cool on my face," she said.

"Glad to hear you're feeling better."

"You ever fold down Maxine's windshield?"

"Just once."

"Shame," Angelica said, her slurring voice betraying her attempt to will herself sober with continual sips of bottled water. "Every car had a folding windshield in the beginning. These Jeeps are the last holdouts." Teddy smiled whenever Angelica offered a nugget of odd trivia. "You can sit behind the wheel and line up your rifle on the hood."

"Not sure if you heard, but we won World War II, Ange."

"I'm talking about hunting. Let me take you out shootin' sometime."

"Nah, I could never point a gun at anything."

"Maybe not. Some things just ain't in your blood. I'm not even sure it's in mine, but my daddy used to take me out in the brush during Duck Season. That's where I got the bug." Angelica reached into her puffy nylon jacket and pulled out a small handgun.

"Put that away before you hurt yourself."

"Says who?"

"Says the twelve ounces of Scotch running through your veins."

"Fine, Mr. Safety Inspector." Angelica slid the small gun into her jacket pocket. "Teddy Brewer, you're a real stand-up guy, you know that?"

"Uh oh, drunk affection incoming."

"No, really, you are. Marissa missed the boat."

"You always gotta bring her up? She's your friend, not mine."

"She ain't mine no more neither. She's Zero's bitch now, so fuck her."

When Teddy and Marissa were on the rocks, Marissa started seeing her new boss. Angelica strongly opposed the sudden direction her roommate's life took, getting into daily shouting matches with her. At first, Teddy assumed Angelica overreacted, envious that her friend landed a guy who owned a popular nightclub in the Castle District. It made sense that Marissa dumped a drunk, degenerate gambler like Teddy and hooked up with a successful businessman. That was before Teddy got to know the man everyone called "Zero."

"He can have her," Angelica said with a snort.

"Yeah. I suppose."

Teddy pulled over in front of Angelica's house, a former farm laborer's bungalow with peeling paint and tin-foil-covered windows. Cyclone fencing surrounded the property, its front yard of tall weeds hiding car parts and land mines of dog shit strewn about. Other than a few derelict shacks, the small home was isolated by razed fields, the next residence ten acres away.

"You wanna know why I always bring her up?" Angelica asked.

"Not really."

"'Cause you always wanna hear her name."

"Oh, please..."

"Marissa! Marissa! Marissa!"

"Dead wrong, Ange."

"Hey, I don't know much, but I know you, Ted." Angelica stepped out onto her gravel driveway. Her last words made her stop and think about her friend and the rest of his night to come. "Go home, Ted."

"Really?" Teddy said with a forced laugh. "You think that I'm gonna..."

"Go home, Ted. Go straight home."

"I'm not the one who's shit-faced here."

"Don't think I didn't notice you checkin' out those sharps back at the bar."

"Did you hear me tell Larson that I was out?"

"Go home, Ted."

"I'll see you at the range," Teddy said, dismissing her concern. "Bring three different guns. Roman wants comparative data."

"Whatever." Angelica stared at Teddy, refusing to follow his attempt to change the subject. "Good night, Ted." She slapped the hood of the red Jeep. "Good night, Maxine."

Teddy promptly shifted into gear, made a U-turn, and drove away, his Jeep disappearing in the night behind a row of cypress trees guarding a neighboring veteran's cemetery.

Angelica Cruz swung open the gate of the front yard's chain-link fence and walked down a dirt path through the overgrown weeds to her front porch, avoiding the old tires, water pump, clutch plates, and transmission case that had long sat rusted and out of view. She trudged onto the covered porch and inserted her key into the lock, taking a moment for a deep breath before entering her home.

8

Bologna Sandwiches

Saturday, August 28, 1999, 12:49 a.m.

The dark, silent interior of the Cruz household looked nearly abandoned, its details seen in the moonbeams streaming in through the front windows. The couch, recliner, and coffee table sat unavailable as always, piled high with packages from the Home Shopping Channel, most never opened. Opposite the door, the south wall was lined with floating shelves that held hundreds of tiny ceramic animals, souvenir spoons, and framed photos, all covered with layers of dust and cobwebs. Angelica dared not clean the knick-knacks for fear of another confrontation. To her right, the west wall had a half-finished coat of teal paint, a home improvement project from years ago, now left abandoned in memory of the man who denied himself the chance to complete it. To her left, the east wall

Lynn Harrod

held the doors to the two bedrooms and the kitchen. She wondered which door led to her mother that night.

"Ma?" Angelica called out. "I'm home, ma!" She hung her puffy jacket on her bedroom doorknob, placed her keys in a bowl on the TV, kicked off her hiking boots, and entered the door to the kitchen.

Rosa Cruz sat under a lone light bulb in the kitchen, at a round oak table that twelve-year-old Angelica singled out at a flea market. Her late father Arturo insisted that his adolescent daughter choose the table as part of a life lesson in self-confidence, encouraging her to make seemingly important choices and stick to them. He also tasked her with choosing the TV, couch, coffee table - even his leather recliner - wanting her to feel a sense of owner's pride in their modest farm laborer home.

"Did you eat, Ma?" Angelica glanced at a green-and-yellow clock on the wall in the shape of a John Deere tractor. It would soon be one o'clock in the morning. "From the looks of the kitchen, I'm gonna guess no. An empty sink in this house?" Her little joke failed to land.

Rosa stared at a cup of tea clasped in her hands. Angelica hovered her fingers over the cup, noting that it was cold. Rosa had likely been sitting there for hours, another of her "off" nights.

"I'm gonna make you something," Angelica said, swinging open the refrigerator. "I hope you like grilled bologna and cheese 'cause that's what we got." She slammed a frying pan on the stove as if that would jolt her dazed mother, but the old woman didn't flinch. She spread mayonnaise and mustard - dots of Tabasco for her - on four slices of white bread and grilled them in the pan. The smell of cooked mustard and hot sauce filled the small, cluttered kitchen. "Just like pop used to make, with mustard bubbling in the pan." The nostalgic smell did nothing to grab Rosa's attention.

Angelica cut the sandwiches diagonally, set them on old rectangular Tupperware plates, and slid them onto the table. She dumped out her mother's cold tea and filled the cup with hot water, plunking in a single sugar cube and a new bag of Chamomile. She sat at the table beside her mother and dug into her bologna sandwich, hoping the ritual of eating together would get her mind working again. Like the other little moments that Angelica punctuated, the act of eating with her daughter failed to bring her back to lucidity.

"Come on, Ma, I haven't seen you all day," Angelica said. She knew it was useless trying to reach her when she fell into a "hole." Rosa only made eye contact when she was able and ready, but Angelica always tried. "I'm going shootin' tomorrow, gonna bring Pop's old Springfield. That thing hasn't seen action in years. Of course, I'll clean and oil it first."

Since the tragic death of her husband Arturo four years prior, during their final Thanksgiving together, Rosa Cruz battled Stage Five dementia, though Dr. Flowers recently told Angelica that her mother's "severe cognitive decline" indicated a gradual slip into Stage Six. Angelica didn't understand the gravity of the doctor's updated diagnosis and had to ask what separated the two stages. Dr. Flowers explained that Rosa's long-term memory loss was now coupled with increased anxiety and confusion, to where she "stalled" several times a day, her brain spinning and rewinding so much that she sat unable to perform basic tasks. At Stage Five, Rosa often saw a stranger when she looked at her only child, at family photos, and even her own reflection. Entering Stage Six, she occasionally forgot little things like how to make toast, change TV channels, and put on her socks. Soon, she would completely depend on the young woman who claimed to be her daughter.

Dr. Flowers recommended assisted living, but Angelica refused to consider the idea. He urged her to research a promising behavioral health program at Easton Medical Center, but the new program had yet to pass trials and wasn't covered by their healthcare coverage due to it being labeled a pre-existing condition.

Angelica subscribed to her late father's notion that any ailment could be fought, that a tough approach of "suck it up and shake it off" would eventually work. Though she still clung to that idea, her blind optimism became more difficult to hold on to.

She tore a corner of her mother's sandwich and fed it to her. Rosa stared into space and took the bite, giving Angelica an ounce of hope, for she rarely responded at all.

"You gotta eat, Ma, I don't care if you're on some new fad diet or if you lost your taste for bologna. You gotta get this down."

She placed the sandwich in her mother's hand. Rosa raised it to her lips and took another bite. Angelica was finally getting through.

"Thank you, Love," Rosa said, looking down at her plate. A fly on the wall might have considered this moment encouraging, but Angelica knew better. Rosa had always called her daughter "Butterfly" or "Mija" and her husband "Love."

"It's me, Ma," Angelica said. "Pop ain't here, remember?" She hated reminding her mother of her father's absence, a tragedy that loomed over their life, but Dr. Flowers insisted that Rosa be continually and gently reminded of the truth if there was any hope of communication, even in fleeting moments. Still, Angelica always used euphemisms like "He's out" and "He's not here," never disclosing that her father lay in the cemetery just west of their house.

Arturo Cruz worked as the Lead Mechanic at CenCal Ag - Central California Agricultural - a large commercial farm in Whitesbridge, overseeing the equipment on four properties for thirty-one years. He took pride knowing that people across the world ate fruits and vegetables maintained and harvested by his machines. He earned the reputation of being able to operate and fix anything, of always keeping a cool head when faced with a challenge. The image of a tall, strong, no-nonsense farmer who could solve any problem as both a natural leader and his family's figurehead was how his friends remembered him. A photo of Arturo in his stained overalls adorned his casket and comprised a fourth of that day's obituaries page. The Easton City Council chose him as one of twelve "Sons of Easton County" for their year-end memorial tribute, the only Mexican-American to ever make the list.

Angelica alone knew her father's distant past as a tormented soldier who served his country in two wars.

Arturo's first tour of duty was in 1953, fighting in North Korea with the 7th Marine Regiment, 3rd Battalion. His second tour was in 1965, fighting the Viet Cong as part of the 10th Marine Expeditionary Brigade. He never shared his experiences with friends nor with Rosa, sparing her delicate sensibilities from the details of the atrocities he witnessed and was tasked with, but he considered Angelica of tougher mettle and told her a few war stories when they sat alone for hours fishing along Lake Royale or hiked the John Muir Trail through the Sierra Nevadas.

Angelica sat at her kitchen table and recalled a few of those stories. Arturo's superiors tasked him with burying their dead in the rain-soaked jungles of Vietnam in the thick of the night. He blessed each of his friends' bodies with a silent prayer and the Sign of the Cross as he slid them into a mud pit he'd dug earlier that evening, giving them the closest thing they'd ever get to a proper funeral, knowing their loved ones could never visit their mass graves. Arturo always looked over his shoulder, always expected a sniper round to find him, as he covered his comrades with mud and leaves. He told Angelica about his first day there, how shocked he felt at seeing truckloads of Vietnamese citizens corralled and abused by those who considered themselves saviors, how his Lieutenant scolded him for expressing remorse in front of them.

Throughout her teenage years, hearing her father's war stories, she wished she could have been there with him. She wanted to protect him, to counsel him during his unimaginable grief. Such an honorable man didn't deserve to be broken down for the sake of duty.

Returning to civilian life, Arturo found work and married Rosa Ramirez, a field worker at CenCal. He soon saved enough money to buy their small house in Whitesbridge next to the Saint Paul Veterans' Cemetery. For thirty-one years, he raised his family there, leaving his past in the jungle but failing to forget. By 1996, at sixty-one, he dismissed the notion of retirement and continued working his fleets of tractors and combines, until the day his body failed him.

On doctor's orders, Arturo was soon forced into retirement, his world narrowing to the small plot of string beans and root vegetables behind his house. Within a year, he was diagnosed with lung cancer. The chemotherapy quickly took its took its toll, emaciating him into a shadow of his former self. His frail body affected his mind and soon his world narrowed further until a red bird feeder hanging on his back porch was all he had the strength to focus on.

Angelica helped him fill the feeder every morning. They'd sit on the porch and gaze up at the bluebirds, finches, and hummingbirds that visited them. Despite his positive attitude and stubborn optimism, it seemed cruel to Angelica that a man who'd lived such a large life was reduced to caring for backyard birds an hour a day. Rosa saw the shift in her husband's life as a good thing. He'd had his fill of duty and hard work and deserved to relax and enjoy simple pleasures.

Angelica knew her father better and was not surprised when he ended his life with an overdose of Abraxane. She found him on the couch one sunrise, his peaceful, sleeping face not fooling her for a moment. She knew her father had woken up before dawn, toddled to the living room, and taken the entire bottle of pills with a final cup of black coffee. As

Lynn Harrod

she kneeled and sobbed, she felt a strange relief. She and Rosa had been robbed of his large, boisterous personality years prior. At least now his pain and struggle had ended. Sadly, Rosa's was about to begin. By the year's end, her usual absent-minded manner spiraled with memory loss and desperate confusion. Dr. Flowers' eventual diagnosis of dementia didn't come as a shock to anyone.

Angelica took another bite of her bologna sandwich, the sting of the spicy mustard and Tabasco bringing her back to the present. She noticed that Rosa had eaten half of hers, fingering her tea cup's handle as if in deep thought.

"You with me, Ma?" Her mother nodded, glanced at her daughter, and offered a faint smile. "How about you eat that other half?"

Rosa shook her head, but picked up the sandwich, anyway. Mother and daughter ate in silence as the John Deere clock on the wall struck one.

9

Lifetime Membership

Sunday, August 29, 1999, 11:56 a.m.

The Easton Rifle and Pistol Club sat seven miles from the nearest shopping center or housing development. Just outside the eastern city limits in the foothill community of Dale Valley, the old shooting range was a favorite among the county's law enforcement and gun enthusiast community. Monty Glass opened the club in 1959 and quickly filled all fifty slots of private membership, comprising mostly locals and a few retired sheriffs. He passed it to his son Mitchell Glass in 1963 shortly before succumbing to heart failure. Like his father, Mitchell ran the club for another decade before selling it to war veteran Big Danny Perkins, an old friend of Arturo Cruz, going back to their tour together in Vietnam.

Arturo enjoyed a Lifetime Membership at the club and was popular with the other members despite only bringing his

Springfield bolt action rifle during each of his weekly visits. Unlike the other members, who were quick to boast of their vast collections of rare and exotic firearms both legal and "special," Arturo sought only to keep his marksmanship sharp leading up to Duck Season. He often brought his young daughter Angelica and her simple .22 rifle with him, smiling as she fired the starter weapon better suited for hunting small game rather than waterfowl.

After Arturo died, Big Danny Perkins extended his Lifetime Membership to Angelica in honor of her father. Having long outgrown her youth-oriented hunting rifle, she usually brought her .45 pistol, more comfortable with the feel of a compact gun, its rate of fire blazing past the collectors' rifles to her left and right on the range.

With the sole exception of Big Danny, Angelica spoke to no one at the club. She lacked both the charm and desire to fraternize with her father's old acquaintances at the range and grew tired of their toxicity, the shameless sexual advances they made. Being the youngest member of the club and its only female, she came to expect it, though she never dropped the hammer in protest out of respect for Big Danny.

Most persistent of the bunch was local contractor Cal Zimmer, a leering man who spent more time talking with Angelica during each session than he had with her father during the entirety of his eighteen years coming to the range. Cal bragged about his restored muscle cars - including a blue-and-white Shelby Cobra certified replica - and his floor safe filled with antique and modern military guns. He often invited her for a supposedly rare peek into his safe, which lay hidden in his bedroom, of course, installed under the floorboards at the foot of his California King bed.

Despite Cal's advances, Angelica continued to visit the range, always keeping to herself. She trained with her chosen pistols, occasionally brandishing one of her father's guns.

That morning, with Teddy on route, she brought her father's trusty Springfield. Shooting the old bolt-action rifle made her feel like he was still there, talking with Big Danny Perkins out front while she stood inside, wearing ear and eye protection, perfecting her aim on 18x10 paper targets depicting head-and-shoulders silhouettes. Though she could easily hit the targets dead-center, she preferred to nail their "arms" and "shoulders," practicing non-lethal tactics. Bored with achieving critical hits on the paper men like a villain in classic Western films, she'd rather incapacitate him like the movies' heroes. Growing up watching *Gunsmoke* and *The Rifleman* on Sunday mornings with her father, it never impressed her to see a man simply shot dead. Far more thrilling was when Chuck Connors expertly blasted the revolver out of a bandit's hands, offering him a fierce warning while also showing off his cool head and intimidating skill. Forget nailing a man in the torso - something she could do with one eye shut - she wanted to shoot the flames out of a row of candles or the caps off flying bottles, just like in those classic TV shows she and her father loved.

Teddy walked in with a small camera bag and joined his friend at her booth at the far end of the range. Like Angelica, Teddy stood out amongst the older members and their male camaraderie, one-upping each other in a never-ending pissing match of stories about their new double-wide RVs, touring motorcycles, and week-long vacations in Las Vegas. Angelica's white tank top with camouflage pants and Teddy's green thrift-store trench coat clashed with the dozen plaid flannel hunting shirts and vests around them. He felt uncomfortable at the range and knew his friend did as well.

"You warmed up yet?" Teddy asked.

"I was warmed up when I got out of bed," Angelica said. "Let's both load up and do this already."

Teddy reached into his camera bag and pulled out his weapon of choice, a large gray-and-white Canon XL-1 camcorder with a long detachable lens. He cleaned the lens and loaded a fresh video cassette.

"What's first?" Angelica asked.

"You're the gun expert here. Just shoot. I'll capture it all and sift through it later." Teddy put on noise-cancelling earmuffs and safety glasses like Angelica's as she held down a red button to send a new paper man down the lane.

Right on cue, at five past noon, Cal Zimmer entered the Easton Rifle and Pistol Club and glanced at the members firing along the range. Like the others, he wore an outfit of plaid flannel, a hunting vest, and cargo shorts, only his was topped with his signature tan fedora to hide his comb-over, and gold-framed aviator sunglasses to hide his crow's feet. He smiled when he spotted Angelica reloading her gun, his swagger shifting to a curious smirk as he approached and noticed Teddy and his camcorder behind the partition.

"Brewer?" Cal said with exaggerated surprise. "I never took you for a gunman."

Teddy's heart raced when he heard Cal's cackling voice before turning to see his fat, freckled face. "There's a lot you don't know about me, Cal."

"I guess the only thing you're shooting is that thing." Cal ran his fingers across the camcorder's lens hood. "Probably better that way. Not sure if I trust a loose cannon like you with a gun."

"Whatever that means."

"You two know each other?" Angelica asked.

"Oh sure, Old Teddy and I have had our share of showdowns," Cal said with a laugh. "Just not with pistols, and not at the OK Corral. Instead, we face off at..."

"This is a gun range, Cal," Teddy said, pouncing on him. "We talk about guns and nothing else."

"Fair enough," Cal said, raising his hands in surrender. "I guess if I were you, I'd want to keep things quiet, too. Whatever happens at Ronnie's Room stays at Ronnie's Room, am I right?"

Angelica didn't immediately know what they were talking about, but she knew both men well and she knew about "Ronnie's Room." She'd bring it up with her friend later in private.

"I finally got the Deville back from the shop," Cal said to Angelica. "Turned out real cherry. Eight coats of candy apple red, like a classy lady's rouge. Red's still your favorite color, am I right?"

"Green," Angelica said. "You're confusing me with someone else, Cal."

"I suppose I am. My mistake. You aren't the only filly's caught my eye." With a nod and a tilt of his fedora, Cal walked away, preparing his guns at an open booth down the range.

Clasping her pistol in both hands, Angelica took careful aim and fired five shots three seconds apart.

BLAM! BLAM! BLAM! BLAM! BLAM!

"Nice," Teddy said, recording every moment. "You were rock steady. Perfect line of sight. I bet every shot landed square in the primary impact area."

"So now you're a gun expert?" Angelica smiled at both her performance and the notion that her friend knew what the hell he was talking about.

"Like I told Cal, there's a lot you don't know about me."

"If you say so, Ted."

Angelica held down the red button to bring in the paper man, revealing that all five shots landed dead-center on the silhouette's heart. "You hear what happened to Rolo last night? I heard he got jacked up by some Castle goons."

"Must have been before he collapsed and bled all over my living room rug."

"For reals?" Angelica whipped off her earmuffs. "Shit, is he okay?"

"He's black and blue and hungover as hell, but he'll live. How'd you find out?"

"Marissa called me." Though Angelica's friendship with Marissa waned over the years, they still occasionally spoke on the phone, each hoping the other would extend an olive branch, something other than a catch-up call. "She told me what happened, something about a big guy named 'Moonlight Marino' getting tossed out of the club. I heard Enzo call Rolo that at the Brickhouse."

"Well, don't worry about 'Moonlight,' he's back at my place eating all my Pop Tarts."

"What about Maxine?"

"What about her?"

"She ain't parked outside, is she?" Angelica glared at Teddy, not giving him time to come up with a lie.

"Okay, now how the hell do you know *that*?"

"You always twirl your keys in your fingers when you enter a place. No keys, I figure something happened, like she broke down again or something like that."

Angelica's simple view of things often made her appear unintelligent or naive but sometimes sharply observant, something Teddy forgot that morning. If he'd remembered, he would have twirled his house keys to keep from fielding questions about last night. She'd put him on the spot, forcing him to quickly choose between crafting a last-minute cover story or laying out the truth. He chose the latter.

"No, she ain't parked outside."

"Did you go home last night like I said?" Angelica sent out a new paper man and waited for an answer. "Or did you go to Smokey's Club with Rolo?" She readied her gun, aiming it down the range, taking in her friend's awkward silence. "I see. So then you went to Ronnie's Room. Is that where Maxine is? At Ronnie's?"

Teddy gave up the idea of shaking Angelica from her line of questions. "I don't know where she is now. But yeah, okay, I left her at Ronnie's..."

BLAM! BLAM! BLAM! BLAM! BLAM!

Angelica angrily fired over her friend's embarrassing confession. "You and Marissa are meant for each other!

You're both fucked up! Do everyone a favor and get some professional help!"

"Hey! You got baggage, so you think you can talk about other people's baggage? Does your mom still walk outside in her underwear? Does she still get lost going to the bathroom?"

Angelica placed her pistol on the shelf beside her, grabbed Teddy by the collar, and slammed him to the partition wall, pinning his throat with her forearm. She started to grab him in a chokehold but let it go, her sympathy for him creeping into her fury. "Watch the mom shit, Ted."

"My bad," Teddy said, his voice hoarse and muffled from Angelica's firm grip. "Look, Ange, you gotta understand, as hard as it was to stop drinking, it's even harder to stop..."

"Then *you* gotta be harder."

Angelica released him and picked up her gun for another round. "Did you get *that* on tape?" Her bravado simmered as she saw him struggle to breathe again. "You good, Ted?"

"Fine," Teddy said with a cough.

"About last night, I mean."

"Yeah. I just needed The Walk."

10

Best Cup of Coffee in Town

Saturday, August 28, 1999, 12:21 a.m.

The night before, in the closing hours at the Brickhouse Bar, Rolo sat at the end of the bar with Enzo. He watched Teddy handle Angelica as she stumbled out of the women's restroom.

"You're not being real ladylike," Teddy said.

"I guess I'm not a real lady." Angelica stood, knocking over her chair. "Let's fight for a beer, Ted. Makes it taste better 'cause I earned it."

"How about I call you a taxi?"

"How about I call you a bastard? A taxi? Am I made of money? Are we the Jeffersons?" She held a spoon like a microphone. "We're movin' on uuuuuup!"

Rolo turned away as Angelica collapsed onto Larson's poker game, ending the evening for both herself and the players. Enzo leaned on the bar, watching the scene unfold.

"Not one of her better nights," Enzo said. "Girl belongs in rehab."

"Don't we all?" Rolo asked. "She always like this?"

"Nah, not always," Enzo said, "but she definitely has her moments, and I seem to be serving at each and every one of 'em."

An hour prior, Teddy's attention turned to the game, making him poor company. They'd finished discussing their class project anyway, deciding that's Teddy would record them on video as they performed routine "personal" activities as Mr. Roman instructed. From there, Teddy would craft stats charts from the footage. Bonehead stuff, indeed. With Teddy distracted and Angelica becoming more belligerent with each passing minute, Rolo left their table and retreated to the end of the bar for casual conversation with Enzo.

"When do you get off, Z?" Rolo asked.

"Not soon enough." Enzo's thick Boston accent always felt like home to Rolo, the proud New York Italian-American from just up the coast.

"After you clock out, let's head over to Jiminetti's. I'll buy us a bottle of limoncello."

"Nah, not tonight, Moonlight."

"My Nonna used to say, 'When life gives you lemons, drink limoncello.'"

"Is that what life's throwing at you right now? A bunch of lemons?"

"A fuckin' orchard, Z."

Enzo waved to Teddy as he helped the drunken Angelica out of the bar. He turned back to Rolo. "Go home, buddy, and I mean go far around your castle this time, you know?"

"My castle," Rolo said with a tired laugh. "Ain't been mine for while. And I can't go home 'cause I'm not even sure where home is nowadays."

"My pop used to say said 'Home is where you take a shit.'"

"The problem is, I've been shittin' all over the place lately."

"Rolo, if you need a place to stay..."

"I appreciate it, brother, but I just need to drink some more, with a change of scenery."

"Yeah, well, the only drink you need right now is a cup of very strong coffee."

Rolo nodded, stood from his stool, and tossed down a Twenty for his drinks with an additional Ten for Enzo. "You're right, Z. Coffee is what I need, and I happen to know where I can get the best cup of coffee in town."

If the crime-ridden Castle District represented the diseased heart of Easton, Smokey's Club laid center as its tumor, a malignant mafioso mass connected to illegal gambling, prostitution, racketeering, and narcotics throughout the surrounding five cities. Long neglected by most of Easton, overlooked by its police, the seedy all-night strip club had an illustrious history.

Lynn Harrod

Smokey's Club began its life as "The Belvedere," a classy dance hall in the 1920s, the neighborhood's golden years, offering booze and dime dances before and during the long dry spell of Prohibition. In the 1950s, it transformed into a teenage juke joint with dueling pianos and rockabilly acts that welcomed the greaser crowd, leather-clad gangs that were feared at the time but tame compared to the present-day mobs. In the 1960s, the dance hall was renamed "The Experience," a psychedelic head trip with go-go dancer cages, black lights over fluorescent murals, and round-the-clock recreational drugs. Shuttered in 1971, it fell victim to vandalism and the elements, serving as a shelter for squatters and later a clubhouse for the Lost Wolves motorcycle club, a group of outlaws that still pass through Easton to this day with their bathtub meth and garbage skunk weed.

In 1974, Smokey Greene bought the property for a song and named it after himself, turning it into an always-open burlesque club. Clues hinting to the club's former lives remained, including the stained, peeling velvet wallpaper, the decorative light fixtures, the steel go-go cages, and the original 1950s jukebox sitting nearly dead in the corner, only its arc of back-lit bubbles still operational.

Rolo ordered a large mug of coffee from the barkeep, taking a long sip before walking it to a table in the back of the room. At this late hour, fresh coffee was rare, and Smokey's brew was normally reserved for Irish coffee, the house speciality. Rolo's oversized white porcelain mug took nearly a fourth of the carafe.

The dimly lit joint could easily seat two-hundred, comprising a semi-circle stage along the north wall, opposite the door. The few other patrons sat across the room from Rolo with their elbows on the stage for an up-close view of the entertainment, a young African-American stripper - Marissa Washington - earning her pay dollar-by-dollar, swaying to the tunes of classic Mötley Crüe.

From the DJ booth, Santiago "Shorty" Domínguez, a bald, muscular Mexican man in a black tank top, noticed Rolo nearly hidden in the shadows, recognizing the big man even with his head bowed over his coffee. Shorty stepped through a beaded doorway into the manager's office, where his employer went over the night's earnings with three associates.

Cristof Anada, known by family as "Nada" and by everyone else as "Zero," was one of the top lieutenants of the Barrio Castillo 9 Kings gang, more widely known as "BC-9." Zero wore a red silk shirt, black pinstripe slacks, and sterling silver jewelry adorning his neck, arms, and fingers. The trim Mexican man smoked a cigarette as he cursed at his desktop calculator, the evening's receipts failing his expectations. Though the club represented a fraction of BC-9's cash flow - most of it coming from sales of weed, meth, and cocaine - he still felt frustration whenever its admission numbers were low. From where he sat, his "working girls" clearly weren't working hard enough.

Shorty knelt beside his boss to grab his attention but waited for him to speak first, as everyone did.

"Please tell me Izzy is back with the drop from Brawley," Zero said. "I need good news from someone for a fuckin' change."

"Don't know if this is good news or not," Shorty said, "but Moonlight is out there, sittin' in the back of the room."

"Alone?"

"Yeah."

"You sure it's him? What's he drinking?"

"Just coffee."

Zero sighed and shut off his calculator. "Yeah, that's him. And no, Shorty, it ain't good news."

Tucked in the corner of the main room, Rolo sipped his coffee, cupping his hands around the warm mug. Tilting it up for another sip, still hazy drunk from his evening at the Brickhouse, he failed to spot the four men approach from across the club, only taking notice as Zero took the seat opposite him.

"Best cup of coffee in town," Zero said.

Rolo nodded in agreement, taking another sip. He set the mug down, clasped his hands, and looked his host in the eye.

"Rolando," Zero said.

"Zero." Like Shorty and everyone else, Rolo pronounced the crime boss's name "SAY-RROW" with a slight Spanish accent. No one dared mispronounce it.

"The last time I saw you in The Castle was, what, four months ago? You were drunk and blabbering on."

"I took care of the blabbering earlier. I'm just drunk now."

"You know what time it is?" Zero asked.

"It's Coffee Time."

"It's Get-The-Fuck-Out Time."

"Last I checked, this place was 24-seven. I'm drinking coffee and enjoying the lady on stage. I might even stuff a buck in her chonies."

"I wouldn't let you touch her."

"Fine. Saves me a buck."

"You here to beg me for a job?" Zero asked. "There ain't no current openings."

"Good, 'cause I ain't BC-9 material."

"On that, we all agree."

"I got a job. A real job."

"Ah, that's right, Moonlight Marino made it out of the Castle, got himself an office job. That might get you a gold star behind white picket fences, but down here it's a joke. One of the legendary Marino Brothers, a fuckin' secretary."

Rolo bolted up from his chair, making Zero's three men step closer, hands over their pocketed pistols. He towered over them, easily the biggest guy in the room, but struggled to stand with blurred vision and a hammering headache. Zero remained in his chair, looking up at the giant mad-dogging him. He reached across the table and picked up Rolo's mug, taking a defiant sip.

"It's sad to waste such a good cuppa joe," Zero said. "I buy this stuff special. It's one of my five vices. A couple of weeks ago, this coffee was beans on a tree on a mountain in Ecuador. It was destined to be a good cuppa joe. It was destined to be mine. Otherwise, it wouldn't be here."

"That's fucking beautiful," Rolo said, trying not to slur his words. "You stay up at night thinking of this destiny shit? Fancy yourself a poet, Zero?"

Zero downed the rest of Rolo's coffee and stood to face him. "That's the trick with destiny, to stop shaking your head and accept it. This club was destined to be mine, otherwise Smokey would still own it. The Castle was destined to be my neighborhood, otherwise you and your brother would still run it. And you're destined to be wherever the hell you are in whatever the hell life you have, otherwise you wouldn't be some office bitch."

Rolo snapped and lunged at Zero, up-ending the table as he reached for his neck. He didn't get any closer than three inches as Shorty and his associates swooped in and beat him to the floor, stomping on him without mercy.

After allowing his men a solid minute to work over the big man, Zero raised his hand to pause the beating. He gestured for them to bring Rolo to his feet.

"I'd love five minutes alone with you," Rolo said with a blood-filled mouth.

"I bet you would."

"That's all I'd need. Five minutes. That's less than you gave Tony."

"If I'd granted Tony Marino a fair five minutes, I'd be dead or crippled. We all know that."

Rolo didn't expect even an ounce of respect for his late brother from Zero Anada, but no one could deny his logic. Tony was a walking Hell On Earth back in the day, especially in a fight.

"You still have Dance Night?" Rolo asked.

"Dance Night?" Zero said with a laugh. "Yes, we certainly do, every first Friday as always. But you have nothing to stake, not even honor anymore."

"You're all I got left in this world. You saw to that."

Zero nodded to his men and they struggled to get Rolo to the door. Shorty kicked the door open as they prepared to toss him outside. Zero raised his hand again for a last word.

"Don't come back, Rolando. Not on Dance Night or any night. Leave me the memory of who you were. Moonlight Marino. The name I respected. These charades we play, this drunk-on-revenge drama, it's no good. Go back to your 'real' office job. You might not be so lucky next time. Destiny. Remember."

"Lucky," Rolo said with a bloody lip and drunken grin. "If you believe in luck, you're gonna need it,"

"Where'd you get that shit? From an inspirational poster on your cubicle wall?"

"And if you believe in destiny, why don't you want me here? Maybe it's *because* you believe in destiny."

Zero had no ready response. He walked away, signaling his men to toss Moonlight Marino out into the night.

Lynn Harrod

11

Some Guys Play to Lose

Saturday, August 28, 1999, 12:21 a.m.

Earlier that night, back at the Brickhouse, Rolo sat at the end of the bar with Enzo as they watched Teddy handle a drunk Angelica coming out of the restroom.

"You're not being real ladylike," Teddy said.

"I guess I'm not a real lady." Angelica stood, knocking over her chair. "Let's fight for a beer, Ted. Makes it taste better 'cause I earned it."

"How about I call you a taxi?"

"How about I call you a bastard? A taxi? Am I made of money? Are we the Jeffersons?" She held a spoon like a microphone. "We're movin' on uuuuuup!"

Angelica collapsed onto Larson's poker game, ending the night for everyone.

* * *

After a long drive through rural Whitesbridge, with Creedence Clearwater Revival playing on the car stereo, Teddy sat parked in front of Angelica's house with his motor running as she stepped out of the Jeep. He hoped she could make it to her front door without assistance. The last thing he wanted was to carry her inside and face an awkward scene with her ailing mother again.

"Go home, Ted."

"Really?" Teddy said with a forced laugh. "You think that I'm gonna..."

"Go straight home."

"I'm not the one who's shit-faced here."

"Don't think I didn't notice you checkin' out those sharps back at the bar."

"Did you hear me tell Larson that I was out?"

"Go home, Ted."

"I'll see you at the range," Teddy said, dismissing her concern. "Bring three different guns. Roman wants comparative data."

"Whatever. Good night, Ted." Angelica slapped the hood of the red Jeep. "Good night, Maxine."

Teddy shifted into gear and drove away, through the countryside down Whitesbridge Road.

Twenty-eight minutes later, Teddy pulled his Jeep up to his garage at the Playa Vista Apartments, a modest property with an Early-California Spanish design in the center of town. Despite the name, there was no beach and no view other than the rear of a shopping mall. He clicked a remote to open the door, drove into the garage, and shut the door behind him. He shut off the engine but remained seated with his hands gripping the steering wheel, thinking about the possibilities of the evening, all the action still to be had on that late Friday night.

He couldn't deny that Angelica was right. She knew him well.

He restarted the engine, reopened the garage door, and backed Maxine out. With his headlights beaming across the row of garages, he stopped to think about what he was about to do, staring at the red fuzzy dice hanging on his rear view mirror.

"Fuck it. Fuck it all."

Teddy shifted into gear and drove away, forgetting to shut his garage door.

* * *

Far down the southern edge of Easton stood the district known as "Chemical Town," the city's industrial zone of factories belching smoke into the sky throughout the day and semi-trailer trucks loading and unloading, coming and going, throughout the night. The air smelled of bleach and soot and rotted meat, a lingering noxious fog so strong that the impoverished residents should have been relocated at the companies' collective expense. Instead, they were ignored by their corporate neighbors and the county's air pollution control board, encouraged by their slumlords to simply remain indoors. Even sealed within their derelict homes, the pungent fumed air could often be tasted with a thick mouthfeel like warm buttermilk.

Teddy drove Maxine over railroad tracks and irrigation canals, under electrical towers, down empty streets lined with chain-link fences and cinderblock walls topped with coils of razor wire. The shiny red Jeep stood out from the countless rows of dormant forklifts, cargo vans, and flatbed trucks, all sandwiched beside two lanes of big rigs passing each other in the night.

He parked in the small gravel lot of a beige, nondescript, single-story building. A small metal sign near the lot entrance announced the property's address as 444 Paradise Lane, something that always made Teddy laugh considering the wasteland that was Chemical Town. Only the corporate overlords reviewing their portfolios would ever see that forsaken edge of the city as any kind of paradise.

Teddy shut off his engine and pocketed his keys. He rubbed his fuzzy red dice out of habit more than superstition, stepped out onto the gravel lot, and approached a lone, red door. While driving there, he'd considered turning around and heading up to Crow Canyon, a large Indian reservation casino on a mountain plateau overlooking Dale Valley. They had plenty of action but continually urged players to make smart choices, including knowing when to quit. Teddy hated that. He hated how they clearly watered down his bourbon after four glasses, suggesting in a whisper that perhaps a club soda was in order. He hated the table limits, the flyers for Gamblers Anonymous hanging next to the bathrooms, and the one-use-only ATMs. They treated him like a child running amok with Daddy's wallet.

A casino's concern for the well being of its players ruined the overall experience for Teddy, diffusing the thrill. It might seem strange and counterintuitive to most that a casino would discourage runaway gambling, but after a player loses most of his bankroll in combat with the dealers, the house would rather he live to fight another day than die on their green felt tables never to return. Repeat business is everything.

Turning his Jeep onto Paradise Lane, Teddy had also considered simply making a U-turn and going home, just as Angelica had repeatedly urged him. Even in her drunken state, she saw her friend's eyes widen upon seeing Larson running a game at the Brickhouse and heard him gasp when Larson stole a towering pot with a last-moment "river rat" Ace.

Whether he went home or up to Crow Canyon, either of Teddy's options would have been safer and wiser than driving through Chemical Town to Ronnie's Room. But there he stood in the wee hours of the night, facing the lone, red door of the nondescript building. Behind him sat a classic Cadillac Coupe Deville with eight fresh coats of candy apple red paint. "Like a classy lady's rouge," Teddy thought, muttering a curse when he realized who owned the vintage car, yet another reason to drive away.

Teddy knocked on the door and smiled at the peep hole, at whoever was about to get a fisheye view of his face. He heard several locks being undone.

Ronnie Mayes, a young brunette Filipina in a dark gray pant suit and heels, with short, wavy black hair, opened the door. Her face turned sour as she recognized Teddy in the dark. Unlike most of the people in Teddy Brewer's life, Ronnie immediately came across as highly intelligent, educated, and astute. Her friends and business partners told her as much, though she disagreed. She may have been smart enough to size up Teddy the second she saw him through the peephole, but naive enough to open the door.

"Lady Veronica," Teddy said, "my long lost friend."

"Not long enough."

"It's Friday night. I thought I'd paint the town red, and such a painting wouldn't be complete without a visit to..."

"Not tonight, Teddy." Ronnie sounded exasperated, tired of his forced charm, barely able to look at his face.

"How have you been? How's Dario?"

"You really wanna catch up?"

"I really do."

"Then come see me at the restaurant during the day. We'll shoot the shit over cake and coffee. I'll make some ube hopia and sweet siopaos. You used to love those. Hell, I'll have Dario join us. How's that sound?" She extended the invitation with a half dose of sarcasm, knowing that Teddy would shoot it down with some shoddy excuse, as he always did, but hoping he wouldn't. His hesitation to respond to her offer cruelly confirmed that all he cared about was getting through that red door.

Ronnie moved to slam that door on Teddy, but he held it open with his foot. She knew he would, just as she knew he'd finally abandon the bullshit small talk and get to the meat of the matter.

"Just gimme a seat, Ronnie."

"You don't need a seat."

"Of course, I don't *need* a seat. I want one. 'Need' is air, water, and shelter. I'm just talking about a simple seat. You got plenty of room in there."

"Cal's here, Teddy," Ronnie said. "You remember the last time you sat across from him?"

"That was months ago! Really, was it that bad?"

"Really, you're asking me that?"

Teddy waited for her to cave as she usually did, giving her old friend another chance. Normally, he pegged his odds with her at 60 percent. That night felt different, closer to 20 percent. He almost expected an intervention.

"Ronnie, if you close the door on me, I'll drive up to Crow Canyon and sit with the Indians, and they'll rake my ass all night long. Here, you can lord over me."

Ronnie's incredulous expression fell away. "I promised Marissa."

"Like she cares about me or any of us anymore."

"She cared enough to make me promise that I'd watch your back."

"That's what you'd be doing! In the room!"

"Look, if Marissa found out..."

"Hey, I pulled the name out of my Rolodex long ago."

Years prior, Marissa, Angelica, and Ronnie were an inseparable trio, traveling the California Central Coast together in the weeks after graduating high school, looking forward to hitting the road to college. Since that innocent age, their lives took painful, sharp turns away from each other, their friendship reduced to occasional phone calls and run-ins at the annual Downtown Easton Street Festival, an event they used to look forward to attending together. Ronnie missed those days and saw Teddy as a remnant of that carefree time.

She looked at his pleading eyes and pursed smile and sighed as she swung open the red door. Her gesture came not from any renewed faith in him, nor from nostalgia, but from getting sick of pulling him up from the cliff's edge while he insisted on waving his arms, his gambling spinning further out of control with each game. She started not to care, or so she told herself.

As Teddy entered the building, she took a quick look around the parking lot before shutting the door and slamming all four of its dead bolts.

Within a small entry room, with dozens of coats hung on hooks embedded in the brick walls, Teddy raised his arms for the massive bouncer to frisk him. "Always good to see you, Randy. I love how intimate we've become."

Randy patted Teddy's legs up into his buttocks, a routine he'd performed countless times. "Gonna be a good boy this time, Teddy?"

"Of course."

"He's here tonight you know."

"Isn't he always?"

Randy looked to Ronnie as if to ask "Are you sure?" Ronnie nodded and walked through a red curtain into the main room. After the perfunctory security check, Teddy handed

Lynn Harrod

Randy his trench coat and parted the curtain with a flourish of his raised arms as if entering his personal domain.

Looking out across the long, narrow room that stretched before him like a great hall, Teddy saw "Ronnie's Room" in all its glory - an underground card room that boasted fifteen tournament-size poker tables, each with four to six players. Two young men shuttled drinks without pause. A middle-aged woman offered massages. A buffet table of pizza and deep-fried finger foods ran along one wall. The ornate oak card tables sat on red shag carpeting surrounded by walls adorned with framed, autographed photos of professional sports legends like Joe Montana, Larry Byrd, Lyle Alzado, Arnold Palmer, and Earvin "Magic" Johnson. They represented a small portion of Ronnie's vast collection of memorabilia, another remnant of her past life.

Teddy walked past the tables, the onion rings, and Kareem Abdul Jabbar's smiling portrait to a barred doorway whose room beyond served as a combination of cash cage, office, and security. Behind the bars sat Benny Bullini, better known as "Bulldog," a stocky old man who smelled like three cartons of spent cigarettes, with a wrinkled forehead like a cracked desert and a snub-nose pistol holstered against his left armpit.

"Happy Friday, Bulldog."

"Ain't exactly Friday no more," Bulldog said in his grizzled, chain-smoker voice.

"Saturday. Even better."

Bulldog smirked at Teddy's bright tone. "Feeling lucky tonight, Teddy? Or maybe you're pumping yourself up 'cause you're feeling a touch nervous?"

"Only the unskilled and unprepared are ever nervous, Bulldog."

"And you ain't neither of those things, eh?"

"Not tonight."

"You know Cal's here, right?"

"Apparently, everyone knows." He grew tired of his friends trying to discourage him, even it came from a place of kindness and concern.

"He's sittin' nine o'clock at Table Six, as always."

Teddy ignored Bulldog's mild warning and slid twenty hundred-dollar bills across the little counter built into the bars. As Bulldog took the money and prepared a tray of gaming chips, Teddy looked back at the tables and spotted Cal near the front of the room. The loud braggart may as well have had a fluorescent sign above him.

"You still got beef with the guy?" Bulldog asked.

"I hate him, if that's what you mean," Teddy said with an awkward smile.

"The guy can be obnoxious, sure, but come on, life's too short to hate any of these jokers."

Teddy thought about it for a moment, something that was long on his mind. "It's hard to say. Some guys you hate because they burned you. Some guys you hate because they took your girl, or just out of mad green envy. With Cal, it's something else. I can't quite pinpoint it."

But Teddy *could* pinpoint his hate for Cal Zimmer. Simply put, he hated Cal because he was a bonafide, full-time, round-the-clock player, a man who made the bulk of his living at poker, and Teddy wasn't. If a buffoon like Cal Zimmer could become a rounder, why couldn't he?

Bulldog slid a clear acrylic tray with $2,000 in gaming chips across the counter, the chips stacked horizontally by denomination in five rows. Teddy picked up the eight-inch tray and stared at it, as if facing his last chance to turn back, to cash in his chips, get in his Jeep, and drive home.

"May the wind always be at your back," Bulldog said, "may time always be on your side, and may you win more than you lose."

"That's beautiful, like an expensive fortune cookie."

"Just be careful, Teddy. I ain't saying you should be scared, but maybe you should be scared."

Teddy glanced at the many games before him, finding himself inexplicably drawn to Table Six.

"Scared money doesn't win, Bulldog."

Teddy spent two hours drifting from table to table, sizing up players and approaching them with different strategies. First, he singled out obvious rookies and handily took their $500 bankrolls within a half-hour. Next, he targeted seasoned players new to Ronnie's Room, players who'd never met him. He check-raised them, taking pot after pot, until they figured out his approach. By then, he'd taken four-grand from them and moved on to yet another table, where he sat with battle-hardened regulars who knew him well. He rubbed his nose, grunted, gritted his teeth, and toyed with the large ice ball in his bourbon, telegraphing fake tells and allowing them small wins until the moment he hustled them out of a five-grand motherlode with a full boat of Kings over Jacks. He soon had to leave them as well, not daring to con a pro for more than a few hands.

Eventually, Teddy stood beside an empty chair at Table Six, the only table with a dedicated dealer and no betting limits. With the dealer sitting at "twelve o'clock," Teddy's awaiting chair sat at three o'clock, opposite Cal Zimmer's seat at nine o'clock.

"I was wondering when you'd saunter my way," Cal said. "You done tinkering and tweaking your play with the rest of the room?"

"A man's gotta build up his stake before enjoying your company, Cal." Teddy's mild praise poorly masked his famous contempt for the man, but Cal still basked in it.

Their dealer, permanently stationed at Table Six, was the stalwart Richie Rocks, a stone-faced, distinguished old man who looked like Ronald Reagan with Coke-bottle eyeglasses. He shuffled the deck with a thorough wash across the green felt surface. Cal smiled at Teddy and the other three players as if he owned the room.

"What's the game, Richie?" Teddy asked.

"You should be asking me that," Cal said.

"Of course."

Teddy forgot that at the No Limit Table the player who last won always named the next game, a Ronnie's Room tradition that honored the rules of Old West saloons and parlors, or so he was told.

"I'm thinking something simple," Cal said. "Forget Texas for a moment. How about a little old-fashioned Cantrell?"

"Cantrell?"

"Five-card draw. Good enough for me. It's no-dicking-around poker with just a touch of mystery."

Teddy nodded and took his seat, placing his $9,000 in chips on the table, their stacks surrounding his highball glass of whiskey. He fed off Cal's confidence, knowing it came from the fact that he never had a day job - his small business front of imported rugs and flooring notwithstanding. He never took a big hit, never felt the sting of a bad beat, at least not in that room. Some said he was a cheat. Teddy didn't think so, but he didn't really care. Cal had a name, and that usually proved enough to psyche out an opponent.

"I know you gentlemen are always up for the occasional high stake," Cal said as Richie Rocks dealt the new hands. He took a split-second glance at his before placing them face-down again. "Why don't we boost the pot this game? Thousand to start."

Despite his tall stacks, Cal tossed a thick roll of cash onto the table, a bold flex the others had yet to see from him. He'd been saving it for Teddy. Their shared history of trash talking and made him Cal's favorite opponent to defeat.

"Cash plays," Richie said, pushing two players to immediately fold. Two others matched. Teddy raised. Cal matched him, prompting the others to fold. Yet again, it came down to Teddy and Cal, a Heads-Up showdown Teddy didn't expect on his first round against the cocky veteran.

"Six-thousand on the table," Richie said.

"Whoa," Cal said. "Exciting stuff. Gets me right here, you know, in the ol' pumper." Cal often spoke like a bad Christopher Walken impression, his classic poker face.

"Cards, gentlemen?" Richie asked.

Teddy threw away one card. Richie dealt him a new one.

"Good luck with that flush," Cal said, tossing down two cards. "Give me some gold, Richie." The dealer gave Cal two new cards.

Teddy widened his eyes, scrutinizing his new hand. Cal kept his cards down and instead scrutinized his opponent.

"Congratulations, Teddy," Cal said. "Win or lose, you've got a good face. You want me to think you're in a pickle. Or maybe you are in a pickle, but you wanna avoid that dotted line, am I right? Don't answer, of course. You're a good face. The question is, are you a good read?"

Teddy placed his cards face-down on the table and stared at Cal, taking a moment to read his face. As if he could see through Cal's hand, Teddy slid a tall stack of chips into the pot.

"Knock it off, Cal. You never could throw me."

"Well, Mr. Teddy Brewer, he's a big boy now, gonna prove it to the room, to Ronnie, to me, hell, he may even prove it to himself."

Cal raised Teddy. The pot grew obscenely tall, the no-limit game attracting a small audience. Ronnie stood by and watched the familiar scene unfold. She subtly shook her head "no" to Teddy, but he ignored her and re-raised.

"Twelve-thousand in play," Richie said, reassessing the pot, his voice steady and calm.

Unlike Teddy and his chips, Cal tossed more cash into the pot, playing off both Teddy and their audience.

"Twenty-thousand on the table," Richie said.

Lynn Harrod

"Thick as San Joaquin fog," Cal said. "Can you feel the electricity in the air? Raising, re-raising, rubbing our chins in deep thought. It's like building the Tower of Babel."

Teddy paused, realizing he was entering a danger zone. No longer was it a question of whether Cal had gems in his hand, but how valuable they were next to his own. He tapped a quick count of his stacks, realizing he had nowhere near enough to match.

"But Babel must inevitably fall," Cal said. "And so we wonder, who's it gonna fall on?" Cal winked at his opponent. "Hey, how's ol' Maxine doing? I bet she's out in the lot right now, waiting for you, waiting for *someone*."

Teddy smelled Cal's trap. The two men locked eyes.

"There it is," Cal said, continuing his taunt. "There's that dotted line I love, the linking of two players, each waiting for the other guy to so much as twitch an eyebrow. It's like chess on coke."

Ronnie shut her eyes as Teddy went all-in, shoving all his remaining chips into play. Not to be outdone in showmanship, he turned to Ronnie and made a grim request.

"Go fetch my coat, Ron," Teddy said.

Ronnie wanted to protest, to refuse him, but she wouldn't dare humiliate Teddy further by governing his game like a babysitter. She walked to the entry room and returned with his green trench coat. Teddy reached into its pockets and fished out his car keys, laying them atop the pot.

"Property plays," Richie said, unflinching.

As Maxine's keys dropped from Teddy's right hand, he revealed his cards with his left - a Full House of Kings over Nines.

Cal didn't bother counting cash or chips to match the value of the vehicle. Instead, he nodded apologetically and slowly laid out his hand atop the keys - four Queens.

Everyone breathed again except Teddy, who sat frozen as Cal swept the pot, carelessly knocking the stacks of chips into the cash. He delicately picked up the keys and exhaled a deep sigh. Dropping his bad Walken voice, he turned to Teddy.

"Sorry for being so obnoxious," Cal said. "It's sorta my thing. I have to be consistent, otherwise I'm a spotted bird." He held the keys up to the light like examining a precious antiquity. "It's all in the glove, I'm sure?"

Teddy nodded a tired "yes," his face pale from the miserably bad beat.

"How about a cab ride?" Teddy asked. "I'd consider it an honorable gesture." The words pained him as they stumbled out.

Cal set down a small stack of chips, his first time touching them since Teddy sat down. Teddy picked them up.

"Why don't you call that lady friend of yours?" Cal asked. "What's her name again? Monica? Melissa?"

"Marissa."

"That's right. Marissa. Forget going home in some shitty cab, you should call her. I hear she'll give anyone a ride nowadays."

Teddy spit out a curse and tossed the damn chips back onto the table. Cal simply grinned as Teddy left, abandoning his highball of whiskey.

Lynn Harrod

Teddy stormed outside, with Ronnie trailing behind him. He headed toward his Jeep. By habit, he reached into his pocket for keys, which stopped him cold.

"I'll call a taxi," Ronnie said.

"Nah. I need this. I haven't walked across Easton for a while."

"Next time..."

"There won't be a next time, Ron..."

"NEXT time, you take your ass up to Crow Canyon. Let the Indians watch you self-destruct, because I won't play sadist to your masochist anymore." Ronnie went back inside, leaving Teddy alone in the quiet night.

The sound of a motorcycle in the distance grew louder until a man pulled up on a sleek, midnight blue Triumph. The driver shut off the engine and removed his helmet.

Larson Williams placed his helmet on his bike's handlebars and walked up to his friend. "Heading in?" Teddy didn't respond. Larson read him for a moment. "I see. Heading out. *The Walk.*"

"The Walk is more of a grim specter than any hit you'll take in there."

"We've all been there, son. Cal Zimmer?"

"One hand," Teddy said. "I don't understand, Larson. It happened so fast. I built up my stake. I know the game inside-out and I play to win."

"And I'm sure you did win, son. You won and you won and you kept on playing. The problem is, some guys play to lose."

Leaving Teddy to ponder his words, Larson entered the building, shutting the red door behind him. The night was dead quiet again as Teddy started his long trek home.

* * *

After a soul-searching walk of over three hours, Teddy returned to his home at the Playa Vista Apartments. The sight of his open garage door served as another harsh reminder of his complete loss. He quietly shut the garage and headed for his front door where another poor devil waited for him.

Rolo lay passed out, sprawled across the miniature porch of the apartment. Teddy stepped over him, unlocked the door, and tried to get the big man to his feet.

"Goddamn, Rolo, get up," Teddy said. He grunted as he shoved his arms under Rolo's armpits and clasped his hands tight. "How the hell did you find me? Hey! Rolo!" Laying there like dead weight, Teddy shoved him inside like a rolled-up rug, barely able to shut the door behind him.

Rolo woke up as Teddy turned on a lamp. He struggled to stand, the light revealing that he'd been beaten bad. His clothes were disheveled and torn, his face streaked with blood, his speech slurred and tired.

"What the hell happened to you?" Teddy asked.

"It's a long, pathetic story," Rolo said with a groan. "Damn, you know what time it is? What happened? Big date?"

"With destiny," Teddy said.

"My destiny is your couch."

"Help yourself."

Rolo crawled onto the couch and shut his eyes. Teddy grabbed some blankets and tossed them onto Rolo's stomach. He shut off the living room light and headed to his bedroom.

"The story about Roland," Rolo said in the dark, stopping Teddy in the dimly lit hall.

"Roland?"

"At the bar, you rambled on about your shitty life. You told us story about your asshole landlord, Roland. You said he was 'running Playa Vista like a slum.' *Playa Vista*. I looked it up, came here, and found you on the directory."

"Okay?" Teddy didn't know what to make of Rolo's random, slurry memory.

"You asked me how I found you."

"Oh, right."

"I hope it's cool if I camp out," Rolo said. "I'm too fuzzy to ask you proper."

"Forget it. Ask me proper in the morning. I just want to go to bed and sleep away this fucking night."

"Wanna hear a secret?"

"Sure," Teddy said, completely spent. "I love secrets."

"You met me at the official lowest point in my life."

"What a coincidence."

Rolo drifted to sleep. Teddy shut off the hallway light and went to bed.

12

Five of a Kind

Saturday, August 28, 1999, 6:33 a.m.

Neither Teddy nor Rolo slept well.

Though he felt exhausted, Teddy lay awake in bed replaying his time in the wee hours at Ronnie's Room, from the moment he saw Ronnie's incredulous expression as she opened the door to the moment he watched Larson enter and shut it behind him, as if forbidding him from following. He especially combed over his defeat at Table Six, reliving that one hand of poker in slow motion, observing every flick of a card, every toss of chips, every eye movement and curled lip and bead of sweat. Teddy had expertly read every player and made the right moves according to both observation and basic poker strategy. His situational awareness at its peak, he felt sure he'd win, and still couldn't fathom how he'd lost. That one hand of poker against Cal

Zimmer would be placed on a pedestal in Teddy's personal Hall of Bad Beats to haunt him forever.

Rolo slept, but never more than twenty minutes at a time. He continually woke up in pain, his head aching with thunderous pangs, his ribcage kicked in sore, his back deeply bruised. Underneath the physical agony, he, too, replayed the events of last night on an endless loop, though his regrets traveled much further back. He relived his drunken confrontation with Zero and Shorty but also thought about his first run-in with BC-9, dating back to that fateful Dance Night at Smokey's, where Tony Marino took his last breath.

Rolo last woke up at half past six, the sunrise piercing the narrow gap between Teddy's thick curtains, nailing Rolo in the eyes. He looked at a large wall clock that resembled a giant pocket watch and grimaced upon realizing the time. He'd managed a collective two hours of sleep. Sitting up on the couch, blankets still folded atop his stomach, he was startled to see Teddy march into the living room and fully shut the damn curtains. Though he'd been in his bedroom behind a door ajar, the slender beam of light struck him as well, stretching across his bedsheets and into his face.

"I'm going back to sleep," Teddy said. "Fuck this day."

Teddy returned to his bedroom and shut the door. Rolo fell back to the couch and unfurled the blankets onto his legs.

"Fuck this day," Rolo said, muttering to himself.

* * *

Rolo once again woke up on the couch, this time with an additional twelve solid hours of sleep behind him, the harsh sunrise through the east window now replaced by the warm sunset through the small window on the front door. Teddy had been awake for a couple of hours. He sat at his formica dining table in front of his open corner kitchen, his camcorder set up to record him playing cards.

"Good morning, Sunshine," Teddy said, still fixed on his little project.

"Ain't no sunshine, brother. It's more like 'good evening,' I think."

"Soon enough. You slept well?"

"Other than the body aches and the nightmares and the busted couch spring up my ass, sure, I slept like a lamb."

Rolo rose to his feet, folded the blankets, and placed them on the coffee table. He joined Teddy at the dining table, curious about what the hell he was doing.

"You're taking Roman's shit seriously," Rolo said.

"It's all I got at the moment."

"I hear you, brother." Rolo realized Teddy wasn't playing cards so much as just drawing from a deck for the camcorder to capture. "How exactly do you play this fascinating game?"

"Not a game, smart guy. I'm just tracking how often I get a picture card. Bonehead shit, like Roman said. I don't feel like coming up with anything else."

"Maybe I'll do something stupid-easy like that."

"I recommend it." Teddy sipped a glass of cheap blended Scotch - his usual sunset drink - as if tiny sips would keep him from plunging over the cliff as the swill had accomplished so many times before. "You feel like telling me who tattooed you last night?"

"Not really," Rolo said. "Not now. I need a coffee and a smoke first. You don't mind?" He prepared a cigar from his coat pocket.

"Feel free with the smoke, but coffee at this hour?"

"Coffee at any hour, brother."

Without taking his eyes off his cards, Teddy reached into a nearby drawer and pulled out an ashtray, setting it in front of his groggy friend. Made of amber glass, etched with red diamonds and hearts, black clovers and spades, the round ashtray displayed the logo for The Dunes Casino, a former resort from the Rat Pack and mob rule heyday of Las Vegas. Rolo looked around the room and saw Vintage Vegas memorabilia everywhere - old casino ads, photos of Frank Sinatra, framed cards from the 1969 World Series of Poker back when it was still called the "Texas Gambling Reunion," a photo of Teddy shaking hands with poker legend Doyle Brunson.

Centered on a shelf encased in Plexiglas sat a thick, red, leather-bound book with a large golden "Q" embossed on its cover.

"How about you?" Rolo asked. "How ugly was your night?" Teddy was ready to respond, but kept quiet, still focused on his cards. Rolo brushed off the tension by changing the subject. "You ever been to Tijuana?"

The sudden shift in topic made Teddy laugh. "Can't say I have."

"You ain't missing much," Rolo said. "A real shithole. It's like the Castle District with tourists. First, they make you walk through the Gate of Doom, like entering a prison. Then comes the bum rush of cabbies, all trying to manhandle you into their cars. You tell the driver to take you to Revolution Street. You get there and now it's the Rolex guys and the fruit ladies and the sad little kids with the sad little flowers. 'Buy this or we starve.'"

Teddy depleted the deck, stopped the camcorder, and ejected the video cassette. He promptly inserted a new one.

"The shops all sell the same shit," Rolo continued, raising his cigar. "The same ponchos and blankets, the same carved wooden statues, the same rows of half-gallon bottles of vanilla extract. And they all claim to have Cuban cigars. Forty bucks, twenty, ten, everything gets cheaper the farther down you walk. One guy says 'Seven.' I give him a flat no and walk away. He yells 'Five!' from across the street. Five bucks for a fuckin' Cuban. Suddenly, I'm thinking why not? So now I'm walking around the Red Light like a dope, smoking a gas-station cigar with a fake Cohiba band."

Teddy slid the camcorder to Rolo and walked into his small kitchen.

"I'm surprised you didn't kill him," Teddy said. "Imagine, someone pulling shit on Moonlight Marino like that."

"You heard of me?" Rolo asked.

"I ain't the only one who rambled on about his shitty life light night."

"Touché."

Rolo took the camcorder into the living room and set it next the folded blankets on the coffee table. He spied a dish full of dice with many distinctive designs from different casinos. "I think I found my bonehead project."

Rolo stayed for the rest of the week as Teddy's guest. He never asked "proper," but words weren't needed between the stoic men. Both mired in the pits of their lives, company was welcome, each man lending his ear whenever the other vented.

Teddy talked about his many years of drinking and how it ruined his life three times over, pushing him to the open road to drift from town to town, each time entering a new life until he drank his way out again. Upon arriving in Easton, his immediate chance encounter with Marissa started him on a clean, straight path, only for it to collapse under the weight of his second vice - gambling.

What Teddy didn't understand is why she'd left him. He blamed her misconception of his gambling, accusing her of being a prude who was ignorant of high-level poker and the sharp instincts and intelligence it demanded. To her, it seemed just as foolish to devote oneself to "playing cards" as it did to the never-ending flip of a coin. To her, Teddy's love of the game was a gripping obsession, and in that regard, she was right. She left him one Monday morning after concluding that he couldn't even acknowledge he had a problem, never would, and therefore had no chance to overcome it. Worse, his bad beats at the poker table encouraged his drinking, which encouraged more play - two demons feeding each other. He thought she regretted being with him to begin with, but her only regrets were not being able to help him pull the twin monkeys off his back, and not leaving him sooner.

Rolo spoke of his older brother, Tony Marino, and how he used to run the Castle District as head of its largest gang, "The Mojo Boys," comprising Italians and Mexicans in an ongoing territorial tug-of-war with the neighboring Black and Hmong gangs. He used to be known as "Tony Says" because of his unquestioned authority and because another Tony Marino - "Tony Pepperoni" - ran a small neighborhood deli that sold pizza by the slice.

Rolo was a young teenager when his brother lorded over the Castle, raking in money through drugs and gambling.

"Nothing you or Sammy Davis would like," Rolo said, looking around at Teddy's Vintage Vegas decor. "Just cock fights, sports, and dice behind Tony Pepperoni's place."

The dynasty of The Mojo Boys came to an abrupt end on a Friday night in 1974, when Smokey Greene took over the club from the Lost Wolves MC and started holding monthly events known as "Dance Night." With Smokey being an African American, Tony feared he might take sides against him in the ongoing turf war, but the old man's right hand - Cristof "Zero" Anada - convinced Tony that money and business were foremost on Smokey's mind, not the particular shade of brown of anyone's face.

Whether or not Smokey was truly neutral, loyal to whoever ran operations through his club and paid weekly tribute to him, had never been uncovered, but ultimately didn't matter. Tony Marino died on the bloody floor of Smokey's Club at the end of that grisly Dance Night, an evening of betrayal capped with a transfer of power. The

Mojo Boys were run out of town or absorbed into Zero's ranks, laying the foundation for Barrio Castillo 9 Kings - the BC-9 - most heartbreaking of which was Santiago "Shorty" Domínguez, Tony's long-time enforcer and confidant. That Friday night in 1974 would forever live in infamy for Rolo, and would be the last time a Marino had any pull in the Castle District for decades to come.

Through all of Rolo's many fantasies of revenge, he never could've foreseen how brutally they would soon come to pass.

Aside from their evening mutual therapy sessions with White Knights cigarettes and glasses of Scotch - neat for Teddy, rocks for Rolo - the new roommates got along with few words. They carpooled to Clarke Adult School in Rolo's truck, filling the cab with cigar and cigarette smoke instead of conversation. Rolo awoke one morning to find a key to the apartment resting on his wallet, giving him silent permission to claim the couch as long as he wished, by which point Teddy had started his daily commute to the ValleyLink Call Center, serving as Tech Support Representative 88. Most nights, Teddy came home to discover loaded, large pizzas, a perk Rolo enjoyed as Assistant Shift Supervisor for Jiminetti's Family Restaurant. He'd lost his "office job" at Parker Printing from one too many hungover mornings.

After a week of procrastinating, Rolo faced Mr. Roman's looming deadline. Sitting on the couch with a case of beer, facing Teddy's dish of dice and the camcorder, he grabbed a fistful of dice and recorded his rolls. Teddy entered from the kitchen, an incredulous look on his face upon seeing the project.

"I thought Mr. Vegas would like the gaming angle," Rolo said. "I mean, you were flippin' cards for four hours."

"Charting poker hands is a little more complex than rolling dice."

"There's a spin to it, brother." Rolo finished his beer, opened another, and set it in front of the camcorder, speaking succinctly into the mic. "Six. This is beer number six."

"That's your spin?"

"I'm charting how my luck changes with my blood alcohol content."

"Like Roman says, if you believe in luck..."

"Yeah, well, I've been tossin' these dice too long to stop now."

Teddy started shutting off lights, getting ready to turn in for the night. He set some clean blankets on the edge of the couch and then headed to his room.

"Ted," Rolo said. "Thanks again."

"It's fine. I got the room, and we don't get in each other's way."

"Just say 'you're welcome,' brother. No need to justify it. We both know you're doing me a solid."

Teddy didn't expect or feel entitled to gratitude and saw a simple "You're welcome" as a flat gesture. "To be honest, you're the best roommate I've ever had."

Rolo felt the same. Further, he often felt like Teddy's own Tony Marino, though he'd never dare say so. "You're getting me all misty now."

Teddy laughed. Rolo smiled.

"Just keep the pizzas coming, big guy," Teddy said.

Teddy entered his bedroom, leaving Rolo to his simple homework.

* * *

With the camcorder hooked to the TV, Teddy sat on the couch and reviewed Rolo's footage of rolling a handful of dice over and over. He drank evening coffee - a new ritual he picked up from Rolo - as he recorded his friend's numbers on a clipboard. He scanned forward to see how much footage remained. Rolo's hand quadrupled in speed. Continuing to zip through the footage, something strange caught his eye.

Rolo's dice landed on all Sixes... nine times in a row.

Teddy kept watching, amazed at the odds of such a thing occurring. Three minutes of video tape later, Rolo tossed all Threes twelve times in a row, followed by all Twos eleven times in a row. The odds of rolling a handful of dice and landing them all on the same number was astronomical. Teddy grabbed a piece of paper and did some quick math.

With twelve dice in each toss, the probability of landing them all on the same number - just once - was one out of 2,176,782,336.

Rolo achieved this thirty-two times in a matter of minutes.

How could Rolo not notice? After so many hours of tossing dice and drinking beer, leaving the recording of data to the camcorder, he never saw the impossible odds he shattered.

Something dawned on Teddy. He walked to his wall of Vegas memorabilia, to the precious, large, leather book with the gold "Q" embossed on its cover, and whipped it open to a bookmarked page.

"Jesus Christ," Teddy said in a whisper, nearly collapsing to the floor. "There it is." He wanted to tell Rolo, but he was out working late and would head to the school directly from the restaurant. Teddy had planned on skipping class for a jaunt up to Crow Canyon Casino, but suddenly realized it could be the most important night of his life.

13

The Tale of Quickie Buckner

Friday, September 3, 1999, 8:05 p.m.

Easton's thick autumn fog rolled in, enveloping Clarke Adult School, as Mr. Roman's students waited in their social groups for the teacher to arrive, late as usual. Rolo and Angelica stood apart from them near the basketball court as Angelica played handball against the east wall of the building.

"I never met a chick with a membership to a gun range," Rolo said, puffing his cigar.

"My pop had a lifetime membership. It cost him a lot back in the day, and no way I'd let his hard-earned go to waste. Besides, the owner is cool with it."

"It's a 'lifetime' membership, sweets, and his lifetime is over."

"Fuck that. They charge for paper men, make you use 'em. They nickel-and-dime you with all kinds of petty shit if you don't pull up in a Range Rover or Hummer."

"Using their paper men makes sense if you think about it. Otherwise, a lotta guys would be shootin' pictures of their bosses, exes, their idiot neighbor, or the President."

"You ever shoot?" Angelica asked.

"Not at a *paper* man."

As Angelica let the morbid reply sink in, Teddy arrived holding the red leather "Q" book. He approached Rolo, keeping his voice low, while Angelica kept slamming her handball.

"I thought you was skipping tonight?" Rolo said. "How'd you get here?"

"I walked," Teddy said as he flipped through the book. "Listen, I've been going over your video."

"Exciting stuff, I know. Did you like the part where I rolled the dice?"

Teddy handed Rolo a piece of paper that was tucked in the book, a graph of his dice rolls. He pointed out several points on the graph.

"What happened right here?" Teddy asked. "And here?"

"I wasn't paying attention. I was tanked. My hand was on autopilot."

"For five minutes, you rolled numbers I've never seen, numbers no one has ever seen. They kept changing before and after, but your streak lasted five minutes. *Exactly* five minutes."

Rolo laughed and shoved the graph back at Teddy. Angelica felt confused.

"Bartender, cut this guy off!" Rolo said, laughing.

"You went for hours and your next best run was ten seconds, and it was only four Deuces. You follow me?"

"It's just five minutes, Ted," Angelica said, not sure what her friend was getting at.

"The odds of landing twelve matching dice just once are in the billions," Teddy said, giving them a moment to absorb his news. Rolo and Angelica didn't know how to respond to his bizarre discovery.

Angelica quickly shrugged it off, a frown across her face. "Dammit, Teddy, you never shoulda went back to Ronnie's. Forget it, Rol, it's just another one of his 'systems.'"

Rolo didn't share her dim view. More versed in dice games than Angelica, he seemed intrigued. Mr. Roman arrived and hurried to the double doors of the school, letting his class in. Teddy looked at the group shuffling into the building, then at the large book in his hand.

"There's more," Teddy said, trying not to sound too excited. "A lot more. It changes everything. I think we all need to skip class tonight."

"For what?" Angelica said, pissed.

"Hold up, sweets," Rolo said. "I wanna hear him out."

"Yes, you do," Teddy said. "But you're gonna need a drink first."

* * *

Teddy led his curious friends back to the Brickhouse Bar, to a corner table by the front window which made it the most visible yet afforded the most privacy. Angelica had tossed her old mountain bike into the back of Rolo's truck and agreed to join them at the bar, if only to skip class. After the turbulent day she had, she felt deserving of a break.

* * *

Angelica awoke that morning to find her mother missing from her usual seat at the kitchen table, the back door swung wide open, letting in the mosquitos of dawn. Barely taking a moment to slap on a pair of sandals, Angelica ran out into the field behind their property in search of her mother. During the four previous times Rosa wandered off in the morning, Angelica found her within a minute, standing perfectly still on the back porch, near a dead well surrounded by tall weeds, or in front of the railroad tracks that bordered the far end of the field.

Angelica sprinted around the open field for a grueling twenty minutes, looking behind every tree, every bush, running along the tracks from Nielsen Avenue all the way to Palm. Only when she returned to the house did she spot Rosa sitting on the roof facing east, toward the rising sun. She'd climbed up crates that were stacked alongside the house for forty years. Angelica saw it as a small miracle that her mother hadn't lost her balance and fallen, or that the crates, brittle and splintered from enduring the elements, hadn't buckled and caved under her weight.

"Jesus H., ma! What the hell are you doing up there?"

Rosa glanced down at her daughter but didn't respond. Angelica had surmised how she got onto the roof, but as she looked up at her mother staring at the sunrise, she pieced together why. Rosa held a red plaid Thermos bottle, the one her husband used to take to work every day. On weekends, Arturo would still use the old Thermos throughout the day as it had become his go-to vessel for both coffee and Pepsi. While watching football on TV, it served as his beer stein.

In 1987, at fifty-one, Arturo hired a service to re-shingle the roof but had gotten into a squabble over the inflated estimate. Angry and determined, Arturo tended to the roof himself. He started well, but lost his balance and tumbled down the roof thirty minutes into the all-day job after the sunrise pierced his eyes and blinded him. He caught himself on the chimney, avoiding a nasty fall onto a wheelbarrow full of garden tools, pulling his right shoulder. Too proud to ask for help, he sat up there for over an hour, trying to will his shoulder back to health. Concerned for her husband yet not wanting to rush him for fear of wounding his already waning confidence, Rosa filled his red plaid Thermos with coffee, climbed the crates, and joined him on the roof. Husband and wife sat together on the eastern roofline and stared at the early-morning sky.

A teenage Angelica saw them from a distance as she returned home from her newspaper delivery route. It was a strange, beautiful sight, and the first and only time her mother dared do anything so risky.

That odd, tender moment from thirteen years prior was alive in Rosa's mind. She once again sat on the house's eastern roofline - red, plaid Thermos in hand - to comfort her embarrassed and anguished Arturo. Seeing her up there, eyes on the dawn, Angelica wondered what memories were attached to the many other times her mother wandered away.

"Don't move, ma! I'm coming up to help you!"

Rosa held the Thermos out to an unseen presence beside her. Since no one took the drink, she stood it in the rain gutter and made her way back to the stairway stack of crates. Angelica waited for her near the top and helped her to the ground step by step.

* * *

After spending most of that day at home, comforting her mother, Angelica welcomed any excuse to skip night school and relax with friends at the Brickhouse Bar.

Rolo agreed to ditch Roman's class and follow his friend's ranting insistence out of raw curiosity. For most of his life, people with strange obsessions fascinated him. Whether it be booze, an obscure superstition, or pangs of regret for The One Who Got Away - Teddy encompassing them all - Rolo often followed an obsession back to its source to see what kind of person governs his life around a thing he so desperately seeks but can never have.

Sitting at the front corner table of the Brickhouse Bar in the prime of the evening, neither Angelica nor Rolo believed what their frantic friend was revealing.

"Impossible," Rolo said. "Can't be done."

"Mathematically impossible," Teddy said. "Do that in Vegas, you'd bust the cage open."

"This is some kind of Teddy joke," Angelica said.

"You said you'd hear me out. Rolo's run was from 1:21 a.m. to 1:26 a.m." He reached into the red leather book and pulled out another graph. Rolo took a moment to decipher it, shocked at its detail.

"Fuck, you rolled dice for ten hours?" Rolo asked.

"Just look, right here, around eight o'clock."

"This ain't good, Ted," Angelica said. "This is voodoo-hoodoo shit."

"From 8:04 p.m. to 8:09 p.m.," Teddy said, "a couple of hours ago, you could say I had a little run of my own."

Rolo continued to scrutinize Teddy's graph. "You got all Threes for a couple of minutes, then you got all Ones for three minutes."

"Is this for reals, Ted?" Angelica asked.

"I wanted Threes, so I got Threes," Teddy said. "Then I wanted Ones, so I got Ones." Facing their confused expressions, Teddy lay the mysterious red "Q" book on the table. "You guys ever heard of Quincy Ray Buckner?"

"As in 'Quickie' Buckner?" Rolo asked. "This was his book?"

"This was his journal."

Rolo opened the book and looked through it in awe. Each page was nearly black from the dense notes that stretched edge-to-edge, the scribblings of a mad man. "Angie asked you a question, brother. Is this for real?"

"As real as it gets. I got it at his estate sale. Everyone else wanted his jewelry, his cars, his antiques. All I wanted was this book."

Angelica didn't share her friends' star-struck gaze at the large leather book. "For fuck's sake, is someone gonna tell me already?"

"Tell you what?" Teddy asked.

"Who the hell is Quickie Buckner?"

* * *

In the winter of 1990, a week before Christmas, a little man in a blue suit and white dress shirt topped with a matching faded Dodgers baseball cap stepped out of a golden elevator and into the crystal-and-marble lobby of the extravagant Faberge Resort and Casino, nestled in the "new strip" of Las Vegas. He'd turned fifty that day and came out, not to celebrate, but to rake his nightly pot and promptly return to his penthouse suite, a lavish room he'd called home for close to a year. Though he never had friends in tow, everyone knew him - both staff and regulars - as he made his way through the thousands of slot machines, past the bars and the sports book, and onto the gaming floor of cards, wheels, and dice. He carried his red leather book marked prominently with an embossed golden "Q" for his first name, continually jotting down notes even as he walked across the crimson carpet.

Quincy had been well known as a full-timer, playing round the clock at every table in every casino. Cards, dice, horses, even slots, he played every inch of the house. He hit it big once in Reno, winning $500,000 on one roulette spin but just as quickly flushed it away. That became his reputation - tall stacks followed by a goose egg, impressive, gradual construction followed by complete destruction, the sadistic cycle of classic gambling addiction. Everything changed for the rest of Quincy Ray Buckner's short life when he moved into the Faberge.

A day earlier, he made headlines when he won $105 Million in the Nevada State Lottery. Long having dreamt of a night in a Faberge penthouse, he permanently moved there, not once realizing it would become his luxurious prison.

Between his continuous notes, he kept checking his watch as he stepped up to a roulette table. The wheelman wished him a happy birthday. The pit boss arranged for a cake - German Chocolate with two candles shaped like the numbers "5" and "0" to be cut and shared with the other players. Without taking a seat and with all eyes on him, the Vegas legend placed a marker on Zero. He made a note in his book as the wheel spun, landing firmly on that illusive green number, landing him yet another record win. The other players and crowd of onlookers cheered, and Security closely analyzed the footage from the four overheard cameras aimed at the famous gambler. No evidence of cheating could be found, and no excitement showed on Quincy's face.

Quincy knew he'd win, just as he always had for close to a year.

The pit boss collected his winnings for him, applying them to his house credit. Constantly fixed on his book, always jotting down notes, Quincy returned to the golden elevator and ascended to his awaiting penthouse which had long lost its luster, just as the games had.

Teddy had followed the pursuits of Quincy "Quickie" Ray Buckner, whose nickname came from his tendency to make one big bet a night before retiring to his suite. Rumors spoke of agoraphobia, unbridled genius, and the madness they usually entailed.

* * *

Angelica and Rolo tried to connect Teddy's tale of the famous gambler to whatever the hell they were being exposed to that night.

"Holy shit, Ted," Angelica said. "It's like you admire the guy."

"I'm fascinated by him," Teddy said. "I'd never use the word 'admire.'"

"The guy was a nut job," Rolo said without hesitation. "He was the village idiot of Las Vegas."

"An idiot worth nine figures."

"So he got lucky at the end. I mean, look at his journal, he wrote every fuckin' thing down. '8:02 p.m. Cracked two hard-boiled eggs into bowl. 8:03 p.m. Ate first egg.' What the fuck is that?"

"Probably the worst case of O.C.D. ever. But I'm telling you, for five minutes a night, he never lost."

"Jesus, it keeps going with his bets," Rolo said, skimming the tiny journal entries. "He wrote, '9:19 p.m. Bet $100,000 on Blackjack. Doubled down on Eleven' and on the next line, '9:20 p.m. Collected winnings.' Every minute was recorded."

"Sound familiar? Ange says I've been hunting Luck all my life. Quickie found it. So did we."

Rolo flipped the pages to the final entry at the middle of the book, its page blackened from spilled ink. It served as an abrupt, mysterious end to Quickie Buckner's life. Hundreds of blank pages followed, the days he'd never see.

"Listen to me, brother," Rolo said. "I'm not one of those obsessed freaks Roman talks about, only sits at third base at blackjack, only tosses dice with his left hand and his right eye closed."

"You mean obsessed freaks like me."

"Sorry, but I refuse to believe in this shit."

"Then believe in what we did. It's not all in my head, I have it on video."

Rolo and Angelica were quiet, not sure what Teddy wanted to hear.

"What do you want us to do, Ted?" Angelica asked.

"I want you to roll the dice again," Teddy said to Rolo. "I need you to."

"For fuck's sake, man..."

"I need to see that streak again. You too, Ange. No camera, no reports. For five minutes I felt like a god. I can't say, 'No big deal, this shit happens' because this doesn't just happen! And I know you're curious because otherwise we wouldn't be sitting here debating right now."

Rolo couldn't deny Teddy's logic and observation even if it was based on something he didn't understand. He knew he'd help his friend follow his obsession, whether to confirm it or shoot it down.

Angelica held more concern. She'd seen Teddy spiral before. He'd lose everything, vow to quit, only to be back at Ronnie's Room or Crow Canyon the following weekend. This felt different. The stakes seemed higher, with Teddy's sanity teetering on the edge. Perhaps if she helped him pursue this Quickie Buckner thing, she could catch him when he inevitably fell.

"Alright, Ted," Angelica asked. "When do we start?"

14

Full House

Monday, September 6, 1999, 3:58 p.m.

Rolo and Angelica sat at Teddy's dining table rolling his vintage dice, their dish between them. They met again when they were all available, Teddy's getting off work early out of excitement for his discovery. Sadly, after hours of rolling dice, none of them could duplicate their streaks.

The camcorder remained in its case, for there was no need to confirm their discovery, at least not in Teddy's view. He felt they each needed to pinpoint exactly when their luck rose to a peak and figure out how they could repeat it. Teddy thought it strange how apprehensive he felt about narrowing down this surreal thing they stumbled upon, as if finding evidence of God but seeking his precise business hours before daring to knock on the door.

Teddy stood by the kitchen sink, staring at the dice. He lit a White Knight and noted the bored expression on his friends' faces as they continued to roll dice with no miracles to show for it, their faith fading by the second.

Rolo cut and lit a cigar, using an ornate silver lighter, gently placing it on the Formica tabletop afterward. Angelica took the lighter and clicked it on a few times, creating its signature metallic ping. She smiled at the tall jet flame.

"Fancy shmancy," Angelica said. "What'd this run you?"

"Three bills," Rolo said.

"For a fuckin' light?"

"Feels good, don't it?"

"A foot rub feels good, you wanna give me three-hundred bucks for one? You can get a Bic at the Circle-K for forty-nine cents."

"Sweets, this is Mr. Fuente," Rolo said, holding up his cigar. "I know that doesn't mean jack shit to you, but it means a helluva lot to me. I ain't smoking a fine Fuente with no liquor store lighter."

"So, you're a cigar snob."

"Forget being a snob, a Bic would destroy the taste, like sucking a car exhaust."

"Teddy uses a Zippo."

"Teddy smokes White Knights. The taste of kerosine is an improvement."

Angelica stopped suddenly, staring at the die she'd been rolling.

It landed on a Four.

"That's three in a row," Angelica said, picking up the die as if it were suddenly made of thin glass. "Is that... something?"

Lynn Harrod

Teddy nodded for her to continue. He and Rolo watched carefully as she rolled another Four, then another.

Four Four Four Four Four Four Four...

Teddy and Rolo quickly rolled dice with no magic results, but Angelica couldn't lose. She keeps rolling Fours.

"Roll something else," Teddy said.

"And bust this streak? I thought you wanted to test how long this thing went."

"Just do it!"

"How?"

"Roll Ones."

"Again, how?"

Before Teddy could think of an answer, without knowing how, she started rolling Ones as fast as her hand could move. After twelve in a row, she called out different numbers, landing whatever she wanted.

"You don't have to say the numbers out loud," Teddy said. "Just think of what you want."

"I'm calling 'em out so you know I ain't bullshittin' you."

"We believe you," Rolo said, staring in disbelief, his cigar dangling from his lips.

"Mama wants a Six!" Angelica excitedly grabbed the dish of dice and flung it high in the air. Over two-hundred dice of different colors and sizes hit the ceiling and fell to the table, some tumbling back into the dish, some falling onto the floor, a few rolling into the next room.

They all turned up Sixes.

The three of them stared at the dice all around them, stunned, eyes wide, as Angelica kept getting any number she called out, not sure what else to do. Teddy ran out of the room and returned with a deck of cards. However, as he stumbled to slide out the deck, Angelica's smile faded. The streak had ended.

Teddy looked at his wall clock, thinking.

"4:07 p.m." Teddy said, jotting down the time on his clipboard.

"Five minutes," Angelica said. "Sorta like you guys yesterday."

"Exactly like yesterday. To the second."

Teddy reached into the fridge and pulled out another of Rolo's beers. Angelica noticed it was his fifth within an hour.

"This thing!" Teddy said. "This amazing thing! It happened to each of us, and for the same amount of time!"

"So what the hell does that mean?" Angelica asked.

"Consistency is control. I bet Rolo can do it again at his same time of 1:21 a.m. and Ange's time is clearly now, from 4:02 to 4:07 in the afternoon. And I'm positive I can do it again tonight."

"And you're positive about that how?" Rolo asked.

"Because I did it twice already." Rolo and Angelica were shocked. Teddy neglected to reveal that earlier. "I nailed down my five minutes from 8:04 to 8:09 p.m."

"Slow down, Ted," Angelica said. "We don't know exactly what this is, why it works..."

"Who cares? If a genie popped out of a lamp and gave you three wishes, would you sit and wonder, 'Gee, What's going on? How can this be?' Hell no, you wouldn't! You'd already be sitting in a new Mercedes or stretching out on the deck of your yacht!"

Rolo nodded in agreement, though Angelica still hesitated to accept something she couldn't fathom.

"What if this is a limited time offer?" Teddy said. "What if we only get this when the sun is in the House of Cancer and Hailey's Comet flies over the Moon? Don't tell me you don't have plans!"

"Plans?" Angelica asked. "What plans?"

"Plans! If-I-Had-A-Time-Machine plans. If-I-Won-The-Sweepstakes plans. You think, what if things turned around for me? What if this shitty world cut me a break for once?"

Rolo listened closely, his friend's words striking a nerve. He picked up his silver lighter and looked at his reflection on its surface, rubbing the bruises on his face.

"I got plans," Rolo said.

* * *

Teddy and Rolo returned to the Brickhouse Bar the following evening, to their corner table at the front. They paused their conversation when Enzo brought them their usual whiskey and beers.

"I see you in here a lot now, Ted-O," Enzo said. "Is it the drinks, the atmosphere, or just my sparkling smile?"

"You could say I'm rediscovering my roots," Teddy said.

Enzo saw customers waiting for him at the bar. He curtsied and excused himself, leaving Teddy and Rolo to continue talking while observing the regular poker game at the large round table near the center of the room.

"I did some more testing," Teddy said.

"What now? Yahtzee? Bingo? Did you win the church gift basket?"

"I solved a Rubik's Cube with my eyes closed and knew all the answers to Jeopardy."

"Maybe you're just a smarty pants."

"Last night, I juggled an entire set of kitchen knives - steak knifes, cleavers, those big chef's knives - ten altogether. I'd never juggled before."

"Maybe you're a natural."

"I had my eyes closed then, too."

Rolo realized Angelica's concern about Teddy's obsessive compulsive tendencies. He wondered what his friend would try next. "Don't look a gift horse in the mouth, brother. No more doing anything stupid dangerous like that. This thing brings us good luck and that's enough. Let's not push it."

"Oh, I say let's push it. More testing. How else are we to know what we can do?"

"Let's stick to the plan for now. We get some scratch, get well, and maybe then we can ponder the limits of the known universe. No more steak knives or whatever other circus act you think up next."

"Okay, but we stick to the plan," Teddy said. "Five against Vegas."

"Three's enough," Rolo said, uncomfortable with Teddy's plans for expansion. "Me, you, and Ange is all we need."

"It's gotta be five. We can cover more ground in a day."

Rolo grunted in disapproval. He and Teddy had been arguing all day, even as they brainstormed a list of candidates.

"And where are we gonna find two guys we can trust?" Rolo asked. "That'd be tough for me 'cause I trust nobody." He looked about the room, at Larson leading his poker game and Enzo laughing as he joked around with customers. It finally occurred to him why it seemed important to Teddy to meet there that night. "Shit, these guys? Tell me you're jokin'."

"They're solid."

"Larson and Enzo? Solid? We hardly know 'em!"

Teddy motioned to Rolo to lower his voice. "You hardly know them. I know them fairly well."

"'Fairly well' doesn't comfort me, brother." Rolo could feel Teddy's thoughts turning in his head as he studied the two oblivious candidates in the room. "Look, you always talk about being a king for a day versus being a god for five minutes, but do you really know the difference?"

"The difference is power."

"Wrong," Rolo said. "When you're king for a day, you share it, brag about it, spread the wealth and throw a big ass party while you can. It's like winning five-grand in a supermarket raffle. But when you're a god for five minutes every day, and your fantasies catch up with your reality, you keep it to yourself. You don't broadcast that shit unless you want a target on your back."

"Calm down. You're being dramatic."

"Am I? The more people we share this thing of ours with, the more risk."

"Well, rest easy, because we won't be sharing it with anyone."

Rolo felt more confused, worrying about Teddy's growing plans. He could never foresee the frightening heights his friend would take it to.

"You're losing me, brother. How the hell do we get these two on board without showing them nothing?"

"Many ways," Teddy said. "I got a decent cover story." He checked the time on the wall clock - a minute before eight in the evening.

"Know any Italian jokes?" Rolo asked, changing the subject. During their time as roommates, it had become their little game. "We got a few minutes to kill."

"Why don't Italians ever barbecue?" Teddy asked, pausing for effect. "The spaghetti falls through the grill."

"Fuckin' racist," Rolo said with a laugh.

"Why did the mafia cross the road?"

"Oh, so we're all mafia now?"

"You really asking me, that? Mr. Moonlight Marino from the Castle District? Folks down there still recognize that name, you know."

"I mean, present company excepted. Besides, I left that life, remember? Or rather, it left me." Rolo took a swig of his beer. "Fuck it, tell me, why did the mafia cross the road?"

Teddy did his best-worst Italian accent. "Fuggedaboutit."

Rolo laughed. "Goddamn, that's stupid. But still funny."

"Your turn. Come on, hit me with an Irish joke."

"Two Irishmen fishing in a boat out in the middle of a lake. They catch a magic fish. The fish says, 'I'll grant you any wish if you let me go.' Without thinking, one guy blurts out, 'Turn the water to Guinness!'"

"Fucking racist," Teddy said, smiling at Rolo's absurd Irish accent.

"He lets the fish go and the lake turns black. They're surrounded by a hundred miles of Guinness. The other guy says, 'Dammit, Shamus! Now we gotta piss in the boat!'"

Teddy's laughter is cut off when he turns to check the time again. Rolo looks at the clock - 8:03 p.m.

"It's just about your time," Rolo said. "Too bad the lottery numbers ain't picked during any of our Fives. What do you got in mind?"

"I wanna show you something." Teddy rose to his feet and approached the poker game across the room, stopping behind Larson's chair.

"I saw you watching us like a hawk, Theodore," Larson said, dealing out a new game. "You want in, I suppose? You sure that's a good idea?"

"You guys got an extra deck? I'll even take your muck, at least ten cards. Just for a few minutes."

"I recommend you avoid all fifty-two of them."

Larson reached into his jacket pocket and handed Teddy an extra deck. He rejoined Rolo, still not sure what he was about to do.

Of the short list of people Teddy knew in Easton, Larson was one of the few he trusted and considered a genuine friend, though Rolo needed convincing. Enzo had always been a good guy, but Rolo saw him as a wild card, unpredictable. He stared at his friend as he returned to their table with the deck.

"I repeat, three's enough," Rolo said.

"The night we met, you said three's a gang. I say five makes a crew."

"So, that's your grand plan? To form a crew?"

Teddy shuffled the deck, watching the time on Rolo's watch.

8:04 p.m.

He dealt cards onto the table, calling out 'Two,' 'Four,' and 'Nine' beforehand, landing each card he wanted. Too easy. He handed the deck to Rolo.

"Now give me four Jacks," Teddy said with a smile.

Rolo dealt four cards. All Jacks.

"Wash the table now."

Rolo spread the entire deck across the table, face-down. He thoroughly washed the table with them, spread them around for nearly a minute.

"Spade Flush," Teddy said, looking around to make sure no one was observing them. "Make that a Spade *Royal Flush.*"

Intrigued, Rolo randomly slid five cards out of the wash and placed them in front of him. He turned them up to reveal a Spade Royal Flush, the highest ranking hand in poker. They even sat in order - Ace, King, Queen, Jack, Ten - just as Teddy had visualized.

Until that moment, Rolo had only seen their discovery affect single cards, never realizing that an entire hand could be called. He stared in disbelief. "Fuck, the odds of that..."

"Are one in 2,598,960," Teddy said. "Even more so, because they landed in rank."

"It don't get no better than a Royal Flush, brother."

"Oh, it's gonna get a lot better."

Teddy waved for Enzo and Larson to join them in the corner.

"Shouldn't we change the world with a thing like this?" Rolo asked, grappling with the impossible power in their hands.

Teddy grinned. "The world can wait."

15

Make Me A Believer

Friday, September 10, 1999, 6:15 a.m.

Over the next two days, Teddy recruited the rounder Larson Williams Jr. and the barkeep Enzo O'Day, searching for their five minutes by having them toss dice in the seclusion of his apartment in the name of "research." He paid them $500 each - easy money from a quick evening trip to Crow Canyon - to test his friends all day while blindfolded, ensuring they didn't glimpse their discovery.

Larson's "Lucky Five" - a term coined by Angelica - took place early the following day over bagels and coffee, from 6:15 a.m to 6:20 a.m. It later made sense that Larson's Lucky Five took place in the morning for he'd always felt the world opened to him in the hours after he awoke each at six sharp.

* * *

Everything in Larson Williams' life had been timed to the minute with a constant sense of urgency. He'd only ever been late once, a tragic moment of regret that remained fresh in his mind and colored his every decision. His younger brother Devon Williams surely shared the pangs of regret from that day, wherever the hell he was now.

The two brothers never knew their mother. Mary Louise Williams died giving birth to Devon when Larson was barely learning to walk. Raised by their widower father, Larson Williams Sr. - a mechanical engineer known to all as "Larry" - the boys followed a strict daily routine.

They awoke at six to a breakfast of two eggs, a slice of ham, and a piece of wheat toast exactly fifteen minutes later, followed by a bus trip during the school year or backyard calisthenics during summer break. Later in the morning came chores comprising a thorough cleaning of the house and garage, with maintenance of the front yard taking up the afternoon. The brothers shared an evening newspaper route, delivering the *Easton County Bugle* by car with their father to over two-hundred residents throughout Brawley. Being the only "Bugle Boys" in the rural area, their subscriptions would often swell past two-fifty, approaching three-hundred households on Sundays.

For most of his career, Larry worked in steel fabrication, creating irrigation tanks and other related equipment for the many commercial farms in Brawley and Easton. Despite being considered a wizard in his field, his passion lay in stock car racing.

Brawley enjoyed a healthy racing subculture that included modified street cars and dedicated stock cars for the weekend circuit, with competitions every other Friday out in the sticks at the popular Brawley Raceway. Larry's employer, Brix Irrigation, sponsored a modified 1987 Buick Grand National that always finished in the Top Ten but never led the pack past the checkered flag. Ever looking for opportunities to shape his sons into responsible young men, Larry brought Larson and Devon to the track and enlisted them as part of his pit crew. Together, the boys refueled the Buick and cleaned its windshield, always mindful of the time for their father instilled in them that "a careless five seconds can change the course of a race and a foolish five minutes can change the course of your life."

From the moment his boys could hold a crescent wrench, Larry methodically taught them how to repair and maintain any machine, lavishing special attention to the art of the automobile, citing "there is no machine more loved by man." Both brothers took to their duties with earnest drive, fantasizing about forming their own team and becoming drivers. Though he'd always leveled with his sons about the ways of life, giving them "the talk" that all adolescent Black boys had to endure, he never had the heart to tell them that the notion of an African American stock car team didn't fit with the "current climate" of the sport, and allowed them their lofty dreams.

On Larson's eighteenth birthday, Larry surprised him with a performance car of his own, a modified 1986 Dodge Omni subcompact known as the "Shelby GHL-S." The boxy little hatchback sedan didn't look like much, but it could tear up asphalt with the best of them, something that mattered more to Larry than any swooping hood or V-shaped spoiler. The car's original name "GHL" stood for "Goes Like Hell," the kind of playful moniker racing legend Carroll Shelby was known for, but Larson's limited edition "GLH-S" stood for "Goes Like Hell S'More," and indeed, the little black boxy car on mag wheels lived up to its name, reaching 60 miles per hour in 6.5 seconds and running the quarter mile in 14.8 seconds. Though the car only became a footnote in racing history, it was considered a collector's item with only five-hundred produced, each instrument cluster personally autographed by Carroll Shelby himself.

The following year, Devon was presented with his own GLH-S identical to his older brother's, right down to their faded paint and weathered interior. Larry had picked up both cars from a collector who'd neglected them, leaving them to rot in a field behind his barn.

The brothers were eager to restore their cars, starting with the body and paint, but Larry insisted they work on their engines and transmissions first for it was a muscle car's muscle that mattered most. They started with Devon's, since it needed less blood and sweat to get it back on the track. After returning the engine to factory condition came five coats of glossy factory black paint and white pin striping. Team Williams Racing then started work on Larson's more laborious beast, returning its performance to the road demon it once was.

Sadly, it would never *look* like a champion ever again.

On July 4th, 1994, Larson and Devon were to report to their father to start work on repainting the older son's weathered GLH-S, but the Brawley Raceway hosted a festival that featured free laps and friendly competition with other high-octane enthusiasts around its newly surfaced track. With their father at home waxing Devon's car to a mirror shine, Larson registered his seemingly unfinished Shelby GLH-S for a race, much to Devon's protest. Because of its dilapidated appearance, Larson's banged-up GLH-S was underestimated by the other drivers, later to be viewed as a "sleeper car," an underdog machine that could blow the doors off most opponents.

With Devon impatiently watching from the stands, always minding the time, Larson went toe-to-toe against a red 1993 Dodge Dayton IROC, blazing past it to the astonishment of the crowd, providing the upset of the night. The spectators went wild, having never seen such an ugly little creature devour a battle-tested street machine. Eager to soak up the night's glory, Larson ignored his brother's pleas to return home to their father working in the garage, which they'd modified with an old vacuum system for body and paint work. The younger brother feared their strict father's wrath, never imagining the far worse scenario that awaited them.

Arriving home at 8:37 p.m. - nearly forty minutes late - they discovered their father sitting cross-legged on the driveway, bent over in agony. He'd succumbed to a failing heart and struggled to breathe. The boys rushed him to the hospital in the same ugly car that had won them victory and praise only a hour before, not realizing until much later that he'd passed the point of no return in the backseat minutes before pulling up to Emergency, his brain suffocating from lack of oxygen.

After a lifetime of being pressed to be precise and prompt, they failed their father by a matter of minutes. From what the doctor suggested as he emerged from behind an ivory curtain to break the news, Larry Williams Sr. might have been saved if only he'd arrived earlier.

Larson blamed himself. If he and Devon had been home during the attack, the outcome would have surely been different. Devon also blamed him. To Larson's dismay, the soft-spoken, even-tempered brothers never had a brawl or a spitting, fuming argument, and that night was no different. Devon simply stopped speaking to him. A week after they buried their father at Saint Paul Cemetery in Whitesbridge, Devon quietly moved out of the house without a word or a note. Larson felt certain his younger brother didn't leave a forwarding address because he couldn't, leaving his childhood home before securing a new one. It didn't fit Devon's personality to do anything with haste, with no backup plan, no consultation, but his spirit broke the evening he found his father's dying heart while Larson carefully backed his prize-winning Shelby into the garage.

A lifelong betting man, Larson had always been a careful gambler with uncanny instincts and the ability to see through people. At first, he put his money on Devon to reach out to him within a month of leaving home. Never had Larson been more wrong when calculating the odds and profiling an opponent. After years of spending every night at card tables, forgetting his past and escaping his towering regrets one hand at a time, it occurred to him that his profile of Devon was all wrong.

His brother wasn't an opponent. They weren't engaged in a battle of wits. There was no trophy or purse at stake. Devon felt he'd lost both his father and brother in the same day and wandered in search of an impossible thing to fill the massive void.

Larson felt the same way because it was his profile as well. He, too, searched for something greater than himself, and in witnessing Teddy's miraculous find thought that perhaps he'd stumbled onto the divine path that could lead him back to Devon.

Enzo O'Day rolled dice in Teddy's apartment all afternoon and evening to no avail. Waking up late the following morning to return to the testing ground, his Lucky Five was revealed from 12:12 p.m. to 12:17 p.m. after he rolled fifty-nine Sixes in a row behind a blindfold. If Enzo had known what he'd achieved, it would have surely been an awakening. He'd have thought back to times in his life when he wished magic was real.

Enzo tended bar from an early age, serving as barback to his father, Brian O'Day, at their family tavern, the famous Pub O'Day in the Beacon Hill neighborhood of Boston. Unlike the rest of his new crew, Enzo came from a large family of four older brothers and two younger sisters, each of them putting in time supporting the family pub. By the time he turned sixteen, Enzo could craft any mixed drink and had stories and jokes to accompany every glass, a gift his father felt was the difference between a garden variety slinger of drinks and a truly special neighborhood bartender.

Brian O'Day served as the strict patriarch of his clan in much the same way Larry Williams did, only with a healthy dollop of dark humor. The O'Days ribbed each other constantly, spewing vile burns across the breakfast table the same way others would discuss the weather or current events. The only member of the family who bowed out of the daily flame wars was Enzo's mother, Elena Domingo O'Day. After migrating to America from Spain, she found work as a server at Pub O'Day during its grand opening week and soon fell in love with her boss, a man full of life whose own family crossed the Atlantic for a new life in a new world a generation back.

As much as Enzo admired his father and modeled himself after him, he had a special bond with his mother, a woman who worked harder and loved more unconditionally than anyone he'd ever meet. He told only G-rated jokes whenever she was in the room yet shared only with her the skeletons he collected throughout his youth.

Alcoholism ran rampant through Enzo's bloodline, from his father to his aunts and uncles to his great-grandparents, and he made every attempt to avoid falling into the same pits his forefathers had never climbed out of. Turning down countless offers of free drinks while on the job, he felt bulletproof, his convictions stronger than any temptation a tourist or Boston U frat boy could offer. If only he'd viewed narcotics in the same vein.

On his twenty-first birthday, his childhood pals failed to push him to indulge in a night of heavy drinking, a feat of restraint he'd always been proud of. Enzo was so busy expertly avoiding rounds of ale and whiskey that he stood unprepared when Faith McAlister, a perfect beauty with perfect red curls and a perfect constellation of freckles around a perfect smile, asked him for an Isle of Skye, an old drink she used to sneak sips of with her sisters in Scotland. So pristine was Faith that Enzo felt taken aback by her offer of crushed morphine in the alley behind the pub. She'd joined him in the alley during his smoke breaks for five nights before revealing her recreational habit.

Not connecting his family's history of alcoholism to the seemingly mild blue powder Faith inhaled nightly, Enzo joined her in a line, one that would stretch ahead of him for years. He limited himself to a finger's length each night, his futile attempt at control, telling himself that he remained firmly at the wheel so long as he never ventured past that three-inch line. He maintained his self-discipline as he and Faith moved into a studio apartment together at the Brighton Street Arms with wedding plans, but the stress of turning the page to a new chapter in his life proved more than he could handle.

Enzo continued to snort morphine one rationed finger line at a time, but soon did so three times daily. He waded into unexplored waters when he hid his growing habit from his fiancée. One summer night, he ventured out for another bottle of morphine pills to crush into coarse powder only to learn that his long-time dealer, Otto Diamond, had been arrested the day before. Otto's brother Marlon had only heroin to offer. Staring at a night of withdrawals, Enzo accepted Marlon's hypodermic needle, even allowing the gaunt junkie to inject him personally just to get him through the following week until he could find a new dealer for his blue pills. Looking back, what frightened Enzo most was the fact that if he knew how much more powerfully heroin would grip him over all those lines of crushed morphine, he'd still have made the same damning choice.

Enzo fell into the O'Day family pits, plummeting farther than any of his ancestors could imagine. Unable to hide his new habit from Faith and unable to halt his spiral, his fiancée took a "break" from their relationship, leaving their studio on Brighton Street to allow her beloved the space he needed to deal with the vicious monkey clutching his back. She returned to her parents' home in Cambridge to both grant Enzo time to heal and to rehabilitate herself.

Their break proved riddled with escalating fights and flung insults and furious late-night phone calls to the McAlister home in the middle of the night. In hindsight, it felt inevitable that Enzo and Faith would cancel their engagement and sever their relationship. When they spoke for the last time, on the front steps of the Brighton Street Arms, Faith had been clean for two months while Enzo continued to fall.

Enzo's sisters disowned him, realizing that the more they reached out to him the more he dismissed them. His older brothers visited him with doses of tough love that went unheard and unfelt. His father Brian had no better luck, his usual manly advice of "suck it up and shrug it off" coming across more like judgmental scolding than loving concern, which all felt hypocritical coming from a well-known drunk.

Enzo didn't truly see the depth of his torment until the night his mother Elena came to visit. She rarely left Beacon Hill, and her sudden appearance on his doorstep washed over him like a wave of shame, a blinding reminder of his wasted youth.

Moving in with her youngest son, Elena cared for him as she had for twenty-five years, preparing his meals and laundering his clothes. She never pressed him for action, always waiting patiently for Enzo to have a moment of clarity, a self-discovery she feared she'd never see.

The first moment came after an argument over dinner. Elena promised mashed potatoes but cooked rice instead. It infuriated Enzo to such an irrational state that he blacked out for a moment and looked down at his mother, her left wrist broken after he grabbed her and hurled her to the hardwood floor. His violent outburst was so quick and foggy from that day's bender that it felt like another man had accosted Elena while Enzo wobbled helplessly on his feet.

The second moment came when Enzo returned home from work to find Faith sitting on the couch while a two-year-old boy played in their former bedroom. His name was Jason, and he was the spitting image of the balding bartender who'd just done a line of coke in his parked car before entering his apartment. Seeing his younger self stacking plastic LEGO blocks on the floor shot a jolt of perspective through Enzo. No longer was he living for the day in a hedonistic lifestyle with no vision beyond tomorrow. He suddenly felt the obligation of generations of O'Day fathers, men who loved the bottle but always loved their children more. That powerful family pride got them through their darkest years, and it now stared at Enzo through the tender brown eyes of a boy who never knew the drunk, the junkie, the violent monster that his father had become.

Faith moved back into the Brighton Street Arms with Enzo and Elena, who remained to care for young Jason while her son straightened his life. He vowed he'd clean up and become the father he knew he could be.

"Make me a believer," Faith said.

For six months, their shared path seemed wide and sunny. Enzo O'Day's demons faded in the sunlight of new family bliss, but never entirely left, waiting for a moment of despair and its persistent demon to rear its head again.

On January 25, 1995, while Enzo lorded over a Super Bowl Sunday at the pub, Elena Domingo O'Day suffered a massive stroke. Faith called the pub to break the news to her fiancée and rushed Elena to Massachusetts General Hospital. Enzo clocked out and grabbed his car keys, but not before taking up the offer of five shots of Cuervo Gold tequila with a group of college kids and bumming a bump of coke from Otto Diamond, who'd been watching the game at the bar, erasing half a year of sobriety in a matter of minutes.

Despite his longer drive, Enzo raced down the streets of Boston and arrived at the hospital in time with Faith pulling up to Emergency. He saw his fiancée running aside his mother's gurney as an orderly wheeled her into the building, but failed to see his two-year-old son picking snapdragons for his grandma at a flower bed by the sidewalk.

Not slowing for a second, Enzo plowed his pickup into the flower bed, pulverizing its concrete walls and ending Jason O'Day's young life. By the time the truck came to a halt, he'd knocked over one of the orderlies tending to Elena and crashed through the double doors of the ER, sending shattered glass into the waiting room. The silent confusion that followed lasted only a minute before the smoke subsided and desperate screams pierced the sky.

A week later, a funeral took place at Mount Hope Cemetery to honor both Jason and Elena O'Day. Enzo refused the honor of being a pallbearer, choosing instead to watch the service from his truck, its bashed front end a constant reminder of the tragedy his life became. As the caskets were lowered into the ground, without a goodbye or apology, he started his engine and drove west, determined to never return out of fear of ruining the lives of his remaining loved ones with what he deemed the "O'Day Curse."

Like Teddy, Enzo drove across the country, searching for something or someone to help him start anew. He drove until his gas tank and funds ran dry, landing him in Easton.

At the Vista Playa Apartments, Teddy had a sense of wonder he hadn't felt since he was a boy. Each of his friends had a Lucky Five. It showed him that perhaps magic did exist in the world, or at least something bigger, some sign of a higher power. He stared at his clipboard, at Enzo's 172 dice rolls, turning up all Sixes, and struggled to remain calm in front of the new recruits.

"We done then?" Enzo asked, taking off his blindfold as Teddy put away the clipboard and returned the dice to the dish on the coffee table.

"Yes, we're done. This is a big help."

"What's all this shit mean for your research?"

Teddy didn't have a ready answer. So far, he'd only tested his discovery with cards and dice, but Enzo's uncanny performance made him wonder what else they were capable of during their predetermined five minutes a day.

"It has to do with luck," Teddy said. "Your luck rises and falls all day. I know because I've charted that, too. But there's another reason you guys are here."

"You mean something besides your class project?"

"Teddy's got plans," Angelica said.

"Oh, I got a lot of plans," Teddy said. "We're planning a trip to Vegas. Big money if you're in. I'll tell you more on the way."

"What's the angle?" Enzo asked.

"We made a lot of connections over there," Rolo said, puffing his cigar. "You'll see soon enough."

Angelica glanced at Quickie Buckner's red journal sitting on its shelf in the center of the Vintage Vegas wall. She knew Teddy's obsessions and fantasies.

"We'll all see," she said.

16

The First Face You See in Vegas

Monday, September 20, 1999, 5:46 a.m.

The multi-level parking garage of the Poseidon Casino and Resort accommodated 3,500 vehicles with ten spaces reserved for RVs, ten for tour buses, and twenty for motorcycles. The top level of the garage offered a panoramic view of Downtown Las Vegas with Circus Circus, the Stratosphere, and the Wynn Resort to the north and the rest of The Strip to the south starting with Treasure Island, the Mirage, and the Venetian.

With sunrise barely arriving, the parking structure still felt relaxed with one attendant half-asleep in his booth surrounded by thousands of empty stalls. The dark, early morning tranquility of the outrageous city would soon buckle from throngs of mid-week tourists filling every space, every room and seat, with coupons and travel deals, promises of free upgrades, swag bags, and a complimentary stack of gaming chips to kick-start their adventurous three-day "Instant Getaway" travel packages. Las Vegas offers every possible incentive during times of low attendance and revenue. Monday through Wednesday in the fall months was akin to Happy Hour in a bar.

A gray minivan ascended the parking garage, passing seven stories of available spots to reach the completely vacant top level, open to the dawn sky. The van parked near a stairwell, the silencing of its engine throwing its passengers into the city's uncharacteristic quiet.

Teddy and his newly recruited crew emerged from the minivan. The nearly six-hour drive started with Enzo at the wheel of the old van, an unregistered derelict he restored upon finding it abandoned in the back lot of the Brickhouse. Rolo took the wheel after their brief rest stop in the desert town of Baker, California, allowing his partners a nap before showtime. The choice of vehicle was instrumental to the plan in the event things went sideways. The group didn't fly or rent a car in order to avoid any digital paper trails that weekend. Enzo's van didn't officially exist, which felt like destiny to Teddy.

They also planned their attire. Teddy and Rolo wore plain button-up shirts untucked over jeans and slacks. Angelica wore a simple black dress topped with a sweater vest. Enzo chose a white Polo and pressed jeans. Larson donned one of his tailored three-piece suits minus the jacket. They'd dressed casual-formal, siding closer to a job interview feel versus high roller or avid clubber.

As they stepped out of the minivan and straightened their outfits, Teddy reached into the center console and pulled out a K-Mart shopping bag.

"You all get a prize today," Teddy said, passing out small boxes to his crew. They opened the swing-top lids of the boxes to find matching digital watches, their little screens encased in black plastic with bands of black rubber.

"You want us to put on these gizmos?" Larson asked, more accustomed to finer timepieces.

"That's why I got 'em," Teddy said. "I synched them and set their alarms accordingly." They put on their watches, Teddy seeing the moment as a chance to address the troops. "Larson, you asked why we needed five for this deal. Rolo, Ange, and I agreed we needed a couple of trustees if we were gonna do Vegas right, come down hard and fast. That's why I wrangled you two fools into the fold."

"I'm fuckin' honored," Enzo said with a smirk.

"You're sure your guys are ready inside?" Larson asked. "They're all in place?"

"I understand your apprehension. It won't feel like it, but trust me, everyone is ready and in place."

Instead of exposing the Lucky Five to Larson and Enzo, Teddy revealed his grand plan as an elaborate inside game. To explain their upcoming impossible wins, he conjured a smoke screen story involving old associates and paid employees.

Angelica knew some card dealers who would stack the decks for them. Rolo had an electronic gizmo that magnetically controlled the roulette wheels, as paid pit bosses looked the other way. The box man at the craps table,

Teddy's old buddy from high school, would provide loaded dice whenever they stood at the table. The most important detail was that all those little cons were choreographed down to the smallest detail, designed to occur in strict five-minute windows as signaled by their new digital watches.

"You're absolutely sure?" Larson asked. "I mean, the floor is likely dead right now."

"That's the idea. Remember, we stick to the plan, follow the schedule, see how this thing unfolds. Between our five-minute windows, there's no wandering, no impulse games. If everything falls into place like I think it will, we'll gather our piles of winnings and go home to celebrate."

"And that's it," Angelica said firmly. "One and done, right?"

"One and done." Teddy led them to the nearby stairwell.

"Let it be known that I don't buy that for a second," Rolo said. "It's one and done if we fall on our asses in there. If we end up taking the house, there's no way we ain't comin' back for another round."

"One and done," Teddy said again. "That's the plan." The crew followed him into the stairwell.

"I wonder," Larson said in his monotone voice. He took a last look around at the crazy buildings all around them before heading down the stairs.

"What do you wonder, Larson?" Teddy asked over their echoing footsteps, hoping his sharp friend wasn't harboring suspicion. "Come on, spit it out. Better here and now than inside at a table."

"I wonder if you can get a decent shrimp cocktail at this hour."

"Shrimp cocktail?" Rolo said. "Try steak and eggs. It's breakfast time."

"In this town, a shrimp cocktail and a Remy Martin is breakfast."

"In a few hours, we'll have have a small fortune," Teddy said. "We can have steak and eggs and shrimp all night."

Larson smirked, still unsure about their operation. "You wanna know the fastest way to leave Vegas with a small fortune? You come here with a large one."

Angelica laughed, which prompted Enzo to offer his own jokes. "Why's it easy to beat Santa Claus at poker?" he said.

"Why?" Angelica smiled.

"Everyone knows he always checks it twice."

Angelica laughed while everyone else groaned as they went farther down the stairwell.

"Enough jokes," Teddy said. "It's almost showtime."

"One more," Enzo said, "something a fellow Irishman will appreciate."

"Alright, let's hear it. Then we put our game faces on."

"An American and an Irishman are playing cards in a bar. The American is losing badly, so he offers a bet. He says, 'I hear you Irish can drink! I'll bet five-thousand dollars you can't drink ten pints of Guinness in one minute!' The Irishman thinks it over, stands, and leaves the bar. The American is confused until the man suddenly returns and agrees to the bet. He stuns the American by downing ten pints of Guinness in a minute. The American said, 'You won fair and square, but why'd you leave first?' The Irishman wipes his chin and says, 'Five-thousand is a lot of money for a man like me. I went to the pub next door first to see if I could do it!'"

Angelica alone laughed at Enzo's old joke as the group reached the ground floor.

"Enough comedy," Rolo said. "We don't move unless we move together, we all got that?" He turned to Teddy, his hand on the door to the casino. "Where to first, brother?"

Without a word, Teddy adjusted his collar, opened the door, and entered the casino with his friends close behind.

The interior of the decadent Poseidon Casino and Resort resembled a liminal space, nearly as empty as its parking garage. Distant slot machines cut the relative quiet, the sounds of the one-armed bandits in "Attract Mode" tame compared to the bustling hours soon to come. The oceanic pattern of the carpeting, comprising shells and starfish over a deep blue background, seamlessly stretched throughout the massive gaming rooms.

With Teddy leading the way, the group passed the city of slots and entered the table area, where cards and chips and wheels of fortune mostly sat dormant at such an early hour. Only two of the fifteen Texas Hold 'Em tables had action, hardcore all-nighters fleecing wannabe whales with two pair and bluffing them with busted straights. They walked past the one active Roulette table, the shuttered Craps and Baccarat tables, and the two barely breathing games of Three-Card Poker.

They continued through the labyrinth of table games until they reached the Blackjack area, where five of thirty tables were active. Usually one of the first games to see any traffic at the start of a day, Blackjack would prove a good testing ground for the Lucky Five on its maiden flight in Sin City.

Teddy singled out a table with one player. "There's one of our guys," he lied. The man sat at first base, to the dealer's left. Angelica, Larson, and Rolo joined him while Enzo killed time at a nearby slot machine.

"The upper ear, that was the worst," said the one player sitting at third base. He spoke fast with a thick Cockney accent, continuing his one-sided conversation with the silent dealer. "Hurt more than the tongue. Took a fuckin' full moon to heal, too."

Teddy and his crew placed their bets, the table minimum of ten dollars, a conservative figure to start. The dealer pulled cards from an eight-deck shoe - a horizontal stack of 416 cards - and dealt a new round with Larson scrutinizing his every move despite Rolo's order not to. Teddy glanced at the peculiar Londoner sitting among them, an obese man with spiked black hair, heavy tattoos, and a black denim jacket torn at the cuffs and collar. Every part of his body was pierced with metal, including a large silver spade earring dangling from his left lobe.

"I hear the belly button is the worst," Angelica said, breaking her promise to refrain from being social and ultimately familiar. To Teddy's dismay, the odd man offered her a handshake.

Lynn Harrod

"Jerry," the man said with a smile, his bottom lip almost completely obscured by a row of silver rings and studs. "Most folks call me 'Scary Jerry,' if you can believe that."

"Angelica," she said, not knowing how else to respond. She remembered afterward that she wasn't supposed to become neighborly with anyone, revealing her actual name, but they hadn't yet come up with aliases.

"Belly button's the most dangerous," Jerry said. "You do it wrong, you pour open like a flippin' piñata. Major vessel there. Forget slittin' wrists, you wanna kill yourself real bad, just slice under your belly button, see where that gets ya. You'll paint the house red before you can dial 911. I botched it once early in my career. Poor fucka went to I.C.U."

"That's what you do? You pierce?"

"I pierce alright, even got a degree in Metallurgy. That's why I'm here. Big trade show. Lots of stickas here, lots of celebs. I stuck Dennis Rodman yesterday."

Rolo checked the time on his black digital watch, as did Larson.

"The trick to making a name in this biz," Jerry said, "is you gotta forget surgical steel. That's for teenie boppers gettin' their ears gunned at the mall. Fuck that, pardon my tongue. I use Implant Grade steel. Pure, premium shit, used for bones and such. No infection."

The dealer won the hand with a King and a Queen. Teddy lost with an Eighteen. Larson and Rolo busted out.

BEEP BEEP.

6:15 a.m.

"Man, I gotta head out," Larson said, checking the time on his beeping watch. "Might as well go out swinging."

"That's the spirit," Teddy said.

"Why not?" Angelica said, sticking to their crude script.

Teddy and his crew laid down different bets - forty dollars, fifty dollars, seventy-five dollars - Angelica going overboard with three-hundred.

"You sure swing hard, lady," Jerry said with a laugh.

The dealer passed out new hands, Larson staring at each card as if willing them to turn up winners. He and his partners won with Blackjacks and a Twenty, while Scary Jerry and the dealer busted.

"Crikes!" Jerry said. "I sure as hell missed the gravy train you all caught."

Larson sat startled as every person at that table seemed to receive what he pictured in his mind. Everyone else contained their excitement as told, except for Teddy, who couldn't help but smile.

* * *

After playing all their Fives that day, Rolo's prediction came to light. Each bet doubled the last, their bravado growing along with their winnings. Larson and Enzo were impressed by the efficiency of the operation, each insider playing his part to perfection. One would never know that all those dealers were on their payroll, rigging every game in precise five-minute intervals. At the end of the night, feeling the rush of making a collective $115,000 in four casinos over a collective twenty-five minutes, the crew ditched their "one and done" vow and voted to remain in Vegas another two days. Even Angelica voted to stay, her starry eyes at odds with her instincts to return home safely while they still could.

Over those three days, Teddy's crew played every resort, great and small, throughout Las Vegas. It led to further excursions in the old minivan, weekdays at first, followed by weeks at a time, until their trepidation had vanished and caution was abandoned altogether. The Lucky Five felt infallible and endless, which they neglected to recognize as the most ominous of red flags. More than anyone else, Teddy Brewer should have known that winning streaks - even seemingly magical ones - all come to a sudden end like rocketing into a brick wall, and the taller the stakes, the bigger the hit.

Eventually, the fateful night would come with the dreaded visitors that ended it all.

17

Three More For The Slab

Thursday, December 20, 2001, 6:17 p.m.

Manny Sanchez looked up from Teddy's journal, jolted out of his trance by the ringing phone on the kitchen wall. The only people who knew how to reach him were his mother and his boss. Though his relationship with his mother had been strained for years, he hoped to hear her voice when he picked up the receiver.

"Hello?" Manny said.

"We got more work," George Armand said on the other line. "A lot more. I'm on route now."

Manny could tell from the background noise and his boss's raised voice that he was on speakerphone while driving to his apartment.

"On route... wait... what happened?"

"Remember that junkie from the Brewer mansion?"

"Marissa Washington."

"Sharp memory, Manny." George knew his rookie shooter would surely remember the two famous gangsters, but he didn't expect him to recall such a minor player from the double murder scene earlier that day, a woman he'd only seen for five seconds.

"What about her?" Manny asked. "Is it about the book?"

"Jesus, you remember that, too, the book she kept rambling about. Nah, it's still missing."

"What do we know about it?" Manny asked, interested only in his boss's reaction.

"Manny, you're obviously fascinated by this kinda shit, and honestly, it's sorta endearing. I used to get star-struck by high-profile cases, too. But trust me, forget that book. If Brewer really did leave her a 'magic' book..."

"Magic?" Manny wondered how much George genuinely knew but had been withholding from him. Was he secretly on his way to arrest him for stealing the journal?

"Magic," George said with a laugh. "Her words, not mine. If he did leave her a mystical book, a cache of money, drugs, anything, we would have uncovered it by now."

"But it's only been a day."

"Sure, but she swears it's in that house, and we turned the place upside down, right-side up, and sideways. The only thing we didn't do was dig up the garden. My guess is that her voodoo book probably doesn't exist other than in her coked-out mind."

Manny glanced at the journal sitting open on his couch, as if waiting for him to return. "Probably not."

"We took her in for questioning and she spilled a lot."

"Like what?" Manny asked, stalling, looking out the front window to see if cops were gathering out front.

"She told us about three other victims, including locations and other details."

"Dead?"

"Three more for the slab," George said. "Pretty gruesome, from what I was told. You gotta expect that when something as big as the Lucky Five comes tumbling down."

"Lucky Five?" Manny asked, trying to control his panic.

"That was the name of Brewer's gang. Don't ask me why."

Manny knew exactly why.

"Who are the three new vics?" Manny asked.

"All former associates of Brewer, according to her. We'll find out when we get there."

"What do they look like?" Manny felt like he intimately knew all of Teddy's old crew and pictured them dead, face-down in pools of blood. The thought pained him.

"Like I said, we'll know when we get there, so suit up and meet me in Whitesbridge."

Whitesbridge.

Angelica.

"George, I'm sorry, but my camera is out of commission."

"That's why you have two."

"This is embarrassing to admit, but B-Cam is dead, too."

"Shit."

"If you can arrange some money..."

"We both know I can't." George grunted in frustration, thinking. "Sorry, Manny, I wish I could get you some funds but my hands are tied until your probation is over."

"So, what do I do?"

"Well, what I gotta do is call a shooter from another station, maybe from Brawley. We'll capture it, don't worry. Meantime, we gotta get one of your rigs up and running."

"Sorry, George."

"Look, I think I can wrangle some gear from a guy who owes me, but I can't break away today. I'll call you tomorrow. We'll work something out at the lab."

"I really appreciate it, George."

"Don't sweat it. I'll see you tomorrow, bright and early."

Manny hung up the phone, grateful for both his boss's understanding and his ignorance, grateful that uniformed officers weren't pounding on his door with handcuffs ready. He turned to the couch and stared at the journal, wondering how the hell a group of friends that discovered a sure thing and rode it for so long could end up murdered all within the same weekend.

He grabbed another beer from his fridge but ignored it as he sat on his couch and buried himself in the journal, picking up where he left off. He could hear Teddy Brewer's voice as he read on.

"The Lucky Five worked flawlessly. I could have doubled down on a Hard-20, went All-In on a Two-Seven off-suit, put it all on the wheel at Double-Zero ten times in a row, and every time I'd still end up raking the pot. Any chip not purple or yellow or brown felt like child's play. Any table less than No-Limit felt boring. Las Vegas became our playground. Dealers remembered us. Pit bosses comped us. I finally felt like a whale. I'm surprised the ride lasted as long as it did. In Vegas, being remembered is good, but being memorized is all kinds of bad."

18

My Girl Maxine

Friday, November 12, 1999, 6:01 p.m.

Chemical Town sat in its eternal shroud comprising the usual Central Valley autumn fog mixed with the year-round pollution pumped high into the air without pause. At dusk, the columns of smoke blended in with the coming night sky, and the reduced traffic made the area seem almost peaceful. Occasional semi-truck trailers traveled down the street to and from the dozens of factories and distribution centers in the industrial zone.

A lone motorcycle - a midnight blue Triumph - roared down the central street, its small frame back-lit by the polluted sunset and dwarfed by monstrous 18-wheelers. Two men sat atop the sport bike as it turned off the road into the small parking lot at 444 Paradise Lane.

Larson removed his helmet and shut off the motor. Teddy removed his and looked around, amused by how nothing had changed since his last dismal visit to Ronnie's Room three months prior. Larson wore his usual pinstripe suit, his "uniform" whenever sitting at a poker table, while Teddy wore a simple T-shirt and jeans, disarmingly casual compared to his Vegas persona.

Teddy flicked his Zippo and lit up a White Knight, took a drag, and stared at the taunting red door, imagining the events soon to come.

"Last chance to back out," Larson said in his usual flat tone. "You're above this now, Theodore. We both are." Teddy didn't respond, didn't even glance at him, grinning as he took another drag. "She may not even let you in, son."

Teddy and Larson had spoken at length about returning to Ronnie's Room. Larson thought hidden cardrooms were now small-time, not worth wasting their potential on. Teddy assured him it would be just for fun, returning to an old haunt for a few hours of cards and conversation, but he knew there was no fooling his sharp, observant friend.

Teddy wanted revenge.

"I'll tell you the truth, Larson. Vegas has given me more than my fill of Me-Winning. What I want now is a heaping dose of Them-Losing."

"Them?" Larson knew who he meant.

"Them. Him. You know, whatever poor sap dares sit across from me."

"Ah yes. *Him*. Good luck with that."

"Still using that phrase?" Teddy asked with a smirk.

"With you standing here amped up like Charles Bronson, it still seems like the proper thing to say. Just remember, we don't have paid insiders helping us in there. You're going to need all your intellect, all your experience, and yes, a little luck."

"I know my way around a table, Larson."

"I don't doubt your skill, son. You're formidable, we both know that. I'm just saying let's keep a leash on it tonight. Agreed?"

"I appreciate your concern, I really do, but forgive me when I say I don't want to hear it again."

"Fair enough."

Larson placed his helmet on his motorcycle and walked to the red door. Randy the bouncer opened the door and allowed him to enter, leaving Teddy alone outside, sitting on the motorcycle to finish his smoke.

Teddy looked at the other cars in the small lot, searching for a particular classic Cadillac. Instead, he spied his old Jeep, Maxine, parked behind some Oleanders. Her convertible top folded down, she sat on new 33-inch swamp tires. Her roll bar was adorned with a row of fog lights, tacky after-market junk he'd never imagine installing on her. The one detail that remained after transferring ownership was the pair of fuzzy red dice dangling from the rearview mirror.

Teddy snuffed his cigarette onto the gravel lot and walked to the door. He knocked once and smiled at the peephole. Whoever looked back at him from the other side left the door shut, likely running to fetch the proprietor. A moment later, Ronnie opened the door but didn't step outside or utter a word. She glared at her old friend as if he'd gone mad.

Lynn Harrod

"Good evening, Lady Veronica," Teddy said, waiting for a response. Ronnie simply stared at him, incredulous, waiting for his latest pathetic pitch to get into the room. Teddy felt like he could read her mind. "Okay, here goes my spiel. I could have taken a cab up to Crow Canyon, or I could have whiskey'd myself to sleep. But here I stand, a new man of reason. I just want a friendly game."

"What you want is a shrink."

"That last big hit I took here was therapy enough. I should learn not to play emotional."

"You should learn not to play," Ronnie said. "Not here, anyway. But hey, if the Indians will have you, I can't stand in their way. Good luck up there."

"There's that phrase again." Teddy checked his black plastic digital watch. Time was ticking away, and his face showed he had to get in that room *now*. "Everyone wishes me luck, but I have the feeling they get off on seeing me lose."

"I would never curse you like that," Ronnie said. "But I gotta say no. You leave me no choice, Ted. Have fun on the mountain. I do sincerely wish you good luck."

Ronnie didn't slam the door in his face. Instead, she stood there looking at him, hoping he'd truly see reason and understand her position. Of course, he wouldn't, not even considering it for a moment.

"Ronnie, you and I both hate Crow Canyon. It's crowded, it's a long drive to the middle of nowhere. You can't get a decent beer, can't get a seat, and when you do, you're shoe-horned between senior citizens leftover from Bingo Night. But there is one thing that Indian casino has over you."

"And what's that?"

"Legality," Teddy said, enunciating each syllable.

Ronnie stepped outside and shut the door behind her. "You threatening me, Teddy?"

"Of course not. I'm just asking for one more chance to win back, not my money, but my self-respect. You want me to beg?" Teddy got down on one knee and hammed it up good, clasping his hands while looking up at her face silhouetted under the lone light above the door. "Pleeeease let me into your illegal card room, Ronnie Mayes, pleeeeeease..."

Ronnie quickly opened the door a crack to shut him up. Frustrated with what she was about to do, she held out her right palm. "I need to see your stake first."

"I understand."

Teddy handed her two Hundreds, spreading open his wallet to show he had nothing more. She took the bills and held them up horizontally.

"This is your ceiling, Teddy. It should get you about thirty games at the low-low tables if you play it right, but that's it. No house credit, no running to the ATM, no making deals with Bulldog."

"I understand."

"If you build a tower with these two C-notes, God Bless. But if you flush it all away..."

"I understand."

"Teddy, it's not that I don't sympathize. It's flat out bad business, letting a guy in here who loses his soul every time. It's like a bartender who keeps serving a lush. People talk."

"I understand."

"And I'm giving you three hours. Speaking as a friend, I'm telling you, it's for your own good."

Teddy rose to his feet and smiled, nodding in agreement.

"Three hours," Ronnie said. "It's six now. At nine o'clock, win or lose, you go home. Do you understand *that*?"

"I'll be snuggled in bed by eight-thirty."

* * *

Unlike Teddy's prior visit, with its packed house full of regulars and weekend warriors, only half the tables in Ronnie's Room saw action that night, with a few at the front table, the rest scattered throughout the room. He walked past them all - not bothering to search for Cal Zimmer - and headed straight to Bulldog at the cash cage in the back.

"Wasn't sure I'd ever see you again, Teddy," Bulldog said. The overhead lights made his side holstered .38 snub-nose shine.

"You'll always see me, Bulldog."

"Yeah, well Ronnie told me you're on thin ice tonight. Makes me wonder why she let you in at all."

"The woman has a soft spot for me."

"Lucky you." Bulldog turned and reached to a counter behind him where an acrylic tray with $200 in gaming chips taking up just two rows sat pre-prepared, quite a downgrade from the $2,000 he started with during his last visit. He slid the partial tray to Teddy. "I'd let you buy another stack but I got my orders."

"Two's all I need," Teddy said. "I probably won't even touch one of them."

"The more cocky you are, my friend, the more I worry."

"How sweet." Teddy took the tray and turned to the tables, catching Cal Zimmer at front of the room at his usual Table Six and Larson in the middle of the room at Table Nine.

"I've never seen Larson at a low-low table," Bulldog said.

"Me neither. I think he's there to give me company."

"How sweet, indeed."

"But he's got nothing to worry about. I mean, Two-Hundred ain't enough to cause a ruckus. I can't play up front with the big boys, so I'll be slumming with the rookies all night, no matter where Larson sits."

"Let's hope so."

As Teddy headed to the tables, Bulldog called out to him. "May the sun shine behind you, may your cards come up Kings, and may you win more than you lose."

"I must ask, where did you find that lovely poem?"

"I just turned the page on my calendar."

Teddy sat in the center of the room at Table Nine with Larson and several other players, overtaken by the smell of the tri-tip roast, garlic potato skins, and onion rings at the buffet just ten feet behind him.

Over the course of an hour, with hands starting at five bucks, Teddy built a decent, legitimate stack from his modest stake, easily outplaying everyone except Larson. He'd normally feel beneath playing against new fish, but he knew the tables would literally turn at any moment. With each win, he checked the time.

Soon, it was nearly eight o'clock.

Ronnie topped off Larson's glass of gin as he ate potato chips from a can of Pringle's.

"A gourmet spread within reach and you're chomping on those?" Teddy asked. "At Brickhouse, maybe, but here?"

"We all have our little rituals," Larson said.

"I never knew you to be that type."

"What type is that?"

"The superstitious type. I thought that was my vice, not yours."

"Every man of sport has his little superstitions."

Teddy held out his hand. Larson poured him a small stack of potato chips.

"You know how Pringles got started?" Larson asked.

"Yeah, they took leftover peels from other companies and mushed them into that shoehorn shape."

"Thanks for ruining my joke."

"Oh, you tell jokes?"

"Occasionally," Larson said with a slight smile that betrayed his stone face.

"After all these years, I had no idea you were funny."

"I can be hysterical."

Cal Zimmer sat in his reserved seat at Table Six, the one No-Limit table, having eyed Teddy and Larson from the moment they entered the room. He'd been playing a group of "fresh fish" for several hours, men rich with disposable income, thick bankrolls ripe for the taking, but lacking in poker experience beyond online tournaments. He craved the challenge of a veteran and saw the duo of Teddy Brewer and Larson Williams as his chance for a thrilling game. After an hour of waiting for Teddy to sit at his front table, he lost patience and wandered to the buffet near Table Nine, making himself a "Royal Root Beer," his signature drink - root beer topped with Canadian whiskey. He nodded hello to the five players and joined them as their sixth, a curious move unexpected by all except Teddy.

"Cal Zimmer, slumming it with the rest of us?" Teddy said.

"Don't want me around?" Cal said. "Do I make you nervous?"

"Nah, it's always a pleasure to see you. It's just surprising to see you here is all, degrading yourself at a low-low table, sitting in the middle of the room with us dregs."

"This is no longer a low-low table," Cal said with a smile. "No fences for you to hide behind any more, I'm afraid."

"We only have one No-Limit table, Cal," Ronnie said from the buffet. "Take it easy."

"Then let this be the one! I declare this the new Table Six! Come on, let's bring ol' Richie over, make this interesting for a change."

"Even Richie gets to take five once in a while."

"Of course! I meant after our hard-working man finishes his well-earned coffee break." Cal turned in his chair to shoot a look at Richie. "If you want to keep pocketing my juicy tips, this is now the scene, maestro."

Richie stirred cream into his evening cup of coffee as he looked to Ronnie for approval. She turned to the players for a group decision. Teddy glanced toward her, keeping his expressionless face. Ronnie stared at him as if to ask, "What the hell are you up to?"

"I mean, if y'all don't mind?" Cal said to the group. "Are we playing poker or are we playing Kindergarten Go Fish here?"

"I'm okay with it if you guys are," Teddy said.

The players of Table Nine nodded in awkward agreement. Ronnie waved Richie Rocks over from the buffet. He covered his coffee with a napkin and carried an almond danish in his mouth as he took the "noon" seat at Table Nine. He cleaned his round eyeglasses on his paisley vest and wiped his hands with a wet nap. Cal handed him the deck.

"You know I like old-fashioned Cantrell," Cal said. "I get sick of Texas. Draw poker is my speed. I like the feel of five cards fanned out in my hand and the power to trade any of 'em."

"No-dicking-around poker, right?" Teddy asked.

"I like a man who remembers my braggart's ramblings," Cal said, slipping into his bad Christopher Walken voice, which meant he was loading his guns and preparing for another OK Corral showdown. "And I adore a man who makes me come to him."

"Is that what I did?"

"I'm here, ain't I?"

"This is now a No-Limit table, gentlemen," Richie Rocks said to the surrounding players, interrupting the little pissing match. "Hands start at fifty dollars. There will be no raise limits. Unless you're prepared to lose your entire roll, I suggest you join another table."

The casual players of Table Nine - first-timers looking only to sharpen their tools - rose from their seats and meandered to the buffet, becoming spectators for a high-stakes game between Teddy, Cal, and Larson.

"And then there were three," Cal said with a laugh. "Three brave fools in a Mexican standoff."

"Go easy on the drama, Cal," Larson said, always unflappable.

"What are you saying, Larson?"

"We aren't titans of industry embroiled in a multi-million dollar deal. We're just three bums playing cards. Check your perspective."

"I think you need to check yours. There's far more than money on the line, ain't that right, Teddy?"

Richie Rocks thoroughly washed the cards across the table, spreading them over the green felt and squaring them back into a deck. As always, he spoke with the gravitas of a referee obligated to explain the rules and promote fair play. "The game is five-draw. Minimum bet is fifty dollars."

Teddy tapped a quick count of his stacks. He'd built his initial stake of two-hundred to just over a thousand, giving him the chips and confidence he needed to continue with his audacious plan.

Cal, Teddy, and Larson tossed in orange chips - worth $100 apiece - as Richie dealt them five cards each.

"Has the stereo always been punked?" Cal asked, eyes on his cards. Everyone looked at each other, not sure who Cal was speaking to in his bad Christopher Walken voice.

Teddy knew.

"How exactly is it 'punked'?" Teddy asked.

"Doesn't remember presets. Color me spoiled, but it's a pain in the ass having to find 95.7 F.M. ten times a day. What happened? Did it get scrambled after a long day of amateur off-roading?"

"I never took her off-roading."

"Pity," Cal said. "I sure have. I had her modded, took her up to the lake last weekend, really put her through the gauntlet. Did you see her out there tonight? She's a real stunner now."

"I saw her. Looks like you had a Pep Boys gift card burning a hole in your pocket. Lots of cheap, after-market shit tacked on. Me, I always buy genuine Jeep parts."

"Not no more you don't," Cal said with a guffaw, expertly turning chips between his fingers.

"95.7 F.M.? Since when do you listen to rap, Cal?"

"One of my lady friends likes the bad boys. You know how it is."

Based on their initial cards, they each tossed in another orange chip and drew two new cards each.

"Loud, ain't she?" Cal asked.

"Loud?"

"Nadine. She's a loud one. No need to look at the tachometer, you can feel in your gut what gear you're in."

"Maxine," Teddy said, correcting him. "Yeah, she's loud."

"Well, I call her 'Nadine,' named after another of my lady friends. She's loud and she's rough, like driving a bumper car with a tractor engine. Ain't exactly a Fleetwood Coupe Deville."

Cal raised another Fifty. Teddy and Larson called. One of Ronnie's boys brought Teddy another bourbon, his fifth of the night. Larson placed his palm over the drink, concerned for his tipsy friend.

"You might want to keep a clear head," Larson said, leaning in close, speaking in a near-whisper.

"I got this," Teddy said, whispering back.

"Yeah, Larson, he's got this," Cal said. "He's a big boy and he's a Fightin' Irish, got Bushmills in his blood."

Larson removed his hand, nodding a silent apology for revealing his friend's weakness.

"Four-fifty on the table," Richie said.

"Yeah, she is loud," Teddy said, never taking his eyes off his hand. "If she was as smooth and quiet as a Cadillac, she wouldn't be a Jeep."

"All called," Cal said, as if he were the dealer. "Drop 'em, gentlemen."

Game over. Cal turned over three Nines, defeating Teddy's two pair and Larson's three Deuces. As Cal swept the pot, Teddy checked the time again, a drunken smile creeping across his face.

"Another round of Cantrell," Cal said as if ordering his chauffeur to circle the estate once more.

Richie gathered the cards and washed them again, taking a full minute to spread them all around the table as the players placed their new starting bets of $50. He squared the cards into a deck and dealt the three players a new hand of Cantrell. Cal quickly raised one-hundred. Teddy re-raised two-hundred. Larson called.

"Six-fifty on the table," Richie said.

"I see what you mean," Cal said to Teddy. "You don't eat an apple wishing it was an orange. That Jeep is a roughneck soldier girl. A Cadillac is an elegant woman in a silk gown. Ands Larson's Triumph 'Three X' is a fuckin' demon. Each machine has its own personality, its own feel."

"Triumph Speed Triple GT-X," Larson said, correcting Cal. "In case you're curious."

"Limited Edition," Teddy added. "Only three-hundred made." Teddy winked at his friend, but Larson found it odd that Teddy boasted about his rare motorcycle.

"My mistake," Cal said. "Whatever it's called, Larson, that sweet British crotch rocket of yours must be quite a ride."

The three men drew cards. Cal gestured for one, Larson asked for two, while Teddy held up four fingers, requesting almost an entirely new hand.

"You always surprise me, Teddy," Cal said with a grin. "I've never seen someone draw four at a No-Limit table."

"That's right," Teddy said. "I'm full of surprises."

Cal raised another two-hundred. Larson folded. Teddy called Cal, dropping two-hundred more on the table, leaving him with roughly two-hundred left for the night.

Teddy didn't upturn at his new hand, leaving it face-down, unknown in front of him. Larson noticed, disapproving of his friend's blind betting.

"Eleven-hundred and fifty in play," Richie said.

"And you're right, Teddy," Cal said. "If I'm pining for a Cadillac, I should just get one."

"Makes sense to me."

"Do you happen to own a Cadillac?" Cal asked, laughing.

BEEP BEEP

8:04 p.m.

Teddy checked his watch and gestured for another bourbon as he finally flipped his cards, revealing four Kings to the astonishment of the crowd, handily winning the round. He shot down his drink and swept the pot, quickly resetting for a new hand. He played on the clock now.

Cal failed to hide his shock and disappointment, his face scrunched inward. He mucked his hand, not bothering to reveal his inferior cards. He winced as Teddy swept the pot without a trace of emotion, feeling so burnt that he didn't spot Teddy barely able to contain himself as the onlookers silently cheered, long wanting to see the infamous Cal Zimmer get his due.

His frustration arose not just from his bad beat, but from confusion. The rumors were true. Cal Zimmer cheated well and often. He'd slipped an Ace into his hand after the draw, but his Full House of Aces over Deuces were narrowly beaten by Teddy's four-of-a-kind.

"Wow, what a hand," Cal said. "This could be a scorcher of a comeback."

"Stay tuned, kids." Teddy checked the time. His Lucky Five felt like a countdown looming over him, echoing in a canyon. With the minutes burning away, there was no time to savor his victory and toy with his opponent. Teddy had to move in for the kill.

"You got a dentist appointment?" Cal asked, noticing Teddy's obsession with the time.

"I gotta leave after this next bourbon, a double, if you please, so I really only have time for one big thrill. That quartet got my juices flowin'."

"I bet they did. You don't get hands like that often, and by 'you' I mean 'you.'"

Larson bowed out of the game as planned, rising from his seat to join the spectators, leaving only Cal and Teddy to square off yet again. Richie Rocks gathered the cards and washed them across the table.

"Heads Up," Cal said. "My favorite."

"I know you're accustomed to high stakes," Teddy said. "Why don't we boost the pot this game? Forget fifty, let's get serious."

"Someone's getting too big for his britches," Cal said. "Let's stick with the minimum fifty and see where it takes us."

One of Ronnie's boys handed Teddy a double bourbon as requested. Moments before, Ronnie had grabbed her server in protest, but allowed it upon hearing Teddy proclaim it was his last hand. Anything to get him the hell out of there.

"Come on, Cal," Teddy said. "I'll either go out with a bang or a whimper. How often do you see that?"

"The latter, I seen plenty," Cal said. "But why not? Let's do this." Teddy had put him on the spot. Though Teddy's stacks stood at around $1,400 - far less than Cal's seven-grand from cheating all evening - Cal had a feeling he was being hustled. After a moment to read his opponent, he nodded to Richie to proceed, his hubris winning over his instincts.

"Once more around the park, James," Cal said to Richie. "Good ol' Cantrell. Give me five solid gold cards this time."

"Teddy won," Ronnie said, extending her arm across the table to halt the game. "Winner chooses next play."

Cal had forgotten about the room's standing tradition of the last winner choosing the new game. He gestured for Teddy to state his play.

"I also get sick of Texas," Teddy said. "The game is now Stud Rollover." The chatter from the crowd ranged from amusement to confusion to shock.

"No Peak?" Cal laughed at the absurd game, one children might play, or drunken pals gathered around a cheap folding table in one of their garages. "You can't be serious."

"Did I surprise you again?" Teddy asked.

"What is this?" Cal asked, peering at his foe. "I thought you were real player."

"We talk about no-dicking-around poker," Teddy said. "Pure poker. This is a pure as it gets. We put our money on the table and let the cards decide who's who."

Teddy could see the apprehension on his opponent's face and was afraid he'd lose his shot at murdering him at his own game. "You can shuffle, if it makes you feel better."

Both Ronnie and Larson wanted to step in and end the game before it spiraled out of control. As Ronnie moved toward the table, Larson grabbed her and shook his head.

"Let him have this, Ron," Larson said, placing his hand on Ronnie's shoulder. "Whatever happens, I'll personally make sure he never comes back."

"I'll hold you to that." Ronnie shrugged him off but remained in the crowd.

"Richie, you can finish your coffee break," Cal said, his eyes locked onto Teddy. "Me and Mr. Brewer will be ready in just a minute." Richie left the table, joining Ronnie and Larson in the crowd. Even Bulldog and Randy watched from afar. "One last thrill, right?" Cal said with a forced laugh.

Cal expertly shuffled the deck for nearly a minute, arranging the deck to ensure himself a high straight. A master mechanic, he'd long practiced the art of deck control and had amassed the skill of a world-class magician.

"Stud Rollover" - also known as "Seven Card Stud No Peak" - is a simple enough game. Players get seven cards "in the hole" - face-down - and take turns revealing them, never once looking at them beforehand, with betting rounds in between. The player with the best of five in the end wins the pot.

"Okay folks, we're flying blind," Cal said to the crowd. "No skill here, gentlemen, just luck. Even a drunk can play."

Ronnie nudged Richie to return to his seat, both to deal and officiate the game. "Seven card stud," Richie said to the room, unknowingly dealing two new hands from a prearranged deck. "No peak. Cards remain in the hole until turned."

Cal turned over a Ten and bet two-hundred. Teddy called and revealed a Queen. With the higher card, he tossed in another two-hundred. Cal called and turned over a King, betting another two-hundred. Teddy countered with an Ace and tossed in another two-hundred. Cal called again.

"Fourteen-hundred in play," Richie said, gathering the muck.

Cal turned over an Ace, setting up his straight. He threw in another two-hundred. Teddy called and responded with another Ace and another two-hundred.

"Two-hundred, two-hundred, two-hundred," Cal said. "This bores me." Cal called and raised another hundred. Teddy called.

"Twenty-five hundred on the table," Richie said.

"I'm rubbing my chin wondering how the hell you're going to continue with just three blacks left to play," Cal asked with a grin. "You keep this up, you know I'm gonna raise, and then you're done, boy."

Larson pushed his way through the crowd and leaned in close to his friend, whispering in his ear. "There's no shame in walking away, Theodore. We win ten times this an hour in Vegas. Let him take it down. Forget this place."

Teddy smiled and nodded to Larson, waving him away, pointing to Cal to continue. Cal flipped over a Jack, creeping him closer to an Ace-high straight, but unable to bet for failing to keep the higher hand. Teddy turned a Ten. Though Cal's hand had more potential, Teddy still technically had the better hand with two Aces up. He plunked another three-hundred on the table, leaving him with nothing left.

Larson and Ronnie were sure they were about to witness yet another humiliating defeat for their friend. Ronnie turned away, unable to watch his morbid masochism again.

Unsurprisingly, Cal called and raised, this time mockingly reaching into his pocket for a single quarter, twenty-five cents more than Teddy had left to play.

"Bad luck getting that Ten," Cal said, unsure but struggling to remain dominant. "I decided not to get carried away with my raise. No sense in being an asshole about it, am I right?"

Ronnie looked at Teddy in apology. Though she felt for her friend, who was seemingly about to die at the table, she begrudgingly held firm to her earlier promise that there would be no house credit for Teddy, not even a quarter. Cal obviously knew about their arrangement. Randy or Bulldog must have told someone who told someone else. Word among regulars spreads like wildfire in a cardroom.

Cal held Ace-King-Jack-Ten. He needed a Queen to get his straight, and a Queen he'd get after some sleight-of-hand during the shuffle. Teddy held Ace-Ace-Queen-Ten. Another Ace was the only card that would give him anything stronger, though it would still be bested by Cal's corrupt straight.

"Forty-one hundred and a quarter in the pot," Richie said, the odd figure rolling off his tongue like nonsense.

"I guess you're out, boy," Cal said. "I mean, we all know Ronnie ain't giving you another penny. So unless you have the keys to a Cadillac Coupe Deville in your pocket, it looks like we're done here."

"All in," Teddy said, a phrase he always relished, as he reached into his pocket and pulled out keys, dropping them into the pot.

Larson's eyes widened upon recognizing the keys to his Limited Edition Triumph Speed Triple GT-X, lifted from his coat in the entry room two hours prior while Randy frisked him. He wanted to bolt forward to halt the game, but something stopped him from interfering, a feeling that the hand would play out in his friend's favor.

"That 'sweet British crotch rocket' parked outside is worth $12,000," Teddy said. "I looked it up before I got here. So unless *you* have keys for a Cadillac Coupe Deville, I don't see many options for you."

"He's right," Larson said, keeping his stone face considering his frustration and rage. "The bike is valued at twelve-grand."

"Are you All-In, Cal?" Teddy asked. "Or are you All-Out?"

Now Cal sat in the hot seat. His remaining stacks couldn't match Teddy's outrageous bet. He knew he still had the game in the bag, but suddenly felt like he stood staring down into an abyss.

"You weren't joking," Cal said.

"About what?"

"About wanting a quick thrill."

"You in or not?"

"Quite a streak you got going. I guess the cards can't run cold all the time."

"No point fuckin' with me, Cal. There's no skill here, remember? Just luck. Even a drunk can play."

"We have fifteen-thousand, one-hundred and a quarter on the table," Richie said, not sure where this was going. The pots at Ronnie's Room rarely rose above $10,000, even at the No-Limit table.

"Ronnie, sweetheart," Cal said, his eyes fixed on Teddy's, still trying to figure him out. "Tell Bulldog to top me off."

"How much?" Ronnie asked.

Cal slid all his remaining stacks into the pot, tapping a quick count as he reluctantly took back his hand. "Seven grand should do it."

"That's two more than I normally allow..."

"Ain't nothing 'normally' about this game," Cal said. "Do I get the marker? Yes or no, sweetheart?"

Ronnie felt tempted to decline his request, both for Teddy's sake and her business. Players sometimes asked for a five-hundred dollar boost to keep them alive, and her limit for house credit had always been maxed out at five-thousand dollars, something she was rarely asked to do.

"You know I'm good for it," Cal said, glancing at Bulldog standing at the back of the crowd.

Ronnie looked to Teddy, who nodded approval. With everyone hanging on her next word, she felt the pressure to keep the tense game going.

"I'll allow it," Ronnie said, to Teddy's relief.

Bulldog retreated to the cage.

"You mind?" Cal said, pointing to Larson's can of Pringles, still sitting on the table.

"Knock yourself out," Larson said.

As Cal poured potato chips in his hand, Bulldog returned with a tray of chips, setting it on the table.

"We have twenty-two thousand, one-hundred, and a quarter in play," Richie said.

"Let's do it," Cal said. He flipped over his last card, shocked to reveal a worthless hand of Ace-King-Jack-Ten-Two. In the world of poker, there's nothing quite as devastating to a seasoned card sharp as a busted straight on the river.

Teddy turned over his last card - a Nine - revealing his hand as Ace-Ace-Queen-Ten-Nine, his simple pair of Aces winning the game.

Cal slammed his fist to the felt and nearly overturned the table, turning all the heads in the room. Not once in twenty-three years of playing poker for a living had he been skinned down to nothing. He sat flummoxed, with no idea where his play went awry. He'd shuffled the deck himself and had been dealt all the cards he carefully arranged, minus the last-minute Queen he needed for a slam dunk. Unsure what went wrong and unable to protest, he shoved his chair away and tried to compose himself as he stood and addressed the many onlookers.

"That's it, ladies and gents," Cal said, his bad Walken voice suddenly gone. "We all hit the skids. I personally never have before now, but it happens to better men. The life of a grinder. Mr. Brewer, enjoy your tall stacks. May you leave with them for a change." Ronnie handed him his coat. Randy held the door open for his exit.

"You ain't hit the skids just yet, Cal," Teddy said. "I wager you got one more in you." As Richie washed the cards, Teddy reached out and swept the pot, leaving Larson's motorcycle keys where they lay.

"Theodore," Larson said with the tone of a stern father. "What are you doing?" He wanted desperately to grab the keys off the table before another move was made. Again, he found himself unable to interfere, as if compelled to allow his friend to hurl himself headfirst into another reckless bet.

Cal knew what Teddy wanted. He could have walked away, he should have, but he felt the Royal Executioner standing over his reputation, ready to drop his axe the moment he walked out the door.

"I hear they call you 'Prime Time' now," Cal said, still standing, his coat over his arm. "You become a hustler, Teddy?"

"Stud," Teddy said to Richie. "Deal him five cards of gold."

Richie Rocks did as he was told, dealing five cards face-down to Teddy and five more where Cal once sat.

Cal returned to his seat and glanced at his cards, keeping a paranoid look at the table, at Richie, and especially at Teddy. His cards stared back at him like a miracle, five cards that surely couldn't be beat. Richie had indeed given him gold, just as Teddy foolishly requested. He smiled, reached into his pocket, and produced Maxine's keys, the prize his opponent wanted all along. He dangled them over the table for a moment, taunting his opponent, before dropping them beside the Triumph keys.

"That looks like a call to me," Teddy said. "That old Jeep is Blue Booked at $11,000, about the same as the Speed Three."

"Speed Triple GT-X," Cal said. "Only three-hundred made."

"Wanna look up the numbers?"

"Oh, I know the numbers," Cal said. "Let's drop 'em, Mr. Prime Time." Cal revealed a Jack-high straight, a hand of "gold" that came straight from Teddy's request.

"You're right, Cal," Teddy said with a drunken smile as he reached for his cards. "It's like chess on coke."

BEEP BEEP

8:09 p.m.

Teddy's eyes widened upon hearing his watch alarm. His Lucky Five minutes expired. He savored his victory a few seconds too long. His last stud hand, still laying face down before him, was dealt before the five ended, but from his understanding it could be anything now.

Everyone stood all around, dead quiet, waiting.

"Larson, you never finished that Pringle's joke," Teddy said.

Larson told his joke deadpan, almost out of pity. "They were gonna make tennis balls, but they got a truckload of potatoes that first day."

"And the rest is history."

Teddy turned over his hand, revealing a Spade Flush, a notch above Cal's straight.

The crowd breathed again. Cal, completely cleaned out, rose from his seat again. He tried to smile it off, but stood on shaky legs. Teddy reclaimed both sets of keys.

"Cal, since this is your first time, I'll tell you from experience... *now* you've hit the skids."

Cal Zimmer, the legend of Ronnie's Room, the rounder so good that he was long suspected of being a cheat, looked around at the faces of pity, at his fellow players turning away to play it off as just another bad beat, a defeat all card sharps contend with. They all knew he'd never experienced such a total loss before, but kept their smart remarks to themselves, waiting for him to leave before going over the game play-by-play, a game that would be remembered for years to come.

Cal put on his coat and exited the cardroom. Teddy gestured for another drink, but both Ronnie and Larson put a stop to his evening.

"Time to go," Ronnie said.

"It's not quite two hours, Ronnie."

"Forgive me, but my watch runs a little fast."

Ronnie walked Teddy outside. He held his keys in one hand, a fresh bourbon in the other, as he walked a drunken line to his Jeep. He took his seat, caressing the wheel, the dash, the mirrors.

"I told ya, Ronnie," Teddy said, "things are different now."

"The only difference between tonight and last time is that you won. You're still reckless. You still need a shrink. All that drama in just a few minutes." She eyed his bourbon, his seventh of the night. "And I see you're hittin' it again."

"Poker wasn't the same without my good friends Jim and Jack."

"Don't come back 'Prime Time.' Take your slow death someplace else."

Teddy laughed and started Maxine's engine, its signature sound soothing, vindicating.

"So help me, I mean it this time," Ronnie said. "Friends or not, you're off the list."

"Lady Veronica, sweetie, no offense, but I'm making my own list now."

Teddy handed her his empty glass, shifted into gear, turned onto Paradise Lane, and drove home.

19

This Thing of Ours

Saturday, December 11, 1999, 8:06 p.m.

Teddy stood near the twelfth street of a roulette table, staring at Red-28, within the aquamarine carpeting and crimson walls of the Poseidon's "Oceanus Room," a private casino reserved for high rollers with a minimum credit line of $250,000. He wore a deep blue suit paired with walnut boots that matched the varnished horn buttons on his jacket.

Staring down at the rows of red and black numbers painted on green felt, imagining the many good and worldly things he could accomplish five minutes at a time, he barely realized he'd just won a hundred-grand betting on Red in the middle of his Lucky Five. Without a crack of a smile or a bump in his heart, he let his winnings ride and watched the ball bounce around the wheel until it spun and settled on Red-28, garnering him another hundred-grand.

During his Five, Teddy could have put everything on Zero, easily multiplying his bankroll with a jaw-dropping 35-to-1 payout, but he avoided scenarios that would attract attention beyond the shock of the onlooking dealers and tourists. The last thing he wanted was his photo and history of wins covered by the *Las Vegas Review-Journal*. Landing such a monumental bet on Zero would draw the attention of the pit bosses. Landing that bet more than once would draw their intense scrutiny, placing Teddy on their short list of Players of Interest. He recalled something Larson once told him, words he'd later record in his journal and etch into his mind as a life lesson - "In Vegas, to be remembered is good, but to be memorized is all kinds of bad."

Across the street, Rolo and Larson played Blackjack at The Palazzo, biding their time until 1:21 a.m. when they'd shift their strategy to doubling down anything over Seven and splitting any pair. Enzo and Angelica, pretending not to know each other, played at Teddy's roulette table in the Oceanus Room, following his lead with varying bets. Though his partners still smiled and cheered at the large payouts, the novelty waned with Teddy.

The Lucky Five had been visiting casinos regularly through the State of Nevada for three months, with every third visit returning them to Las Vegas. Sometimes they went for a night, other times they booked a weekend. A few daring trips lasted a week. Regardless of how long they were "working," each road trip felt never-ending, as if traipsing through a limitless berry patch with carte blanche.

With Cal Zimmer's humiliating defeat behind him, a yearning for closure that used to elude and overwhelm him but now felt like a distant memory, Teddy never went back to Ronnie's Room or Crow Canyon Casino. He thought about Larson's assessment during their last night at Ronnie's, about how those many back-alley cardrooms and Indian poker tables suddenly felt small time. Never in his farthest reaching fantasies did he imagine he'd view Vegas the same way.

BEEP BEEP

8:09 p.m.

Teddy peeked at his black digital watch, tucked out of sight under his cufflink sleeves. He'd make a few more modest bets before retreating to the penthouse suite he shared with his four partners.

* * *

The Poseidon penthouse defined pure opulence with high, painted ceilings accented with gold leaf trim and a wall-length window offering a panoramic view of The Strip below. The entire crew, dressed to the nines, gathered for a lavish meal. Larson sat in the lounge area, speaking to Room Service on the phone. He carefully chose their evening's dishes, designing a feast destined for the long dining table being set up near the grand window by two servants. Rolo tipped them a Fifty each as they left. The moment they walked out of the suite, a discussion began at the table between the crew's three founders, an exchange that would soon turn from celebration to confrontation as their two other partners joined them.

"What's our neighborhood?" Angelica asked.

"Five-hundred," Teddy said, careful not to let Larson or Enzo overhear. "Altogether, we've played about sixty minutes, so if you do the math, we're each earning a hundred-grand an hour."

"Jeez Louise," Angelica said.

"It's only gonna get better. I'm already cookin' up Phase Two."

"I'm glad you're gettin' a kick out of thinking ahead, Ted, 'cause you sure ain't diggin' our gains no more."

"What's that supposed to mean?"

"I seen your face when we score a big win," Angelica said. "You look almost bored. It's gonna give us away. At least pretend to be excited."

"That's not boredom you see on my face," Teddy said, defensive, stretching the truth. "That's me looking forward, designing our next move."

"If you say so."

"Teddy Brewer, our master strategist," Rolo said, halting the tension. He poured himself a Scotch from the wet bar by the window. "Every gang's gotta have the man with the plan."

Angelica often winced at hearing her group of friends referred to as a gang but forgave Rolo's comment, figuring it was how the brother of a former crime boss saw all circles of friends. If only she knew how true Rolo's words would become.

Enzo stepped out of the bathroom, adjusting his ill-fitting button-up shirt, not used to dressing even casual-formal. Larson took a seat at the table while still ordering their dinner, perfectly at home in his tailored three-piece suit.

"Shrimp scampi is fine," Larson said on the phone, "and two bottles of Chateau Cheval-Blanc St. Emilion. Get us the '98 if you have it. If not, grab something within five years."

"You guys were talking about our take?" Enzo asked, having faintly heard only the first half of the conversation. "Toilet flushed when you started talking' numbers."

"Adding everything together, we're making about ten-grand an hour," Teddy said, crafting a lie he hoped would seem believable. Enzo's beaming, ignorant smile told him the number would work for now.

"Beats the tip jar at the Brickhouse," Enzo said.

Everyone laughed, not just at Enzo's joke, but at how far they had come in such a short time.

"Beats the call center," Teddy said. He quit ValleyLink months prior without ceremony. No farewell lunch, no mid-morning supermarket goodbye cake to be shared among the staff. He simply resigned and walked out the door on a Wednesday morning, out to Maxine waiting for him in the lot, a sudden feeling of release and freedom overwhelming him.

"Beats the restaurant," Rolo said. He left Jiminetti's a day after they discovered the Lucky Five, stepping out unnoticed during dinner rush. He placed his name tag on the hostess's podium and walked out the door without looking back. His coworkers assumed he went for a smoke break, never imagining that the next time they'd see their former Assistant Shift Supervisor was when every news outlet in the country covered a nationwide manhunt for him.

Angelica quit her job at Douglas Auto Parts. Unlike her partners, who had long been fed up with a nine-to-five existence, she put in a proper two weeks' notice and even trained her replacement. She didn't want to burn bridges since she still didn't comprehend the potential of the Lucky Five, seeing the success of their road trips as a temporary windfall. It also wasn't in her nature to suddenly leave her coworkers hung out to dry, scrambling to find a last-minute new hire.

Enzo still worked part time at the Brickhouse Pub out of loyalty to its owner, Jeff Wolf. Jeff hired Enzo without looking into his background even though Enzo had confessed - over a round of Irish coffee - lurid details of his life that would make most potential employers slam the books on him.

Similarly, Larson remained part-time on the roster at Bower Auto Group, the largest chain of new and used cars in the Easton-Brawley area. Larson's domain centered on their fleet of exotic sports cars and motorcycles, the "toys of rich men," as he called them. He stayed on their books because they granted him the ability to set his own hours based on his leading sales figures. Selling family sedans and minivans warrants full-time presence, but taking customers with disposable income out on private test drives for a Ferrari landed in on-call, part-time territory.

"Ten-thousand an hour," Larson said, mulling over the number. "I would have thought we were earning more."

"We got a lot of people on the payroll," Teddy said, keeping up his cover story of having an armada of insiders aiding them at specific hours of the day.

"Of course."

Teddy assumed he'd be able to deceive Enzo for as long as he wanted, keeping him from realizing their discovery, but

Larson proved to be a challenge. He was sharp, good with numbers, and an expert at gambling. Eventually, he'd have to confide in him.

Rolo stepped into his bedroom and returned with a small Armani shopping bag, the white-and-gold bag he had during his rampage at the Lady O' Luck Motel earlier that very night. His partners weren't aware of his personal "test" of the Lucky Five, a test beyond the boundaries of a card game, and wouldn't be privy to it until much later.

"Our take would have been more," Teddy said to further assuage Larson's confusion, "but Rolo was M.I.A. for a while." Teddy turned to Rolo as he rejoined his crew at the dining table. "The plan was to do everything together, remember?"

"That was before we actually did everything together!" Rolo said, to everyone's laughter. "Forgive me, but I needed some time alone to think... and to do some shopping."

Rolo reached into the Armani bag and pulled out small cubical boxes covered in gray velvet. He passed them out to his partners. Angelica opened hers first, anxiously whipping off the hinged top. The lights from the chandelier glittered off of the gold watch in her hand. She looked around at her friends who all received luxury watches identical to hers. Rolo slid up his sleeve to reveal he was already wearing his.

"Rose gold and platinum," Larson said, examining his timepiece. "That was certainly quite a shopping trip, Rolo."

"The salesman was certainly quite nice to me."

"I bet he was. He'd be tripping over himself to sell you just one. I can imagine his excitement when you asked for five."

"Shiny," Angelica said with a smile.

Enzo saw more than their beauty. "Shit, how much did these trinkets cost?" He put on his extravagant new watch. "A few grand each, yeah? Probably cost more than my car!"

Enzo could never have guessed that the five custom luxury wristwatches cost $60,000 each, though Larson knew their value well.

"A lot more than your car, Z," Larson said.

"I figured, I mean, you said these are gold, right?"

"No biggie," Angelica said. "They gave my pop a gold watch when he retired." She turned to Rolo. "But they're real nice, big guy, don't get me wrong."

"It's more than just the gold, Angie," Larson said, puzzled as he realized what he held in his hands. "These are Blancpain."

"Blanc... what?"

"Blancpain. Villeret Reveil GMTs, the evolution of their Carrousel Phases de Lune and the Calendrier Chinois Traditionnel. They offer the same movement, the same internal design, but encased in rose gold with platinum trim."

Teddy and Rolo glanced at each other, shocked - nervous - upon hearing Larson's extensive knowledge of the watches, afraid that Rolo's lavish gift would give away their subterfuge.

"Forget the price tag," Rolo said. "That's all that everyone sees. Their real value is underneath. Flip 'em over."

Angelica again was the first to respond, like a child with a new toy. She turned over her watch to find an inscription.

"The digital Casios Teddy got us are fine for the Average Joe Tourist," Rolo said, "but we're staying in the Rainman suite, and Rainman don't do black plastic."

Enzo read his strange inscription. "High Noon 12:12 p.m. to 12:17 p.m."

"What's this mean, Rolo?" Angelica said, reading her inscription.

"Read it out loud."

"Tea Time 4:02 p.m. to 4:07 p.m." Angelica laughed. "I get it." She realized that all of their watches were inscribed with playful names followed by their Lucky Five times.

"Well, I don't get it," Enzo said.

"Angelica is now 'Tea Time'," Rolo said. "It not only reflects her five-minute window but also her dainty demure."

Teddy didn't approve of these custom gifts that pinpointed everyone's Fives, but had to play it off as if he, too, seemed confused. "I'm not sure I get it, either."

"Rooster?" Larson said, amused, trying to decipher his inscription.

"What else are we gonna call our early morning man?"

"Okay, so of course I'm 'Prime Time,'" Teddy said, feigning that he just figured it out. "Smack in the middle of the evening. So what do we call you, Rol?"

The suite's door chime interrupted Rolo's response. Larson answered the door, allowing a young man in an aquamarine vest to push a loaded cart into the room. He smiled and nodded as he popped open two bottles of Chateau Cheval-Blanc St. Emilion, the precious 1998 vintage as Larson had requested. The French Grand Cru poured a ruby red and smelled of fruit, herbs, and dried flowers.

As everyone took glasses of the fine wine, Larson tipped the server well as he left. With wine and Scotch in both hands, Rolo walked to the panorama window and looked up at the Nevada night sky.

"You were saying?" Larson said to Rolo. "What do we call you?"

"Yeah, big guy, what's your fancy rosy gold watch say?" Enzo asked.

"You guys know I already have a name. My brother came up with it, called me 'Moonlight' back when we ran in the Castle. He said it was from some old Motown song, but I like to think it was because we were only really together at night. He introduced me around as 'my little brother Moonlight.' I liked the name, and it stuck. In the grand scheme of things, I now know why."

The crew shared a long silence, like a moment of pause for Rolo's memory. As always, Angelica broke the quiet, this time with a toast.

"Here's to us," Angelica said, "the five luckiest people in Vegas."

Everyone clinked glasses except Larson, who paced in front of the wide window, deep in thought.

"Larson?" Angelica said. "Come on and toast with us."

"We keep using the word 'luck,'" Larson said, "but by definition, luck is about the chances of something happening or not happening."

"What's that mean?" Teddy said, unnerved as their friend followed his suspicions.

"Luck isn't a factor with us. When we're on the clock, playing during our specific windows, there's no question how the cards will come up. There are no odds when the odds are a hundred percent."

"The odds of winning are a hundred percent, sure, our inside guys make sure of that. But there's always the chance things go south."

"No, there isn't." Larson paused in tense silence as everyone looked across the table at each other in confusion. He continued slowly, knowing his words sounded crazy. "We don't... we don't have any insiders helping us, do we?"

The group looked at him curiously, particularly Rolo.

"How do you propose we've been making ten-grand an hour?" Rolo asked with a forced laugh. "If we ain't got no dealers on the payroll, I mean."

"I'm not a fool, Rolo," Larson said, his voice flat and without emotion as usual. "I know with no uncertainty that we're raking in far more than ten-thousand hourly. That's what's bugging me. But, of course, you already know all this."

"Larson," Teddy said. "Sorry to sound like an ass, but what the fuck are you talking about? How do you think our set-up works?"

"I don't exactly know. But back home, from 6:15 to 6:20, your early morning man... well... he can't lose."

Teddy and Rolo glanced at each other.

Shit, he's figuring it out.

It never occurred to either of them that Larson Williams, a long-time rounder, would play cards on his own during his Five in the casinos and cardrooms back home.

"I usually dream of Halle Berry at six in the morning, but our trips here have upended my sleep schedule. So now, at breakfast, I'm at Crow Canyon working a rake table. During those five minutes, I'm ordering mimosas and getting straight flushes. Do we have insiders at the Indian reservation, too?"

"Maybe we do," Angelica said, not knowing how else to help curb her friend's suspicions.

"Yeah, and maybe you have insiders at Denny's, where I'm playing a God-like game of solitaire. Or at my house, where I'm getting all the answers to *Who Wants To Be A Millionaire.*" He turned to Enzo, who stood with his head down, staring into his wine glass. "Come on, Z, tell 'em yourself."

"Yeah, I noticed the same thing, too," Enzo said, as if ashamed to admit it. "During my five minutes, crazy shit happens to me, and not just at a card table."

"Whatever black magic you stumbled into," Larson said, "we all need to know about it."

The five of them stared at each other, waiting for someone to fess up. Finally, Rolo nodded to Teddy - the subterfuge had ended.

"You heard of Quickie Buckner?" Teddy asked, still anxious about revealing their discovery to two more people. It felt like revealing the location of buried treasure as opposed to metering out the loot.

"Of course," Larson said, unsure. What that legendary madman had to do with their mysterious operation escaped him.

"Alright, boys, your Christmas present is coming a little early. Just keep an open mind as we tell you this."

20

House of Cards

Friday, December 17, 1999, 7:38 p.m.

Teddy drove his red Jeep down Olive Avenue, passing industrial streets and houses built during World War II, straight into the heart of the Castle District. At that time of night, the sight of the aging, shuttered Castle Theater sent jolts through his nerves. He'd always avoided that part of Easton, driving past it with a sense of dread, but that night he was on a mission.

For weeks, with the nightly twin beeps of his gold watch, he thought about something Rolo said from the start - "This thing of ours is bigger than a card game." As he drove, he kept replaying Rolo's words, allowing them to embolden him as he ventured into gang territory.

Teddy parked near the entrance of a dirt lot, along a row of tall Oleander bushes, a good distance away from Smokey's

Club, a long cinderblock building with blinking neon silhouettes of naked women, their colors changing and pulsating with the beat of the muffled music coming from inside. He checked his new gold watch and grew nervous as the time approached eight o'clock. Being a Saturday night, the place was packed with a few dozen cars parked around him, a few customers clustered outside, smoking.

A bouncer stood at the door, a tall, heavy-set man known as "Joey Rose Garden," so named because of the pink wine stain birthmark spanning the left side of his face. The large man made a curious look as Teddy came into view. They recognized each other from Ronnie's Room.

"Joey Rose Garden," Teddy said. "Since when do you work this door?"

"About six months," Joey said. "Never thought I'd see you here, Teddy."

"Why is that? I'm a man and there are women inside, beautiful women who take their clothes off, from what I hear."

"Yeah, but there ain't no action," Joey said with a smile. "No wagers being thrown down, not for cards anyway."

"What then?"

"Dance Night," Joey said. "But you gotta get an invite."

"I heard about that. Betting on flesh and blood instead of cards ain't my speed. Still, you gonna invite me?"

"Nah, I already used up my Plus One this time around. Maybe next time?"

"Maybe, but I think I'll still go in. It's been a while since I've been to a naughty place like this. What's the minimum?"

"Two drinks is all," Joey said.

"Two drinks is all I need." Teddy raised his arms, allowing Joey to pat him down, if only for appearances.

"Have fun... Prime Time."

Teddy entered the club, a place he'd long known about but never imagined walking into, particularly at night. The dark, smoke-filled joint was packed with a crowd of men sitting in a semi-circle against the stage, leering at the lone dancer working the pole above them. A few loners sat scattered about the room, staring intently at the entertainment from afar. Classic rock blasted from worn out overhead speakers, so loud and distorted that Teddy couldn't tell it was AC/DC's Brian Johnson screeching "All Night Long." He made his way to the bar that ran along the east wall, to the right of the door, where Curly, a stocky bartender with tight black curls, red suspenders, and a bicycle mustache pointed to him as he approached.

Teddy thought to stretch across the bar and yell in Curly's ear to be heard over the thumping music. Instead, he simply gestured a "V" followed by a "C" with his fingers - two whiskeys. He pointed behind Curly to their literal top shelf, making it clear he didn't want their standard booze. The bartender grabbed a bottle of Gentleman Jack bourbon, not Teddy's first choice, but good enough. He hadn't come to drink, anyway, or so he told himself.

Teddy tossed two Twenties down for the two bourbons, shooting one on the spot, gaining a touch of the liquid courage he needed. He held the other glass as he leaned over the bar and waved the bartender closer.

"I need to see Missy!" Teddy yelled into his ear, barely heard over the music.

"Missy's done!" Curly yelled back. "She already danced tonight!"

"Still here?"

Curly didn't hear him, or acted like he didn't. Teddy slammed down a Fifty to grab his attention.

"Still here?"

* * *

Eleven minutes later, after having slugged his second bourbon followed by a third and fourth, Teddy stood in the relatively quiet back hall, his fifth whiskey in hand. Curly stuck his head into a dressing room.

"Missy!" Curly yelled, his grizzled voice contrasting with the bright mirror lights and the pastel lace and sparking sequins of the dancers' outfits. "One of your admirers wants to see you." The stocky bartender promptly left Teddy alone in the hall, a long stretch of cinderblock walls that led to an adjacent building.

Marissa Washington stepped out of her dressing room in jeans and a T-shirt, the most "normal" she'd appeared to Teddy in years, though she still had her big, slightly frayed afro, part of her stage persona.

"Hey, Tumbleweed," Teddy said.

"You know I can't talk to you in here." Marissa seemed exasperated, looking down the hall.

"So let's take it outside."

"I can't, I got the stage coming up."

"Curly said you were done."

"Curly's got a big mouth." Marissa looked down the hall again and peeked between the curtains into the main room.

"Come on, Marissa. You can't talk to me for ten minutes?"

"You got five, Teddy."

"Perfect."

* * *

Teddy and Marissa stepped outside into the dirt lot. Marissa slapped Joey Rose Garden on the back as she shut the door behind her.

"Gimme a heads up, would you, Joe?"

Joey knew exactly what she was asking and would oblige her as best he could. "Keep your pager handy, Missy."

Teddy led Marissa out into the dirt parking lot, near Maxine at the Oleanders by the street. Her stern face betrayed a smile upon seeing the familiar red Jeep that held pleasant memories, though she kept her nostalgic feelings hidden behind frustration and urgency. Teddy should not have come.

Teddy had ordered yet another bourbon on his way out, his slurred speech telling Marissa that he'd had his share.

"How's school?" Marissa asked, running her hand across Maxine's front fender. "Still there, I hope?"

"I'm giving school a break. Never was comfortable in a classroom. I'm back to being an entrepreneur."

Marissa felt disappointed but not surprised. "You mean you're back to humpin' a poker table all night."

"There's worse things to hump," he said pointedly, slightly defensive.

"Like the bottle?" Marissa eyed his drink. "You need to take it easy, Teddy."

"I'm always easy."

"Let's get on with it. Trust me, you don't want him coming out here."

Teddy grew angry at Marissa's anxiety, as if she didn't believe in him or care to spend even a few minutes around him. The sixth glass of Gentleman Jack surely fueled his bravado. "Piss on Zero, with his fake leather and gold-plated jewelry. He doesn't fool anyone."

"Ronnie laid some news on me," Marissa said. "She says you bottomed out at her place again. You lost Maxine to Cal Zimmer, of all people."

Teddy smiled wide and leaned against his Jeep. "Ronnie apparently didn't tell you the sequel. I'm back, Marissa! Like a fuckin' heart attack, I'm back!"

"This is the shit that ended us. You get a streak, and it always brings you 'back.' Good luck, Hail Mary, but it ain't bringing us back."

"Does it occur to you that maybe I keep trying with us because you keep staying with him? Do you know, I mean really know, who this guy is? Does anyone really know Zero?"

Marissa thinks about her answer for a moment, looking back at the club as if Zero and his soldiers would come storming out at any moment. "Yeah, I do. He's the guy that isn't trying to change me. He's the guy that loves the real me. And he knows exactly who he is. So you caught a good run. Now we're picking out drapes?"

"It ain't just another good run, Marissa."

"You know what you are? You're the janitor who calls himself a Sanitation Engineer, the lush who calls himself a wine connoisseur. You're not a poker donkey, no way, you're a high roller! A full-timer. A bonafide pro."

Teddy pulled a thick wad of cash from his jacket, holding it up for Marissa and anyone else watching, only for her to turn away. He checked his gold watch again.

"From a friend to a friend," Teddy said, "I'm telling you, asking you, to leave the Castle. Tonight. I got your back. If you need more, there's plenty more, while you get back on your feet."

"I didn't know I was off them."

Marissa looked at the money in Teddy's hand. She couldn't deny the temptation.

BEEP BEEP

8:04 p.m.

"You'd rather dance for it?" Teddy asked. "Then dance for me. You can dance the Blue Danube in a golden silk gown. I told you, I'm rolling now. I'm a name. You heard of Prime Time Brewer?"

Marissa thought about that a moment. She seemed a little more at ease with him, less on guard. "That's you? So the hump became a whale."

Teddy looked down at the three-thousand dollars folded in his hand, not sure if he should continue with his mission.

"Humor me, Marissa. If a genie popped out of the ground and said you can have anything, I mean anything." He waved the cash. "And don't say money. I mean things you've always wanted, things you dream about, because Marissa, that genie is real. He comes to you for five minutes each day and gives you whatever you want. You just gotta know when your Lucky Five is."

"My 'Lucky Five'?" Marissa smirked, amused, curious where this was going.

"You gotta believe me, Tumbleweed. Right now is my five minutes." Teddy set his drink on the ground and took a deck of cards from his pocket. He clumsily dropped a card, watching it stab into the dirt like a knife. The sight of it gave him an idea, and he kept dropping cards as he spoke. "You ever think about those moments when miracles happen?"

The cards fell such that they started to form a house of cards. He kept casually dropping more, adding to the house.

"Miracles? You're religious now, Teddy?"

"Follow me on this. A housewife flips her car. Kids trapped inside. The car's burning. She lifts it with her bare hands. A skydiver's chute fails. He falls ten miles, hits the dirt, walks away without a scratch. It could be something as simple as finding ten bucks in your pocket or hitting every green light on the way to work. Everyone has these little stories, and if you think about it, they're all five minutes long. These five minutes happen every day."

Teddy kept dropping cards as Marissa absorbed his words.

"I do have one of those stories," Marissa said. "I guess if I had five lucky minutes, it would be a couple of hours from now at ten thirty-six."

* * *

Along a winding river in the woods, a skinny little African American girl - a young Marissa - waded into the cool, running water at night.

"I was nine," Marissa said, continuing her talk with Teddy. "I was camping in Florida with my family. We swam in the Aucilla River at night when the sun wasn't beating down on us. I remember the water was the color of coffee but cool like peppermint. We stayed up late, the one time we weren't rushed to bed."

Marissa's father, Harv Washington, a big man with a thick, bushy salt-and-pepper beard, shared a case of beer with friends by the barbecue. He stood surrounded by his wife, children, cousins, aunts and uncles, as his daughter waded waist-high in the river a hundred feet away. He turned to keep an eye on Marissa, barely able to make her out in the moonlight, in time to see her suddenly swept away by the current.

Everyone in the Washington family panicked, screaming for Marissa to swim back to shore. Harv rushed into the river to save his young daughter, but the water quickly overtook him as well.

"The rapids grabbed me like two giant hands. My daddy jumped in and the hands got him, too. We could barely see each other in the dark, struggling to keep our heads above water. Suddenly, the water seemed calm. I didn't know how to swim, but there I was, this little beanpole, saving us both. It was like the river guided me to him."

Young Marissa grabbed her drowning father. With painful effort, she pulled him to shore. Her extended family and other campers ran to help them. Young Marissa caught her breath and looked at her pink plastic Hello Kitty watch, cracked and frozen forever at 10:36 P.M.

"My cheap little watch busted when I hit the rocks. Ten thirty-six."

* * *

Standing in the dirt lot in front of Smokey's Club, Marissa emerged from her memory, her personal miracle. Teddy could see the revelation in her eyes.

"I can't explain why, but I actually believe you, Teddy. I believe that this 'Lucky Five' is real, that during your time you can have anything you want in this world. But you can't have me."

Holding the cash in one hand and the deck of cards in the other, Teddy had no words. He felt the pull of the Lucky Five bringing Marissa emotionally closer to him, but it wasn't enough.

BEEP BEEP

8:09 p.m.

Teddy looked at his gold watch in defeat. Perhaps he'd try to connect with Marissa again another night. Perhaps it would be futile each time. Surely, years of an estranged relationship couldn't be repaired in five minutes.

Marissa felt her pager vibrate. She checked its tiny screen and saw only a single zero sent by Joey Rose Garden - a warning.

Zero Anada stood outside the door of his club. He saw Teddy and Marissa near the street and walked across the dirt lot to them, passing Marissa as she returned to the building.

"Hello, Zero," Teddy said flatly.

"I heard somebody was hanging around by the street gunnin' for me," Zero said. "I never figured it to be you."

"No one's gunnin' for no one."

"So it's 'Prime Time' now? You got yourself some juice. Good for you, little man."

Marissa reached the club and opened the door. She turned for one final goodbye glance as she stepped inside, leaving the two men alone on the outer edge of the parking lot.

"What are you doing here, Brewer?" Zero asked. "This ain't your neighborhood. You and your pal Rolo keep popping up."

"I can't speak for Rolo, but don't worry, I won't be back."

"I knew you'd see things my way."

"For the record, it's because I see things *her* way."

Zero picked up Teddy's bourbon off the ground and handed it to him. He waited patiently as Teddy downed the remaining booze and returned the glass. Zero nodded and walked back to his club, turning for the last word.

"For the record, I don't give a shit. Stick to your slot machines, Prime Time. And pick up that mess."

Zero swung open the door and entered his club. The mess he referred to was the elaborate three-tier house of cards that had formed at Teddy's feet. Teddy dropped the one card left in his hand, causing the house to collapse.

Defeated, Teddy sat in his Jeep, taking a moment to breathe, gripping the steering wheel in anguish. From the corner of his eye, he saw movement in the darkness of the Oleanders. Wisps of smoke rose from a cigar as a man approached. Teddy recognized him as he emerged from the bushes.

"Rolo?" Teddy asked. "I thought the big dancing night was yesterday?"

"Tonight will be even bigger."

Rolo wore the same thing he wore to Smokey's the night before, a long tank top over canvas pants and combat boots, this time topped with an overcoat. He looked badly beaten, with dried cuts and gashes across his face. His gruesome wounds startled Teddy.

"Christ, is all that from last night? What kind of mess did you fall into now?"

"Nothing I can't clean up."

"You sure about that? This place seems like bad luck for you, bad luck for us both."

"You know how we feel about luck, brother."

"Want me to stick around?" Teddy didn't want to spend another minute there, but felt obliged to support his friend in whatever foolhardy plan he'd concocted.

Rolo took a puff of his cigar and looked at the club's door in the distance. "You and me, we're friends, yeah?"

"Of course."

"Then you gotta trust me when I say I don't want my friends anywhere near here tonight. That's why I came early, brother. To warn you."

Teddy pieced together Rolo's morbid plans. "Aren't you the guy who said I should let things go? Look forward? What are you gonna do here?"

"You'll have to read about it in the papers tomorrow."

"Forget about whatever shit went down last night, Rol. Dance Night is over. What's done is done."

"You of all people should understand the need to right the wrongs," Rolo said, eyeing his friend's Jeep. "Go home, Ted."

Teddy nodded, started his engine, and drove away.

Rolo returned to the Oleanders, obscured in shadow.

Earlier that day, Teddy told Angelica that he planned on visiting Marissa at Smokey's Club. She promptly called Rolo, wanting him to talk sense into Teddy, convince him to stay away from his ex and her criminal circle. If anything went down between Teddy and Zero, it would take more than five minutes to survive an onslaught from BC-9 goons.

Rolo understood her concern. He'd experienced Zero's full wrath firsthand the night before and wanted to be sure his friend was far from the club before starting his personal apocalypse that night, a payback brutal even by Castle District standards.

Rolo cut and lit a new cigar, checking the time on his gold watch, its inscription reminding him he still had a few hours to wait. He'd spend those next hours in the shadows, observing every man who walked in and out of Smokey's.

21

Dance Night

Saturday, December 18, 1999, 12:41 a.m.

The night before, on the first Friday of the month spilling into Saturday, Rolo had returned to Smokey's Club in the heart of BC-9 territory, ignoring Zero's threats. Whereas his last four visits were during reckless, drunken stupors, a death wish not far from his wandering mind, this time he came stone cold sober, armed with the Lucky Five.

Tonight would be different.

Leaving his leather overcoat and pistol locked in the trunk of his sedan, he entered the club wearing only a tank top, canvas pants, and army boots. He didn't think he'd need more.

Rolo walked up to the door of the club and greeted Joey Rose Garden, the two large men looking like twins. Joey had a history with The Mojo Boys - with Rolo's older brother Tony

Marino - and couldn't bring himself to turn Rolo away as he'd been ordered. Rolo counted on that.

"Let's get physical," Rolo said, putting his arms up so Joey could frisk him. Joey patted him down only in the event they were being watched. Rolo was clean.

"You know Zero said you're not allowed in the club no more," Joey said. "You sure you want in?"

"Fuck the club. I'm here for the ballroom."

"For Zero?"

"Ain't nothin' on me, right?" Rolo said. "A guy needs more than his fists and gusto to take on BC-9."

"Then why'd you come?"

"You know why."

"Do yourself a favor, Moonlight, and just let this shit go. He ain't worth your time, and the world's better with you in it. I bet Tony would say the same."

Rolo normally took offense to anyone who dared tell him what his late brother would think, but Joey Rose Garden was an old friend who Tony respected. "I appreciate it, Joey, and everyone keeps tellin' me the same thing. Maybe I'll just go home. Maybe I'll just heat up a Hot Pocket and watch Columbo re-runs. You think Tony would want that?"

"Actually, yeah. I do."

"You'd have made a good brother, Joey." Rolo saw the worry on his old friend's face. "Got a knife on you?"

"Yeah. Why?"

"Hand it over."

Joey pulled a small folding knife from his pocket. "I took this from a guy earlier. You sure you want it?"

"Relax, I don't plan on using it. If shit goes south, I can tell them I stuck it at your throat to let me in."

Joey handed Rolo the small knife and nodded. "Thanks for thinking ahead. Just watch yourself, Moon."

"Always do." Rolo opened the door but turned to his concerned friend. "You said Zero wasn't worth my time."

"He ain't."

"You're wrong, Joey. He's worth exactly five minutes."

Rolo entered the dark strip club, which had a tenth of the patrons compared to the packed parking lot. Zero, Shorty, and the rest of their soldiers were nowhere in sight. Rolo knew where they were as he followed a storm of noise coming from somewhere deeper in the building - the sound of a rowdy crowd.

Rolo made his way through the club, past the bar, past the stage, into the back hall of dressing rooms that led to the adjacent building.

The sound of the crowd rose to chaos as Rolo entered a large round room filled with frenzied spectators gathered together in the club's infamous "ballroom," so called because it served as a grand dance hall in a past life, complete with mirror balls and go-go dancer cages. The mad crowd waved money in the air with Shorty Domínguez collecting every dollar. It all looked just as he remembered from his youth. Back then, when Shorty was still a grade-school runt, it was a preteen Rolo who collected the bets for Dance night.

For Tony.

Railings surrounded the dance floor, which now served as a fight arena, holding back the intense crowd as men dragged away a beaten, bloody man, the loser of the recent bout.

Rolo paused, stopped by another bouncer, who rubbed his fingers in the universal "money" gesture, but Rolo wasn't there to place a wager. He pointed to the dance floor, and the bouncer pointed to a line of men.

Rolo stepped in line behind Juan Macaba, a young, muscular, shirtless man jogging in place, pumping himself up.

"What're you here for, man?" Juan said, huffing and puffing as he spoke.

"I don't know anymore. You?"

"What else? To get out of debt!"

"You know that's impossible, right?"

"I ain't afraid!" Juan yelled.

"I believe you, brother."

"I can beat it! Believe that!"

"There's only one way to get out of Zero's pocket, and it ain't this."

Rolo looked up at the former DJ booth, sitting high above the dance floor, and saw Zero and his bodyguards with a view of all. Like any good ringmaster, Zero held his arms up high and used a microphone to address his audience, his words echoing across the room.

"Dance Night continues!" Zero bellowed into the mic. "Who's ready to dance? Who's got the agility and the hostility?"

The dense crowd went nuts, everyone in their savage state. Shorty held out his palms out to Juan, startled to see Rolo in line behind him. Juan took off his rings and watch, removed his wallet from his back pocket, and handed it all to Shorty, but it wasn't enough. Shorty reached down Juan's shirt and ripped out a crucifix necklace.

"Jesus is banned tonight," Shorty said. He shoved the brash hopeful into the middle of the dance floor, oozing with bravado.

Shorty ran across the floor and climbed up the steps to Zero in his tower. He dropped Juan's possessions into a shoebox and nodded to Zero that Juan was ready. Zero noticed the crucifix and picked it up, examining it. He looked down at the lone fighter, hushing the crowd.

"Juan Macaba!" Zero yelled into his mic. "You think you can just dance your way out of here?" The crowd roared, feeding off Zero's exhibitionist machismo.

"Get 'em out here!" Juan yelled back. "One, two, three, four of 'em, I'll take 'em all!"

Zero held up the man's crucifix necklace for all to see. "There's no superstition here! You fight by my rules, not yours! Now let's bring out my Devils!"

The crowd ramped up again as three huge "Devils" - Zero's men dressed in red overalls - entered the dance floor with baseball bats in hand. Juan Macaba faced them in a boxer's stance with his fists raised halfway up his face, his elbows tucked into his sides. Not waiting for the Devils to make the first move, Juan bolted forward and threw a haymaker at one of them, sending him hard to the floor. As he followed with a stomp to the skull, taking the Devil out for the count, Juan felt the meat of a bat strike his temple. He shrugged it off, swinging wildly, his vision a haze.

The screaming crowd loved every moment of the beastly brawl between Juan and the two remaining Devils as they slammed each other to the wooden dance floor of the old ballroom. Juan grinned as he held his own against his opponents, his ferocity and fighting prowess matching or exceeding the armed goons pitted against him. He could see his years of training and harnessing of bottled rage finally paying off. Defeating Zero's men meant the collective debt of the Macaba Family would be wiped clean, and would remain clean, for Juan vowed never to be in the pocket of BC-9 ever again.

What Juan didn't realize, but soon would, was that his challenge had been orchestrated from the start. Dance Night had never been about fair fights for a chance to erase debt. Instead, it stood for rigged wagers, extortion, and entertainment, in that order. Zero's Devils were told to keep the fight going for five minutes, building the storm of excitement and the betting thereof, offering the illusion that someone actually could beat Dance Night, or at least come close. It felt like getting out of Zero Anada's debt was possible, and no exploit is more profitable than false hope.

Like all theater, Juan's fight reached its second act. The two remaining Devils ceased pulling their punches and went in full tilt, attacking their prey in concert, their wooden bats loud against Juan's skull. The crowd's support for the underdog's early success turned to excitement at witnessing shocking violence.

Savoring the roars from the masses surrounding the oval dance floor, Zero nodded to his men to close the curtains on Juan Macaba, to enter a third act that would feature his defeat, perhaps his death.

As Rolo watched the fight unfold, marching mercilessly to its final act, an empty feeling came over him. The piercing sounds of the arena faded in his mind until all was silent. Rolo looked around him and suddenly saw the frantic crowd, the circling Devils, and Zero up on high all in slow motion, taking him back long ago, to another fight in that room.

* * *

In December 1974, a fourteen-year-old Rolo Marino stood in that old ballroom, the rambunctious crowd much the same, back when Smokey Greene first acquired it from the Lost Wolves biker gang and renamed it after himself.

Young Rolo gripped the railing as he watched pairs and trios of fighters on the dance floor, men who fought to get out of debt with the Lost Wolves or Smokey Greene or the budding Barrio Castillo gang, all partners in the club's criminal activities.

The many local fighters looking to clear their debts that night were merely the undercards for the main event of Tony Marino, leader of The Mojo Boys gang, fighting his former friend and new rival, Cristof Anada. Tension from that pairing came from Cristof's recent promotion to Captain for Smokey's new partner, Barrio Castillo. The winds of change saw a transfer of power, with Tony and Zero teetering at its center.

Old Smokey himself served as the evening's ringmaster, speaking to the crowd from the DJ tower above the dance floor. A short African American man in a vest and bow tie,

Smokey didn't look like much to contend with, but underworld denizens knew his background as an enforcer in Los Angeles and his new role as Godfather of the Castle District.

"Good evening, my friends," Smokey said to the crowd below. The man needed no microphone, nor did he need to yell. When Smokey Greene spoke, the room hushed and waited to hear what he had to say. "Tonight, we have a very special event, two men who aren't fighting to wipe the slate clean. Rather, they're looking to take over the slate." He raised his voice to punctuate the importance of the bout. "In one corner we have the chief of The Mojo Boys, Tony Marino! In the other corner, we have the new captain of the Barrio Castillo, Cristof Anada!" The crowd cheered, most screaming for Tony, as the two combatants entered the fenced-off dance floor.

Tony stood tall and lean in a white tank top and sweats, every inch of his frame built with muscle, ready to strike. He looked to his younger brother, nearly lost in the crowd, and smiled to comfort him, as if there was nothing to worry about. Even at the tender age of fourteen, Rolo knew his formidable big brother was not infallible, not in the Castle, a world where honor held no currency.

"Who the hell set this up?" Tony asked Zero, the two former friends standing face-to-face on the floor. "Because I sure as hell didn't."

"Smokey put it together," Zero said, "at my request."

"Why, Zero? Why you doin' this?"

"You ain't stupid, Tony. You know exactly why."

They waited for Smokey to start the fight, Tony looking bewildered but determined, Zero pumping himself up to go insane once the flag was dropped. Smokey held a red handkerchief in the air, waiting for all bets to be placed. Young Rolo normally gathered the fistfuls of cash waving in the air, but Smokey sidelined him for tonight's main event, citing a conflict of interest.

"Call it off," Tony said, angry and confused. He hadn't been told he was fighting his friend until he walked in the door twenty minutes earlier. "It ain't too late to put this shit behind us."

"You scared?"

"Scared of losing my partner, yeah."

"Partner?" Zero said in disgust, the word stabbing him in the heart. "I was just your Number One soldier! You ain't never had no real partners, Tony, not other than your kid brother!"

"Call it off! Walk away!"

"There ain't no callin' this off," Zero said, swallowing his hesitation, "even if I did walk away."

"What the fuck's that mean?"

With no more cash being thrust into the air, Smokey's men called all bets closed and nodded to their boss up on high. Smokey grinned and dropped the red handkerchief. It drifted back and forth like a feather, the two opponents watching it touch down onto the wooden dance floor. The moment the flag came to a rest, they crouched into fighting stances, Tony still confused, waiting for more. He was twice the brawler Zero was. It made no sense to pair them.

"Last time, Zero," Tony said as he and his former ally circled each other. "Why the fuck you doin' this?"

Zero ignored his old friend's question and lunged forward with a front kick to Tony's left thigh. Tony countered with an elbow smash to the back of Zero's neck, sending him flat on his stomach to the floor.

"Stay down, Zero!"

Zero flipped over and kicked Tony's ankle, forcing him clumsily to the railing. In seconds, as Tony fell to one knee, Zero leapt to his feet and rushed him, landing two jabs and a knee to the stomach.

"You asked me why," Zero said, hovering over Tony. "It's 'cause you got something I want!"

Tony grabbed Zero and pulled him in close, turning the boxing match to a brutal wrestling bout. Slamming Zero's face to the floor, he pulled his head up by his hair and screamed in his ear.

"You already got a piece of my territory!" Tony said. "All you'll ever need! What the fuck do I got that you want?"

"I want your everything!"

Zero bit Tony's hand, drawing blood from the veins atop his knuckles. Once Tony's grip loosened, Zero grabbed his forearm and bent it back, forcing Tony against the railing again.

Both men were skilled, each landing blows in the vicious fight. Tony soon gave up trying to reach his former friend and quickly dominated the ring. He knocked Zero down flat to his back and turned to his younger brother in a victory scream.

Young Rolo cheered as his big brother once again proved himself to the Castle. Like Main Street shootouts in the Wild

West, up-and-coming gangsters often challenged each other in the old ballroom, seeking to make names for themselves. Tony Marino had been called out on the dance floor many times, each fight ending with his victorious banshee cry to Rolo.

In the shared moment between brothers, Rolo's sudden look of shock made Tony turn in time to see three Devils rushing in with wooden baseball bats.

Tony gave them a hell of a fight, but was soon overpowered. Smokey's men beat him down until he lay on the floor, conscious but unmoving. They restrained him as Zero groggily rose to his feet across the floor.

Young Rolo looked to Smokey for help, but the money in the old man's fist made it clear he wasn't stopping any fight. The crowd roared as the fourteen-year-old jumped the railing and ran out onto the dance floor, clutching his older brother, trying desperately to get him to his feet. The Devils scooped up young Rolo and locked him in a go-go dancer cage at the base of the tower. Rolo shook the cage violently to no avail, forced to watch his brother's merciless four-on-one beating. He screamed and cried until his voice was spent and he could barely breathe.

Only another minute passed - the minute that would shape the rest of Rolo Marino's life - before Tony fell for the last time, landing on the hardwood floor in a bloody thud.

Zero pulled something out of his pocket and held it up for all to see - an Ace of Spades. He flung it onto Tony's body and turned to the crowd, soaking up their frenzy.

"Barrio Castillo Nine Kings!" Zero yelled, ringing in a new era in their underworld, the public founding of the BC-9 gang.

Though Rolo remained stuck in his cage, he knew his big brother had fought to his death, his lifeless body lying like a blood-soaked rag doll as the crowd cruelly cheered.

* * *

Rolo shook, jostled from his grim memory as Juan Macaba fell on the dance floor for his last time, his face smeared in blood. The three Devils picked him up and looked to Zero for a decision. The BC-9 boss simply nodded once, signaling one of the Devils to lift his bat and strike Juan in the face with a final crack of bone, knocking him out cold. Screams from crowd dropped to a muted chatter as they dragged him off the dance floor.

Rolo turned away and looked up at the tower to find Zero staring at him as he brought the microphone to his lips. His deep voice echoed from the loudspeakers.

"Now we get to the main course," Zero said. "It's about time you stepped onto the floor, Moonlight."

The crowd reacted curiously to hearing "Moonlight," his name still holding weight in this world. Shorty held out his palms as he did with Juan. Rolo handed him his wallet, necklace, rings and - with a moment of hesitation - his gold watch. He checked it first, smiling at the perfect timing.

Lynn Harrod

Rolo entered the dance floor as Shorty returned to Zero's side atop the tower. Zero noticed the extravagant watch and took it from his lackey, examining its fine details.

"Moonlight Marino!" Zero said into the mic. "Back from a long vacation in the world of wholesome goodness and nine-to-five righteousness. Back from the dead."

The crowd came alive, cheering louder than ever. Zero waved his hands to the crowd, hushing them, until the cheering died to a sea of whispers.

"You're not in my pocket, Rolando. Your brother paid whatever debts your family had. So tell me, what are you fighting for?"

"For my brother, Tony Marino!" Rolo yelled. He turned to the crowd. "I'm taking over where he left off!"

The crowd began to chant "Moonlight," much to Zero's annoyance. Shorty spotted something on the gold watch. He handed it to his boss, pointing out the odd inscription. Zero once again silenced the crowd.

"Moonlight 1:21 a,m, to 1:26 a.m." Zero looked down at Rolo, figuring things out. "That's right about now, isn't it?"

Rolo hid his concern and tried to bluff away the inscription. "That's my fuckin' name and time of birth."

"Well, this is my fuckin' house! You fight by my rules! No superstition!"

Zero pointed to the base of his tower, to the steel go-go dancer cage that remained over the years. Four of his Devils grabbed Rolo and locked him in.

BEEP BEEP.

1:21 a.m.

Zero noticed the watch alarm and looked at it curiously. "We'll get to you, Moonlight, don't worry. We just need to wait five minutes." He looked out at the anxious crowd. "Until then, bring out the next dancer!"

The crowd cheered as Shorty approached the next man in line, a tall, thin African American named Dreg, who handed over his possessions and stepped onto the floor. Rolo strained to break out of the go-go cage, pulling the bars with every bit of strength he could summon.

Dreg put on an impressive show against two Devils. At one point, he briefly knocked a Devil to the floor and turned to Rolo in a victory screech just as Tony had years before. The fight continued with Dreg falling to the Devils while Rolo struggled with the cage, reliving that horrific night from his youth. After another minute, Dreg collapsed and remained sprawled across the floor, out for the count. The Devils dragged him off to the cheers of the crowd.

BEEP BEEP.

1:26 a.m.

Zero looked at Rolo's watch inscription again, piecing together the two alarms.

A Devil unlocked Rolo's cage, noticing that he'd impossibly started bending the heavy steel bars apart. Another minute and he would have been free.

The crowd grew silent as Rolo reentered the dance floor, hanging on Zero's next word.

"Time's up," Zero said. "Now we'll see if Moonlight still shines in the Castle."

The crowd roared as three Devils ran in and attacked Rolo. He slugged one Devil, sending him against the railing. A

Lynn Harrod

second grabbed him from behind. He elbowed him to the chops and struck the third. Despite his Lucky Five having passed, Rolo still fought like a bear, prompting Zero to summon three more Devils. They gave up advancing on him one at a time, all six working together to brutally beat him down with their bats.

Rolo could barely stand, taking hit after hit on his back, his head, his legs, until he slumped to his knees. The Devils looked up to Zero for a decision. Zero thought for a moment. From his tower, he looked down at Rolo as if to ask him, *What now?* Rolo stared at him, daring him to continue, revolted at the notion of mercy. Zero obliged him by nodding to his men. One of them slammed Rolo to the floor with a crack of a bat against the back of his skull.

The crowd became silent again, stunned as Zero climbed down from the old DJ booth and stepped onto the floor, a gesture they'd never seen. As he stood over Rolo, Zero seemed distraught, disappointed.

"Let it be known that it took six of my Devils to fell this man." Zero tossed Rolo back his gold watch. Unlike with the other fighters, no one dragged him away.

"Dance Night is done," Zero said to the crowd. "The Moonlight is gone."

Zero and his Devils left Rolo alone in the middle of the dance floor, curled in agony, the crowd looking on in shock and pity.

22

Irish Coffee and Killer Darts

Saturday, December 18, 1999, 6:12 a.m.

The historic Monarch Building sat prominently in the Grace District, a neighborhood of old Downtown Easton lined with former warehouses, machine shops, and storage buildings, all over-designed with exquisite masonry, artisan stone fixtures, and ornamental windows. The Monarch came from an era when architectural aesthetics still mattered, when artists worked alongside carpenters and bricklayers to erect something beautiful, even if it was just a parking garage or fire station. Seventy years past its prime, the industrial neighborhood that paralleled interstate railroad tracks was left to rot as City Hall expanded north in a classic case of urban sprawl. Most of the original structures of the Grace District were razed and turned into parking lots for no one, a far cheaper alternative to the upkeep of classic architecture.

In the early 1990s, real estate developers saw the crumbling old buildings of Grace - the ones spared from the wrecking ball - as an opportunity to cash in on a revived public interest in historic landmarks. Immense industrial buildings that had been derelict for decades were gutted, brought up to code, given fresh paint and the IKEA touch, to be served up to young urban professionals looking for something hip and cool, old and new, worthy of a magazine spread and sky-high rent. The trend of building lofts in former warehouses and garages transformed the Grace District, filling it with restored residential units that were yet to be filled.

At fifteen stories, The Monarch stood as the tallest of the city's original buildings. Once the crown jewel of Easton, it devolved to become the centerpiece of desolate, high-crime streets that skirted the revitalized Downtown Center.

Larson Williams lived in a loft on the top floor, with a panoramic view of Easton, Brawley, Dale Valley, and Whitesbridge. Within his upscale, modern studio home, with its vaulted ceilings and restored original brickwork, one wouldn't know the encasing streets were overflowing with homeless tent villages propped against barbed-wire fences along the railroad and small street gangs fiercely territorial over their two-block pieces of turf.

He often referred to his loft as his "ghetto penthouse," a suite comprising Units 15A and 15B that he enjoyed but never considered a home. He saw the loft as part of his business, a comfortable workspace that happened to house his bed and clothes.

Each morning, Larson awoke at 6:00 a.m. with a carafe of fresh coffee waiting in his kitchen, a timed event he set up the night before. He had wheat toast with marmalade and two cups of black coffee while completing his daily crossword puzzle, a strict ritual that started in his early adolescence.

BEEP BEEP

6:15 a.m.

Larson glanced at his gold watch sitting in its velvet-lined box atop the kitchen counter. The luxurious, noisy trinket that beeped twice every morning - and what it represented - still felt like a novelty, not yet integrated into his tight routine spanning forty years. He'd always assumed he was a grandmaster at morning crosswords, but the Lucky Five forced him to reconsider his prowess. He admitted to himself that at no other time of the day could he have known that a ten-letter word for a pleasant experience was "salubrious."

After breakfast, he showered and shaved. He chose his suit for the day, another ritual from his youth, one instilled by his late father who equated a suit and tie with success and self-respect.

BEEP BEEP

6:20 a.m.

Once dressed, Larson went to work for Bower Auto Group. Some days, he put in time in their glamorous showroom, but most days he logged onto his laptop computer and finalized sales online. Most his clients didn't live in the Easton area, with several residing out of the state. They had disposable income and usually bought their indulgent toys sight unseen, trusting Larson as if he was their personal servant. He took care of the research, location, inspection, sales, transaction, and transportation of the exotic cars in his inventory. A wealthy client would contact him, describe what he wanted, and find a bright yellow Lamborghini in his driveway three business days later. If delivery occurred within two weeks of a client's birthday, Larson would arrange for an oversized bow to be placed atop the car.

After six phone conferences and two dozen faxes, Larson's part-time workday was done, usually before noon. That day, it would run a little longer. His new partner, Enzo O'Day, was also his latest client, buying small vintage roadsters and motorcycles once the money rolled in from their Nevada road trips.

Enzo arrived at The Monarch and hit the door buzzer on the ground floor ten minutes to noon.

"Z?" Larson asked over the building intercom.

"None other, pal," Enzo said. "Gonna buzz me in?"

"Come on up. I'm in 15A."

Larson pressed a button, allowing his friend entry with a mild buzzing sound. In the three minutes it took Enzo to reach the top floor, Larson played a round of poker on his favorite website, *All-In Online Pro*, a site he kept open twenty-four hours. He'd either play several games at once or simply watch others play, usually while he ate dinner or performed his evening calisthenics, always taking meticulous notes on strategy and psychology. Every aspect of gambling intrigued him, and his new crew fit perfectly into his obsession. His four partners fascinated him likewise, though his permanent poker face would never reveal it.

Larson heard a knock on the door, followed by the chime of the doorbell. He quickly answered.

Enzo entered the loft, impressed by its upscale tone and minimalist decor. "Not exactly what I expected."

"What exactly did you expect?" Larson asked, amused.

"I dunno, something more military. I mean, you kinda come across as a drill sergeant."

"Out of respect to our nation's troops, I'll take that as a compliment."

"But it is Spartan, and that's totally you, pal."

"Out of respect for the ancient people of Sparta, I'll take that as a compliment as well."

Enzo walked around the large loft, his red-and-white track pants, jacket, and Air Jordan shoes clashing with the loft's black marble sculptures, polished hardwood floors, and framed photography. Larson's fascination with his friend extended to his choice of attire. Despite looking so casual in his street clothes, Enzo's Nike outfit - a collector's item - equaled in value to Larson's designer ensemble.

"The Jag came in okay?" Enzo asked, still perusing the loft like a museum.

"Of course."

"I mean, I don't doubt you, pal, but a lotta things can happen on the road."

Larson sat at his computer and checked the status of his friend's order, a British "Racing Green" 1969 Jaguar E-Type Roadster designed by Enzo Ferrari, his friend's namesake. "It's being brought here now. It just left the dealership."

"How long was it there?"

"An hour."

"Damn, you guys take this shit seriously."

Lynn Harrod

"We certainly do," Larson said with a laugh, "but I had things expedited for you."

"Because I'm your boy?" Enzo asked.

"That's right."

"Is that coffee I smell?"

"Absolutely. How do you take it? Creamy sweet or basic black?"

"Irish."

Larson readied a small goblet from his liquor cabinet and poured a second serving of fresh coffee. He added two sugar cubes and a healthy pour of Irish whiskey, topping it with a careful dollop of heavy cream, its bright white foam contrasting sharply with the black coffee. He joined Enzo by the front windows overlooking Old Downtown and handed him the decadent drink.

"And they say I'm the bartender of the group!" Enzo said, taking the coffee. "Watching you make this was like watching a master perform a Chinese tea ceremony. This is perfection in a glass, my friend."

"That's high praise coming from you. I imagine you've made quite a few of these."

"You got that right. I made thousands of these, day and night, back home at Pub O'Day."

Larson thought about his friend's first name, how it matched the designer of his exotic sports car on route. "I don't meet many Boston Irishmen named 'Enzo.' Your Bostonian accent is as thick as your Irish pride. I'd never peg you as an 'Enzo.' I admit, it confounds me."

"Then the names of my brothers and sisters will blow your mind! I got two kid sisters, Lucia and Giana, and four big brothers, Mateo, Giovani, Nuncio, and Carmelo. I'm the runt of the litter, smack in the middle of the boys and girls."

"What's your father's name?"

"The Honorable Mr. Brian O'Day."

"Honorable? He was a holy man?"

"Sure, you could say that," Enzo said with a laugh. "His church was an old-fashioned public house, his pulpit an oak counter with built-in beer taps, his congregation a bunch of half-wit drunks come in from a Celtics game. Good ol' Father Brian O'Day, happy to sermon you at Happy Hour."

"I'm guessing it's your mother who's of foreign descent."

"She was a gourmet blend of half-Italian, half-Portuguese. She and my Pop had an agreement - he'd pick where they'd raise the family and she'd choose all our names and raise us proper old country."

"You speak any Italian or..."

"I picked up enough Italian to survive if I were ever air-dropped over Rome. No Portuguese, though. That shit's tough, like Spanish spoke backwards." Enzo walked up to a vintage dart board on the front wall of the loft, noticing not one hole in it. Larson had hung it up purely as a decoration. "This is a sin where I'm from! Never once used?"

"Let's use it now." Larson opened his desk drawer and revealed the new box of darts that came with the board. He handed it to Enzo.

"These never been used, either, I suppose."

"You shall be the first, my Italian-Portuguese friend."

"Well, get ready for an Irish hooligan ass-kicking. We're the best dartists in the world, you know."

"Dartists?" Larson smiled at the colorful term.

"Artists with darts! You good with 'Killer' rules?"

"Sounds good to me." Larson watched his friend unbox the ten-year-old darts, his thoughts wandering back to their talk of "home."

Enzo stood roughly eight feet from the board and marked it by dropping the small box at his feet. He tossed a dart with his off-hand, hitting a single-eight. Larson stood at the box and threw a single-three with his off-hand. The basic rules of "Killer" stated they would take turns attempting to hit double the other man's initial number.

"Is it still home, Z?" Larson asked. "Boston, I mean."

The motor-mouth Enzo didn't have a ready response for the simple question. He lowered his dart and looked at all of Larson's framed black-and-white photographs of strangers throughout time, wondering where they all ended up.

"Rolo says home is wherever you take a shit," Enzo said with a smile. "His brother told him that. Angie says home is where her mom is. As for Teddy, who knows? I assume home is wherever he's playing cards or rollin' dice 'cause action is all he fuckin' thinks about."

"What about you?" Larson asked, his tone always flat, straightforward, covering his emotional bond with Enzo.

"It'll always be Boston. That brownstone I grew up in, where a lot of my folks still live, that'll always be home no matter where I go. To me, 'home' is people, not four walls and a roof. And those are my people over there."

"You ever going back?"

"No," Enzo said, his energy suddenly sapped by the thought of never setting foot in his hometown again. He'd revealed his sordid past to Larson long before, his drinking and drugs and the deaths of his mother and infant son, but never talked about a return to his roots. "I could only come back in shame, and that would ruin everything I remember. So, nope, I ain't never going back to Boston."

Larson saw the sorrow in his friend's face and realized he shared it, though he kept it well hidden. "I apologize if I brushed against a delicate subject."

"It's alright, pal. Delicate conversations are the only ones that matter, you know? So, how about you?"

"Me?"

Enzo threw a double five.

Larson threw a single-ten.

"Damn, we suck," Enzo said. "So much for me being an Irish dartist."

"What about me, Z?"

"As nice as this place is, I know it ain't your real home. It certainly don't feel like it."

"You're quite perceptive."

"Hey, I come from a family of bartenders! We see and hear everything."

"What do you see here?" Larson asked, gesturing to the well-appointed walls around them. "You asked me what I consider home, if not this loft. I'm sure you asked that knowingly. What do the generations of bartenders in your blood think?"

"I didn't mean nothing by it, Larson."

"I take no offense. I'm genuinely curious."

"Alright, let's see." Enzo looked at a bookshelf of framed photos and took one off the middle shelf, one of the few in color. "If I had to guess, I'd say this is home for Mr. Larson Williams. Devon is home, am I right?"

The photo depicted Larson and his younger brother Devon posing next to their pair of Dodge Omni Shelby GLH-S sport hatchbacks, Larson's badly needing paint and body work, Devon's in sterling showroom condition, though both cars were formidable little beasts. The two brothers stood with their arms over each other's shoulders, looking like twins, beaming with pride at the work they'd performed on Devon's car.

Enzo threw a double-nine.

Larson threw a triple-two.

"My father took that picture," Larson said. "We'd just finished three months restoring Devon's car. As far as I know, it remains one of the finest Shelbys in the world."

"As far as you know?"

"It's been a while since we spoke."

"You mean since your Pop died." Enzo knew his friend's stone face hid regret and sorrow. "How come you guys never got to yours?" Enzo had long been familiar with Larson's dented, scratched, primer-gray sports car. "I mean, it runs like Days of Thunder but looks like shit, no offense."

"My father passed on before we could get to it. And yes, that's when Devon and I disconnected."

"That happens, pal" Enzo said. "When my Elena and Jason died..." Enzo paused for a moment upon saying their names, as if offering a moment of silence. "My big brother Mateo rushed to the hospital to kick my ass. I wish he had. Instead, he looked at me like I was a fuckin' blight on the world. We went our separate ways for four years. It broke my family's heart, and it spilled mine wide open, 'cause Mateo and I grew up like best friends."

Enzo threw a double-ten.

Larson threw a double-seven.

"My God, we suck hard," Enzo said with a laugh.

"Four years? So you did see him again."

"He moved to Montpelier, about nine hours up from Boston. I figured that was about as close to home as I was willing to go."

"How was Mateo when you saw him again?"

"Dead," Enzo said, nearly halting their conversation. "I stayed at a motel in Montpelier for three weeks before I had the courage to reach out. By then, news was he had a heart attack. All us O'Day men get them, I just didn't think he'd get his so young. He was still technically alive when I saw him in the hospital. I spoke to him, apologized for being a shitty brother, no idea if he heard me. He died the next day."

"I'm so sorry, Z," Larson said, treading carefully. "What would you have said if you'd made it in time?"

"Honestly, I got no fuckin' clue. Knowing me, I probably would have stayed in that shithole motel until I heard he was dying." Enzo removed all the darts from the board, returning three to Larson. "Despite my bright disposition and radiance of energy, I'm a coward, Larson."

"I wouldn't say that."

"I failed my family in every way you can count, and in the end, I failed Mateo."

"You went back, booked a motel, intent on reaching him. So you didn't go all the way. You made the effort, you just didn't close the deal. I don't think that makes you a coward."

"He's gone, ain't he?" Enzo said with a grunt. "Ain't no going back home for me now."

"You know about Devon and my father. Am I a coward, too? Am I a fool for not seeking him out?"

"I dunno, are you? I mean, can you still reach him?"

"I have his number."

"Then, sure, maybe you are a coward. I mean, you guys were peas in a pod growing up. Do you wanna throw that away? Do you wanna end up like me?"

Enzo stood eight feet from the dartboard and readied his next throw.

"What would you have me do?" Larson asked, his monotone voice betraying a soft yelp, his eyes revealing he was prepared to do anything to avoid repeating his friend's mistake.

"Call him, Larson."

"You see yourself as a coward, but I don't possess even half of your courage, Z."

"Nah, you got more, pal. You're smart, logical, and Devon is out there waiting for you to knock-knock on his door, even if he don't act like it. Don't let it slip away, 'cause believe me, it will."

Enzo saw the struggle in his friend's eyes and turned to the dartboard on the wall as if he could connect them. "You're a betting man, right? How 'bout we make a bet?"

Even in grief, Larson famously never turned down a wager, and Enzo preyed on it.

"What do you propose, Z?"

Enzo held up his darts. "If you win, you get my Jag being delivered to us right now. I'll sign it over to your name the second it gets here. If I win, you call Devon."

Larson thought about the bet for a moment. It seemed lopsided, pitting a valuable, vintage roadster against a simple phone call, though he realized it was actually his fear of losing Devon all over again, renewing his pain, that sat on the line.

"Check this out, I'll throw in my cut of the next take," Enzo said, sweetening the pot. "Next time the crew heads to Vegas, you get my share."

"If I win."

"You got it."

"Why such large stakes?"

"It's been a while since a bet gave us a thrill, am I right?" Enzo read his friend perfectly. "This is a genuine, juicy, high-stakes bet. How can either of us refuse?"

Enzo needed a six to win.

Larson needed a sixteen.

Enzo stepped aside and offered the next throw to his old friend. "I'll even give you next toss, pal."

"You're on," Larson said with a nod, reluctantly cementing their wager. He threw his dart, hitting a triple-four.

Enzo stood with his toes against the small box on the floor, ten feet from the board, and froze like a statue. After nearly a minute, Larson threw his hands in the air, out of patience.

"What are you waiting for?" Larson asked.

BEEP BEEP

12:12 p.m.

Enzo pulled up the right sleeve on his track jacket and looked at his gold watch, identical to Larson's sitting on the kitchen counter. Barely looking at the dartboard, he quickly threw a double-three, winning the match. He tossed his remaining two darts together, both nailing the same spot.

"Looks like you got a call to make," Enzo said with a grin.

"You... timed this with your Five?"

"I did."

"You little trickster. You hustled me, Z."

"Irish hooligan, remember?"

Enzo approached his friend's desk and picked up the cordless phone that sat between the computer and the fax machine. He pressed its large green button for a dial tone and held it out to him. "I hustled you, yes. You can slug me in the face, but a bet's a bet. You'll thank me later."

Larson squashed his frustrations, realizing that Enzo may have been a conniving weasel, but he did him a great service. Only his honor as a gambler could trump his anxiety and fear.

Larson dialed Devon and waited for an excruciating five rings before his younger brother answered.

"Larson," Devon said on the other end of the line.

"Hello Devon," Larson said. "I just wanted to see how you're doing."

"I'm fine, as I will continue to be." The younger brother spoke just as monotone as his older brother, betraying no trace of emotion. "No need to check on me, though it's appreciated."

"Shall we get together this weekend?"

"What for?"

Larson's mind raced, coming up with several convoluted reasons they should meet, concluding that none of them would work. Devon would deflect them all.

"I challenge you," Larson said, realizing the one thing that neither of the Williams Brothers could turn away.

"Challenge me? To what?"

"Meet me at the track," Larson said. "Tomorrow morning. Six o'clock."

"And if I don't?"

"Then you forfeit, and you'll never get another chance to beat me at anything."

Larson held the phone to his face, staring at Enzo sipping his Irish coffee. He clutched the phone with sweaty hands, hoping that his challenge would work but expecting a cruel rejection.

"Challenge accepted. Six o'clock."

Devon promptly hung up.

Larson placed the phone onto his desk and looked at Enzo, grinning on a barstool in the kitchen.

"So, it's on?" Enzo asked.

"It's on."

Enzo nodded and sipped his coffee. Larson walked to his computer and checked the progress of his friend's delivery.

"The Jag is turning the corner," Larson said. "It'll be here in a minute."

"Perfect timing."

BEEP BEEP.

12:17 p.m.

"How long have you had this con planned?" Larson asked.

"For a while, pal. I mean, I didn't really want the Jag."

"Then... why?"

Enzo downed the rest of his Irish coffee and set the goblet on the counter, not sure how to respond. "You ain't like me, Larson. You didn't do nothing to deserve losing your brother. I just wanted to make sure you didn't end up in a shitty motel on the edge of town years from now, banging your head to the wall 'cause you blew your last chance at family. You deserve better."

"I guess bartenders really do see and hear everything," Larson said, still reeling from the sudden turn of events, the heartfelt scam that forced him to act. "Thank you, Z."

Enzo couldn't help but smile at his anxious friend. "I told ya you'd thank me later."

23

Sleeper Car

Sunday, December 19, 1999, 5:50 a.m.

The sun rose over the Brawley Speedway, a modest, three-quarter-mile, oval dirt track with berms at both ends. The old track shut down in 1998 after a fire took out the skybox, concession stand, a grove of Acacia trees, and four competition cars on blocks in separate bays. City inspectors had issued several safety violations that year, all of which were ignored. The fire ensured that the speedway's racing days were over.

Larson parked his weathered Shelby GLH-S in the shade of the remaining Acacia tree on the edge of what used to be the parking lot. He shut off his engine at 5:50 a.m. and waited for his car's twin to arrive. Exactly ten minutes later, Devon's pristine Shelby turned off Whitesbridge Road and entered the lot, coming to a stop beside Larson's. Devon shut off his engine, returning the speedway to the silent dawn.

The Williams Brothers stepped out of their cars and faced each other, their first time together in four years that felt like twenty.

"Good morning," Larson said.

"Why the challenge?" Devon asked.

"It feels like unfinished business. We always said we'd pit our cars against each other on the track."

"It's unfinished business because your car is unfinished," Devon said. "And because Father's life ended unfinished. We said we'd race for him once both cars were completed, to see which of us would be the Lead Driver."

"Team Williams," Larson said with a mutter, remembering the name of their outfit.

"None of that happened. There is no Team Williams. So I asked myself on the way here, and I ask you now, why the challenge?"

"You're wrong. Team Williams is standing right here. Father would want that."

"Since when do you care what Father wanted?"

"I made one mistake," Larson said, raising his flat voice. "I was selfish for one night, and suddenly I don't care about us?"

"You don't get it, Larson," Devon said, his flat tone giving way to long-pent grief. "It wasn't just one mistake! You dismissed Father's orders many times!"

"I defy you to give me an example."

Devon wanted to get back in his car and drive away, change his number, and forget he ever had a brother, but the "challenge" of facing their past and the lust for competition in his blood compelled him to stay, even if he could barely look Larson in the eye.

"An example, please." Larson forced himself to stare into his younger brother's eyes, even as he turned away.

"As far back as I can remember, you were always Father's Number One!" Devon startled himself with his outpouring of emotion. "The faster runner, the stronger athlete, the honor student, the ladies' man. You had all the awards, all the potential. While you grew up under Father's wing, it never occurred to you to look down and see me in your shadow."

"I was always proud of you," Larson said, blindsided by his brother's confession. "And I thought you were always proud of me."

"You were proud of me? The guy who everyone knew as 'Larson's brother'? The guy whose father referred to as 'my other son.' Why would you be proud of a walking, talking afterthought?"

"I'm sorry you felt that way, but believe me, the only person who saw you that way was you."

Larson immediately regretted saying "you" so many times, turning Devon's pain back on him. He'd felt for his little brother and couldn't deny any of the things he said. As he looked at his anguished face, it pained him to realize he'd always felt he was indeed his father's "Number One." It never occurred to Larson that he came in first in everything. He never sought the accolades or crave the attention. He simply fulfilled his obligations to his strict father's standards of excellence and assumed Devon felt the same. The two brothers had been fiercely competitive since they were children, vying for their father's subtle nod, sometimes followed with a smile, but while Larson viewed their ongoing contest as an affectionate rivalry, Devon saw it as his inferiority being rubbed in his face again and again...

"You're right," Larson said, halting his whirlwind of revelation and regret. "I never thought of how you must've felt. We both did our best for him, but it didn't dawn on me how it hurt you. I'm sorry, Devon."

Devon didn't expect any kind of sympathy from his older brother. He assumed they'd meet, run the track, Larson would win, and they'd go their separate ways. Still, he agreed to meet there at the edge of the abandoned speedway, with the ounce of hope that perhaps he could finally beat his brother, and in that triumph get a moment of clarity, or at least closure.

"We came here to race, didn't we?" Devon asked. "Or were you thinking of a staring contest?"

"Me and you, side-by-side on the track."

"I had her upgraded, you should know. Shift linkage, brakes, intercooler. Bumped the turbo to a T3/T4. Full suspension swap. Bored out the 2.2-liter to a 2.5. Clocked her at 310 horsepower, 135 more than yours."

"With that power-to-weight ratio, it may as well be a thousand horses. I bet it takes off like a rocket when you open it up."

"Like I'm launching to the moon," Devon said, defiant.

"You practically rebuilt it," Larson said with a smile of admiration. Devon didn't return the expression.

"I did a lot more than all that. Seven donor cars went into turning this little machine into a land-based cruise missile."

"I'm surprised you kept the stock wheels and tire size."

"I wanted it to at least *look* like Father's work."

"But underneath everything, it's all you, Devon."

Devon expected no recognition, but hid his surprise behind his struggling stone face. "You sure you still want that challenge?"

The younger brother's upgraded car now stood as the superior machine, but the older brother had always been the superior driver.

"You should be proud," Larson said. "This is your car, not mine, not Father's. Now that I see what you've done, how much you've grown, it truly will be a challenge."

"So shut up and race me." Devon pulled a small firecracker from his pants pocket. "Three laps. Win or lose, I'm never coming back here again."

* * *

Three minutes later, as the sun peaked over the horizon, the two 1986 Dodge Omni Shelby GLH-S hatchbacks sat at the starting line of the faded, hardpan dirt track, their engines hot and purring like lions waiting to pounce. Devon lit the long fuse of the firecracker and hurled it out the window in front of them. A moment later...

BANG!

The Williams Brothers stomped on the gas and let their Shelbys loose on the oval track, hurtling forward down a long straightaway. Devon soared ahead, expertly making the first turn several seconds before Larson, his car nearly vertical, high on the berm. He extended his lead further on the second straightaway, drifting through the second turn at 90 miles per hour, taking the first lap.

Larson drove with the effortless skill and precision of his youth, as if his last winning race - the victory that overlapped his father's stroke - took place yesterday. Despite his flawless driving, Devon's car pulled further away with every second, approaching 110 miles per hour.

BEEP BEEP

6:15 a.m.

Larson passed the finish line with a fiery roar of his 2.2-liter I-4 turbo engine, completing the first straightaway in the blink of an eye, whipping the next turn with ease. Within his Lucky Five, his four-cylinder engine screamed like a war machine, yet his wheels glided across the dirt track like a sled on ice, closing the gap in seconds. Upon the next turn, approaching the second lap, Larson drove up the berm to pass and pull away from his brother, his lead growing as if he'd been granted ten times his horsepower.

Devon watched the rear of Larson's beat-up, primer-gray Shelby become smaller as it impossibly gained distance, repeating the first turn as if it were locked on rails. His big brother would somehow win again - as he always did - despite having the vastly inferior car.

Leveling on the final straightaway, Devon reached down to his right and twisted the nozzle on the manilla canister mounted to his center console, releasing a volatile 40-percent mixture of nitromethane and methanol into his engine, a surprise move he'd been saving for the finish line. Rather than meter out the boost as planned, he spun the nozzle completely, opening up his GLH-S to its full potential, even though a sudden final turn loomed before him.

Devon quickly caught up with his brother as they entered the last turn, their cars rising up the berm as if clinging to a sheer wall. Their cars parallel, the two men looked at each other as they spun their steering wheels to the right, drifting sideways through the 180-degree turn, rocketing toward the finish line.

Devon's dangerously rich nitro mix proved too much for his engine, bringing its temperature to a whopping 400 degrees before bogging it down and blowing the coolant system, overheating it in a flash. With smoke bellowing from the hood and the steering wheel shaking as if the drivetrain was flying apart, Devon lost control of his car high on the berm, spinning wildly over the top into the empty former stands of the speedway.

Larson sped toward the finish line, focused on completing the race, when he was halted by the deafening sound of his brother's crash. He skidded to a full stop fifty yards from the end and jumped out of his car to see the frightening sight of Devon's GLH-S laying upside down in the bleachers engulfed in bellowing black smoke. He sprinted to his brother's wreck and impossibly ripped off the driver's door like tin foil, pulling him out and carrying him over one shoulder across the dirt track as the car's overworked engine caught fire behind them.

The two brothers sat on the track and struggled to breathe as the upgraded, showroom-condition Dodge Omni burned in a towering blaze, tall flames licking the wooden roof of the old stands. If the shuttered Brawley Speedway was a decaying eyesore before, it would lay utterly destroyed by the morning's end.

Devon stared at his burning, upended car, the car he and his brother and father restored together, and felt a wave of panic overtake him. In that moment, he didn't care for his own well being, rather the preservation of that little car. Though he knew it was a lost cause, he wept as if allowing the last remaining memory of his childhood burn in a pyre.

"It was my fault!" Devon shouted. "I did it!"

"You used nitro, I know," Larson said. "You ran it too rich, poured it on too thick. It's okay."

"It was my fault Father died!"

Larson held his sobbing brother, assuming his newfound guilt came from shock. "It was no one's fault, but between us, I shoulder more of the blame. You know that. If we had been there in time..."

"It was me!" Devon yelled. "I killed him!"

"You're talking nonsense. Just calm down and breathe."

"You don't understand! I was supposed to fill his prescriptions! I had the fuckin' papers in my pocket!"

Larson looked his brother in the eye with sorrow and sympathy mixed with confusion. "Devon, he had everything he needed..."

"No! I was supposed to get his meds! His Plavix and Jantoven and Lipitor, but I didn't. His pillbox was empty, but I wanted to race at the track alongside you. I wanted to beat you in front of everyone. I wanted to prove that I could be the Lead Driver for Team Williams."

Larson released his brother's embrace, not sure what to make of the confession.

BEEP BEEP.

6:20 a.m.

Larson heard his gold watch signaling the end of his Lucky Five, but ignored it. A mystical five minutes seemed pointless now. "Father had his drugs. He was meticulous about it."

"I was in charge of his refills," Devon said, panting, letting the long pent-up words pour out. "I was supposed to pick them up days before, but I stayed up night after night tuning my engine, upgrading everything I could. Didn't think about him once. All I could imagine was passing you on the track, showing everyone that I mattered. Me! Devon Williams!"

Like his brother, Larson had always been logical, focused, self-centered, intent on being the best to satisfy his strict father. In his selfishness, he didn't see his little brother's longing for acceptance, and he didn't realize the pressure he wrestled with.

"Why would he keep quiet about his medication running out?" Larson asked.

"Because it was another test," Devon said, catching his breath. "Everything was a test. He gave us tasks and expected us to complete them. He never micromanaged us. I thought he'd chew me out, tell me what a fuck-up I was, and I was okay with that. I never thought he'd..."

Devon choked while trying to finish his thought, admitting to himself for the first time that he shared the blame for his father's early death. While they were celebrating Larson's win at the track that tragic night on July 4th, 1994, it struck Devon too late that their father had gone nearly four days without his heart medication. At the last minute, he urged Larson to forget the race and return home, but ultimately, it wouldn't have made a difference.

"It's over," Larson said, clutching his brother's hand. "It's in the past."

"And it's my fault."

"No. Father was no fool. He kept careful records, knew precisely how long he'd gone without his medication. He should have gone to the drug store himself and not rely on his teenage son to pass some absurd 'test.' Father should have reminded you to pick them up, to save you the grief and save his own life. Instead, he stubbornly wanted to turn it into another goddamn life lesson."

Devon caught his breath, torn by his brother's logic. "I failed him."

"He failed us!" Larson yelled. "Father allowed you to forget your responsibility only so he could lecture you about it, make you feel guilty about disobeying him. He got his wish, and here we sit, grappling with guilt, each of us feeling we caused his death. But it takes more than one childhood mistake to bring it all to an end. Believe me, I've examined it from every angle. Neither of us are to blame."

Devon nodded and sighed as he watched his beloved car burn.

"You were going to win again," Devon said, looking over at Larson's car near the finish line.

"Does it matter? Look around. The crowds are gone. The speedway is gone. Father is gone. It's just us now. It's been just us for years."

"Look at my car."

"Every day, I buy and sell cars five times more powerful and a hundred times more valuable than our Shelbys. It doesn't matter. They're just machines. Father didn't work on a couple of Omnis because he treasured them. He treasured us, in his own way."

"You really believe that?"

"Look at all the old photos he took. He snapped plenty of pics of the cars, sure, but a hundred more of you and me working on them together. Father didn't see his 'Number One' son or his 'other son.' He saw Team Williams Racing. That was his dream."

Larson walked the short distance to his car parked behind them. He pulled out his car phone and called 911 to report a fire at the old race track on Whitesbridge Road in Brawley, hanging up without providing his name. He returned to his brother, his suit dirty from sitting on the track.

"Can you give me a ride home?" Larson asked.

Devon laughed at the silly question. "Sure, but my car's overheated. We'll have to wait for it to cool down."

"Your car is over there," Larson said, pointing behind them with his thumb.

Devon looked at his brother's car, sitting silently fifty yards from the finish line. "You're giving me your Shelby?"

"I use my motorcycle to get around, hardly drive the Shelby any more. I mean, look at it. It needs a lot of work."

"Why would I want your car?"

"Because you're going to fix it, upgrade it, turn it into the little track monster it was meant to be. You're going to make it bigger and badder than the one barbecuing in the stands." Devon laughed, something Larson hadn't seen since they were kids. "It's something I never had the heart or talent to do."

"By the time I'm done," Devon said, "this little Shelby will be on the cover of *MOPAR Muscle Magazine*."

The brothers rose to their feet and walked toward the banged-up, primer-gray car, the smell of burning oil and rubber behind them as the fire finally diminished.

"I may need a little help," Devon said, "if we're gonna do it right, anyway."

"I'll check my calendar. I think I can pencil you in."

Larson smiled and handed his younger brother the keys to his ugly, beloved GLH-S. Devon sat behind the wheel and started the engine, its fine-tuned purr sounding almost magical. Larson sat beside him in the passenger seat. The two drove off, leaving the burning wreck behind for the firefighters to handle.

"That's gonna be expensive," Devon said, taking one last look at his ruined race car smoldering in the bleachers.

"Don't worry, little brother," Larson said. "I got it covered."

As Devon pulled onto Whitesbridge Road, Larson's car phone rang. He glanced at its monochromatic screen, sure he would ignore whoever it was, considering his reunion with his long-lost brother.

It was Teddy.

"Theodore," Larson said on the phone. "Should I be alarmed by the fact that you're calling me so early in the day?"

"Yes," Teddy said on the other end of the line. "If I'm alarmed, you should be, too. You heard about last night? Actually, about four hours ago."

"No. What's this about?"

"I thought you read the newspaper every morning."

"Usually, but I'm with my brother right now. I left before the paper came. Why?"

"Devon? Glad to hear you two are talking again."

"Baby steps," Larson said, sensing that Teddy's attempt at small talk delayed terrible news. "Son, are you going to tell me what's going on?"

"When you get a chance, read today's front page."

"I'll be sure to when I get home," Larson said, turning over scenarios in his mind. "Care to give me a quick summary?"

"It's about Rolo, Smokey's Club, and a big fuckin' mess."

24

Read About It In The Papers

Saturday, December 18, 1999, 8:14 p.m.

"You and me, we're friends, yeah?" Rolo stood hidden in the shadows of the Oleander bushes on the far end of Smokey's dirt parking lot. Zero and Marissa had just returned to the club.

"Of course," Teddy said, sitting behind the wheel of his Jeep, having just failed to win back his ex-girlfriend.

Rolo wore a long tank top over canvas pants and combat boots, just like on Dance Night nineteen hours before, this time joined by an overcoat and a bulging back pack. Teddy stared at the dried cuts and gashes streaked across his friend's face.

"Then you gotta trust me when I say I don't want my friends anywhere near here tonight," Rolo said. "That's why I came early. To warn you."

"Aren't you the guy who said I should let things go? Look forward? What are you gonna do here?"

"You'll have to read about it in the papers tomorrow."

Teddy knew whatever his friend had planned, it would end badly for someone. He also knew there would be no changing his mind. He started his Jeep and drove away.

Rolo returned to the Oleanders, obscured in shadow, stepping through the bushes to his truck. Two weeks prior, he purchased a sleek, black, customized Lincoln and proudly drove it everywhere, but kept the old pickup for times when he needed a low profile. Only a fool drives around the Castle in a flashy car while on the job, and tonight was business, even if it was stained with a vendetta.

Rolo spent the next three hours in his truck watching every patron come and go - street gangsters from G Street, weekend warriors from the northern suburbs, drunk frat boys from the university, silent three-piece suits from Bankers' Row. He kept a tally of how many souls the club held at any moment, kept notes on how many were innocent, one-time lookie-loos, how many simply sought some forbidden excitement before returning to their wives and classrooms and nine-to-five cubicles, and ultimately how many were violent street trash who deserved to die.

He fielded three hours of texts from Teddy, his mobile phone's little six-line screen displaying simple messages discouraging him from bringing further attention to himself, which would eventually compromise the crew. Teddy offered counsel and even offered to help with "the mission," but Rolo ignored the messages, replying only once as he stepped out of the bushes at 1:13 a.m.

"HEADING IN NOW. IF I DON'T SEE YOU TOMORROW, IT'S BEEN FUN, BROTHER."

Rolo's face, battered and swollen from Dance Night less than twenty-four hours prior emerged from the shadows as he reentered the edge of the lot, the rest of his body cloaked by his long, black overcoat. Far fewer cars sat out front, most of the patrons gone. He checked his gold watch in the moonlight as he stepped over the pile of playing cards Teddy left on the ground. He approached the door of the club where Joey Rose Garden sat on a busted barstool smoking a cigarette, the wine stain birthmark across his cheek seen clearly under the lone light above the door.

"My favorite bouncer," Rolo said, shaking his old partner's hand. "We meet again."

"Moonlight, I'm everybody's favorite bouncer."

"I've always wondered, 'Joey Rose Garden,' why do they call you that?"

Joey rubbed his wine-stained cheek. "I guess it's 'cause I smell so sweet."

The two men laughed. Rolo pulled a cigarillo from his coat pocket and held it out to Joey. "Light me up?" Joey flicked a Bic lighter and held the flame out for his friend's miniature cigar. Rolo winced at the sight of it. "A fuckin' Bic? That's all you got for me? For a fine smoke like this?"

"Take it or leave it, fancy pants," Joey said. Rolo leaned in and puffed his cigarillo over the lighter, its tall flame highlighting his swollen, bruised face. "Damn, Moon, they really jacked you up bad last night."

"Not bad enough. I'm still standing, ain't I?"

"I wouldn't think a guy would come back so soon after a beatdown like that. Hell, I wouldn't think a guy even could."

Indeed, Rolo's injuries from Dance Night extended beyond cuts and bruises. He endured a concussion, two cracked ribs, and a blurry right eye, but he felt determined to return to Smokey's before even considering a hospital.

"Shit, first Teddy tonight, now you again," Joey said. "What you two got cookin' up?"

"What's that supposed to mean?" Rolo asked, taking a slow draw from his cigar while checking the time.

"It means I know you're runnin' a crew together."

"Oh, you know that for a fact?"

"I know lots of things," Joey said.

"Teddy was here lookin' for love. I'm lookin' for anything and everything else, gearing up for a wild night."

"How wild are we talking?" Joey asked, a concerned look on his face.

Rolo blew cigar smoke above him and thought about what to do with Joey. He'd been a long-time friend, a former Mojo Boy loyal to Tony back in the day, but he worked for Zero now. He might help or he might complicate things.

"It's gonna take me about seven minutes to smoke this Kentucky Cheroot," Rolo said, "after which I'm gonna enter the club. I might not walk out, Joey, but I can tell you that no one else will." He looked at Joey, anxious for his response. The bouncer stared at his old friend, hoping for a punchline. He considered talking him down, but quickly realized the grim scenario unfolding in his friend's mind was already on rails.

"What should I do?" Joey asked with a flat tone that implied he wouldn't help him but wouldn't stand in the way either.

"Look away, like last night. Look away from a distance."

"Got your own knife this time? My pockets are empty. They find out I let you in again, I'll be in a world of shit."

Rolo reached into his coat pocket and revealed a ten-inch survival knife, wickedly jagged on one edge and laser sharp on the other. "I got one, sure, but I promise, no one's gonna give you grief 'cause like I said, ain't no one walkin' out."

"I believe you," Joey said, staring at the intimidating blade. He nodded, snuffed out his cigarette, rose from his busted stool, and walked away, across the gravel lot. As he started down the road, he turned for one last look at Rolo, as if it would indeed be his last.

Rolo stared at the door, focused on the muffled rock music coming from inside. He checked his gold watch and counted down the seconds as he pulled two sawed-off shotguns from his long coat.

BEEP BEEP.

1:21 a.m.

Rolo entered the club.

* * *

Inside Smokey's, Rolo stood in front of the door, blocking the exit, twin shotguns in hand. The club ran business as usual with classic Def Leppard blaring from the fuzzy sound system, a lone dancer on stage, and a few patrons gazing up at her from their seats.

No one noticed Rolo.

A plain-clothes guard patrolled the bar area, passed behind the patrons near the stage, and meandered toward the entrance. He froze upon seeing Rolo, his large frame made larger still by his loaded overcoat and back pack. In that blink of an eye, Rolo recognized the guard as one of Zero's Devils from Dance Night, one of the three additional, unmasked men brought out to finish him.

The startled guard reached for either his gun or two-way radio, both items holstered at his side. Rolo didn't wait to find out which, raising a shotgun and blasting him point blank. The powerful gutshot sent his body over a table covered with empty glasses, overturning it with a loud clatter, piercing the music.

Def Leppard continued to rock and wail as everyone in the club whipped around and quickly scattered to the dark corners like cockroaches, ducking behind speakers, tables, booths. As he had foreseen, each man who remained in the club at that dismal hour had a gun on his person and prepared to unload it on him. Rolo didn't rush to cover or to dispatch them. He didn't need to.

With bullets flying by his face, he waited for the dancer to scramble off stage and out of sight before he returned the greetings, seemingly out in the open and vulnerable to even the least experienced marksman in the room. Gunfire split apart the wood beams, chairs, bar mirrors, neon signs, but none so much as grazed Rolo Marino's body.

Rolo blasted the men indiscriminately, firing at them from an arm's length away, annihilating each of them with a face full of buckshot. No screams of pain, no pleas for mercy, each man was one shot, one kill. Their bodies soon lay motionless, awkwardly sprawled out across the stained wooden floor as Rolo advanced through the club.

Curly the bartender hid behind the counter, his own shotgun at ready. He trembled as he waited for Rolo to pass so he might bolt up and shoot the man in the back from ten feet away, a plan he had in the back of his mind for years in the event the club was ever raided by rivals. He fired two slugs at Rolo's upper back. As they left his barrel, he somehow instantly knew he'd impossibly missed his mark, nearly cutting a pillar in half. Rolo turned, his eyes red with rage. He lowered his gun, rushed forward, and ended Curly's life with the vicious knife through his throat.

The room became a storm of gunfire, clashing with the ongoing, thumping rock music. Though the men crouched behind cover were scared, none of them could conceive that Rolo "Moonlight" Marino, the man at the center of the storm, the man who stood outnumbered 20-to-1, would soon pick them all off as he continued his death march through the building like a juggernaut. One by one, Rolo killed the patrons foolish enough to still be there at that hour of reckoning. A few of them stood, tossed their weapons aside, and raised their hands, but the gesture proved futile. Each of them met a violent demise with no trace of mercy, their killer frighteningly close at the pull of the trigger.

His shotguns depleted, Rolo dropped his back pack and pulled out twin sub-machine guns. Out of either bravery or desperation, another of Zero's Devils seized that moment to rush him. Rolo threw him off and peppered him in a blind fury as he entered the back hall.

The four dressing rooms in the hall had no other exits. Dancers cowered in corners against cold cinderblock walls, half-naked, their hearts pounding wildly, as they waited for Moonlight Marino, the long-dormant, monstrous legend they'd known about for years, to finally come for them like the fabled bogeyman in the night. To their confusion, he merely peered inside the rooms, saw only dancers, and moved onward down the long hall toward the old ballroom.

In the last dressing room, a second guard cowardly held Marissa in front of him as a human shield. Rolo didn't bother sharpshooting the man or reasoning with him. He sheathed his guns, walked up to the guard, pulled Marissa away, and snapped his neck, nearly crushing it in a brutal twist of his clutches.

"Everyone out!" Rolo yelled to the dancers. After a moment of hesitation, the women scurried away, abandoning their wallets and purses as if offering tribute to the demon showing them mercy, allowing them passage.

More men fired at Rolo from the main room, their bullets shredding the curtained entrance to the hall. Rolo briefly doubled back to address the bold fools.

While the dancers fled in terror, crouching through the main room and out the front door, Marissa split from the group and ran further down the long hall into the vast ballroom where Zero and his last stand of seven men knelt behind overturned steel tables, guns at ready in sweaty hands. Shorty kept to Zero's side, seemingly ready for anything but hardly prepared for what lumbered down the hall in what sounded like an approaching battalion.

Zero alone stood up when he saw Marissa bound into the room in hysterics. Shorty gestured for her to take refuge behind him. To her shock, Zero shook his head. Rather than offer her safety or comfort, he held up his palm, halting her in the center of the dance floor.

"You stay right there, sweetheart," Zero said.

"Are you for real?" Marissa glared at him, incredulous. "I came to warn you!"

"No warning necessary. Every one of us with eyes and ears knows where the man is headed."

"He's headed right here! Right now!" Marissa looked at her boyfriend as if he'd lost his mind. She ignored his command to remain on the floor and started for the corner Shorty pointed out, only to stop at the sight of Zero's gun pointed at her.

"I told you to stay put," Zero said in a flat tone.

Marissa couldn't believe what she was hearing. "Who should I be more afraid of? You or Rolo?"

"That ain't Rolo storming up here," Zero said as the dark realization overtook him. "Not no more. That's Moonlight Marino, and you'd be wise to always fear him over anyone."

"He's right, Marissa."

The deep voice immediately silenced everyone, coming from a large shadow that loomed in the doorway as if it had always been there, haunting the ballroom like a malevolent spirit. Moonlight Marino stood with his last remaining gun in his right hand as he faced Zero and the last of his men.

"Everybody hold up!" Shorty said, but his command left his lips a moment too late as one man fired wildly at Rolo, only to instantly receive a bullet to the bridge of his nose.

"Enough!" Rolo's booming voice echoed across the ballroom. He locked eyes with Zero, his fiery stare piercing his prey's courage. "How many more of your soldiers do I gotta cut down for you to face me like a man? I came for you, Zero, to finish what you started years ago. No one else needs to die."

"So finish it," Zero said, angry at his own fear, daring his nemesis by remaining on his feet, his body exposed in the harsh overhead lights from the tower above.

To Zero's surprise, Rolo tossed his gun into the hall behind him. He walked to the center of the dance floor and stood in front of Marissa as if to shield her from the rain of gunfire sure to follow.

"Let her take off," Rolo said. "Then you come meet me out here on the floor."

"You think you're calling the shots now? I lord over this house! Not you! Not no one else!"

"You'll lord over a burning graveyard if you don't come out here. No guns, no games. Just you and me."

"No guns?" Zero said with a curious, forced laugh. "You always had a flair for theatrics, Rolando." He stepped out from behind his cover and walked out onto the dance floor, his hand firmly gripping his pistol. "You don't really believe I'd come unarmed, do you?"

"I'd expect nothing less from a weaselly punk like you."

"Bold words from an unarmed man facing a Glock."

"Back when you betrayed Tony, you probably thought that was your moment. But you're wrong, Zero. You've been wrong for a long time. This is your moment, right now."

"Yours as well," Zero said. "That's what this is all about, right? Your big, fuckin' shiny moment of glory?"

"You're the one who's gonna be immortalized tonight."

"No more of this posturing bullshit." Zero walked up to Rolo, pressed his gun to his forehead, and pulled the trigger.

CLICK CLICK.

Rolo slapped the pistol away, sending it flying to the south wall. "Got anything else? Now's the time. Take your shot."

Zero pulled a knife from his coat and repeatedly slashed and jabbed at his opponent, to no avail. Rolo snaked the blade from his grasp and hurled it high to the tower like a massive dart, taking it out of play.

"Looks like it's just you and me on the dance floor now," Rolo said, "how it was always meant to be."

"It's you and me and your magical five minutes," Zero said. He nodded toward Marissa. "A little black bird told me all about it."

Rolo hadn't foreseen Zero's knowledge of the Lucky Five. He tried to downplay it. "What the fuck are you going on about now?"

"She told me about Teddy, but I figured you two are partners now. I put together the rest."

"What'd you put together? Tell me."

"That you discovered some mystical thing where you're Super Fuckin' Italian Stallion for five minutes every night. I'm fairly certain that's right about now."

"And here I thought you hated superstition."

"You thought wrong. I've always been a superstitious freak. It's one of my five vices. It's why I never allowed it in my fights. I'm not gonna get beat by some bum because he's got a photo of his dearly departed mother in his pocket."

"You really believe this?" Rolo asked, not expecting Zero's fearless stance.

"Every power player believes this. The clouds in the sky. The Zodiac. Every king has some kind of rabbit's foot. Those are the only people who really take chances. But I took The Castle with my own hands, not with a crystal ball or some magic minutes. It was destiny." Zero's words became filled with rage. "And now you're gonna cheat it away from me? Your brother tried with honor, but you, you have no honor! So of the two Marino Brothers, I respect the dead one, and I spit on the one trying to take over."

Rolo paused for a moment to digest Zero's words. "The trick with destiny is to stop shaking your head and accept it. If you were destined to run the Castle, you wouldn't be stalling right now."

Zero stared in awe as Rolo reached into his pocket and pulled out a bent, soiled playing card - the Ace of Spades. "Damn," Zero said in an exhale. "I never thought I'd see that again."

* * *

In 1974, on the night Tony Marino was beaten to death in a cruel betrayal by a newly appointed Zero and Smokey's Devils, an adolescent Rolo wept from the go-go cage just off the floor. Smiling ear-to-ear, with a faint sympathy tugging at him, Zero unlocked the cage and allowed the boy to run to his big brother in a futile attempt to revive him. It would be Rolo's final sight of his brother before seeing him days later, peaceful in his coffin, moments before being lowered into the ground.

As Zero turned away, raising his arms in victory, soaking up the heartless cheers from the frenzied crowd, he missed the moment Rolo picked up the fateful playing card from Tony's body. It became a souvenir that locked Rolo into a life of revenge, waiting for a night when everything aligned in his favor, a night that wouldn't come for decades. To the young boy, the large, black spade in the center of the card represented a bullet meant for his brother's former friend and murderer.

* * *

Thirty-five years later, Rolo stood once again in Smokey's ballroom, in the middle of the dance floor, now a level playing field, holding that same blood-stained Ace of Spades. He glared at Zero.

The dread of that large, black spade didn't escape Zero as it came full circle before him. He stood in shock, helpless, his pockets empty. "Someone shoot this motherfucker!"

Shorty held out his hands and gestured for the men to stand down. They obeyed and made no moves, watching the tense scene unfold. One by one, they slowly stood from their cover, no longer part of the melee.

"I said shoot him!" Zero said, turning to his soldiers. Their stone faces belied their fear and apprehension.

"Moonlight!" Shorty said. "You leave us out of it! You hear! How long you known me? Check my gun, I didn't fire a single shot! Not in here, not out there!"

Perhaps from gained insight from within his Lucky Five, Rolo somehow knew Shorty's words were genuine. He nodded to Shorty, remembering how he'd been loyal to the Marino Brothers once, and knowing he'd be loyal now.

Zero stared at his captain with venom in his eyes. "You turncoat bitch! All of you! You gonna let a little voodoo get your panties wound up? His magic charm won't last forever!"

BEEP BEEP.

1:26 A.M.

Zero grinned upon hearing the gold watch's alert. "And there it is. You said I was stalling, Rolando, and I admit, I sure as Hell was. I was runnin' out the clock on your five fuckin' minutes of immortality."

"So was I."

Rolo's murderous Lucky Five had come to an end, but rather than meet it with fear and anxiety, he relished the moment. He'd been waiting for his time to expire, counting down the seconds in his mind. Over the previous 24 hours, since his brutal beating at Dance Night, he planned to use his Five not to kill Zero but to merely clear the path. "You don't have your soldiers no more, and I don't have my 'rabbit's foot.' It's just you and me on the dance floor, how it was always meant to be."

Zero lunged at Rolo, who easily manhandled him into a bear hug, slamming him to the hardwood floor, crushing his

Lynn Harrod

ribs. Zero gasped for air as he grabbed at Rolo's legs, trying to trip him, but he stood steadfast like an immovable statue. Rolo reached down, picked up Zero, and tossed him across the dance floor like a marionette. Blood spewed from Zero's mouth as he landed hard to the floor. He struggled to stand, his left leg and right wrist broken, only to collapse back to the floor, barely able to breathe.

"You wanna do me like this, Rolando, then do it." Zero feigned a slight smile. "All those drunken nights, stumbling in here to pick a fight, this is what you've always dreamt about."

Rolo brought Zero to his feet and shoved him against the go-go cage with a loud clang. "I'll tell you what I've always dreamt about. For years, I thought about locking you in this cage, mowing down your lieutenants, and setting this shithouse on fire, forcing you to watch your empire die in flames... but I think I'll keep it all instead."

Rolo slugged Zero in the stomach, sending him sliding down the steel bars of the cage. He looked back at Shorty and the rest of Zero's soldiers, as if giving them one last chance to intervene. Not one of them offered their former boss salvation.

Rolo grabbed Zero's legs and dragged him back to the dance floor, four feet from the center. Zero instinctively knew exactly where his broken body laid.

"This is the spot, isn't it?" Zero asked, wheezing, knowing his question was among his final words. "This is the infamous spot where we last saw the mighty Tony Marino. How dramatic. How fitting."

"No, Zero," Rolo said as he walked to the south wall, retrieving Zero's discarded pistol and returning to his helpless opponent. He pointed the gun down at Zero's face. "From this moment on, this is the spot where we last saw the pathetic Cristof 'Zero' Anada."

"This ain't right," Zero said in a fading voice. "This ain't my destiny."

"When you tell him about destiny, tell him how I got you. Tell him how you lost everything in five minutes, how Moonlight Marino took it all back. Tell him destiny's a bitch at the other end of the gun."

"Tell who?"

"Tell Tony. He'll be waitin' for you on the other side."

Marissa screamed as Rolo pulled the trigger, ending the decades-long feud with a single shot. He tossed the Ace card onto Zero's lifeless body, dropped the gun, and walked out of the ballroom.

Shorty left his stunned men and hurriedly followed his new boss.

25

The Last Face You See in Vegas

Thursday, January 6, 2000, 9:11 p.m.

Teddy traced the gold-and-white diamond pattern of the elevator walls, their criss-crossing lines perfectly joining the matching carpet at his feet. He noted the absence of any kitschy ocean motif in the elevator or in any of the upper floors of the resort. It made sense to him. The weekend tourist crowds, with their strollers and souvenir hats and buffet coupons got tacky dolphins and starfish plastered on their walls while serious players like him saw gold leaves and white diamonds when they stayed at the Poseidon.

Teddy knew his attention to such details often served to distract him from the persistent feeling that the proverbial rug was about to be pulled out from under him. The Lucky Five gang had swept through all the major casinos in Vegas and, despite their efforts at discretion, had become known in gambling circles, a fact that weighed on Teddy's mind throughout the day.

Larson lived in the high-stakes card rooms, playing for hours between their Fives, even entering poker tournaments. Angelica chatted up everyone from cocktail waitresses on break to custodians sweeping around the slots, introducing herself with variations of her name, though not varied enough. Enzo held court in the sports book, regaling the staff with wild anecdotes and generous tips, the result of bathroom coke binges and downing entire bottles of whiskey and gin. Resort staff and management called them by name and had their usual food and drinks brought to the table immediately upon arrival. A few veteran players adept at seeing through their opponents even connected some of them, tying Teddy to Larson and Rolo to Enzo. A clear sense of their history came through in body language, conversation, subtle smiles and nods, all pulling down the facade of strangers together in a game of chance.

Their identity as a group of five later seemed all but cemented, not in a casino, but on the streets of Las Vegas when every resort hosted street events and evening fireworks in a combined citywide New Year's Eve celebration. Drunk and away from their card tables, sports books, and roulette wheels, the crew felt at ease welcoming the new year and new millennium together out in the open. It never occurred to any of them that even in outdoor crowds at night, mixed in with nearly half a million revelers, they could be spotted, photographed, and cataloged. Their actions could've been credited to simple recklessness, but their careful plan to remain inconspicuous started to feel like paranoia after the

Lucky Five made them feel empowered and invulnerable beyond their designated times. This irrational sensation led them to share a penthouse rather than book separate rooms, another unwise decision.

Teddy looked through the elevator's rear glass wall, at The Strip far below, becoming smaller, more distant, as he ascended to the penthouse suite of the Poseidon. He caught the reflection of the two other men in the elevator with him, Rolo and their personal concierge, as his partner ordered dinner for the evening.

"Find some decent steaks," Rolo said to the young man who took careful notes in a day planner. "You pick the cut, just nothing you'd see on the buffet line."

"How do Prime Black Angus ribeyes sound?"

"Can you manage a King Cut?"

"Absolutely."

"Sold. Gimme five of those with the works. And I got some shirts waiting at Harland's. Bring 'em to me on hangers. I don't need 'em in cute bags or boxes this time."

A soft tone came from the ceiling as the elevator doors slid aside on the thirty-sixth floor. A long, beige hallway stretched out before them, having only four white doors spaced widely apart. They led to separate suites, each occupying an entire fourth of the massive penthouse level.

The concierge shut his day planner and remained in the elevator, nodding to Teddy and Rolo as they stepped out. While the elevator descended behind them, they stared down the hall, puzzled by what waited for them. At the end of the hallway, in front of the last door - their crew's suite - stood six men in black suits.

"Friends of yours?" Teddy asked in a near-whisper, hoping they weren't soldiers from a rival gang looking to take Rolo's head back to Easton. At 9:11 P.M., neither of them were anywhere close to their Five.

"Brother, if they were 'friends' of mine, we wouldn't have made it out of the elevator."

Teddy and Rolo stood at the elevator and simply looked at the six men in the distance. Behind his back, Teddy brushed his finger against the call button, trying to decide between flight or conflict. Rolo chose for him as he started down the hall. Teddy abandoned the button and followed, walking beside him as a partner rather than behind him as if he were a shield. A seventh man stepped out from behind the group. He looked peculiar, familiar. He had scars on his face, kept his arms crossed, and smoked a Briarwood pipe, the kind Sherlock Holmes might pensively smoke as he worked a confounding case. Like the classic detective, the strange man paced in front of his entourage, deep in thought. Upon closer view, Teddy and Rolo recognized him from their first morning in Las Vegas, seemingly a lifetime ago.

"I remember you," Rolo said, thinking he was the last man he'd expect to see on the elite's thirty-sixth floor.

Scary Jerry, the talkative body piercing artist from the blackjack table, smiled at his guests. "Hard to forget ol' Jerry," he said in his thick Cockney accent, his tone warm and pleasant as if he were greeting old friends. He wore a gray silk dress shirt over pressed black slacks and polished low-top black leather boots, a striking contrast to his outrageous punk rock appearance from their earlier introduction, though he still had tattoos and piercings abound.

Jerry nodded to his six men behind him. Two of them promptly frisked Teddy and Rolo, relieving Rolo of his pistol.

"Sorry about the touchy-feely," Jerry said, "but I like to keep things as civilized as possible for as long as possible." He took the pistol from his guard and examined it in his hands, running his fingertips across its shiny stainless steel and hardwood-paneled grip. "Real nice piece. That must make you Moonlight Marino, which means your compadre here is Prime Time Brewer."

"You know us," Rolo asked, "but should we know you?"

"You shouldn't, and under better circumstances, you wouldn't. I'm the one friendly face in Vegas that you don't wanna meet, and it should be our mutual hope that you never see me or my associates again after tonight."

Jerry turned, walked through his men, and swung open the wide door to the penthouse. Bowing and extending his arm like a proud host, he gestured for his guests to enter their home first. Upon following them into the lavish suite, Jerry shut the door and nodded to his men again.

Without warning, the six guards - two of them dwarfing Rolo - restrained and viciously beat Teddy and Rolo to the marble floor, kicking them in the stomachs and stomping on their heads. All Teddy could do was raise his arms to shield himself from the attack while his partner lay beside him curled in a ball.

The guards picked them up and brought them to the semi-circular sofa in the sunken lounge at the center of the room, shoving them down onto the white velvet cushions, a welcome respite after being pummeled on the hard marble.

Jerry sat in a chair across from the sofa. "Takin' a beatin' should be a regular kinda thing." He took a casual puff of his pipe. "It's good for your constitution." He turned to one of his men who flanked the lounge. "Bring us a drink. Something brown."

Jerry waited patiently, eyeing his guests, as the guard walked to the bar by the grand window. He poured three highballs of bourbon and brought them to the lounge, setting them onto a glass table. Jerry took his drink. Rolo took the other two, handing one to Teddy, trying to appear as if he still had some semblance of dignity and control.

"You know my name," Rolo said, downing his bourbon in a single slug. "But do you have any idea who I am?"

"Yeah, we got an idea alright. That's why I'm here and not in front of a Porterhouse and potatoes."

"Does the Poseidon eventually rail all its high rollers?" Teddy asked, holding his drink without interest. His fear replaced his usual craving for booze with a sudden need for clarity.

"The thing is," Jerry said, "even with the highest of high rollers, is that they bet big, they win big, they spend big, but you wait long enough, you see they still lose. When they don't, they start to 'smell' as we say."

"Is that right? So we smell because we don't lose enough?"

"Not at all, mate," Jerry said with a smile. "It's because you don't lose at all! Not when it counts, anyway, when the pot's fat enough to choke a horse. You see, that's what happens to a real gambler, who plays with skill and strategy. He loses. But he takes it like a champ, dusts himself off, and works on a comeback. Even Magic Johnson missed the hoop sometimes, but he trounced enough Celtics to make up for it. Imagine if a team never missed a shot, made it through an entire season without a single slip. The other teams would demand an investigation."

"So, the 'other teams' sent you?"

"I don't have Poseidon towels in my bathroom, if that's what you mean. I'm what you'd call an 'Executive Trustee' and I represent the best interests of a number of joints you blokes have been to. Can't say which, of course, but it's safe to say that the City of Las Vegas frowns on your operation."

"Our operation," Rolo said, feigning an amused laugh. He defiantly rose to his feet and took his empty glass back to the bar.

"Can we arrange a sit-down with your higher-ups?" Teddy asked, keeping Rolo in the corner of his eye.

"Scary Jerry is as high up as you're gonna get, mate. Believe me, you don't wanna get no higher."

At the bar, Rolo poured another bourbon. As he returned the bottle to its lower shelf, he reached into a drawer, only to find it empty. He looked up at the group and saw Jerry holding up a silver .38 snub nose pistol.

"I got your pea shooter right here, Moonlight," Jerry said, dangling the gun over the glass table. He set it down and sipped his drink. "We turned your room upside-down, downside-up, many times, over many of your visits."

"You violated our privacy?" Rolo said, as if that sin would somehow outweigh Jerry's accusation.

"What were you gonna do with that little thing? Shoot us all? Was that the plan? Shoot us in your hotel room, then go downstairs and belly up to the baccarat?"

Jerry nodded to his men again. The two largest advanced on Rolo and beat him against the grand window, the sparkling lights of The Strip silhouetting the brutal attack. Without a weapon or his Five, Rolo abandoned the idea of fighting back, correctly surmising that it would only escalate the scene.

Teddy remained on the sofa, unflinching as his anger grew. He stared at Jerry as he puffed his Briarwood pipe, returning the tense stare.

"We're not gonna have to tenderize *you* again, are we?" Jerry asked.

The guards tossed Rolo back onto the velvet sofa. He glanced at the small pistol on the glass table, its chambers empty, no doubt handled before they arrived.

"To answer your question," Jerry said, "I do know about you, Moonlight Marino, King of The Castle District in Easton. You're no different than the boss of the Bloods in Compton or the Grand High Poobah of the Hell's Angels. I could nail you for that gun, but we're being civilized, right?"

"I thought you were a body piercer," Teddy said.

"A nice side gig. Gotta degree in Metallurgy. Comes in handy when you need to stick a poor fucka harsh without killin' him. But being an Executive Trustee, now that's where my heart lies, and my wallet."

"How about a thicker wallet?" Rolo said.

"Like I said, you're no different. If you were, you'd know what my employers are capable of, and you'd know that I'm untouchable. This was peachy, but now my serious face." Jerry finished his drink and set his glass on the table before stating the bottom line. "Standard offer. You lose your active credit, which I imagine is nearly the whole lot, take whatever you cashed and check out in an hour. I assure you, it's a very generous offer. I personally voted to drain you of everything, but the desert gods are in a good mood."

"I think it's because we've become high profile," Teddy said. "You can't have bad publicity, railing a big name, letting everyone know how good we cleaned you out, because you can't prove a goddamn thing."

"It's never about proving anything, Prime Time. If we don't like the smell of your Speed Stick, you're out. 'Right to Refuse Service' and all that. Of course, they want this kept quiet. Like I said, we're being civilized here."

"You have a very memorable face," Rolo said in a dark tone. "Hard to forget Scary Jerry."

"Wouldn't want you to," Jerry said, dismissing the threat. He bent down and leaned in close to Rolo. Jerry's beard of silver rings, earlobes stretched with platinum hoops, and cheeks covered in sharp studs made him an intimidating sight. "I want you to always remember this very memorable face 'cause the next time you see it, if there is a next time, will be the last time you see it. We share an understanding?"

Rolo didn't respond. He simply locked eyes with the man as if burning his wild visage into his brain.

"We do," Teddy said, looking to end the confrontation and regroup with his crew.

Satisfied, Jerry rose and nodded to his men, sending them to the door. "Gents, if you're seen in any of my employers' casinos in sixty minutes, we'll flush the cash from your pockets and strip the soles from your shoes. Sixty-one minutes and, take my word, there will be a comeuppance the likes of which will ring from here to Easton. Same goes for your clan."

"Our clan?" Teddy asked.

"The pretty Mexican girl, now she's a real Chatty Cathy, that one. Then there's the tall Blackie in the spectacles, sits at the table all night like a poker-playing robot. We can't forget the bald drunken idiot. I can't decide if he blows more cash on Patriots games or if he blows more on blow. All three of 'em are livin' the life down at the cabana. Actually, by now they're probably in a conference room gettin' tenderized." He pocketed his spent pipe and straightened his silk shirt. "Twenty years in this racket and I gotta say your operation was tip o' the top. I had my best and brightest scour it for weeks and we never nailed it down. Some said maybe you ain't pulling a con, but I said you gotta be, and you got greedy. Ain't that the tale of every crook's been caught."

Jerry and his guards walked out of the room without a glance back. They slammed the door shut, compounding the shared silence between Teddy and Rolo, still sitting on the white velvet sofa. There were no words, only the gut punch of being stripped bare by the casinos they'd spend months fleecing.

Teddy's thoughts felt like that door slam, like the end of a long narrative, words that would later be scrawled in the back of his journal, formerly Quincy Ray Buckner's.

"Just like that, our Vegas days were over. I think we all knew it was inevitable. The end didn't sadden me like I figured. Better than Quickie's exit."

26

Midnight Tacos

Thursday, January 6, 2000, 10:05 p.m.

Teddy and Rolo didn't bother searching the resort for their partners. They trudged to Rolo's black full-size SUV on the top floor of the Poseidon's parking garage and waited. After Jerry and his guards were through with their friends, they'd have nowhere else to go. Teddy laid across the back seat, failing to calm his nerves with a nap.

Sixteen minutes later, at 10:21 P.M., Angelica, Larson, and Enzo walked across the parking garage, a single duffel bag between them. After their confrontation with Jerry's men, they were locked out of the penthouse, their key cards failing to even summon the private gold-and-white elevator. Angelica's duffle bag, filled with their damp swim trunks and shirts after their time at the pool and cabana, was all that remained for them to carry home. They'd fortunately made the choice of changing at the cabana earlier that evening. Otherwise, they'd be traveling home in their swimwear.

Without a word, Enzo limped to the SUV and joined Rolo in the front seat, while Larson and Angelica sat in the back with Teddy, Angelica having the third row to herself. They took a moment to look at each other, at the many bruises and cuts they all suffered from their abrupt and violent expulsion.

Teddy could barely form a thought, wanting only to get the hell out of that fucking town, its garish, towering signs of blinking lights and glowing neon now taunting him. The sound of the SUV's engine cut the tense silence, followed by Larson's grim observation.

"Of all the bad beats in my life," Larson said, turning to Teddy, "this is the big one, and of course, you're sitting here next to me."

"Are you saying I'm bad luck?" Teddy said with a forced smile, failing to lighten the mood. "You know what we always say about luck."

"I'm saying maybe we should start believing in luck after all, because we sure as hell need it now." His parting thought would be the last words spoken for the next several hours.

Rolo shook his head in disbelief, still reeling from the drastic turn of events. He shifted into Drive and made his way down the parking garage.

* * *

The Lucky Five gang left Las Vegas, heading south in the night down Interstate-15, meandering through the dark desert. They passed the town of Mountain Pass, which comprised an enormous rare earth mine, and through the town of Baker, known for having the world's largest thermometer. They, too, haunted Teddy, as if telling him he didn't belong in Nevada, he never did, and to never return. With only the SUV's headlamps to light the way, the absolute darkness between the towns stretched into the seemingly endless desert.

Teddy stared out the window at the void that surrounded them. It felt like the car simply sat idling in a vast, empty room. Such a pointless, dead-end scenario aligned perfectly with his despair, his loss of everything both physical and emotional. The confident casino whale known as Prime Time Brewer had been ejected from the paradise he'd sought for so long. Only Teddy Brewer remained, the uneducated, middle-aged loser with failed dreams of being a winner, foolish fantasies of fame and respect among his peers now gone.

Scary Jerry had exiled the gang after an all-day marathon of gambling, but before any cash-out and before the arrival of their lavish dinner, a parting meal denied. Teddy imagined their personal concierge returning to their penthouse suite with the five King Cut Black Angus ribeyes Rolo had ordered, curious about where his wealthy guests had disappeared to. Teddy wondered what happened to those glorious steaks. He thought of telling Rolo that he hoped they went to a good home rather than the Dumpster, but he chose not to drudge up that recent, miserable memory.

With the group exhausted and hungry, Rolo pulled over in the small, lifeless town of Barstow, California - roughly halfway to Easton - and into the triangular parking lot of the

Cactus Inn Motel, a crumbling, eighteen-room relic with exaggerated "googie" post-modern architecture from the golden age of Route 66. Angelica thought it looked like George Jetson's car had plummeted to the ground and been abandoned to the elements. Larson thought it resembled the back end of a classic 1950s car with tail fins of stucco and burnt-out neon tubes pointing up to the clear night sky, its millions of stars unobstructed by the usual light pollution of a larger city. Enzo wondered why there was no cactus in any part of its abstract, angular design. Rolo neglected the building's appearance and instead imagined rows of beds to fall into.

Teddy looked at the old motel and saw only a shithole, a retreat of last resort that offered their only respite. Though they'd traveled 161 miles from Vegas, to Teddy, the Cactus Inn Motel felt like a million miles from the penthouse suite at the Poseidon Casino and Resort.

Rolo had cash in his office at Smokey's Club, and everyone had cars and other valuables to sell once they made it back home. Otherwise, they had a total of $128.00 between them as Rolo shut off the engine in the nearly empty parking lot. The paltry sum booked them two rooms for the night, each with two full-size beds, and bought two bags of tacos from Robertiro's Mexican Food nearby on Main Street. Angelica considered the small, 24-hour corner restaurant a godsend, the former 1960s burger stand looking more like a shanty shack now with its crude, hand-stenciled sign and patchwork paint barely keeping up with the nightly graffiti. Larson also welcomed the all-night taco stand, preferring its simple, greasy street fare served in wax paper and tucked into white bags over the more opulent meal they had planned. Though he certainly enjoyed the finer things in life - a pitcher of martinis paired with a fine cigar - he never considered himself a steak-and-lobster man, and he never felt comfortable dining with linens and silverware and crystal champagne flutes underneath a chandelier.

To the group's surprise, they had plenty of quality liquor to go with their asada beef and carnitas, to help deaden and drown their sorrows. Teddy had ransacked the bar of their penthouse as he quickly gathered his things, filling his suitcase with top-shelf bourbon, Irish whiskey, vodka, and tequila. He abandoned his four expensive "Rat Pack" suits, however, leaving them behind for housekeeping to find in the morning. The sight of his custom-tailored outfits disgusted him in his depression, as if they symbolized all that he'd lost.

Rolo, Larson, and Enzo took their bag of tacos and most of the booze to Room 11, with Enzo volunteering to take the spare, roll-away bed by the bathroom. Teddy and Angelica retired next door in Room 12.

"What now?" Angelica asked ten minutes later, her soft words the first attempt at conversation by anyone since fleeing Vegas.

She and Teddy quietly ate their tacos with motel water glasses of añejo tequila and single-barrel bourbon, the juxtaposition of luxury and ghetto somewhat absurd. A banged-up four-drawer dresser served as their table, an old 13-inch TV between them.

"What now, Ted?" Angelica asked again as she sipped her tequila.

"What do you mean?" Teddy said, struggling with his overstuffed taco. "We're done. There is no 'what now' that I can see."

"So we lost Vegas. We still got the Lucky Five."

"I don't know if you've noticed, Ange, but the Lucky Five is camped out in a shitty motel in the desert with twenty bucks left in our pockets, and that's all going to gas up Rolo's beast in the morning."

"I ain't talking about the gang or whatever we call ourselves. I'm talking about our thing, you know, our five minutes a day?"

"What now is we get some sleep. Rolo will be snoring through his Five in about an hour, and I imagine Larson will forgo his time when the sun comes up. Ain't no games to play at six in the morning, not around here."

"I mean when we get home," Angelica said. "We can still do *something* with the Five."

Angelica's faint optimism passed Teddy's ears. He thought about Rolo, who achieved his dream of avenging his brother and reclaiming the Castle District. He knew Larson had always preferred to play it straight at the table, valuing the thrills and skills of a proper game rather than easy money from a sure thing. Enzo seemed happy enough to be alive and still able to walk after his run-in with Jerry's goons and would surely be welcomed back at the Brickhouse. Angelica could continue using her Five to connect with her mother each afternoon, hoping that their daily talks would eventually stick.

Teddy's dream alone seemed forever dead. The thought of returning to the small-time tables at Crow Canyon, cuddled up against old ladies fresh from bingo, shoved a sharp pit in his stomach, and Ronnie's Room stood well out of his reach, what with his reputation as a whale and rumors of being a cheat. None of the other, smaller poker rooms he frequented would have him, either. Even if they allowed him entry, such small stakes and small players could never make him feel at home the way the big rooms of Las Vegas did. He felt like a one-hit-wonder rock star who packed arenas for a year but now couldn't even secure a gig at the community center or county fairgrounds.

What did Dean Martin do in the winter of his career?

Dean continued to live a full life, retiring with the respect, legacy, and vast fortune he made, something Teddy lost along with his credit and clout. All he had left in the world was his embarrassment, his infamy, and four equally miserable people in tow.

"You told me from the beginning," Angelica said, "the Lucky Five is about more than money."

Teddy remembered his words well. He remembered the night he tried to use his Five to rekindle Marissa's affections only to achieve a tepid friendship based on pity and regret. It seemed the magic only went so far with both love and money.

Teddy finished his second carnitas taco, washing it down with a full glass of bourbon. He placed his third taco in the mini fridge - breakfast come morning - left his napkins beside the old TV, washed his hands, and got into bed. Sleeping in his dress shirt and slacks felt uncomfortable, but the booze and the fatigue from the long drive would soon counter that.

"So you're saying we're done?" Angelica asked. "That don't sound like Prime Time Brewer to me."

"There is no Prime Time Brewer. Not any more."

"You know what I mean."

"I know exactly what you mean, Ange. Remember the pathetic little man you went to night school with? The dreamer? The man who wanted it all and figured, eventually, he'd land his jackpot? That pathetic little man is back. He's your roommate tonight."

Angelica put down her taco and stared at her friend. "Enough with the drama. We still got our thing. What's our next move?"

Teddy looked at Angelica, her eyes still wide, still hopeful that they could pivot their amazing discovery toward a better future for them all. He wanted to tell her to focus on her goals that didn't include riches, to focus on what truly mattered, but didn't have the spirit or energy for a late-night pep talk.

"I can't think right now," he said. "I just want to sleep, all the way to check-out time. Maybe another miracle will appear tomorrow to make up for how badly I fucked up this one."

"Ain't just you, Ted. We're all hurtin' here."

"Good night, Ange."

Teddy rolled over and passed out within a minute.

27

Raising The Stakes

Friday, January 7, 2000, 11:55 a.m.

Late the next morning, the gang awoke nearly a half-hour after the eleven o'clock check-out time and left their rooms another twenty minutes later. The housekeeper graciously saved their adjacent rooms for last after Larson asked for time to take much-needed showers. The motel's meager Continental Breakfast of pre-packaged muffins, donuts, cereal, styrofoam cups of coffee, and trail mix bars ended an hour prior. Their leftover tacos would have to sustain them until they returned to Easton.

The group piled into Rolo's SUV and headed across the street to Elmo's Gas and Snax, an eight-pump gas station and mini-mart on the corner diagonally opposite the Cactus Inn Motel, selling gasoline at the inflated desert price of $1.59 per gallon. Every dollar they had between them - just over twenty bucks - would fuel the SUV for the rest of their trip. Rolo entered Elmo's to pay for the gas, his Twenty filling only half of the SUV's tank, allowing them 270 miles on the road, just enough to make it home.

"I invited that Judas to my parties!" Enzo said as he fueled the SUV, remembering times he ran into Scary Jerry and his charming crocodile smile. "He ate my food, drank my whiskey, and he sold me this..." He reached into his pocket and pulled out a diamond earring for all to see. "This fuckin' thing cost me three-hundred clams!"

"Why'd you buy it then?" Anglica asked.

"I dunno, maybe 'cause three-hundred wasn't so much a week ago."

No one knew Enzo hosted wild parties at the Poseidon's rooftop pool while the rest of the gang worked the tables downstairs. He didn't invite them to his impromptu celebrations for he didn't want them to see him snort lines of cocaine off a glass patio table or pop ecstasy under the black strobe light of the dance floor. The remaining population of Las Vegas, however, was free to attend and Jerry had joined the drug-fueled parties twice. He stayed up late with Enzo, sipping champagne and doing Jell-O shots, all the while getting to know him - and his companions - quite well.

"So you were the leak in the boat?" Larson asked.

"Come on, pal, who here wasn't?"

Rolo felt betrayed by the revelation but let it go, knowing as Enzo did that they surely all had secret, private sessions away from the group, as the patrons of the Horseshoe Lounge and Lady O' Luck Motel - living and departed - could attest to.

"Scary Jerry has a killer instinct," Larson said. "He pegged us on Day One, the first time we took a table."

"He pegs everyone," Teddy said. "It's what he does." Sitting in the front passenger seat of the SUV, he looked at the rest of his gang. "Did they rough you guys up bad?"

"Pretty bad," Larson said. "For a moment, I thought they were going to kill one of us to make an example."

"They almost broke my fuckin' leg!" Enzo said. Jerry's men had thrown him across a conference table, dangled his legs off the edge, and stomped them without mercy.

"That's because you tried to bribe them. There's no swaying that bunch. They're well taken care of."

"Hey, you know I had to try."

"You need to read a room better, Z."

"Yeah, well, I ain't the poker genius you are."

Teddy spotted Rolo emerging from the mini-mart.

"I ate lobster for the first time yesterday afternoon," Angelica said. "An hour ago, I choked down a cold, greasy taco. Ain't this the Quickie Buckner life? From rags to riches to rags again."

"We got it far better than Buckner," Larson said. "His deal was rags to riches to dead."

"How did Quickie die?" Angelica turned to Teddy. He hesitated to answer, interrupted before he could.

"I guess we should feel lucky," Enzo said, eyeing Rolo as he returned to the car. "We had our moment in the sun. Most bastards never see the insides of a penthouse, am I right? I mean, the astronauts who were shot up to the moon never went back, but they were lucky to be up there once, you know?"

"NASA didn't beat their asses and strip their pockets when they returned," Larson said.

"I'm with Larson," Angelica said. "After yesterday, this crew of five don't feel so lucky." She cursed as she strained to take off her pantyhose.

"Now that's not real lady-like," Teddy said with a grin, recalling their milestone night at the Brickhouse Bar.

"I guess I'm not like a real lady," Angelica said, laughing, also remembering her drunken exchange from that fateful evening. "I was so wasted last night, I slept in these damn things, but there's no reason to wear 'em out here. Let these desert creeps see my hairy legs."

"How about we try another town?" Enzo asked as he finished filling up the SUV. "Fuck Vegas. Plenty of other casinos."

"They've had time to blacklist us all the way around," Rolo said, joining the dismal conversation. "We're likely made from Crow Canyon to Atlantic City at this point."

"Rolo's right," Teddy said. "We're done. No casino or cardroom will have us now, maybe not even the Indian joints. We might as well..."

BEEP BEEP.

12:12 P.M.

Enzo looked at his gold watch, a cherished gift from Rolo, the one thing of value he had left in the world from their days as high rollers. He laughed at the fact that his Lucky Five just started, during their forced retreat from Vegas. "Hey guys, it's my Five! Want to rob the gas station? I'll stay here and cover you all!"

The group laughed, their first moment of levity since their exile. Angelica turned to Teddy, whose quiet laugh quickly dropped away as he stared at something across the street.

"What do you think, Ted?" she asked, amused by the notion. "Knock over Elmo's? Clean out the register and snag some frozen burritos? Next we hit a 7-Eleven? Start rebuilding our empire!"

"One Slurpee at a time," Enzo said with a tired smile.

Teddy found no amusement in their words. He stepped one foot out of the SUV, ever focused on a small glass door across the street that seemed to beckon him. "Rolo, you got a piece?"

"If you really wanna take down Elmo's Gas and Snax," Rolo said with a laugh, assuming Teddy continued the gag, "I got a snub-nose in the glove. Help yourself."

Teddy didn't laugh along with his friends. He quickly opened the glove compartment and pulled out the small, silver snub-nose revolver.

"Umm, it's called a joke, Ted," Angelica said, suddenly concerned.

"The gun's dry anyway," Rolo said. "Why don't we all calm down..."

Teddy turned to Enzo. "Keep sight of me, Z."

"Wait, what are you gonna..." Enzo's reply was cut off by Teddy's reckless haste.

Without hesitation, without a thought or consultation with his comrades, Teddy ripped Angelica's pantyhose in half, pulled it over his head, pocketed the snub-nose, and ran across the street to the small business he'd spied - a branch of Cal-Neva Trust Bank.

Lynn Harrod

Rolo instantly realized his partner had crossed a line, past the point of no return. He quickly tossed the other half of Angelica's pantyhose to Enzo and nodded for him to follow.

Enzo suddenly shook as he stepped out of the SUV and clumsily pulled the pantyhose over his head. He had to sprint to follow Teddy to the small corner bank, sure to keep his eyes on his foolhardy friend. "Shit, shit, shit," he said under his breath as he ran across the street in the morning sun, tailing Teddy, trying to ignore the slowed traffic and curious pedestrians all around.

Teddy ran into the bank like a madman, swinging the glass door to bang against its adjacent window. Enzo remained at the entrance, terrified to enter but also scared to lose sight of his friend during his Lucky Five. Confused and fighting off a panic attack, he imagined being manhandled by the police, standing trial in court, being sentenced to prison by a cold judge sitting up on high. He desperately wanted to rejoin his friends at the gas pumps and get the hell out of that shitty little desert town, but he inexplicably remained, keeping sight of Teddy in the face of his overwhelming fear.

At Elmo's Gas and Snax, Rolo jumped into his SUV and started the engine. Larson and Angelica sat frozen in the back seat, wondering what was going to happen to their comrades.

A moment later, Teddy burst out of the bank with a waste paper basket. He kept his pantyhose mask on, as did Enzo, as the two men ran back to the SUV, its engine running.

Teddy sat in the front passenger seat as Enzo scampered into the back with Angelica and Larson. Rolo shifted into gear and sped down Main Street, merging onto I-15 South.

No police pursuit followed as the SUV's engine roared, Rolo driving well past the speed limit, passing dozens of cars on the highway. Teddy peered inside the small plastic trash can for his first look at the bounty.

Teddy Brewer, an uneducated, middle-aged man who dreamed of being the next great poker champion, walked into that small bank with a small revolver and ran out with $65,710.00 in assorted bills, some in wrapped stacks, some in clumsy piles, all crammed into a flimsy waste paper basket. He didn't realize there was no need to run out of the Cal-Neva Trust Bank. He could have simply walked - he could have stopped in the middle of the damn street to tie his shoes - during the impossible protection of Enzo's Five.

Unbeknownst to the crew, there had been no resistance during the brief heist. The security cameras jammed. The alarm died. The tired, aging, lone guard had coincidentally just entered the men's room, his hearing aid temporarily glitched. Teddy imagined the old guard emerging from the toilet to find the bank's staff and patrons quiet, flat on the floor in horror.

The morbid image amused him.

Teddy held up fistfuls of cash. "There's gotta be high five figures here! All taken in sixty seconds! From a hole-in-the-wall bank!"

"What the hell were you thinking?" Angelica said.

"Whoa, what's with the hostility?"

"You've fucked us!" Rolo yelled, turning off the I-15 and heading west on the CA-58. He passed car after car on the highway, stomping the pedal to the floor, trying to get as much distance from Barstow as he could. "It's one thing to run shit from the Castle or to fix a card table, but robbing a bank in broad daylight?"

"Don't you see?" Teddy said. "It came to me last night when my mind kept racing, kept going back to the moment we pulled up to the motel, when I first saw the bank. I woke up around 4:00 a.m. and walked around that little bank. I knew it'd be peanuts during one of our Fives. That's when it dawned on me - cheating casinos, robbing banks - what's the difference?"

"You're out of your fuckin' mind!"

"Listen to me, Moon..."

"Open your eyes! You said it yourself, we're done, Ted!"

"No, we're not," Teddy said, raising his voice above the racing engine. "I know we're not! How can we dismiss this?"

"I feel it, too," Enzo said, surprising the frightened group. "Those guys didn't see it coming, and they ain't chasing after us. Don't ask me how I know, but they're back there right now, scratchin' their heads, wondering what the hell just happened."

"What about witnesses?" Larson asked. "There were plenty of eyes around."

"None of them will remember shit," Enzo said, suddenly energized by the modest heist. "I can't explain it, but Teddy was never gonna get caught. None of us are."

Rolo, Angelica, and Larson sat unconvinced, still waiting for a police car to rush them from behind, sirens blazing. It never came.

Teddy didn't count the money. He simply clutched the waste paper basket and peered in at the loose cash. It wouldn't be until another half-hour down the road, at a lonely Pilot Travel Center in Kramer, California, that the gang pulled over to count the take. They waited with tangled nerves as Teddy laid out the money in the folded-down rear seat. Seeing all that cash blanketing the SUV's interior made them uneasy, as if a police officer would walk up to them far out in a dirt lot, see the money, and call for backup. It felt as if Fate would eventually catch up and compensate for failing to apprehend them in Barstow.

Teddy completed the count. "It's about what I thought."

"How much?" Angelica asked.

"I somehow knew it was north of fifty-large."

"Dammit, how much, Ted?"

"We're looking at $65,710.00."

"Roughly thirteen-grand a piece," Larson said some quick math.

"Oh, we're splitting it now?" Teddy said. "Half an hour ago, you guys were pissing your pants, cursing at me for taking some initiative."

"Is that what you call it?" Rolo asked, incredulous.

"Hold on, it was me and Ted-O that went in," Enzo said.

"True, but all five of us were at risk," Larson said. "You and 'Ted-O' didn't run to another car and drive off into the sunrise together. You hopped in *this* car, which makes us accomplices. So, yes, we split the take."

"You sure, Larson?" Teddy asked. "Aren't you afraid that the cops will surround us at any second?"

"I was afraid, but... I don't feel it anymore."

"Feel what?" Angelica asked.

"The heat. I felt it all around us back in Barstow, but the farther away we got, the more I realized how completely Enzo's Five covered us."

"Me, too. I guess."

"It sounds crazy," Teddy said, "but I feel like we could shoot someone in the middle of Times Square during one of our Fives and never get pinched for it."

"Let's not get carried away," Rolo said despite secretly having committed multiple murders during his own Five. "We ain't hitmen."

"What are you thinkin', Larson?" Enzo asked, confused. Larson had no response, still processing their morning.

"Ange is up next," Teddy said, "in about three hours."

"Wait, what happens in three hours?" she asked.

The rest of the group instantly knew.

* * *

Rolo's black SUV sat in another dirt lot, this one in the nearby town of Boron, fifteen minutes further down CA-58. A short distance away stood the Desert Citizens Bank, a California branch of the Nevada-based financial institution.

Up to that pivotal moment, the gang had not continued fleeing down the highway but killed time in Kramer, waiting for Angelica's mid-day Five. They had lunch at a Burger King across the street from the Pilot Travel Center, listened to Creedence Clearwater Revival on the stereo, played cards on the hood of the SUV. Rolo purchased a discount DVD from the travel center and played it on the car's built-in entertainment screen - *The Godfather Part II* - his favorite movie.

Just before leaving Kramer, Teddy spotted a police car pull into the Pilot lot and took yet another risky gamble much to his companions' dismay. Feeling empowered by their take from Barstow, he dared to walk up to a California Highway Patrol car and ask the two officers inside what they knew about "the Barstow robbery all over the radio," the daring daylight robbery having quickly made the local airwaves. As he predicted, the police had no identification to go on, no vehicle description, no credible eyewitnesses to the noontime heist. Despite Teddy's persistent questions, they looked at him without a trace of suspicion.

Rolo drove them down the highway to Boron, to a spot out in the open a short distance from the Desert Citizens Bank.

BEEP BEEP.

4:02 P.M.

Angelica pulled one leg of her ripped pantyhose over her head, wondering if she even needed to do so. She looked to her crew to see who would actually enter this second bank. To her surprise, Larson volunteered. He put on his makeshift mask - the second leg of the pantyhose - and walked into the small bank. Angelica watched from the door as Enzo had earlier.

This last-minute heist proved slightly more challenging. Two young security guards stood inside, armed and alert. Larson spotted them through the glass door before his glance was returned, but dismissed his mounting panic, putting all his faith in the Lucky Five. To be safe, he held Rolo's snub-nose revolver at his side, its chambers empty, as he entered the bank.

Rolo, Teddy, and Enzo waited with breath held in the front seat of the idling SUV, a wave of fear washing over them with a distant, almost muted feeling.

Larson emerged with a bulging canvas sack. He didn't run to the car. He walked briskly, defiantly, never looking back, with Angelica alert at his side. No one followed from the bank. Its magnetic security door malfunctioned, locking in the guards, staff, and patrons during the gang's departure.

Larson and Angelica stepped into the SUV, Angelica taking up her permanent spot in the third row. Larson returned Rolo's gun.

"Let's roll," Larson said calmly. Rolo shifted into Drive and continued west on CA-58.

"What happened in there?" Rolo asked of the two-minute bank heist, twice as long as their previous one.

"Details, please," Teddy said.

"I had to threaten them," Larson said, disturbed by his own words. "Two guards, six tellers, eighteen patrons. I pointed the gun at them and they cowered as if I were the Devil Incarnate."

Indeed, the terror that swelled in the hearts of the security guards was something neither man had ever experienced in their collective twelve years of service. The staff feared for their lives despite being protected by bulletproof glass three-and-a-half inches thick. The patrons dropped to the polished tile floor and froze in the fetal position. Larson had a stone expression showing through his pantyhose mask as he pointed his small, empty snub-nose at everyone. From their terrified expressions, it may as well have been a lit cannon.

Eighty-seven minutes later, on the southern outskirts of Bakersfield, with no one in pursuit, the gang pulled over again, this time at a Sonic Burger on White Lane. A quick count revealed their take from the Desert Citizens Bank added up to $52,925.00. The trepidation they felt only hours before had been replaced with feelings of accomplishment and curiosity. Enzo felt surprised at the low dollar amounts these banks had on hand.

"I always figured a bank's vault was loaded," Enzo said. "I mean, in the movies, they're stacked to the ceiling with millions."

"Hollywood bullshit," Teddy said. "Especially these small, rural banks. You gotta hit up a big city bank, gotta time it right. Most days are business as usual, but certain days of the month they're flush with cash."

"Where to next?" Enzo asked, stuffing the money back into its burlap sack.

The rest of the group pondered his question with nods and grins. Angelica alone had reservations about where the Five was taking them. "Is this what we've become? We're only a day out of Vegas and suddenly we're bank robbers?"

How naive she is, Teddy thought. She's still scared, still expecting to get caught and hauled off to prison.

"Nah, this is it," Rolo said, taking command of what felt like an escalating day sweeping them along. "No more of this road gang shit. We made some of our money back. That's enough for now."

"For now," Teddy repeated.

Over the next few weeks, the Lucky Five gang didn't bother looking for a new cardroom or casino. They didn't think to test their discovery against the state's many dealers and pit bosses who'd been put on notice about these five blacklisted individuals. Instead, they followed their new path of banks and credit unions, executing carefully timed five-minute robberies without incident.

During Enzo's noontime Five, they took $70,000 from the California Workers Community Bank in Dinuba and another $46,000 from the Mesa Park Credit Union in McFarland. During Angelica's mid-day Five, they stole $81,000 from Berk and Associates Bank and Trust in Tulare, $90,000 from Frontier Savings in Taft, and a whopping $200,000 from Rombank Incorporated in Visalia. Each heist lasted less than two minutes and felt like easy money with no comeuppance, a feeling of freedom and immunity they hadn't felt since their early days in Las Vegas.

Despite their seemingly perfect crimes, they agreed on one rule - nothing within the Easton city limits. "We don't piss in own backyard," Rolo said.

Though they no longer had Scary Jerry monitoring their every move, they felt their growing fame as eyewitnesses who saw them moments after their Fives came forth, their recollections gradually coming together like a mosaic under police questioning.

Unlike the four men of the crew, who carried no concerns, trusting completely in their shared discovery, Angelica clearly recalled their false feeling of unchallenged power as they rolled through Vegas casinos. She remembered their sense of empowerment as hubris, overconfidence, ending in a confrontation that could have easily turned fatal. Meeting Jerry's guards in the Poseidon's cabana, being taken to a conference room for intimidation and terror, suddenly seemed like a slap on the wrist compared to what could be waiting for them at the tail end of a string of bank robberies.

Her pleas to end their crime spree fell on deaf ears. Of course, the Lucky Five would forever protect them. Of course, they'd be safe if they stuck to their timed heists and left well before the clock ran out. The power of their shared miracle proved itself each time. All they needed was to act with more caution than they had in Nevada. Despite her caution, Angelica felt compelled to contribute.

Most alarming, not once did anyone in the crew consider using the Lucky Five for something other than personal gain. Fleeting thoughts of benefiting the world came and went, silenced by an inner voice. Perhaps it was the tormented ghost of Quickie Buckner. Perhaps it was simply greed. The Lucky Five not only instilled power, but an insatiable lust that would continue to spiral.

If only Teddy and the rest of the group had listened to Angelica and not dismissed her trepidation as a pessimistic vision of doom. Perhaps they'd all live to enjoy their riches well into old age, working together to achieve personal dreams that went beyond grand theft larceny. Sadly, they were blinded by the apparent ease of the heists and could never anticipate the consequences of their actions, soon to strike them like a tsunami.

28

American Dreams Broken

January 2000 - October 2001

Over the following year and a half, the five unlikely friends spent less time together, feeling the heat of a newly formed state task force created to investigate and take down the masked gang hitting small banks across Central California. Some nights, that heat felt as if it was rushing toward them from around the next corner, with officers canvassing the rural neighborhoods surrounding their targets. Though the men of the gang still didn't agree with Angelica's doomsaying, they believed that a low profile was the best move after so many heists in such a short time. "Low profile" turned out to be a loose term as the five members of the gang went their separate ways to pursue new goals based on lifelong regrets.

Rolo reformed his brother's old gang, "The Mojo Boys" and expanded it well beyond the streets of the Castle District, soon becoming the chief crime lord of the Greater Easton Area. Led by his born-again lieutenant, Shorty Dominguez, the soldiers of Moonlight Marino took the gangland territories known as The Docks, West Side, The Quarry, and The Bluffs, overthrowing their self-appointed lords in bloody skirmishes. Seen as an underworld messiah, Rolo rallied the loyalty of every gangster in the Six-County area, conquering it all five minutes at a time. Word spread that his troops seemed invulnerable after midnight, no one realizing the raids always occurred from 1:21 to 1:26 a.m. The money came at blinding speed, enough to last the rest of their great-grandkids' lives. In time, money wasn't enough. Rolo wondered if anything would be.

Larson and Devon resurrected Williams Brothers Racing, securing and modifying a fleet of six Dodge Daytona coupes and headhunting top talent for a hand-picked stable of drivers and veteran pit crew. Together, the two brothers reentered the world of NASCAR. They placed well at the Auto Club Speedway in Fontana, California, the Los Angeles Memorial Coliseum, the Phoenix Raceway in Avondale, Arizona, the Sonoma Raceway, and even the legendary two-and-a-half mile track at the Indianapolis Motor Speedway. With each successful race, they felt determined to strike a major sponsorship deal through a series of underdog wins and the glowing publicity thereof.

Enzo opened "Brian's Bar and Grill," a glossy new tavern meant to ignite a franchise. Initially modeled after his family's original Pub O'Day, development soon retooled Brian's into a hip modernization of any Old Boston neighborhood joint with the college craft-beer crowd in mind, authenticity be damned. Named in honor of his late father, the first Brian's sat in the secondary anchor space of "North End Boulevard Shops," a sparkling new shopping center in Brawley. It offered a family-friendly atmosphere, featuring steaks and burgers and the widest selection of beer and liquor in town all complemented by faux antiques nailed to the walls, nightly entertainment, and foot traffic pouring in from the nearby nightclubs, fashion boutiques, and the primary anchor business, the Royale-21 movie theater.

Angelica continued to connect with her mother, Rosa. Now independently wealthy and able to stay home with her at all hours, she positioned her Lucky Five as the starting point of deep daily conversations, soon seeing her mother's lucidity extend beyond five minutes. At first, she planned to move her mother into a luxurious home in North End and hire a full-time staff to tend to her every need, but felt the change of her surroundings would further confuse and disorient her. If she had any hope of overcoming Rosa's mental issues, it would have to be in the familiar environment of their long-time Whitesbridge home. She wanted to have the old house completely remodeled, but feared the construction crews would disturb her mother and interfere with her progress. In the end, Angelica dipped into her fortune to buy only a red convertible Corvette, placing the rest of her cash in her father's steamer trunk. Though the dream she pursued seemed less ambitious than her partners' flashy goals, they were no less challenging or life-changing.

Teddy revisited his past relationship with Marissa Washington, who abandoned her career as an exotic dancer after Rolo reclaimed Smokey's Club. She now served as a

Lynn Harrod

receptionist for the Carlson Automotive Group, the third largest car dealership in the state, working toward a sales management position. Teddy entered the lot several times under the guise of shopping for a new Cadillac, insisting each time that he be shown the latest models by their newest sales trainee. Since he always arrived shortly after eight o'clock, during his Lucky Five, Marissa always seemed to more than willing to show him their latest models.

For the duration of 2000, all seemed well. The humiliating exile from Las Vegas long behind them, they used their discovery to chase their true, deep desires, attempting to course-correct the many wrong turns they took so long ago. Sadly, like Quickie Buckner before them, they realized that the Lucky Five comes at a cost, that the universe balances its miracles with equal tragedies. During the spring and summer of 2001, the former gang saw their carefully stacked achievements and wealth tumble away.

Rolo may have claimed new territories five minutes at a time, but his reputation grew at all hours, calling the attention of both the local police and the state task force. More aggressive each day, the authorities seized his properties and arrested his soldiers who'd become more akin to cult followers in light of Moonlight Marino's impossible power in the wee hours of the night. Within a month, the boundaries of his empire were brought back to the four streets that surrounded the Castle District.

Williams Brothers Racing suffered an unimaginable loss as two of its prized drivers perished in an infamous pile-up at the Knoxville Raceway in Iowa that landed three others in the Intensive Care Unit and two others in the morgue. Among those hurt was Larson's lead driver, little brother Devon Williams, who was flown to the Burn Unit of Fort Sanders Regional Medical Center. A pending deal with Chrysler was indefinitely shelved in the fallout of the tragic race.

Brian's Bar and Grill lived and died as a single location as talks of franchising fizzled after Roman Ivanov, the Chief Financial Officer of BBG LLC, embezzled six-million dollars and fled the country. Compounding this loss, the Royale-21 theater complex filed bankruptcy, vacating the primary anchor spot in North End Boulevard Shops, reducing Brian's foot traffic to a trickle. Enzo's bar bled money every night, with no cash reserves to fall back on.

Teddy's repeated attempts to reconnect with Marissa never extended beyond his Five. With each pleasant conversation, as she showcased the features of a new sedan and laughed at his goofy jokes and half-clever observations, he could never get her to fall in love with him again after his gold watch beeped a second time. He blamed the time limit of the Lucky Five, never once accepting the fact that she'd simply moved on and was no longer interested in a desperate man mired in regret, more infatuated with his vices and obsessions than any meaningful relationship.

So it was, after nearly a year away from the high crimes of cheating casinos and robbing banks, after a year of digging deep into their hearts and mining their fleeting dreams, that the Lucky Five gang of Easton, California had succumbed to hard times once again. It would have served them well to forget about their discovery and strive to better themselves and the world around them, to rebuild their lives without exploiting others. It would have saved them all to truly keep a low profile, grateful to have forfeited their found miracle in exchange for the rest of their lives. But it's one thing to avoid risk and live in safety, and another to turn one's back on what seems like easy riches waiting for those bold enough to take them.

29

Long Green Hour

Wednesday, October 10, 2001, 6:05 p.m.

Teddy sat at his old table, nestled in the corner by the front window. He glanced across the mostly empty room, over the booths and little square cafe tables, at the one large round table in the joint, just off the center of the room. He felt dispirited to see no poker game, no players laughing and teasing each other with Larson Williams lording over them. Teddy saw only six empty wooden chairs where his peers once sat, neatly pushed in under the table.

Teddy turned toward the long bar against the west wall, not recognizing the bartender. The stone-faced young man served a shaker pint of dark beer to a patron, erroneously tapping it without head, a rookie mistake the old barkeep, Enzo O'Day, would have laughed at.

Other than those nostalgic omissions, the Brickhouse Bar sat largely the same. A mix of classic rock and 1990s Top-40 pop came from a bookshelf stereo behind the bar. A stainless steel, ventless, automated fryer in the opposite corner silently cooked French fries, onion rings, and jalapeño poppers to order. In the back room, a game of pool could be heard, the dense resin billiard balls clacking wildly against each other during their initial break. A young couple sat two tables away, making timid small talk, clearly on a first date. Three middle-aged women at the end of the bar giggled quietly over their margaritas from the young bartender being "a little cute" and them being a little tipsy.

Life went on at the Brickhouse Bar, business as usual, just as it did before Teddy first stumbled into Easton, continuing while he and his friends graduated to what they considered bigger, more worthy venues for their lives. He sat in quiet awe. How humbling and sobering it felt to realize that he and his friends were ultimately meaningless to the life of that neighborhood joint, a welcoming place they once viewed as their clubhouse.

Similarly, the Vista Playa Apartments still stood with a new tenant likely occupying his former home, Apartment 128. ValleyLink Call Center, his old employer, relocated to the Bay Area. Jiminetti's Family Restaurant, Rolo's long-time haunt, shut its doors. Despite the heights the crew reached with their discovery, they were destined to be merely a blip in time, a footnote on the pages of Easton's history.

* * *

In the months that followed everyone's collective failures, the Lucky Five gang had eventually agreed to gather at "Brewer Manor," Teddy's mansion in North End, a grand house secured during their prime era in Vegas, maintained by his cash reserves from their trail of busted banks.

The crew entered the estate and stared in both admiration and amusement at the spectacle of it all - the Greek statuary lining the long, winding driveway, the topiary animals dotting the immense lawn, the decadent French Renaissance design of the house. None of it seemed to fit the man they knew simply as Teddy, though it seemed to serve his towering alter ego, Prime Time Brewer, known as a famous gambler, notorious criminal, and elusive mob boss.

The purpose of that evening meeting at Brewer Manor was to plan a series of "Five" jobs to rejuvenate their cash flows and restart their failed ventures. Despite their desperate woes, none of them were eager to return to bank robbery, coordinated gambling, or any kind of heist or con that could be scrutinized by the authorities. It had been a curious miracle that none of them had been identified and apprehended, considering how infamous they'd become. From a combination of the gang's hubris and the loose lips of witnesses and criminal informants across Central California, the state task force finally had names to match the ring of bold, masked thieves.

Much to everyone's dismay, their Lucky Five nicknames had become their mob aliases. "Prime Time," "Rooster," "High Noon," and "Tea Time" were on FBI watch lists. Near the top, of course, was "Moonlight," the one member of the gang suspected of far worse crimes - drug trafficking, racketeering, prostitution, and illegal gambling. It seemed only a matter of time before their aliases would be connected further to their legal identities.

Though the group rejected the reformation of their rural bank tour, they agreed to working together one more time so long as it resulted in a payday hefty enough to settle their debts and pave the rest of the days. Sitting in Teddy's grand Game Room, they decided they'd all be in once that special lead had been found. Until then, they were to remain separate and hidden within their legitimate lives.

* * *

Teddy sat at his corner table at the Brickhouse, thinking back on that meeting at his estate. He knew he'd convinced his partners to agree to one more job likely because of the notion that there was no job big enough to satisfy them all. They'd nodded yes to an unobtainable goal, out of loyalty, as if to appease their de facto leader. In the back of his mind, Teddy felt the same way. That one final big job simply didn't exist, and it felt easier to shake hands and agree to wait for an opportunity they secretly knew would likely never come rather than admit that their days together had ended.

After many evenings toying with tourists on the mountain at Crow Canyon Casino, accepting the unspoken retirement of the Lucky Five gang, it came as a surprise when Rolo called him out of the blue to discuss a new lead. Fittingly, he'd chosen to meet at the Brickhouse Bar, the same place they first explored their discovery together and later planned their Vegas takeover.

Rolo walked into the bar and looked around for a moment, silenced by both the changes and stagnation of their old hangout, just as Teddy had pondered moments before. Without bothering to search for his friend, he made a beeline for their usual corner table against the front window.

"Been a while since I walked in here," Rolo said, taking off his leather overcoat and sitting opposite Teddy.

"They say it's a mob bar now. Word is 'the Italians of the Castle' are running everything."

Rolo smiled at the rumor. "'The Italians of the Castle.' Shit, I'm the only one with red Sicilian blood pumpin' through my heart. Everyone else is black something or brown something else."

"Word is the Marino Boys are back."

"I heard. 'Marino Boys,' 'Mojo Boys,' hell, even 'BC-9,' they can say whatever they want. Some people even say Tony is still alive, along with Elvis and Tupac and Jimmy Hoffa, I'm sure. That's all fine and good. Let him live on."

"Why the meet?" Teddy asked, down to business, unsure if he wanted to hear the answer.

"I got another job for us, the big one we talked about."

"I've been thinking about that. I'm not sure everyone really wants that one big job."

"Everyone? Or is that how you feel?"

"No jobs," Teddy said, planting his foot firmly on the floor. "I got my money."

"What about the others?"

"The others will survive."

"Don't matter, 'cause it ain't about money. It never was. It's about 'more.' At least hear me out." Rolo waved to a passing server, summoning a petite Latina with a round tray of empty glasses. "Two Rolling Rocks and another... whatever the fuck he's having..."

"Whiskey," Teddy said. "Bushmills 21."

"Of course," Rolo said with a smile. "Another whiskey for the Irish hooligan. Make it four fingers. He'll need it."

The server committed their simple order to memory and took her loaded tray to the bar. Teddy followed her with his eyes, watched her open Rolo's two bottles of beer behind the bar.

"You still drink that shit?" Teddy asked.

"You have the balls to call Rolling Rock shit?" Rolo said with mock anger.

"It was shit then and it's shit now. How can you choke it down after sipping vintage single-malt at the Bellagio and fifty-dollar cocktails at the Poseidon?"

"This place, coming here, got me cravin' a simple bottle of pissy swill. I can't explain it. All I can say is that even a globe-trotting gourmet occasionally gets the itch for a Quarter Pounder when he sees the Golden Arches. Nostalgia can be a powerful thing."

The young woman returned with her tray, carrying the two bottles of beer and a highball glass of whiskey. As she set the drinks on the table, Rolo paid her while subtly nodding to front window beside them, to the tall building across the street. Teddy turned, confused to see only the Easton Monument Bank.

"We agreed," Teddy said, looking his friend in the eye. "We don't piss in our own backyard."

"I'm telling you, this is the job," Rolo said. "I scoured four states for that one big score, and I kept coming back here."

"Easton Monument."

"The one and only."

"It's easily the biggest bank we've ever looked at, the most secure, smack in the middle of Downtown just a stone's throw from a police substation."

"You really worried about all that?" Rolo asked with a grin. "During the Five, it might as well be the Three Little Pigs' straw house."

"And we're the Big Bad Wolves?" Teddy said with a laugh. "I dunno, I'm not sure the rest of the crew will sign up for yet another bank."

"It's not just another bank and it's not just another job. This is the kind of job movies-of-the-week are made of. We're looking at one-point-eight, maybe two-mill, just sitting on the table, waiting for you to grow a pair. You ever heard of 'Long Green Hour?'"

Teddy shook his head and sipped his whiskey, trying to act uninterested.

"When the treasury pumps in new money, it sometimes collects the old money, to retire it. Certain banks in certain cities act as hubs."

"And Easton Monument is a hub?"

"They're a hub for eighteen banks across the six counties. They have the best security, the strongest vault, the highest insurance."

"The highest risk," Teddy said, looking around to ensure no one was listening.

"To any other crew, sure, but again, none of that means jack shit to us. You know that better than anyone."

"Who's your intelligence on this?"

"Don't worry, I got a solid source," Rolo said, annoyed with Teddy questioning him. "They get the new bills first. They confirm the delivery, count the cash. Then they return the old bills, but there's a window before they get picked up by another truck, between sixty and ninety minutes. That's 'Long Green Hour.' Happens every two years. These hub banks have ten times the cash during that window. Their vaults are filled, and their cows..."

"Cows?"

"They call 'em 'Cash Cows,' these little rolling tanks, look like armor-plated shopping carts. They're used to carry the cash from the tellers to the vault across that big-ass bank. I guess they don't trust the managers to simply carry that shit."

"What about these Cows?"

"During Long Green Hour, they'd loaded, about to burst with that new cash while the old bills sit stacked high in the vault. It's low-hanging fruit."

"Yeah, but that orchard is gonna be a bitch."

"I don't think so. Brother, if anything was ever worthy of the Five, this is it. But the playbook I got penciled out is big. All five of us gotta be in there, masked, armed, and ready, to make it work."

Teddy looked out the window at the grand old bank across the street. He sighed as he warmed to the idea. "Do we know when that ninety-minute window is?"

"For the past six years, it took place in the middle of the afternoon... around four o'clock."

"Angelica."

"Bingo. My source says it'll be the same this year."

Teddy looked at the bank, its towering pillars and three-story windows intimidating, almost daring him to come take its treasure. "Up to two-mill?"

Rolo smiled, knowing he had him, which meant he'd have everyone.

30

Time's Up

Thursday, December 20, 2001, 10:04 p.m.

Manny Sanchez sat in his studio apartment with his legs outstretched on his Murphy bed, its frame and mattress lowered from its inner wall compartment for the night. He had Prime Time Brewer's red journal spread open across his legs which helped hold his fifth bottle of beer tucked between his thighs. He'd been reading the book all day and into the night, mesmerized by the intimate details of the infamous Lucky Five gang. After getting to know each of the players involved, their dashed dreams, their continued failures in the shadow of their miraculous discovery, Manny reached the page that would finally reveal the missteps on what many deemed the pivotal moment in the gang's life - the doomed Easton Monument Bank job.

Teddy had touched on the heist in his first entry, but left it halfway through the experience, likely because it pained him to relive that afternoon within the early pages of his journal, just as it pained Manny to read it. From the many headlines and TV news coverage a year prior, he knew the outcome of that botched operation and didn't look forward to seeing it unfold in his mind as he continued further into the book. Still, that day secured its place in the city's history, and drew Manny into it.

Some local news channels called it the most daring daylight robbery in the history of the city, detailing the criminals involved and the unprecedented take carted away from the bank. Others focused on the heroic efforts of the civilians, the tragic loss of life, and the statewide manhunt that followed.

Manny continued reading, as if Teddy himself beckoned him to join them back on that day.

"Rolo once told me he has to cheat death every day. I asked him if it was the cliché about knowing you're alive. He said no. In the Castle, nothing feels better than cheating someone, and Death is as good a sucker as anybody."

BLAM! BLAM! BLAM!

As the shots were fired at him, ringing out across Easton Monument Bank, Rolo shut his eyes tight underneath his pantyhose mask, accepting his fate for the briefest moment.

He slowly opened them, realized that he stood unharmed, and spotted Angelica across the bank. She'd regained eye contact with him through the teller windows.

Off-duty Easton police officer Robbie Sullivan clutched his smoking pistol tight as he still lay on his side on the floor, not sure what the hell was happening. He'd just fired repeatedly at Moonlight Marino from a few yards away. Not only did he miss Marino, but the large gangster once again seemed unconcerned about the cop, just as he had a minute earlier.

"Don't move!" Sullivan said. "Stay right there!" To his bewilderment, the gang of thieves ignored his command - and his gun - as they regrouped in the center of bank, Larson pushing the bank's heavy, wheeled "Cash Cow" with sudden haste.

Afternoon Tea Time was about to end.

"All of it?" Rolo asked.

"Not all," Larson said.

"Then get the fuck back in there!"

"No time," Teddy said, helping his partner wheel the loaded cow to the bank's side exit.

"Godammit!" Rolo's eyes fixed on Sullivan, his gun still raised.

"I said hold it right there!" Sullivan yelled again. He pulled the trigger on the gathered gang.

CLICK CLICK.

Rolo walked up to Sullivan and clutched his pistol, still in hand, and turned it inward toward the officer's head.

"Just so there's no confusion..." Rolo said, seething, squeezing the man's finger wedged against the trigger.

BLAM!

The screams that echoed throughout the grand bank signaled the turning point for the Lucky Five gang. Never had the gang killed someone. They never needed to. So complete was their otherworldly invincibility during their Fives that violence never reared itself. Even ammunition was barely needed.

"He's dead!" a woman hysterically screamed. "He's dead!"

In his fury, wallowing in his self-hatred for publicly succumbing to fear moments ago, Rolo had killed off-duty city police officer Robbie Sullivan, shooting him point blank in the forehead with his own gun. Even the black magic of the Lucky Five couldn't erase the public execution, witnessed by dozens, that would stain the gang for the rest of their lives.

Bart Reed, the old retiree working as a part-time security guard for the bank, vomited from terror, expecting the next bullet to pierce his skull. From his experience, all it took was that first kill to trigger a cascade of bullets from a gang teetering on edge. He knew most organized heist crews avoided violence, but he also knew that when it was deemed necessary it usually ended with guns blazing.

Alice DeVoss, the bank's manager, froze in shock upon seeing the pool of blood slowly growing like a deep red halo behind Sullivan's head on the marble floor. Her mascara streaming down her weeping face like black tentacles, coupled with her thousand-yard stare, made her look lost and deranged. In her mind, she also imagined Moonlight Marino and his cronies unloading their weapons onto the staff and customers to ensure no witnesses remained.

Nora Castillo, a senior citizen sitting cross-legged on the floor, hugged her tote bag to keep her Chihuahua "Pee Wee" calm inside during the gunshots and the screams and the overall feeling of fear that dogs can sense. Scared that Pee Wee would jump out of the tote bag and sprint across the floor in fright, she wrapped her arms tight around the bag, hoping she wasn't suffocating the poor little thing. Many emotions swirled in Nora's head, yet throughout her plight, she kept coming back to the one woman in the gang. Even behind the pantyhose mask, she seemed familiar to her.

"Goddammit, Moon, we gotta move!" Angelica said, staring incredulous as Rolo raced back to the open vault to carry as much cash as he could handle. "We got no time! We got to fuckin' move right now..."

BEEP BEEP.

4:07 P.M.

Angelica looked down at her gold watch in a sudden wave of panic. She whipped her head to a large wall clock above the bank's main entrance as if it would disprove her timepiece and grant her another minute. The grim realization soon flooded her with dread - her Five had expired - yet there she stood in the middle of the largest bank in the San Joaquin Valley with three-dozen terrorized people surrounding a bloody corpse only thirty feet away.

She looked to the side exit and saw Teddy, Larson, and Enzo step outside with the cow. She looked to the vault behind the tellers and saw Rolo rushing out with his crossed arms loaded with stacks of cash. Without thinking, she turned to the security cameras mounted ten feet apart on every wall, to the cowering staff knelt within an arm's reach of an alarm button, and to the old security guard now considering taking action despite it seeming inconceivable to him moments before.

Finally, she looked to the old woman who'd been staring at her since the heist began.

Nora Castillo slowly released her grip on her tote bag, the little dog within remaining inside like a good boy. Upon the synchronized beeps of the gold watches worn by each of the thieves, she now recognized the young woman's voice clear as day.

"Angelica!" Nora said with a pleading whimper. "Why do you do this?"

Angelica turned away from the woman. She ran to join Rolo as he emerged from behind the tellers' counter and poured half his haul into her arms.

"Moon! Time's up!"

Before Rolo could tell her he very well knew her Five had expired, he spied two uniformed police officers come in through the main entrance across the bank. He clumsily handed all his cash to her.

"Forget this!" she said. "We gotta go!"

Rolo pulled two guns from his coat pocket and fired at the cops as they took in the scene and pulled their weapons. The customers between them screamed, their faces pressed against the floor as bullets flew over them. Angelica felt a searing pain in her left thigh, felt blood trickle into her boot. Rolo darted in front of her, grabbed her by the waist, and threw her behind a desk, taking a bullet across his face as they both ducked behind cover.

Lynn Harrod

Angelica sat flat on the floor, her arms carrying a small fortune. Beside her, Rolo's bloody face made him look more demonic, his chin and left cheek split open.

"Moon," she said, her words a faint whisper in the gunfight. "Moon, something happened..."

Enraged, Rolo returned fire with both guns, the shootout going back and forth until the two officers slumped down to the floor, dead. He helped his partner to her feet and guided her to the side exit.

"Moon!" she said, resisting his pulling her by the arm.

"What is it?" Rolo asked, looking around frantically as if the National Guard would pour into the building at any moment.

"I been made."

"What? Who?"

"That old lady," Angelica said, as if withholding the woman's name would somehow protect her. "She knows my ma."

"You sure?" Rolo asked, as if offering her one last chance for a U-turn. "Ange, tell me, you absolutely sure?"

"She called out my name." As the words left her lips in a gasp, her tone feeble and helpless, she knew she'd just doomed Nora Castillo.

Rolo turned to look at Nora, now holding Pee Wee in her arms. The little dog had finally come out of the tote bag. It would be the last time the little Chihuahua would see his caregiver alive.

"Can you make it to the van?" Rolo asked.

Angelica nodded. "What are we gonna do?"

"Get to the van. Don't worry, Angie. You'll make it."

"What about you?"

"I'll clean this up, make sure she takes your name to the grave."

Angelica cried as she carried the bundles of cash to the side exit. Through the glass door, she saw her partners outside, slamming the rear doors of their unmarked van. She turned around and pushed the door open with her backside...

BLAM!

With her body halfway out the door, Angelica looked toward the gunshot only to see the large frame of Rolo running toward her, blocking the grisly scene he left behind.

"Don't look!" Rolo said. "Just go!"

"Rolo..."

"Just go!"

Distant sirens grew closer as all five members of the gang got into their van and drove away, turning down alleys and back streets on a route Larson had scouted days before, eventually reaching a garage he secured only sixteen blocks away.

In the bank, Alice DeVoss ran to tend to the old woman while her staff and customers rose to their feet, keeping their distance from the three other bodies. Alice stopped a few feet shy of Nora Castillo, seeing with no uncertainty that she lay dead, her little dog whimpering in her arms.

* * *

The Easton Monument bank robbery was the biggest and last job of the Lucky Five gang. Rolo's homework, estimating roughly two million at stake, was off by an additional eleven million old and new bills sitting in that under-protected building. The gang had taken nearly all of it, and the state task force felt emboldened enough to double their efforts to hunt down the dangerous crew.

The robbery-turned-massacre was seized upon by every crime journalist coast to coast with round-the-clock coverage. News outlets created logos for the gang, accompanied by signature jingles and sound bites from witnesses. Footage from the security cameras, which reactivated in the final minute of the heist, played in endless loops on all channels. The heights and frames of the thieves were scrutinized. Experts tried to read the lips of everyone present, hoping for some small detail that would lead to further intel that could bust open the case.

What gained the most coverage, even more than speculation about the notorious gang, were the lost lives from that tragic afternoon.

Eddie Franks and Rich Juarez, the two uniformed police officers nearest the crime scene when the bank's silenced alarm suddenly kicked on, were on their way back from speaking at an elementary school. Robbie Sullivan, the off-duty cop in the Yankees cap, had been at the bank to make a withdrawal to buy a new crib and stroller while his wife waited in the car with their two-month-old daughter, Molly.

Arguably, the most remembered of the victims was Nora Castillo, the beloved den mother for the Easton University Eagles softball team. Nora had just turned seventy-five, commemorated with a big party thrown by the team in her honor. Besides supporting her niece's team, Nora also volunteered at St. Nelia's Church just north of the Castle District, offering her time to patients with dementia. She regularly made house calls, including to the Cruz household in Whitesbridge, where she cared for Rosa Cruz weekly. The congregation often remarked lovingly about the pair, "Nora and Rosa," as kindred spirits.

* * *

Manny put down the journal, feeling sick at the intimate details of the Easton Monument Bank Massacre. Like everyone else who followed the news, he'd known about the landmark crime for months, but never imagined the desperation and brutality involved. It made him nauseous to think of what Angelica must have gone through, what the rest of the crew must have felt as they fled the scene, leaving those dead bodies in their wake.

He looked at the microwave oven in his corner kitchenette for the time - well past midnight. Despite the late hour that came after a long day's work and further hours of reading, Manny didn't feel tired. Being immersed in the journal seemed to energize him, pushing him to continue.

He turned the page and allowed Teddy to continue his life story.

"Police officers are nine-to-fivers like anybody. They punch in, take a lunch, punch out, and go home. Your tax dollars at work.

You wanna see real motivation behind every badge? You wanna see them go above and beyond the call of duty? Kill a cop. It's like daring every uniform in every precinct to come and get me, motherfucker. It's like fifteen murders rolled up into one. Suddenly, after a year of anonymity, after a year of blindfolded blue boys chasing ghosts, the sky was falling all around us. That damn task force followed every lead and were now unleashing the dogs on us and anyone remotely connected. Forget worrying about running out our Lucky Five minutes, the clock was now ticking on our lives."

31

Last Meal

Monday, October 22, 2001, 4:13 p.m.

The Easton Monument Bank heist had been designed to be the crew's last outing together, one huge final job to fill everyone's coffers for the rest of their lives. They'd soon learn they'd stolen north of $13 Million from that massive vault, certainly enough to sustain them for the foreseeable future, with an even split giving them nearly three million each.

After fleeing the bank, the crew piled into Larson's van and zig-zagged through the labyrinthine inner streets and alleys of Old Downtown before ducking into one of his properties surrounded by vacant, derelict buildings, less than ten minutes away. The former produce warehouse from 1935 had been converted into an automobile dealership in 1956 only to be gutted and retrofitted into a machine shop in 1972. Larson acquired it three months earlier, removed the old lathes and drill presses, and turned it into storage for his growing fleet of classic cars. To store their getaway vehicle - a plain, brown panel van - among vintage Ferraris, Porsches, and Jaguars seemed quite the contrast until Larson pointed out that both the van's cargo and its role in the historic heist easily made it the most valuable vehicle in the collection.

The five partners stepped out of the van, their pantyhose masks in hand, and breathed deeply and at ease for the first time all afternoon. The police sirens sounded distant and fading. There would be no arrests that day.

"Holy shit, I'm alive!" Enzo said with a mix of exhilaration and wonder, tied together with his bundle of frayed nerves. "I thought we was done! I mean, when our watches went off at the end and I was still standing there inside the joint, I thought we was over and done!"

"But we kept pushing," Larson said. "We stuck to the plan, we kept pushing ourselves onward, and now we're here."

"The only thing we were pushing was our luck," Teddy said in a huff. "What the fuck was that all about back there?"

It took a moment for the group to realize that Teddy had asked Rolo the direct question.

"You're lookin' at me?" Rolo said, offended that Teddy would so openly call him out.

"You stayed past the Five! You could've gotten killed! Worse, you could've gotten the rest of us caught!"

"None of that happened or ain't you noticed?"

Teddy stormed up to the giant gangster. "The goddamn plan was for everyone to be in the van, motor running, before the Five was up. Instead, you ran back to the fuckin' vault!"

"Because you couldn't do something simple like load all the cash into the cow, which was also the goddamn plan, by the way. So we took off at six minutes instead of five. So what?"

"You don't believe that, Rolo. 'So what?' That extra minute changed everything!" Teddy felt boiling rage at both his partner's actions and his attempt to now brush it off. "Look at Angie's leg! Look at your face!"

"We'll live."

"Can't say the same for everyone! We got four dead bodies in that bank! We got witnesses and cameras rolling! Do you know what that means for us?"

"Nothing." Rolo turned to open the rear doors of the van, his cold, curt response silencing Teddy. "It don't change nothing. We were wanted crooks before and we're wanted crooks now."

"We're wanted *murderers* now! Forget stealing the bank's FDIC-insured money, we killed an old lady and three cops!"

Rolo reached in and pulled the Cash Cow to the rear of the van. Enzo and Larson silently helped him lower the heavy, wheeled tank to the floor. "None of you ain't killed no one. That's on me."

"Don't play it like that, Rolo. You aren't stupid."

"The video will show it was all me."

"When they ambushed Bonnie and Clyde, did the federal agents stop and think that the rest of their gang in that car hadn't actually killed anyone? Did it matter? When they opened up their Tommy Guns from all directions and blasted that car to Hell, did it even cross their minds?"

"This thing's locked up tight," Enzo said, patting the steel-reinforced cow, fumbling with its lock, trying to distract from the heated argument.

"Let's keep it down, gentlemen," Larson said. "I'd hate for our sanctuary to be blown because someone jogging by heard two men shouting about killing and thieving."

Rolo didn't look at Teddy or any of his partners as he used his entire will to squash his jagged pangs of frustration and guilt. He knew well that he alone strayed from their precise plan, that he let his anger take over against that off-duty cop in the Yankee cap, and that his insistence on taking every last dollar led to his and Angelica's injuries and the deaths of four people. But as much as he knew he'd thrown them headlong into a deadly new chapter in their lives, he meant his earlier assessment that nothing had changed, at least not for him.

Rolo "Moonlight" Marino had been a cold-blooded killer before they stormed that bank, before the bank even entered their radar. As lord of the Castle District, leader of his late brother's Mojo Boys, he and his men had killed dozens of rivals over several months, with many bystanders fallen as collateral damage. The four additional lost souls that afternoon had changed nothing, or so he told himself, making no eye contact with his paranoid partners.

"Don't act like we didn't have blood on our hands already," Rolo said, "before today, before we got booted from Vegas."

Teddy felt confused, unsure of the secrets his friend chose to clumsily spill. "What are you talking about?"

"Don't pretend you didn't know about the Lady O' Luck, or Smokey's Ballroom, or The Docks, The Quarry, The Bluffs. Plenty of blood still soaking those floors."

"Z's right, we can't open it," Larson said, knowing instantly that he failed to subvert the tense subject. "We need to wait until Teddy's Five to bypass this lock."

"Lady O' Luck?" Teddy asked, ignoring Larson. He thought back to a morning he woke up in their Poseidon penthouse when he turned on the TV and saw the headline story on *KTNV-13 Action News* - "Six Dead at the Lady O' Luck Motel" - the day after Rolo gifted the group the gold watches. "The motel slaughter? That was you?"

For the past ten minutes, as Teddy and Rolo argued, as Enzo and Larson examined the Cash Cow, Angelica had retreated to the north wall and sat on a workbench, hugging her knees while she thought about Nora Castillo. For once, she felt grateful that her mother's memory failed her daily for she likely wouldn't remember the nice old lady from the church, the caregiver with the little Chihuahua who paid house calls to ensure Rosa Cruz had hot meals, books, magazines, and company over coffee cake. The mention of the Lady O' Luck Motel shook her from her trance.

"You killed those college guys?" Angelica said in an exhale. "Way back then?"

"Don't believe the news, Angie," Rolo said. "Those boys weren't from any college. They were grifters and they had it comin'. They put me in a room where it was gonna be me or them. What would any of you have done?"

"I wouldn't have stepped foot in that room to begin with," Teddy said, realizing the play-by-play from that night in their

Lynn Harrod

early days. "You left us for a while for some 'alone time.' You were fishing for grifters, weren't you? Testing your Five?"

"Gimme a fuckin' break..."

"You wanted them to come at you so you could see how far you could take the Five. That's how you were so sure of what it could do, that it was 'bigger than a card game.'"

Rolo entered the back of the van and grabbed the loose stacks of cash he took from the vault by hand. He tossed them atop the wheeled tank between Enzo and Larson.

"Forget that!" Teddy slapped the cash to the floor. "Answer my question, Rolo!"

"Oh, you asked a question? It sounded like you got it all figured out!"

"Did you hunt those grifters to test your Five?"

Rolo looked around at his partners. They'd given up trying to de-escalate the argument and were now fixed on him.

"It's a simple question, Moon," Larson said. "Did you mark those men that night?"

"I never wanted to be the next high-roller hot shot," Rolo said, dropping all pretense as he finally turned to the group. "All I wanted was to reclaim the Castle. It's all I wanted from the beginning. While you were all having the time of your lives, sippin' martinis at the craps tables, I thought the Five might get me what I really wanted. Turns out, I was right."

"You selfish prick," Teddy said with fiery eyes. "We're connected now. You put us all in harm's way, and for what? To chase your bullshit dream!"

"Don't you take a piss at me! Because you fucked up your shot with Marissa all over again! Your poker wins, your fancy suits, your new rep, not even the power of the Five could convince her to take you back. Even a fuckin' Wednesday-night stripper knows when to throw away a losing hand."

The crew stood frozen in silence as Rolo's razor sharp retort landed. Teddy rushed his partner. The two men fell against the Cash Cow in an ugly brawl, grappling atop the stacks of Hundreds spread across the concrete floor. After rolling over each other twice, their arms locked, and Rolo quickly gained the upper hand. He knelt on Teddy's chest and pummeled him without mercy, striking his skull against the floor, fueled by the anguish of all he'd lost and all the atrocities he'd done and could never take back. Enzo and Larson tried to pull him off Teddy, but the giant shrugged them off like rag dolls as he threw haymakers down at his partner, helpless and bloody.

"Stop it, Moon!" Angelica screamed from the workbench. She stood holding a long-barrel revolver, pointed at Rolo's head from twenty feet away. "Get off him! Now!"

Rolo paused his brutal beating and turned to her, grimacing at the sight of her wounded leg. "You gonna shoot me, Angie? Is that what's going on? After I saved your ass? You get caught in a gunfight, get popped in the leg, and suddenly you're a stone-cold killer now?"

"Like Ted said, we're all killers now, thanks to you."

"You don't got it in you." He stared at her, almost daring her to pull the trigger.

She stared back at him, unflinching, tracing the brutal slash across his cheek and chin from the last-minute bullet that grazed him at the bank. "I haven't shot no one yet. Don't you be my first."

Rolo recognized the determination on her face for he'd had the same expression the night Tony died. Looking at her down the barrel of her gun, he knew she'd shoot him if she had to, just as he would have shot anybody to protect - to bring back - his older brother.

Rolo released Teddy and rose to his feet. He offered Teddy a hand, but the help was unwelcome.

Teddy stood on his own, spit out a glob of blood, and stared at his crew as if he and all around him had collectively lost their minds. "It wasn't supposed to be like this! It was just about the money! No one was supposed to be ruined! No one was supposed to be dead!"

Teddy's fierce rant put everything into focus. Beyond Rolo's violent actions, despite the vast, illicit fortune between them, each person in that garage realized that the Lucky Five had burned them all, an albatross of false hope and baited rewards.

Larson's dream of forming a racing team collapsed in grand fashion, the respect and admiration of his brother Devon fading again. Enzo's fantasy of running a bar like the one he grew up in failed to reunite his family, ultimately feeling empty and deserving of having its doors shuttered. Angelica's wish to reconnect with her mother ended as abruptly as it reformed, over and over each afternoon, making it clear there would be no going home again for Rosa. Teddy's vision of a future with Marissa never had a chance, for she knew his rehabilitation, his rebirth as a better man, was never genuine. Rolo's rise to power, his expanded criminal empire, came at the steep cost of all their lives as a nationwide manhunt for the Lucky Five gang shifted into high gear, the many trails of blood all leading back to them, standing in that old garage.

"Here's the deal," Enzo said, taking charge for the first time. He sounded exhausted and exasperated, as they all did. "We tend to your wounds. We wait until Teddy's Five kicks in at eight o'clock, open up this fuckin' tank, split the take, and go our separate ways. The end."

"It's not safe to carry that much cash around right now," Larson said, unsure.

"We'll figure something out. But right now, that's the only play I can see. It's all we got left."

The group stood in a circle, their eyes locked as if any one of them was destined to be their final undoing.

"Anyone have issue with Z's plan?" Larson asked.

After a moment of silence, Rolo rubbed the gash across his face. "First aid kit?"

"In my office, down the hall."

Rolo walked away, tossing his bloody pantyhose mask in a trash can. He left the garage and entered a hallway to one of Larson's office spaces. A moment later, Larson recognized the sound of Rolo collapsing on his couch.

"You alright?" Larson asked Angelica. "Need me to pull out that bullet?"

Angelica clutched her bleeding thigh. "I think it went through. I just need time with that kit, too."

"I got a few of them. Let me know if you need help."

"Thanks."

"Anything else?" Larson said to the group, hoping there was no more murky air to clear.

"Pizza or Chinese?" Angelica asked suddenly, not sure what else to say. "I don't know nothing else that delivers."

"Whatever you order, I'll eat," Teddy said, also retreating to the office down the hall.

Enzo grabbed a stack of Hundreds off the floor and tossed it to Angelica. "Order a lot, whichever you decide. I could eat a horse." He walked into the car collection, to a red, vintage Cadillac Coupe DeVille, and laid across its front bench seat of white leather. Larson simply sat in the back of the van, his legs hung over the side.

"Chinese it is," Angelica said, pocketing her revolver. As she picked up the nearby wall phone, it occurred to her it would likely be their final night together. She'd later observe that their tense last meal as a crew of friends was far more than Quickie Buckner eating his pathetic hard-boiled egg, alone in his penthouse tomb before turning a gun on himself.

32

All Luck Runs Out

Saturday, December 8, 2001, 6:20 p.m.

Six weeks after the five criminal partners parted ways, they felt like they were living in quarantine. Teddy remained at Brewer Manor throughout the day, seldom venturing out even after dark. Rolo moved into his office beside the old Ballroom at Smokey's Club, a troop of his most loyal soldiers standing at his door. Enzo bought a pleasant, unassuming suburban home in Brawley and remained indoors with the window blinds down. Larson kept to his loft on the fifteenth floor of The Monarch, a few blocks from the garage that housed his collection of vintage automobiles. Angelica stayed close to her mother, paying her extra attention should she wander away again.

The gang assumed that the many eyes and ears tracking them stepped closer each day. They hoped the intense heat on them would become a cold case in time, reducing the manhunt to the level of missing kids on milk cartons or wanted posters on the walls of post offices, but none of them were naive. Though it remained unspoken, the consensus stood that this manhunt would continue unabated to its five ends.

With news coverage at an all-time high, state and local authorities that had been working in concert to investigate and capture the crew held a press conference that revealed its clever, if not cheesy, operational code name - "California Adjunction Tactical High Crimes" unit, better known as "CATCH." Though sounding as if written for a comic book or action B-movie, it offered better optics in the public eye, pitting the gang and its ilk against a memorably named opponent to root for. Public support for the task force suddenly seemed important because the daring, mysterious crew soon gained "fans" as it became legend from the many bizarre, emerging stories being connected by crime enthusiasts, and because the pursuing authorities looked like Keystone Cops in the press. The many financial institutions robbed by the gang, fielding a wave of harsh PR from seeming like easy targets, pressured law enforcement to double their efforts.

Sound bites often included sensational headlines such as "CATCH Edging Closer to Capturing Lucky Five" and "Governor Vows to CATCH Lucky Five." Rolo regretted arrogantly announcing their group's name at Easton Monument, but knew the media surely would have created a colorful handle for them, anyway.

After nearly two months of round-the-clock news updates, editorials, expert interviews, and shelves of books analyzing the gang's modus operandi, the heat seemingly dropped away with its plummeting TV ratings. Even with the manhunt packaged with us-versus-them narrative, Middle America soon grew tired of yet more updates with no definitive resolution, their faith and trust in law enforcement waning. In short, the audience wanted an ending to the bloody, epic story, and were changing channels when none was offered. Worse, rumors of dirty cops and bribed officials spread, explaining how impossibly elusive the Lucky Five gang seemed to be.

Enzo O'Day felt more comfortable leaving his Brawley house for short trips to the supermarket or the corner liquor store. Missing the feel of tending bar, he even started inviting his old Brickhouse coworkers to join him in his new backyard patio, complete with outdoor kitchen and premium sound system, for barbecue and beer and loud, dirty jokes around a late-night fire pit. He hosted poker games, pay-per-view boxing nights, and weekday gatherings he called "Foo Foo Cocktail Club." He made himself the life of the party, which disguised his need for the safety of numbers. Surrounded by friends who'd always show up so long as he stocked his buffet table and tended his open bar, Enzo felt a sense of normalcy. In the corner of his mind, however, he couldn't fool himself for long, and hid firearms in the walls and ceiling vents of every room.

The concealed guns, human shields, and heightened fear failed Enzo. During the early evening of Saturday, the fifth of December, Enzo and twelve of his guests were killed in a storm of bullets during the first hour of what was to be his all-night birthday bash. Most fell in the living room and kitchen while Enzo locked himself in the bathroom, desperately trying to pry the cover off the ceiling vent to access the pistol that lay inside. He'd planned to install either a panic room or escape tunnel in his new house, but procrastinated with both, leading to the day he needed them. Among his last words were his cursing aloud for not following up on his plans.

Enzo never saw his killers, for they never entered the bathroom. The wooden door may as well have been styrofoam as it ripped apart from the incessant blasts of an automatic rifle. Following calls from neighbors, CATCH reportedly arrived on the scene shortly after the fact, though it seemed clear to all that only a well-armed troop of officers could have pulled off such a melee. Officially, CATCH credited a rival gang for the multiple killings, never wanting the public to think it served as cold-blooded revenge for the deaths of three of their fellow officers and an example to all organized crime.

Within a week of Enzo's death, on an early Sunday morning, a cross-country cycling club discovered the twisted, mutilated body of Larson Williams in the foothills of Dale Valley. Wearing an outfit of black-and-red leather adorned with matching half-helmet, he laid face-down on Live Oak Road a short distance from his wrecked Triumph Speed Triple. Local police surmised Larson had taken his cherished motorcycle out for a country drive in the clear morning air and fell victim to a drive-by shooting with at least two assailants. Once again, CATCH arrived late to the scene and credited the killing as a gang-related hit, denying speculation that it was a vengeful comeuppance from a joint police organization with the morbid agenda of showing the world what happens to cop killers.

The string of assassinations widened its circle to include anyone remotely connected to the gang, including all known accomplices and associates. A day after Larson met his end, the denizens of Ronnie's Room met theirs, laid to waste without warning. During a slow night, an evening of fourteen regular players spread among four games, a death squad armed with assault rifles entered the illegal cardroom at 444 Paradise Lane in Chemical Town. As seen by security cameras, the squad wore tactical vests unneeded in such a tranquil space as they burst in through the red curtains and opened fire on the room.

The body of Ronnie Mayes sat in a corner, her bloody hands clutching a taser. Benny "Bulldog" Bullini lay slumped over a chair in the cash cage, a shotgun inches out of reach. Randy the Bouncer held only a gold cigarette lighter, taken unaware, the first to die as he stood guard near the door. Across from Randy's post, the lifeless body of Richie Rocks stretched halfway out of the restroom, the old card dealer taken by surprise as he exited the toilet. At the front of the room, sprawled across the cards and chips at Table Six, lay Cal Zimmer, the once regarded rounder, now dead from boasting of his playboy lifestyle in the worst place on the worst night.

As leaked by CATCH, local news blamed the cardroom massacre on gangs from The Quarry and The Docks, spinning a tale of territorial war sparked by the Castle District's attempts to muscle their way across the Central Valley. CATCH held a press conference to announce their shock and dismay at the tragic loss of life, dismissing the many rumors that ran askew of the broadcast news. Some speculated that the joint task force learned from informants that Prime Time Brewer frequented Ronnie's Room and was there solely for him, the deaths of the staff and players merely collateral damage. Others believed CATCH took no chances and assumed every soul in that room watched over Prime Time, each player harboring a grudge against the police with a gun ready to protect their beloved friend. The PR campaign worked as the Court of Public Opinion ultimately decided it must surely have been a mob hit. Such dark, backroom gambling halls are known for them.

* * *

At her Whitesbridge home, Angelica Cruz lay across her bed, unmoving, her eyes open wide, staring up at the ceiling.

She was in shock from Teddy's news.

"Anyone remotely connected?" she asked, gripping her cell phone close to her face, hoping Teddy was exaggerating. "All known accomplices and associates? You think I should worry about Ma?"

"When they got to Enzo," Teddy said, "they wiped out everyone at the party."

"Party?"

"His birthday. Ain't that for shit."

An alternate reality swam in Angelica's mind. She'd received an invitation to that party, but made the tough decision to pass. She held her phone between her right cheek and shoulder as she reached into her bedside table and pulled out two revolvers. Despite her many years training with firearms, the sight of the long silver barrels made her uneasy. She would likely have to use them soon. "Ted. You ever think maybe we're going crazy? Like Quickie Buckner? Maybe that's what did him in. Maybe the secret, the catch to the Five, is that it makes you crazy."

"We're not crazy," Teddy said. "We're in Survival Mode. It feels crazy, but that's where we are."

"What do I do? If anyone comes for me here they're gonna…" She ran out of breath as the words raced out. She couldn't finish her grim thought.

"Leave your mother to the nurse and get over here. I got Rolo coming over now. We'll cover each other during our Fives. That's the closest I got to a plan right now."

"When can I come back home…"

"You can't," Teddy said. "If you want to keep Rosa safe, you'll pack a bag, get your ass over here, and let her go because right now you're the last person in the world that she'd be safe around."

Angelica wiped away a tear, blurted "okay," and promptly hung up. She grabbed a small, packed suitcase she'd prepared days prior, slid her two guns inside its front pocket, and searched the house for her mother. She found Rosa sitting in front of their new 70-inch TV, its high-definition widescreen and Digital Dolby surround sound wasted on an old episode of *The Andy Griffith Show*. Angelica sat on the sofa beside her mother and wrapped her arms around her for the last time, realizing that Teddy was right, that being so close to her would further jeopardize them both.

"I'm going out now," Angelica said, her soft voice quivering with fear and shame. "I'm gonna have Lydia come over. You stay here and watch TV, okay? No going outside while I'm gone."

"But it's almost time for tea," Rosa said, confused, knowing that this young woman looked after her, unsure why she did.

"Lydia will make you lunch."

"What will she make?"

"I dunno, but we got everything in there," Angelica said, nodding to the kitchen. "Just tell her what you want."

"How do I know what I want?"

"That's a good question, Ma. I wonder the same thing myself sometimes."

Rosa never took her eyes off Andy Griffith as her daughter gave her one last kiss on the forehead, picked up her suitcase, and headed out the front door. Though the old woman sat lost in the small black-and-white TV town of Mayberry, she hoped the nice young woman would return soon.

Angelica stepped out of the house and walked to her shiny, red Corvette parked in the driveway, facing the street. The convertible top remained stuck in the lowered position, something she wanted the damn dealership to fix if only she could risk showing her face in public. As she sat in the driver's seat and started the powerful engine, three men emerged from a sedan parked by the mailbox. Angelica shut off her engine, returning the rural road to silence. She knew why those men were there and felt grateful that they waited for her to walk out of the house before making their move.

She glared at the three men standing in front of her car. One of them pointed his gun. The sight of the weapon on her property threw her into a defiant rage.

Angelica spit out her words with venom.

"You touch my ma, and you're fuckin' dead..."

BLAM!

Angelica reeled back, shot in the gut at the top of her ribcage, pressed to her seat. She sat motionless, breathing in bloody wheezes, leaning against her steering wheel. Her still eyes faced the three men as they got back into their sedan and drove off. She watched the car travel alone down the country two-laner as she struggled with her final gasp for air.

33

Point of No Return

Friday, December 21, 2001, 4:44 a.m.

Manny Sanchez looked up from the journal, at the digital clock beside his bed. The red display of "4:44 A.M." startled him, the alarm set to ring in less than ninety minutes, starting a new work day.

Had he really been reading for ten hours? His eyes burned from fatigue and his every movement ached, the six-pack of beer long spent from his system. As Teddy's obsession with the Lucky Five grew within the pages of that journal, so did Manny's.

He flipped through the remaining pages and decided he'd forgo sleep to finish the book. He continued reading as Teddy recounted his final chapter...

"We thought life would be our oyster once we got everything we wanted. Trouble is, we could never get everything we wanted because - like Rolo said - it was always about 'more.' This thing of ours wasn't just bigger than a card game, it was bigger than everything, anything we could conceive. I hope Heaven isn't as disappointing."

Manny looked again at the enclosed photo of Teddy and Marissa in their early days, smiling beside the "Welcome to Las Vegas" sign. The happy couple looked ever more unrecognizable after getting to know them better within the journal.

"The one thing I can't do from 8:04 to 8:09 P.M. is travel back in time. I wouldn't have asked out Marissa. I wouldn't have studied poker. I wouldn't have taken an interest in Quickie Buckner. And I wouldn't have uncovered and shared the secret. I'll probably be dead and gone by the time someone reads this, and I'll die knowing it's no longer about being invincible for five minutes. It's about being a target, being paranoid, the rest of the time. Angelica was right. This is a curse that devours men in shame, a secret that drives them mad. No one should know their Lucky Five."

34

Lonely Christmas

Wednesday, December 19, 2001, 6:40 p.m.

Teddy sat at his ornate oak desk in the grand library of his mansion, surrounded by towering bookshelves that touched the ceiling. His gold watch rested in a box lined with white velvet next to a glass of Irish whiskey, both items within reach. He loaded a fresh cartridge of ink into his silver fountain pen, quickly shoving it in, and wrote a new entry in his journal - the second half of Quickie Buckner's massive book. His hands scrawled words across the page in a blur and it unnerved him to realize that his handwriting now matched the feverish scribblings of his predecessor, but he couldn't help it. He hurried to express his thoughts, feeling his time winding down, as if something or someone was about to take it all away.

"You still have your gold watch," Rolo said over Teddy's shoulder. The sudden, deep voice startled Teddy, causing him to mash down on the pen's nib, spilling a river of ink across his page.

"Shit shit shit!" Teddy picked up the book to let the pool of ink pour onto his desk.

"Sorry about that."

"No, it's my fault. I loaded the pen in a hurry, probably flooded it."

"On edge, brother?"

"I'd be crazy not to be."

Rolo picked up his partner's watch and read its inscription. "I remember picking this out for you. I rarely buy gifts for anyone. My brother always said it was bad luck, like only completing one half of a trade."

"I figured it was a Christmas present." Teddy said, trying to hide his brief fright.

"Shit, I forgot it's almost Christmas. I suppose I shoulda brought you something."

"Forget it," Teddy said, looking behind Rolo. "How'd you get in here?"

"Your man let me in. He recognized me as your friend, something you're supposed to do."

"Dammit, I told Donny to buzz me if someone showed up, no matter who. This task force business has got me up nights. Maybe they got to him."

"So, you're blaming the help?"

"When it comes to Donny, yeah, I am."

Rolo laughed. "Want me to spank him?" He pulled aside his coat, revealing a black gun in a belt holster.

Teddy calmed himself and shook his head "nah." He took the handkerchief from his front pocket and used it to blot the excess ink on his journal before finishing his latest entry on the remaining white of the page. He spoke to his friend as he wrote. "We gotta hit the road and start over. Easton ain't safe for us. Hell, this whole state has us in its sights."

"Agreed." Rolo looked around the library, at the luxury in its details, sad to see it for the first and likely last time. He'd only seen the front parlor during his one prior visit. "When do you wanna leave, brother?"

"Tonight."

35

Last Request

Friday, December 21, 2002, 5:24 a.m.

Manny Sanchez held Prime Time Brewer's journal in his hands, disheartened to see the remaining pages blank. Through the book, he'd traveled with the Lucky Five gang for two years only for the journey to end with a final page stained with spilt ink like a puddle of black blood. He felt that he got to know the five thieves intimately, saw them as friends, and couldn't bare to close the book as if to finalize their deaths.

He knew Rolo Marino and Teddy Brewer never left that house alive, the shocking sight of their bodies together on the floor of Brewer Manor still fresh in his mind. He knew their plans to flee Easton never came to pass, never had a chance, and that they met their mysterious, grisly ends in the mansion's Game Room less than an hour after Teddy fittingly bookmarked his last journal entry with Rolo's Ace of Spades. Surely, CATCH or a rival gang caught up with them and turned the plush rug of the luxurious Game Room into their shared deathbed.

Perhaps Manny could forget the carnage he saw the morning before and imagine the two old friends surviving and starting over on the East Coast, the book's final black page offering an open ending. Perhaps he could learn some vague moral from Teddy's memoir and avoid a similar path of self-destruction.

He looked at the digital clock across from his bed. George would expect him within the hour for another day of shooting photos at gruesome crime scenes throughout Easton, none of which would rival the dismal fates of his new friends. The thought of working a shift in the wake of so many deaths sickened Manny, as if expected to work after five members of his family died that week.

He walked to his phone on the kitchen wall and called his supervisor, almost feeling compelled to. He spoke with a weak, quivering voice, not entirely theater.

"George... It's Manny... I can't come in today... I'm not feeling so good... I think I'm gonna throw up, actually."

"No problem," George said. "I know there's a bug going 'round. A couple of other guys caught it. And I know I certainly don't wanna catch it. You just sit tight. We got everything covered."

"Thanks, George. I appreciate it."

"It's a crazy morning, anyway. Be glad that you're stuck at home."

"What do you mean? What happened now?" Manny couldn't fathom yet another bombshell after the entire gang had been brutally killed.

"Your hero, Prime Time Brewer…"

"Teddy?" Manny said.

"I see you're on a first-name basis now," George said with a laugh. "Yes, Teddy Brewer."

"What about him?"

"We're all scratching our heads about it. The medics never seen anything like it. Neither have I, and I've seen it all."

"What about him?" Manny asked again, holding his breath.

"He's in ICU at Easton Memorial."

* * *

The sprawling new campus of Easton Memorial Medical Center stood on the edge of North End like a futuristic city on the horizon. Most of its patients enjoyed disposable income and hearty healthcare, including members of the City Council and card-carrying members of the community's business elite. Still, none of the staff were accustomed to the high profile and media circus surrounding their newest patient.

On that otherwise calm, mid-December morning, mob boss Teddy "Prime Time" Brewer, victim of what seemed to be a fatal gunshot, was rushed into Emergency with a police escort and dense cluster of reporters close behind. At the city morgue the night before, on the late evening of Thursday, December 21st - nearly 24 hours after the City Coroner called his official time of death at the mansion - Teddy's lifeless body grabbed hold of his hand, clutching at a last thread of life. His eyes opened wide to the shock of the morgue dieners at 8:04 p.m.

Manny knew exactly what happened. Teddy had been declared dead but had not yet left this world, and his Lucky Five granted him one last day and one more chance for the doctors to save him. As impossible as it seemed, Teddy Brewer still lived, if only for another few hours.

Manny rushed to the hospital and ran into the ICU, determined to meet Teddy by any means. He lied to the Admissions Clerk, claiming he was Teddy's cousin and best friend. He lied to the doctor, citing how close he was to Teddy and that a visit from him might offer encouragement for the patient to keep fighting. The nurses halted him in the hallway with strict rules about visiting patients in critical condition, but he weaved elaborate stories about Teddy's last request to be with family, to see his most trusted relative one more time. He even lied to police officers, explaining that he represented Easton P.D. on a case against the Lucky Five gang and that speaking with Brewer in his final hours alive was paramount to apprehending a dozen known criminal associates.

Manny effortlessly deceived everyone with a convincing tone and unbreakable conviction, the red journal clutched in his hand at each step. One-by-one, he circumvented every obstacle until he stood at the foot of Teddy Brewer's bed.

Staring at the infamous crime lord, barely conscious as he glanced at the machines keeping him alive, Manny felt a familiarity he knew was unearned yet felt crucial.

Out of respect for someone seemingly so important to the patient, and out of the knowledge that he would likely not survive the day, Teddy's doctor allowed Manny a private half-hour with him as journalists and officers waited in the hall.

"My journal," Teddy said, his weak voice wheezing and fading. Though the Lucky Five had kept him alive, it did nothing to augment his strength or prolong his survival beyond that morning.

"I'm Manuel Sanchez of Easton P.D.," Manny said with a lowered voice, not knowing how else to introduce himself. Though they were alone in the one-bed intensive care room, he didn't risk someone overhearing.

"Ah, so you're a cop," Teddy said with a slight smile. "Congratulations, you finally got me. You part of that two-penny task force?"

"I'm not with CATCH, and I'm not exactly a cop. But I am investigating you."

"You must have a lot of questions for me, Mr. Sanchez. I'll tell you whatever you want to know, but you better make it quick. I'll be checkin' out soon."

Manny didn't know how to proceed, but didn't need to. Teddy caught sight of the red book in his hand and knew precisely what this young man wanted.

"You read my journal?" Teddy asked.

"Yes."

"All of it?"

"Every page."

"Then you have all the answers you need."

"Almost," Manny said. "What happened after your last entry? I can't explain why, but I must know."

Teddy recognized the desperate, tragic, nearly feral look in Manny's eyes, for he first saw it in his bathroom mirror two years prior, the look of someone struggling to make sense of the discovery, how it worked, how it bent men's morals and steered them to madness.

"What happened is I died," Teddy said. "Rolo died. My crew died. That's the end of our story."

"No!" Manny looked around and calmed himself though he felt their time quickly running out. "I don't expect you to explain how it worked, how it felt, how it warped you and landed you here. I just need to know what happened the other night, Wednesday, December 19th."

Teddy coughed and reached for his bedside table. "After they brought me here, I wrote another page for the journal. I had to. The doctor thinks it's gibberish, the scribblings of a dying man. It's yours, if you can make sense of it. Take it, learn from it, and don't share a word of it with another soul." He reached into the drawer of the small table and pulled out a single sheet of paper, crumpled and dense with illegible, almost microscopic writing from top to bottom, front and back. He handed it to his visitor. The doctors and nurses had dismissed it as merely a pen randomly scrambling across a steno pad, an outlet for the immense pain Teddy endured, but Manny could read it as clear as if it were typed.

Manny straightened the page, looking upon it like the Holy Grail. So focused was his gaze that he barely reacted when Teddy started to convulse and clutch his bedsheets in agony, barely able to breathe. Manny picked up the call button attached to the bed but paused, instead allowing Teddy his final desperate gasps for air.

An hour before, Manny stared at the incomplete journal and fantasized about Teddy and Rolo surviving their night at the mansion. Now, with the man's final thoughts on paper, firmly in hand, Manny hoped that Teddy would fade away, narrowing the list of people aware of the discovery so that he alone knew the secret.

Teddy started to moan as his body went through its death throes. Manny quickly pocketed the paper and returned to the hall, offering no pleas for help to the awaiting nurses and reporters. "He needs his rest," he said as he gently shut the door behind him. The many waiting faces nodded in understanding, believing him to be a grieving, close family member.

Another seven minutes passed before the medical staff, overwhelmed by the media frenzy of the crowded hallway, noticed on their consoles the lack of any signal from Teddy's room. By then, it was too late to save him.

Four minutes later, Manny walked across the parking lot to his car, the rain pattering down on its roof as he started the engine and drove home.

* * *

Upon returning to his studio apartment, Manny buried his face in his hands and screamed, ashamed at his cruel, inexplicable inaction as Teddy died again. He sat on his sofa and pulled the crumpled page from his coat pocket, the unofficial last entry of Prime Time's Brewer's journal. He read the bizarre writing made on his hospital deathbed, hanging on every word as if reading a bible passage.

36

No More Games

Wednesday, December 19, 2001, 6:52 p.m.

"We gotta hit the road and start over," Teddy said, sitting at the desk in his library. "Easton ain't safe for us. Hell, this whole state has us in its sights."

"Agreed." Rolo looked around the library. "When do you wanna leave, brother?"

"Tonight."

Teddy quickly finished what would be the penultimate entry of his journal, writing as fast as his hands could move underneath the black splatter of ink. He pulled a pencil from his desk drawer, placed it in the book, and started to shut it only for Rolo to stop him.

Rolo reached into his inner jacket pocket and revealed an Ace of Spades. He tossed the card into the book, marking Teddy's page.

"That's how a player marks the days of his life," Rolo said. He returned Teddy's watch, sliding away its velvet-lined box. "Put it on, for old time's sake, no pun intended."

Teddy looked at his watch as if admiring it for the first time. He hadn't worn it in weeks, though its two alarms signaling the start and end of his evening Lucky Five could be heard throughout the silent house daily. He placed it on his wrist and thought of their early days when the future seemed wide open and full of promise, and their takeover of Las Vegas felt never-ending.

"Did you convince Angie to get her ass over here?" Rolo asked. "I'm surprised that girl ain't been got yet."

"She's on her way," Teddy said, unaware that he would never see her again. "She'll be okay. The girl knows how to take care of herself, tougher than both of us put together."

"I hear ya, brother, but it doesn't matter if she's fuckin' Wonder Woman. CATCH is on a rampage. They'll set half the state on fire just to smoke us out. Forget about spotting black choppers in the sky, I keep expecting a sniper bullet to the back of my skull."

Teddy knew Rolo was right. Though Angelica proved more of a survivor than Enzo or Larson, or the poor devils at Ronnie's Room, it seemed only a matter of time before the countless CATCH agents and officers hunting them would uncover her identity and raid her home. The thought of her being gunned down made him sick. "I gotta get outta here. I need some air."

"You know you ain't going nowhere, Ted..."

"Just come with me."

Teddy grabbed his glass from the desk, a second glass for Rolo, and a bottle of cognac from the bar behind him. He walked out of the library. Rolo followed, looking around to ensure they were truly alone.

Teddy led his friend out onto a rear balcony overlooking Lake Woodman, a man-made lake created exclusively for the two-dozen majestic homes that surrounded it. At first, Rolo felt confused to be on a balcony since they stood on the first floor of the mansion, but he quickly realized that the grand home sat at the edge of a bluff. The first floor transitioned into the second floor toward the rear of the property.

Teddy poured two glasses of cognac and handed one to his partner. "Merry Christmas."

"Nothing from Santa Claus, but hey, sharing a drink with a friend, that's what it's all about, brother."

"That and we're still above ground."

"Here's to not bein' dead... yet." The two men smiled as they clinked glasses and took a sip together.

The cool night air prompted Rolo to pull a cigar from his coat. He cut and lit it as he took a seat by the edge of the balcony. "California has gotten to me. I can't bring myself to smoke indoors no more." He offered a cigar to Teddy, who refused by revealing a pack of White Knights. "Brother, you still smoke those things?"

"If you can still drink your Rolling Rocks, I can still smoke my Knights."

"Fair enough." Rolo reached over, flicked open his lighter with a metallic ping, and lit his friend's cigarette.

"Besides, I only smoke 'em when I'm stressed."

"Stressed about what?"

"Are you joking?" Teddy asked. "We got a list of shit to stress about."

"I know that, a long-ass list, what I'm asking is what item on that list is on your mind right now."

"This place. This town. We need to have our heads examined still squatting here. We gotta get hit the highway. "

"We never had to worry about no task force before," Rolo said, puffing his cigar. "I figured maybe the Five was protecting our asses round the clock somehow. But I agree, our time here is over."

"I'm thinking of going back east."

"Back to your people in New York?"

Teddy felt unnerved hearing "your people." He wondered how much of his past Rolo had uncovered. "Nah, not New York. Somewhere further up the coast, like a Cape Cod beach house on a big plot of land with a nice garden in the back yard."

"Sounds like a pretty postcard."

"The luxury I look forward to is having a goddamn phone again!" Teddy laughed, glancing at the time on his gold watch. "I live in North End, in this house, but I have to send Donny down to the 7-Eleven to make a fuckin' call."

"Welcome to my world, Prime Time. My guys make all my calls, too. "

Teddy thought about his phone call earlier, when he spoke with Angelica. Though he made the call from that remote convenience store two miles down the road, he later viewed it as a reckless move.

"Get yourself one of those new portable phones," Rolo said.

"I thought about it, but those things can be traced to the house, plus any nearby surveillance might pick it up."

Rolo looked at the exquisite back yard below them, at the lap pool, hot tub, and guest house. "How many banks you got it in?"

"No banks," Teddy said, avoiding eye contact.

"I thought your brilliant plan was to have your man stash it off-shore?"

"Not after Enzo's accountant fucked him over. No way."

"So where is it?" Rolo asked. "Tucked in your mattress?"

"Even a California King isn't big enough for half that take."

"Half? You didn't split it?"

"If I had, Larson's share would be lost now, wouldn't it?"

Rolo couldn't believe what he was hearing. When the crew left Larson's garage in the wee hours of the night after the Easton Monument job, everyone felt nervous about having the cash on them. Rolo and Teddy each took half the lot, intending to split it among the crew, nearly three-million apiece. "What about Angie?"

"I gave her fifty-grand the next day. She was too scared to take any more."

"So you're saying you fucked them over?"

"I'm saying the plan was to hold it a while," Teddy said, growing defensive, "to keep it tucked away until things cooled off. Sorry Larson died before we could follow up, but that's how it turned out. I didn't pay Enzo, either. Did you?"

"Not yet. We were supposed to take care of that together, remember?"

"It's good that you didn't, 'cause Enzo's gone."

Rolo reeled from yet another bombshell. "I thought Z headed back to Boston after his big birthday party?"

"He never left that party. Don't you follow the news?"

Rolo puffed his cigar and stared out at the lake, wondering what other secrets Teddy held. "Shit's worse than I thought."

"Look, you keep his share, okay?" Teddy finished his White Knight, snuffing it in an ashtray sitting between them. "See, this is why we should've moved first, then split the pot, 'cause you never know who's gonna get pinched."

"Or worse."

They heard the doorbell chime, echoing throughout the house. Teddy looked in through the glass doors, curious, as the doorbell chimed again. After a third chime, Teddy rose to his feet. "Where the hell is Donny?"

Teddy downed the rest of his cognac and headed back inside. He walked through the library but paused at his desk, the sight of his exposed journal seizing his attention. A sudden feeling of dread compelled him to take the book to the cathedral window at the back of the room and tuck it into the hidden compartment he built into its hollow window sill.

After hiding the journal, Teddy left the library, passed through the Game Room, and reached the front door. He peered outside through a side window, shocked to see who stood there in the cold.

He opened the door and let Marissa Washington enter. In her disheveled dress and frizzed afro, she looked as if she rushed there with little notice.

"Marissa, what the hell..."

"Angie called me," she said, looking around the house. "Teddy... it's..."

"Angie called you? She's supposed to be here." He turned and shouted into his house. "Donny? Where are you? What the hell am I paying you for? Donny!"

"Teddy!" Marissa said, silencing him. "It's about Angie."

She pulled Teddy close and whispered, in case there were others within earshot, updating him on what happened to their mutual friend, about the men who came to her home and the shocking events that followed. His heart raced from hearing the details.

Without another word, Teddy took Marissa down the hall, through the next door, into his elaborate Game Room. She stopped him at the entrance when she saw Rolo sitting at a poker table. He nursed a bottle of beer while shuffling a deck of cards, glancing up at a large wall clock that resembled a giant pocket watch.

Teddy and Marissa entered quietly, Teddy sensing fear in his ex-girlfriend upon seeing Moonlight Marino, lord of the Castle District, sitting there. Teddy understood why she hesitated to be around him after the bloodbath at her former nightclub. He sat across from Rolo, curious about the sudden tension in the air.

"Cognac is fine, but I needed my Rolling Rock," Rolo said, shuffling cards.

"Hello, Moon," Marissa said.

"Didn't think I'd ever see you again, Missy. Still dance on Wednesday nights?"

"My dancing days are over."

Rolo dealt cards for himself and Teddy. "Where the hell is Angie? We need to regroup and figure things out."

Teddy checked the time on his gold watch as they played their hand. Holding his cards, Teddy seemed lost in thought.

"What's eating you, brother?" Rolo asked.

Teddy thought of keeping his revelations private, but realized it would be pointless now. "It's this task force of fools they put together. They got to us pretty hard and fast these last few weeks. I mean, for the past year they couldn't find flies on shit. Like you, I figured the Lucky Five was protecting us. But suddenly they're poppin' us off one-two-three. It makes me wonder."

The two men finished their round, Rolo winning with two pair. He gathered the deck and handed it to Teddy.

"Killing cops tends to motivate people," Rolo said.

Teddy shuffled the deck and dealt two new hands face down while Marissa stood behind him, watching in anticipation. "Rolo, just for a giggle, why don't you lay your piece down on the table for me."

Rolo paused and looked his friend in the eye with a quiet laugh. "It's your house, brother." He reached into his coat pocket and pulled out his gun, setting it down on the center of the green felt tabletop. "Where the hell is that soldier girl?"

"Tea Time ain't coming."

Rolo seemed shocked. He eyed Marissa before returning Teddy's glare. "So she's 'Tea Time' now? Not Angie no more? What the hell happened to her?"

"Angie's in the hospital."

* * *

BLAM!

Angelica Cruz reeled back in her Corvette, shot in the gut at the top of her ribcage, pressed to her seat. She sat motionless under the afternoon sun, breathing in bloody wheezes, leaning against her steering wheel. Her still eyes faced her three assassins as they returned to their sedan and drove off. She watched the car travel alone down the country two-laner as she struggled with her final breath.

She helplessly slumped forward, her arm knocking the stick shift into neutral, sending the sports car slowing rolling forward into the street until it bumped to a stop against a cluster of trash cans. She summoned all her draining strength to reach for her cell phone beside her, her hand failing to make it. Unable to move, barely able to breathe, she drifted off...

BEEP BEEP.

4:02 P.M.

Angelica opened her eyes, breathed deep with renewed life, the bullet in her ribs held at bay. She again reached toward the cell phone but passed it to grab the twin pistols from the front pocket of her suitcase. She strained to stand up in her convertible, her feet planted on the driver's seat, her back braced against the top of the windshield, and took careful aim at the sedan down the road. In an exhale, she fired three quick shots at the distant car.

The sedan continued down the rural road for a moment before suddenly swerving, crashing into an orchard. Not stopping to reflect on her impossible marksmanship, she picked up her phone and made a call.

"Hello? Yeah, I been shot... hurry please... Whitesbridge Road... near Peach... There are three men here... They're all dead."

She hung up and painfully climbed out of her Corvette, limping down the road to her assassins. Upon reaching the wrecked sedan, she readied her guns and examined the carnage.

The driver sat dead from a headshot. A second man laid across the backseat, also victim of a headshot. A third man sat in front passenger seat, alive but severely wounded from a shot to the neck. He opened his door, fell out of the car, and crawled face-down across the dirt into the trees, struggling to breathe with each movement. Angelica soon stood over him, blood oozing from her own gunshot.

"You ain't cops," she said, noticing their plain clothes, tank tops and baggy jeans. "You work for Jerry in Vegas? Scary Jerry?" The man on the ground turned over for one last look at the sky, his face sending shivers through Angelica. "No. You guys ain't cops, and you ain't from Vegas." She didn't twitch a muscle as the dying man pointed his gun up at her and pulled the trigger.

CLICK CLICK CLICK.

She recognized the fatally wounded man as Shorty Domínguez, former captain for Zero Anada, current Lieutenant for Moonlight Marino. Her first thought was to curse this man for betraying Rolo after he spared him during the massacre at Smokey's Club.

It took another few seconds for her to realize the truth.

With tears streaming down her face, she pointed one of her guns at Shorty and executed him on the side of

Whitesbridge Road, a quarter-mile from her home. Though she stood in the middle of her Five, she collapsed to the dirt clutching her pistols, staring at the three dead men sent from the Castle District. The sounds of an ambulance's siren was the last thing she heard before waking up in the Emergency Room of Easton Memorial Hospital three hours later.

Realizing she'd survived, her first thought was to call Teddy, but he'd only been using pay phones lately. She called her former best friend, Marissa, and begged her to go to North End to warn Teddy about Moonlight's betrayal.

* * *

"She's in ICU," Teddy said to Rolo, staring at him across the poker table. "Shot in the chest, just below her heart."

"Fuck, when did this happen?" Rolo asked.

"A few hours ago. She's alive, and her hitmen are dead, thanks to her Five. Shitty timing on their part."

"Hitmen?"

"That's right. Not cops, not CATCH agents, but hitmen."

"And they're all dead?"

"Your boy Shorty is gone, if that's what you're wondering. He's laying in a drawer in the morgue right now."

Rolo didn't respond. He thought about asking why Shorty would do such a thing, why he'd go rogue and take out one of them. The knowing expression on his partner's face made the notion feel futile. Instead, Rolo gave up playing dumb. He simply sat back in his chair and puffed his cigar.

"Tell me, Moon," Teddy asked. "Why Larson first?"

Lynn Harrod

* * *

Larson sped down Live Oak Road, a tree-lined country two-laner in Dale Valley, his motorcycle humming with mechanical precision. Despite cruising along well past the speed limit, a black SUV crossed the double-yellow line and raced past him. He slowed to allow the SUV to pass.

When it merged in front of him, its rear window slid down, and the long barrel of a shotgun protruded forth. Larson felt the shot before he could react. He and his motorcycle tumbled violently down the old road until they finally came to a rest in front of a large acacia tree on the sandy shoulder. He stained to sit up, to remove his helmet.

A short distance away, the SUV screeched to a halt. Larson squinted in the morning sun, shocked to see Rolo Marino step out of the vehicle holding the smoking shotgun. The large gangster approached Larson, sprawled out across the pavement. Rolo pointed the shotgun at his face and pulled the trigger.

* * *

Randy the Bouncer sat half-asleep on his stool in the velvet-lined entry of Ronnie's Room. He tucked a wad of chewing tobacco between his cheek and gum, his attempted transition from smoking two packs of smokes a day. Behind the red curtain sat four tables of players, tended to by Ronnie and Bulldog with old Richie Rocks dealing the game at the lauded

Table Six. With the latest hand over, Richie excused himself for a bathroom break, leaving Cal Zimmer and his opponents to entertain themselves with bullshit small talk about Cal's new fishing boat.

Unlike the rest of the room, Randy the Bouncer never saw it coming. A bullet pierced his forehead the moment the door burst open. Men in tactical vests over tank tops and jeans poured in and mowed down the players and staff, nailing Richie at the bathroom door within seconds, stepping no further than five feet from the red curtain.

* * *

"And why Ronnie's joint?" Teddy asked, sipping his cognac, a quiet fury burning in his brain. "I still haven't figured that one out."

"If it's any consolation," Rolo said with a stern look, taking a moment to relight his cigar, "Larson wasn't the first. The first face I wanted to revisit was our friend from Sin City. I wanted to give him some new tattoos."

* * *

On a desolate desert road eleven miles south of the Las Vegas city limits, Rolo's black SUV idled as his men attached a steel chain to its trailer hitch. The chain split into ten smaller chains, each attached to the many gold and silver ring piercings of Scary Jerry. The Executive Trustee laid bloody across the pavement. He wheezed, his eyes widening as he heard the master chain being secured to the SUV with a loud clank.

Sitting in the back row of the SUV, Rolo looked out the open rear window at his victim who'd been "tenderized" by Shorty and his men moments before being thrown to the cracked pavement. Rolo nodded his head and the SUV lurched forward, inching its way down the road. He smoked a cigar as the vehicle picked up speed, dragging the helpless man behind. Rolo rolled up his window as Jerry's screams rose to an agonizing pitch.

* * *

Rolo tossed a silver spade earring onto the poker table for Teddy and Marissa to see, encrusted with dried blood. Marissa looked across the table at Rolo as if he were the Devil himself.

"So what are you waiting for, Moonlight?" Teddy asked defiantly. "You're the lord of the Castle District. You took out half our crew, and you got me dead bang."

Rolo didn't answer. He simply puffed his cigar.

"And why the body count?" Teddy asked. "This can't be about Easton Monument. I mean, no one's gotten their cut yet. You and I got all the money."

"It's not about the money, you know that as well as I do. It's about too many kings in the castle, too many knowing the secret." He turned toward Marissa, sending chills through her. "I bet Missy knows. Hey, does she know about Enzo? I mean, it was the guy's birthday."

Marissa looked at Teddy, who had no ready reply. She realized with horror what Rolo insinuated.

* * *

Enzo's quaint suburban house sat adorned with colorful streamers and balloons for the evening, decorations fit for a child's birthday. Two folding tables covered in green paper tablecloths held an impressive spread of barbecue, pastries, and drinks, with a two-tier chocolate rum cake sitting at one end. His guests, all former coworkers from the Brickhouse Bar, listened to thumping techno music while waiting for the guest of honor to come out of the kitchen.

Enzo returned to his guests with a tray of twelve fresh "Irish Car Bombs" - half-pints of Irish Stout accompanied by shots of whiskey. Everyone grabbed a beer and a shot, dunked the shot glasses into the pints, and quickly downed the decadent drink to great applause from those who waited for the next round.

Upon setting the empty glasses back onto the tray, the doorbell rang. Enzo quickly ran to let in another guest. He smiled and embraced Teddy at the doorway, urging him to come in and join the next round of car bombs. He introduced his friend and partner to the many friendly faces, some recognizing him from his nights at the Brickhouse.

Teddy shook hands while glancing at his watch.

BEEP BEEP.

8:04 P.M.

Without warning, Teddy pulled a revolver from his jacket and opened fire on the crowded room indiscriminately. Everyone fell unaware, shot point blank in the head before they knew what was happening. A few men rushed Teddy, tried to wrestle the gun from his grip, but found him to have the strength of a gorilla. Teddy shoved them away and plugged them dead.

Enzo dropped his drink and ran to the bathroom at the end of the hall, slamming and locking the door behind him. He heard the shots and screams throughout the house as he fumbled with the air vent, desperately trying to reach his hidden gun.

With the rest of the house laying dead on the floor, Teddy walked down the hall to its last door. He pulled an automatic rifle from his coat, took aim at the wooden door, and blasted it without mercy. Firing the powerful weapon within his Five, the first two bullets fatally struck Enzo in the head and chest, felling him instantly, though Teddy kept the trigger depressed until the magazine ran dry, ensuring that his former partner would never emerge from that bathroom.

"Happy Birthday, Z. I'm sorry it ended this way."

Hearing no sound from the other side, Teddy returned to the living room, grabbed a piece of rum cake, stepped over the dozens of bodies, and walked out of the house without a glance behind him.

Teddy reached over his poker table and grabbed Rolo's gun from its center. He pointed it at Rolo, who sat unmoved by the threat, while Marissa stood speechless from the shocking reveal.

"Is he lying, Teddy?" Marissa asked, keeping an eye on the intimidating gangster sitting across from him.

"You're looking at me with fiery eyes, Missy," Rolo said, "but there's two devils at this table. Why do you think Teddy left New York? That's our connection. Everyone likes to think I'm the born thug in town, but your boyfriend here was a point man in the Bronx Association..."

"That's enough," Teddy said.

"...until he played the ponies with the wrong man, got himself a gun, got greedy. It's like Scary Jerry said, ain't that the tale of every crook's been caught."

Marissa backed away from the table, staring at her ex-boyfriend with new eyes, not sure what to believe.

"Teddy didn't clue in," Rolo said, "that you can't so much as paper-cut a made man in the Bronx unless you got Italian blood. Poor Teddy, all he's got is ten pints of Guinness in his veins."

BEEP BEEP.

8:04 P.M.

Teddy looked at his gold watch and smiled, still pointing Rolo's gun across the table. He felt curious and confused to see his former partner smiling as well, but shrugged it off as misplaced hubris. "You fucked up, Moon. My Five just kicked in. Just like with your boys, that's some shitty timing for you. All your preening and posturing, your ferocious front, your play-acting as a legitimate mob boss, all for what? To show

Lynn Harrod

the world that you're Tony's equal? To show everyone that nobody fucks with Moonlight Marino? It's sad, really. What's your play now?"

"Teddy, what the fuck's going on?" Marissa asked from across the Game Room, though the terrifying situation finally dawned on her. "He's not lying, is he? About Enzo?"

"To answer your earlier question," Rolo said, glancing at Teddy's watch, "that's what I was waiting for."

BLAM!

Marissa stood rooted to the floor, confused, unsure what just happened. It took her a moment to realize that of the two men sitting together, Teddy had just been shot under the table by Rolo, who revealed a snub-nose pistol.

Teddy slumped forward, his gun tumbling to the floor. He looked at his gold watch, failing to understand how he could get shot during his Five.

"Cards turn cold?" Rolo asked. "When I had your watch earlier, I took a moment to set it back for... daylight savings time? Whenever that rolls around."

Teddy looked up at his old wall clock that resembled a giant pocket watch. Its wide, white face stared down at him, displaying the correct time - 7:34 P.M. - a half-hour before his Lucky Five.

Rolo pointed his gun at Marissa. "For the record, baby, you're a beauty, but I don't know what Teddy and Zero ever saw in you."

He pulled the trigger.

CLICK CLICK.

Confused, Rolo fired again, to no avail. The snub-nose he just used to kill his partner now sat useless in his hand.

Marissa eyed the gun at Teddy's feet and scrambled for it. Rolo bolted up from his chair, knocking it over, and rushed toward her, reaching her the same moment she grabbed the gun and pointed it at him.

BLAM!

Rolo instantly froze and fell to his knees. He clutched his chest wound in disbelief. With one last confused look, he collapsed to the floor, dead.

Overwhelmed, frightened, Marissa tossed the gun away and knelt beside Teddy - still alive but barely breathing - sure to keep her distance.

"Are you afraid of me, Tumbleweed?" Teddy asked, barely able to string a sentence. "Because I am." He laughed with a cough, fading fast as he looked down at his dead partner. "You found your Five. And it's just where you thought it'd be."

Marissa didn't know what to make of his final words, her mind a whirl. "What are you talking about, Teddy?"

"You remember? The river? When you saved your pop?"

Marissa thought back to that pivotal moment in her childhood when she flailed helplessly in rapids of the Aucilla River in Northern Florida, late at night, back to when her father Harv Washington jumped in to save her only for the little girl to miraculously save them both. Upon dragging her father to shore, she looked at her plastic Hello Kitty watch, lit by the moon, busted and forever stuck at 10:36 P.M.

"Yeah, I guess," she said, confused. "But I figured it was ten thirty-six."

"Yes," Teddy said. "In Florida."

Marissa looked up at the wall clock.

Lynn Harrod

7:38 P.M.

"Amazing, isn't it?" Teddy said. "What are the odds? With this thing of ours, I guess anything is possible."

"I don't understand." Marissa stood shaking, staring at the clock, trying to make sense of it all.

"You know the most tragic thing?" Teddy said as blood filled his lungs. "We could've changed the world. We could've cured cancer or helped the homeless or solved world peace, but none of that shit crossed our minds. The Lucky Five didn't slowly drive us crazy. It made us crazy from the start."

Marissa's mind spun as she saw Teddy's life fall away. She rose to search for a phone to call an ambulance, but Teddy grabbed her arm.

"He was right, you know," he said. "There are indeed two devils in this room. As I look at you now, my Tumbleweed, I wish I could kill you, bring you with me. I wish I could keep you from knowing my precious secret." Marissa cried, terrified by the terrifying, dying man she thought she knew. "Don't cry, Marissa. Since you already know it, there's a book I want you to have. I want you to learn from my many mistakes. It's hidden in this house. Promise me you'll find it."

Marissa crouched beside him and nodded her head, agreeing to his dying wish. "I promise, Teddy."

"Ironic, isn't it? You're in the middle of your Lucky Five right now. You can have anything you want. But you can't have me."

Teddy smiled and shut his eyes, his body beside Rolo, their blood pooling together. Marissa dropped to her knees and sobbed, torn by loving a man who'd become a monster, a man she'd briefly considered returning to.

37

A New Player

Friday, December 21, 2001, 8:13 a.m.

Manny Sanchez reached the end of the final page in silence, as if the rest of the world offered a moment of remembrance for the many lives lost. He set it on his Murphy bed, unable to touch it again. He knew the curse of the Lucky Five, how it empowered, but ultimately destroyed a group of friends and all who crossed their path. It pained him to realize that the ruin didn't lie in the nationwide manhunt, nor the grip of the notorious Castle District, nor the long reach of Las Vegas mobsters. Prime Time Brewer, Moonlight Marino, and their associates corrupted themselves and ruined each other, the corruption now reaching Manny as he sat dazed on his bed.

Perhaps the Lucky Five had indeed always been a curse, a malevolent marvel that drove men mad with greed and obsession. Perhaps Teddy's notion that everyone has a Five, but that no one should know it, was the lesson to be learned from the journal. Through his logic and intellect, Manny knew the moral of the story, but it didn't matter.

He looked around at his meager studio apartment, at the two busted cameras on the sofa and the empty fridge beside him. He spoke the truth when he told George he felt ill, ready to vomit, but the large, red journal with its gold embossed "Q" still beckoned even as it sickened him.

He reached into a bowl of coins on his bedside dresser and pulled out a Quarter. After staring at the coin for a moment, he tossed it onto the bed.

Tails.

Manny kept "tails" in his mind as he flipped the coin again, landing it onto the bed between his legs. He flipped the coin again and would continue to do so until he saw his life take a dramatic turn nearly nine hours later, at 4:57 P.M.

KEEPERS
OF THE
NIGHT
GARDEN

a novella

LYNN HARROD

Lionheart Park Retirement Village offers its residents a luxurious resort setting with quaint cottages by the sea. Within this paradise is a profound sorrow, a need to feel loved again. Eloise spends her time in the garden caring for the flowers and statues. Her lonely routine takes a turn when she finds a wounded crow that changes the everyone's lives. Family can be found in the unlikeliest of places in this novella by veteran writer Lynn Harrod.

Keepers of the Night Garden
Available on
www.deerwoodpress.com

About the Author

Lynn Harrod is an award-winning writer, artist, filmmaker, and educator with over 30 years of experience crafting shorts, essays, and screenplays. His characters often find their worlds spun sideways by a startling revelation.

Lynn was awarded the PRSA Image Award of Excellence and has placed in the Quarterfinals and Semifinals of the Nicholl Fellowship, the Finals of the Nevada Film Office Competition, the Semifinals of the Writers' Network Competition, and twice in the Semifinals of the FadeIn Awards.

Born in Texas, raised in California's San Joaquin Valley, educated and trained in Hollywood, Lynn is a writer and partner with Only Human Productions, where several of his works are in development. When he's not spending time with his wife and daughter, or writing all night on his patio, he's usually having a pint with friends.

www.ingramcontent.com/pod-product-compliance
Lightning Source LLC
Chambersburg PA
CBHW072021020726
47501CB00006B/1896